The past is with you. Always.

PATRICIA POTTER
"...will thrill lovers of the suspense genre
as well as those who enjoy a good romance."
—*Booklist*

"The Potter treatment...is pure action and
excitement, and the characters are
wonderful."
—*Midwest Book Review*

"One of the best."—*BookBrowser*

Praise for
PATRICIA POTTER
and her bestselling novels

"Pat Potter proves herself a gifted writer . . . creating a rich fabric of strong characters whose wit and intellect will enthrall even as their adventures entertain." —*BookPage*

"Patricia Potter looks deeply into the human soul and finds the best and brightest in each character. This is what romance is all about." — Kathe Robin, *Romantic Times*

Broken Honor

"Palms will sweat and hearts will race . . . This well-written crossover novel will thrill lovers of the suspense genre as well as those who enjoy a good romance." —*Booklist*

"Although Potter is better known for her historical romances, this bracing romantic thriller proves that she's just as comfortable writing in the contemporary arena." —*Publishers Weekly*

The Perfect Family

"The reader loses all sense of time as they become entangled in a web of mystery Ms. Potter spins in *The Perfect Family* . . . Flawless characterizations . . . You are holding a work of art when you pick up a book by Patricia Potter." —*Rendezvous*

"This is a novel that will long be remembered by those who read it." —*Midwest Book Review*

continued . . .

The Black Knave

"Patricia Potter has taken a classic plotline and added something fresh, making her story ring with authenticity, color, exciting action, her special humor, and deep emotions. *The Black Knave* is *The Scarlet Pimpernel* with twists and turns that make an old story new."

—*Romantic Times* (Top Pick)

"I couldn't put it down! This one's a keeper! Pat Potter writes romantic adventure like nobody else."

—Joan Johnston

Starcatcher

"Patricia Potter has created a lively Scottish tale that has just the right amount of intrigue, romance, and conflict."

—*Literary Journal*

"Once again, Pat Potter demonstrates why she is considered one of the best writers of historical novels on the market today . . . Ms. Potter scores big-time with this fabulously fine fiction that will be devoured by fans of this genre."

—*BookBrowser*

Twisted Shadows

Patricia Potter

JOVE BOOKS, NEW YORK

TWISTED SHADOWS

A Jove Book / published by arrangement with
the author

PRINTING HISTORY
Jove edition / January 2003

Visit our website at
www.penguinputnam.com

ISBN: 0-515-13439-2

A JOVE BOOK®
Jove Books are published by The Berkley Publishing Group,
a division of Penguin Putnam Inc.,
375 Hudson Street, New York, New York 10014.
JOVE and the "J" design
are trademarks belonging to Penguin Putnam Inc.

PRINTED IN THE UNITED STATES OF AMERICA

10 9 8 7 6 5 4 3 2 1

prologue

She was running for her life. And the lives of her children.

She clutched the twins, one in each arm, her purse slung over her shoulder. *A cab.* She had to reach a cab.

She knew she would soon hear footsteps behind her. Heavy. Hurried. Her guard—her husband's guard—would discover she'd left the doctor's office through another door. His life would be as much at risk as her own if he failed. If he lost her.

This would be her one and only chance to escape her husband. She knew that. If she failed, he would kill her. He would find out what she knew—and to whom she had given information—and then dispose of her as his family had disposed of irritants before her. Fear eddied in her stomach. Her breath was short from both terror and the exertion of carrying two eight-month-old babies, their necessities and the largest purse she owned. It contained everything she could carry without giving away her intention. Unfortunately, her possessions did not include a weapon.

Nick squirmed, protesting her protective hold. For a

moment, she feared she would lose her grip. She stopped, balancing him on her hip, getting a stronger hold on him. In a moment he would start wailing. That would probably inspire Nicole to do the same. Each always followed the other's lead. They reached out for each other when separated. They seemed to take comfort in each other's company.

A loud wail now would be disastrous. She cooed quietly to him, frantically balancing the two heavy babies.

She started down the steps again, trying to run without dislodging the two children. She feared the elevator. She could be trapped in an elevator. *No, the stairs are safer.* She'd spent days considering her options, the best escape route. And, hopefully, preparing safeguards.

But her husband was unpredictable. He would be so angry, he wouldn't care that his actions could send him to prison. Or send the policeman who served the family to the electric chair.

She heard a door slam above her.

Joey. Such an innocuous name. But he was not an innocuous man. He was a made man, a man who had killed before. That she was a woman would mean little to him, particularly since his own life might well depend on his stopping her.

One more floor.

She was wearing tennis shoes that made no noise. She had purposely been hitting tennis balls just minutes before returning to the side of her twins. Then she'd used a heating pad on Nick's and Nicole's faces to simulate a fever.

Her husband was out of town. So was her father-in-law. When she'd screamed that the children were sick with high temperatures, she'd finally won permission to go to the doctor. She'd been to the pediatrician before. She knew the offices. She knew a way out that avoided her so-called bodyguard in the waiting room.

"Bitch!" Joey's voice roared down the stairwell.

She could see the door below her. She moved faster than she thought possible, shifting, Nick again as she grabbed for the knob and jerked the door open.

Nick wailed loudly.

Another curse echoed from the stairwell as she ran across the lobby. *Please, God, let the cab be there.*

She'd called from the nurses' station, ordering a cab, promising an extra fifty if it waited outside the professional offices for a woman with two babies. If it wasn't there . . .

She darted between people, bumping one. "Taxi waiting," she muttered, then made the door. She turned to see Joey bursting out from the stairwell door.

Nicole started wailing, too. Tracy knew that every eye was on her. She'd already started thinking about what she would do if Joey caught her. She would yell "Kidnap." If some brave good Samaritan . . .

And if there was gunfire? If she caused an innocent's death . . . ?

Someone entered the revolving doors, and she jumped inside one of the partitions. Then she saw the taxi. Waiting in front of the building.

She ran for it. Nick almost fell as she pulled the door open and lurched inside, dropping her son on the seat and locking the door.

"Go," she screamed.

She heard Joey's voice behind. "Stop, dammit!"

The cabbie turned to her.

"Go," she said again, even as she heard the waver in her voice, even as she clutched the babies closer to her. "For God's sake, go."

He hesitated, then stepped on the pedal and darted in front of an oncoming car.

A horn blew long and hard.

The cabbie swore.

Tracy Edwards Merritta sat back and tried to calm a screaming Nick.

She struggled to take a normal breath, then looked back. Joey was frantically trying to wave down another cab.

"Where to, lady?"

"Filene's, please. Side entrance." The department store wasn't far from a Boston MTA station. She would go in one door of the store, depart through another and disappear.

Nicole stared at her, thumb in her mouth. Nick complained loudly.

But they were safe.

For the moment.

one

Samantha Carroll didn't frighten easily.

Still, apprehension rippled through her as two men walked into the western art gallery she owned with her mother.

She could tell at a glance they weren't ordinary tourists or typical art lovers. They wore expensive dark suits and highly polished shoes rather than casual slacks or shorts and trendy T-shirts. Yet one look at their faces told her they weren't salesmen, either.

The one in his mid-twenties wore his hair slicked back, a gold chain around his neck and a flashy watch that looked like a Rolex on his wrist. The other one had well-groomed graying hair and face. Their eyes were hard. Without humor. Without friendliness. They looked like hunters, but not the kind who were after deer or elk.

Western Wonders was unusually empty in the midst of the summer tourist season. The last customers had just left. Had the two men waited until the customers departed? She moved toward the panic button that was linked to the police dispatcher.

She didn't know why all the bells in her head were ringing. No one would rob her small gallery. Nearly everyone paid with credit cards, and the bulk of the store's business came through the web site she'd designed. She kept the finest pieces locked in secure storage, bringing them out only when she knew she had a viable buyer.

Sure, she had some ready cash, but not enough to attract a daylight robbery. The gallery had some nice western art, but no one would drag armloads of paintings or heavy sculptures out the front door and onto the main street. At least, she'd never believed so. Not in Steamboat Springs, where major crime was nonexistent.

Her apprehension deepened as the two men browsed among the paintings but seemed to have little real interest in them. Their gazes continued to roam back to her, studying her as a collector might before pinning a butterfly to a board.

She resented it. She resented anyone who diminished her. And these men were doing just that.

Sarsaparilla wandered in from the storeroom, swishing her great bushy tail. The once stray cat who now believed herself queen of all she surveyed investigated the two strangers and rubbed against the trouser leg of the older man.

He immediately jumped back, his right hand going to the inside of his suit jacket.

Her heart leaped into her throat. "Sarsy," she scolded, forcing herself to stand fast and not show the reaction her cat's behavior prompted. Sarsy sensed people who disliked cats and went out of her way to irritate them.

Sarsaparilla gave her an indignant look, then slunk back into the other room.

"Is there anything I can help you with?" she finally asked the men. "A particular artist? Or style?"

The older man nodded toward one with a thousand-dollar price tag. "This any good?"

If she'd any doubts about his interest before, she didn't now. The painting was very good. Anyone with even the faintest interest in art would know the lighting was exceptional. The moonlight depicted in oil seemed to glow.

She looked toward the door again, willing someone else to come in. "It's the work of a local artist who is becoming very popular," she said, unable to keep the edge from her voice.

"I'll take it," the man said.

She didn't want to sell it to him. The painting was one of her favorites, an oil of a snow-covered mountain at night. A wolf peered out from the shadows of a stand of trees, as if ready to begin a night's prowl.

The men reminded her of that wolf. Prowling after prey. "I'm sorry," she said. "It was sold earlier today. I haven't put the sold sign on it yet." Now *she* would have to purchase it herself. It was in Western Wonders on consignment, and she'd just cost the artist a sale.

His cold dark eyes studied her. He didn't believe her.

The hair on the nape of her neck stood up; a shiver ran down her back. "If there's anything else," she said, "I'll be glad to help you. Otherwise, I'm going to close for lunch."

"It's three," the man noted skeptically.

"I was busy at lunchtime."

"Are you the owner?"

"My mother and myself," she said.

"Mrs. Carroll?"

"She's my mother, yes," Sam said, growing even more wary.

"And your father?"

"I don't think that's any of your business."

The speaker looked surprised, as if he'd never been corrected before. He glared at her.

The younger man glanced out the door, as if keeping watch.

"He's not dead," the older man finally said.

"I beg your pardon?" She felt the bite of anger. She had always been slow to anger, slow to allow any emotion to take control. But when she removed the leash, she could be a holy terror. That was one reason she disciplined herself.

"Your papa ain't dead." The younger man joined the conversation. "Not yet."

The older man gave him a warning glance but didn't correct him.

Both were obviously crazy. "I think you'd better go," she said, her hand once more moving toward the panic button. "I do want to close."

"I wouldn't do that," the younger man said. "Keep your hands on top of the table."

How could he know about the button?

"Or?" she asked.

His eyes glittered.

The older man broke in. "I don't think your mother would appreciate it," he said softly. Somehow he was more menacing than the other.

"Why?" she challenged him. She felt trapped and afraid, and she was furious with them for causing it. She hated the feeling. Hated the fear that was growing. She'd always prided herself on conquering fear. Or ignoring it.

"She has some secrets," the man said. "Secrets she might not want to share with this town." The words were poisonous. Cold. Deadly.

Her mother? Her protective, good-citizen mother? Her best friend? Since her father's death, the one person she trusted above all others?

"You must have me confused with someone else," she said. "I asked you to leave. Now I am telling you."

"Your mother's been lying to you," the older man said. "She committed bigamy years ago. David Carroll was not your father."

She shook her head, denying his words rather than questioning them. David Carroll *had* been her father. In every way. She'd seen her birth certificate when she entered college.

Yet the older man had planted the smallest seed of doubt with his quiet certainty.

"Now I *know* I want you out of here," Sam said, feeling a desperate need to disconnect from this situation before it became too real. She went to the door and held it open. Neither man moved.

She wasn't quite sure what to do. She could continue to stand there, looking like a fool, or go outside and yell for help. The younger man moved in front of her, neatly herding her back toward the interior while the older one closed the door, turned the sign to CLOSED and stood in front of it, arms crossed, feet apart.

"I'll call the police," Sam said through clenched teeth, her doubt being drowned by their arrogance. She hated personal conflicts, but she'd never been timid. She'd sailed down mountains on skis, spent days alone in the deep woods, climbed mountains. She knew how to fire a pistol. It completely went against the grain to let these men intimidate her.

Still, they did. They reeked of . . . violence.

They made no move to back away. The younger man stepped between her and the phone. She tried to weave around him.

He blocked her.

She turned to the older man, who seemed to be in charge. "What exactly do you want?"

"Your papa is dying. He wants to see you."

"My father died two years ago."

"Carroll *wasn't* your real father."

Despite the softness of his voice, his statement was like a boulder dropping. The absolute conviction made her feel it was dropping on *her.*

"No," she denied, her voice not quite as strong as before.

She flinched as the older man reached in his pocket, pulled out an envelope and placed it in her hand. "Open it," he commanded.

From the corner of her eye, she saw a couple pause in front of the shop, looking at some of the paintings in the windows. "I have customers," she said, the envelope burning her fingers.

"Hell with them," the man said. "This is more important."

"To whom?"

"To you. To your real papa."

"Who *are* you?"

"Just messengers."

As much as she didn't want to give them the satisfaction of acceding to their demands, it seemed the only way to get them to leave. She opened the manila envelope. A photo fell out.

She stooped, picked it up and looked at it. A new shock jolted her. A pretty young woman sat in a chair holding two babies. A darkly handsome young man stood behind her. It was an old-fashioned pose. The man protecting his family.

The woman was her mother. She was at least thirty years younger and her hair was long rather than short, but the wide cornflower blue eyes were unmistakable. She was also wearing a bracelet Sam immediately recognized. Her mother always wore it.

Sam found herself compelled by that photo, by the two children. One was dressed in pink. One in blue. They sat in their mother's lap. The girl beamed at the camera; the boy stared impatiently. His eyes were the same blue as those of the little girl beside him. And of the man standing behind them.

From the snapshots of her own early years, she knew she was one of those babies. The other . . .

"Your brother," the man said. "Your *twin* brother."

Her legs started to crumple under her. The younger man

reached out to steady her. She shook him off and stumbled past him to the desk, and this time he let her. She studied the photo again, then looked farther into the envelope. Three more items. Copies of two birth certificates. She chose the top one.

None of the names was familiar. Mother: Tracy Edwards Merritta. Father: Paul Merritta. Baby girl: Nicole.

Date of birth: August 15, 1967. Place of birth: Boston. Weight: four pounds, three ounces.

She looked at the second one. Same mother and father. Baby boy: Nicholas. Born four minutes earlier than the girl. Weight: four pounds, nine ounces.

The fourth item was a photo of a well-dressed man with dark hair and dark blue eyes just like her own. She could tell the photo was more recent than the family portrait. The cut of the casual sports jacket gave it away.

"Your brother," the older man said again.

She was too stunned to move, to speak, to react. She wanted to deny it. Accepting the pronouncement meant her entire life was a lie. Her mother had lied to her. And her father. He would have lied as well.

But these men said he had not been her father after all. At least, not her biological father. Though she knew he certainly had been her father in every important way.

This was some really twisted joke. It would be easy enough to create phony birth certificates. Computers could do anything these days.

Yet something clicked inside her head. She'd always had an odd feeling that something was missing from her life, as if she were not quite whole. She'd dismissed it as her longing for siblings and an extended family.

Her mother had said she had been orphaned and raised in a foster family. Her father's mother and father had died in an accident before Sam was born. No uncles. No aunts. No grandparents.

A flash of recognition leaped in her heart when she

looked at the boy in the family photo. But that was because they looked alike, she told herself. *Remember what a computer can do.*

But who would possibly attempt such an elaborate and cruel hoax?

She touched the birth certificate. "I have a copy of my own. It's different. It says David Carroll is my father."

The man smiled. "They can be forged."

"My point exactly," she said. "*One* of them has been."

"Granted," he said. "But the picture doesn't lie."

"I know what computers can do. Anyone could take my mother's photo, make her younger, doctor photos of the children."

"But why make the effort?"

"You tell me," she said, trying to keep her voice steady.

The door rattled. She jumped, her nerves jangled. All three of them looked toward it, but the tall man blocked her view. Someone was not taking the CLOSED sign seriously.

Her mother? But her mother was on a buying trip to Taos. Sam wouldn't be able to reach her. Possibly not until tomorrow.

The door rattled again, and she managed to slip around the two men. *Terri.* Her best friend who helped with the books at Wonders.

"Get rid of whoever it is," the older man ordered.

"It's a friend of mine. She knows I'm here alone. She can see you two. She won't leave now, not without knowing I'm all right. You look . . . intimidating. If I don't open the door, she'll go down the street to police headquarters."

"Then tell her you're all right and get rid of her."

"No." She felt more in control now. Terri would do exactly what she'd said. Her friend would be as suspicious of the two men as Sam had been when they first entered.

The older man gave her an odd look of approval. "Your papa doesn't have much time left. He's real sick."

She forced her gaze away from him and back to Terri. Her friend had capped her eyes against the sun and was peering inside. In seconds, she would be running down to the police station.

Did Sam want that?

No. Not until she talked to her mother. Not until she made some sense of something that made no sense.

She knew she had to find out whether there was even a thread of truth to their tale. She had to know whether she had a birth father she hadn't known existed. And a brother. Not only a brother but a twin.

How many years had she dreamed of having a big brother?

No, it's impossible.

Ignoring the two men, she went to the door and opened it. Terri had been leaning against the door so hard she stumbled, then caught herself. Her gaze shot to the two men, then she turned back to Sam.

"What's wrong?" Terri asked, starting to back out the door.

"Miss Carroll was giving us a . . ." The younger one said, glancing at Sam, obviously expecting her to supply the rest of the excuse, as if there were no doubt that she would.

"Private viewing," Sam said, hating to give him even that much.

"A private viewing," her visitor concurred. "We're just leaving." He turned to Sam. "We'll get back to you about that picture tomorrow."

The two politely passed Terri but left an aura of menace behind them.

The tension in the shop dissipated noticeably, and for a brief moment Sam wondered whether the visit had happened at all.

two

A nightmare?

Sam wanted it to be. But the photo of the family together, and the one of the self-assured young man who
stood alone, were all too real.

Had her mother and father lied to her all her life?

She avoided Terri's questions about the two men, saying only that they seemed intent on finding work from a
certain artist.

Terri wasn't satisfied. But she took one look at Sam's
frozen expression and asked no more questions.

Terri Faulkner had been her best friend since grade
school. They told each other everything, or almost everything. A history teacher in the local school, Terri was also
a whiz at math and moonlighted as bookkeeper at Wonders. The arrangement helped both of them.

Terri's interruption had been a godsend. Oddly enough,
Sam hadn't felt—except for a brief few moments—in
physical danger. But she had been terrified of losing her
composure, of showing weakness to people she suspected
would use it against her.

She tried to listen to Terri, but she was still numb. It was as if a bomb had exploded her world. Shock deadened every other emotion.

"Still game for the books?" Terri asked.

The question startled her. She had forgotten that they'd planned to go over the books this afternoon, then have supper at The Hitching Post.

She shook her head. "Something's come up. Maybe tomorrow."

Terri looked concerned. "Anything wrong? Those men looked a bit weird, as if they'd stepped out of a movie."

Sam tried a smile. "I had the same feeling. But they turned out to be rather ordinary. They were looking for a painting."

She almost vomited after Terri left.

She closed the shop early, scooped up the cat and drove the ten minutes to her home, but questions haunted her all the way.

An elaborate hoax or the truth? And if it was the former, why would anyone go to so much trouble? Neither she nor her mother had any enemies. At least, none she knew of.

Her eyes kept wandering back to the envelope on the seat beside her. She could still see the photos in her mind's eye. The children looked to be less than a year old. Still, wouldn't she remember something? Wouldn't she remember a brother? Even at that age.

Maybe she had. Maybe that's why, as a child, she used to reach out her arms after a nightmare, and no one would be there.

A sense of overwhelming loss invaded her.

She started to relax as she neared her house. Her dream home. She had put her heart into every log as it was being built. The house sat at the foot of a mountain, and the view was particularly spectacular from the back porch and back balcony.

Once inside, she poured herself a glass of wine, which she seldom did when alone. Then she sat down and

watched the sunset, but it didn't have its usual tranquiliz-
ing effect. Abruptly she stood and padded down the hall,
through the living room and up to her office in the loft.

She had the photos. She had the name of Paul Merritta.
And Nicholas Merritta. She turned on her computer, then
accessed the Internet. First a general search, then she
would go to the credit bureau she used to research buyers
and sellers who used the Western Wonders web site.

Searching "Paul Merritta, Boston," she found a huge
number of articles and started reading.

Hours later, she knew more than she wanted to. Her
blood ran cold as the knowledge sank in. She realized now
why those two men had so inexplicably alarmed her. Although never convicted, Paul Merritta had been consis-
tently linked to organized crime in Boston. There was one
news photo of Merritta being led into a police station in
handcuffs. He was later released after a witness disappeared.

She knew what that probably meant. She'd read enough
books about organized crime. She paused, then searched
on "Nicholas Merritta." She found he'd changed his last
name to Merritt, and was a partner and vice president of a
medical supply company in Boston. Although some stories
suggested he was possibly connected to his father's activities, nothing had ever been proved.

He had served in the army during the Gulf War.

That surprised her. With his family's money, why would
he choose to serve in the military?

She studied one of the few photos she found of him online and ran it off on her printer, then sat back.

She had heard that twins sometimes shared a unique
bond, that each knew what the other thought—even when
separated by thousands of miles. She immediately
searched under "twins" on the Internet. That led her to
"multiples," which led her to identical and fraternal twins.

"Multiples" seemed to be the politically correct description.

Twins, whether fraternal or identical, she read, often develop their own language — called twinspeak — that only they could understand. Twins were less prone to loneliness than nontwin siblings because there was always someone at hand who was going through many of the same experiences. Often, twins maintained their special bond throughout their lives.

On the other hand, said one article, although fraternal twins shared the same uterus, they were no more similar than any other set of siblings. Their shared experiences promoted the bond.

Then she moved to the message boards on the multiples site, and skipped through the posts. One mother of fraternal boy/girl twins said there was definitely something between them, like "a kinetic energy bounced off each other."

She turned the computer off and stared at the blank scene, her thoughts in turmoil. If the men's story was true, she had shared the earliest minutes, hours, weeks, months with a brother.

She'd lost years with him. A lifetime.

At that moment she knew she'd accepted the tale as possible. She could have a twin brother. Her biological father could be a mobster, possibly a killer.

Was that why her mother had left him? But how could she have left her son?

Sam must have been very young when it had happened or she would have felt something other than a vague loss over the years.

Paul Merritta wanted to see her. Had he known where she'd been all these years? Had he ignored her existence until it was important to *him*?

If it were true, she kept reminding herself.

She looked around her office, which occupied the top

floor of her home. The house wasn't large, but it *was* her dream house, realized after she'd wandered about the Northwest for eight years, taking first one technology job, then another, each time earning a substantial salary and obnoxiously valuable stock. But she had been seeking something she couldn't identify.

When her father died, she'd had enough of a nest egg to return to the picturesque ranching community to help her mother with the gallery that had been near bankruptcy after her father's illness. She had taken Western Wonders online, developing a web site that drew both buyers and sellers. With the increased exposure to a global market, their profits doubled, then tripled. Now ninety percent of their business came over the Internet.

The gallery was her mother's life and love, and it was her mother who usually tended it, while Sam concentrated on the web site. But Sam occasionally staffed it when her mother traveled, looking for promising new western artists.

How did those two men know I would be there today? And my mother wouldn't?

She shivered again, realizing that someone had been watching her when she wasn't aware of it. Had her phone been tapped or her house bugged?

You've been watching too many movies.

She looked out at the dark, quiet street, the shadowy mountains behind it. Several hours until dawn.

Perhaps a good run would help clear her mind. Sam went into her bedroom, pulled on a pair of jogging pants and shirt, and slipped out the back door. She hesitated for a moment, aware of a new wariness, then shook it off. Steamboat Springs had a negligible crime rate, which was one reason she loved it. She felt safe in every nook and cranny of the valley. She seldom even bothered to lock her doors. She did now, though, pocketing the key in her pants.

She ran a mile, then turned back down the street that

fronted her house, her footsteps pounding on the pavement and echoing along the street. Faster. Faster. Run away the emotions that were bubbling just beneath the surface.

Had she heard the truth? Or a lie?

Did she really have a brother?

She approached her house. Her perfectly sane world. Her sanctuary. She'd never realized she felt that way about it before. Now she did. Her pace increased yet again and she felt moisture dampening her clothes.

The light in the living room was still on. The one in her office was off. Just as it should be.

She would make a cup of hot chocolate, then try to sleep for several hours.

She unlocked the door, went into the kitchen and poured milk into a saucepan to heat.

A sound intruded. Upstairs in the loft. A creak. Soft. Stealthy.

Sarsy. It was probably only Sarsy.

Still, Sam held her breath, listening. Another slight sound. A footfall? Or Sarsy jumping from a perch? But Sarsy's paws wouldn't cause a creak like that, not unless the cat brushed against something. Maybe that was it.

It had to be. "Sarsy," she called.

No answering meow. No sound, except for the pounding of her heart that seemed to radiate out from her, filling the space around her. She searched through cabinets and found a rolling pin. It was the closest thing to a weapon she had in the house except for knives, and she wasn't about to prowl the house with a sharp knife in her hand.

The rolling pin gave her some courage, that and her knowledge of self-defense. She would probably call herself all kinds of an idiot in a few moments when she found Sarsy alone and safe and playing hard-to-find.

She climbed the stairs to find the cat and, she admitted, to quiet her own fear.

The computer was blinking. She thought she had turned it off. But she'd been distracted.

Then she noticed the neat pile of papers on her desk. They were not so neat now. She knew she hadn't touched them earlier. Sarsy again? She released a stifled breath. That was probably the noise: Sarsy jumping from the desk.

She started to call the cat again, but no sound came from her throat as she heard a noise behind her, then felt a driving pain at the back of her head.

It was still dark when she woke, and she knew she'd been unconscious for only a few seconds. A glancing blow. Nothing more.

The door was open and she stumbled up to look out. *Nothing.*

Her head ached. She touched the bump on her head. No blood. Just pain.

She'd heard a noise, seen the computer and the papers . . . and she'd felt a blow, then nothing. . . .

She walked unsteadily to the phone, pausing as a wave of nausea washed over her. She leaned against a wall for a moment, then picked up the receiver. The buzz sounded unusually loud. At least it worked.

She dialed 911 and reported the burglary, giving her address and name, trying to keep it as matter-of-fact as possible, even though her head was spinning and her mind was having difficulty accepting that someone had actually invaded her home and assaulted her.

"Hang on to the line until you hear the sirens," the operator directed her. "Talk to me. Tell me what happened."

"A prowler. In my office. I'd . . . been jogging."

She looked down. She was still wearing the jogging clothes. They were still damp.

"Miss Carroll . . . talk to me." The operator's voice was still calm but now it had a note of urgency.

"I'm here," she assured the operator. She heard a siren. "I think the police are here," Sam said.

"Stay on the phone until you know. . . ."

She looked outside as a squad car pulled up in the driveway and two officers approached. "It's the police," she assured the operator. "Thank you."

An ambulance stopped at the curb behind the police car. Lights now glowed in several neighboring houses.

Her head pounded as she led the officers and paramedics inside and to the kitchen, where she sat down. One of the officers went through the house to make sure it was empty as the paramedics started asking questions. Sarsy suddenly appeared and wended in and out between her legs. "She was in a closet," said one of the officers who'd returned. "Didn't find anyone else. I don't suppose you know if anything's missing."

She shook her head.

She suffered through endless questions and probing. The police were obviously concerned. They were used to burglary, but this was an assault as well.

"We'll be talking to your neighbors," one said. "See whether they saw or heard anything. We'll keep in touch."

The medics finished with their examination. "A bump, but it doesn't look as if the skin was broken. You should go to the hospital and have it checked."

Sam shook her head. "It's nothing. I'll see my own doctor," she promised.

"Then you'll have to sign this form," one medic said. "It absolves us of responsibility."

"In case you die," added the other.

She didn't appreciate the humor. Undeterred, she signed the form. She wanted to know whether anything was missing. She wanted to talk to the two men who had visited the gallery earlier.

She thought about mentioning them to the officers, but then she would have to explain everything, and she couldn't do that, not until she knew more. Steamboat Springs was a small town. The permanent residents all knew one another, particularly the merchants within the city limits. How could she tell these two officers that her mother might be the ex-wife of a mobster.

What if none of it was true? What if she destroyed her mother's reputation and life for a lie? Silence, she decided, was the better part of wisdom.

Instead she thanked them after they promised to send over some fingerprint technicians and asked her to inventory her valuables and report anything missing.

After they all finally left, she sat down in a chair.

What to do?

She knew head injuries could be dangerous, but she had been out just long enough for the prowler to get away. Maybe he'd meant no serious bodily harm. She just wasn't going to wait all day in an emergency room. Any sign of dizziness, though, and she would ask someone to drive her there.

She carefully locked the doors, then started to look around, anger mounting with every step.

The assault had been an invasion, not only of her house but of her sense of safety.

But nothing appeared to be missing. Not the silver Indian jewelry she favored, nor the western paintings that were the only items of value in the house.

She looked at her watch. Seven-thirty. She phoned Terri, who always rose early. No one answered, and she decided not to leave a message. What would she say, anyway? She was no more ready to confide in her friend than she was in the police—not without more information.

Her head pounded.

She had never lied to the police before, even by omission. She was one of the world's most upstanding citizens, having gotten only one traffic ticket in her life and that at the bottom of a hill in a speed trap. Something inside her rebelled at the thought of breaking a law.

Her mother would be driving in this evening. She thought about trying to reach her on the cell phone, but her mother seldom kept it charged. Besides, Sam wanted to be in the same room with her. She wanted to see her face.

This was going to be a very long day.

She went back downstairs to the kitchen and glanced at the pan of milk. The bottom of the pan had burned. One of the policemen had probably turned it off, but the scorched smell permeated the kitchen. *Coffee*. Coffee would be better anyway. But when she tried to fill the carafe with water, her hand shook. She looked at the offending part of her body. It shook even harder.

"Damn," she muttered to herself.

She set down the carafe.

The two men said they would return to the store today. She had to go there. She had to know if they were the ones who had invaded her home. They probably wouldn't admit it, if they had, but she wanted to ask the question. She wanted to show them she could not be intimidated.

Still, she didn't move.

Her world had tipped over. She didn't know where the dangers lay. Unlike the challenge of hiking and skiing on risky trails and runs, the dangers of this situation couldn't be anticipated. And she feared the emotional ones far more than the physical ones.

Who am I?

She gave up on the coffee and went to stare at the framed portrait of her mother and father that hung above her fireplace mantel. She had commissioned a painting of them on their twenty-fifth wedding anniversary and had ordered a copy for herself.

She had been twenty-four then, and just hired at a ridiculously high salary at a technology firm because she had the ability to combine marketing skills with computer innovation.

Twenty-fifth anniversary. She'd held a huge surprise party for them. Her father had been handsome and her mother looked so much in love. They'd always been extraordinarily close. That was eleven years ago. If the tale she'd been told was true, that anniversary was a lie as well.

She studied the man she thought she knew so well. David Carroll had been the ultimate westerner. He'd loved the outdoors and took the family camping, swimming, fishing and hunting. He had been the one who started calling her Sam, though her mother always insisted on Samantha. But though he loved the outdoors, he had a genius for mathematics. Sam had always wondered why he'd settled for such an undemanding job as business manager for a small gallery in a remote valley in Colorado. Had Paul Merritta been the reason?

Sarsaparilla rubbed against her legs.

"You're useless," she said. "I need an attack cat."

Sarsy meowed plaintively, telling her she'd tried to point out danger yesterday in the gallery but had been rebuked.

"I know," Sam said with a sigh, wondering whether she was really having this conversation with the cat.

The gallery. She could go there. But she seemed unable to leave the house.

Normalcy. How she craved it right now.

But there was none. She no longer felt safe here. Even Sarsy seemed unusually nervous.

Then she thought of the computer again. It had been on, when she was pretty sure she'd turned it off. Maybe her assailant had left some clue. She went up to the loft and checked recently opened files. The times posted indicated someone had used the computer after she had. He'd apparently backtracked her own search on the Merrittas.

But why?

Then she looked at the papers. She'd noticed before the assault that they'd looked different. She skipped through them. Nothing there of any interest except to her.

She turned to her desk drawers. The top drawer had also been invaded. She kept two credit cards there for easy access when ordering for the gallery. They were still there, but again not where she always left them.

Her throat tightened. Her personal address book was missing.

She searched every drawer, every corner, every space between the drawers, between the desk and the wall. She was puzzled at first, then angry and finally frantic.

It was gone!

She sagged into her chair, trying desperately to find an explanation.

This was a personal invasion and more frightening than if a string of pearls or a painting had been taken. They were things. Her address book was the bits and pieces of her life.

Why would anyone want that?

three

FBI agent Nathan McLean felt anticipation bubble up inside him. It was a rare emotion after all these years of one defeat after another.

He leaned forward in the chair as he listened to the tapes from the taps on Paul Merritta's multiple hones. Nate and Gray Evans, his partner, had been listening nearly all night, but only this conversation caught their attention.

"I don't know if she'll come willingly." Nate recognized the voice as belonging to Tommy Camda, one of Merritta's most trusted lieutenants.

"She saw the birth certificates?"

"Yes, Mr. Merritta, and the photos."

"How did she react?"

"She didn't believe it. Not at first. She believed your wife's . . . husband was her biological father."

"Dammit!" Paul Merritta's voice sounded as strong as ever. If the rumors that he was sick were true, it wasn't evident in this exchange.

"I left the envelope with her. I told her I would get back to her."

"Her mother wasn't there?"

"No, I waited until she went out of town."

"Good. She'll turn the girl against me." A pause. Then, *"What's she like?"*

"Smart, but then you expected that. Not easy to rattle."

"You didn't try . . ."

"No, sir. I did exactly as you told me."

"Did she ask any questions about me?"

"No." The answer was regretful. As if Camda would have preferred to give any other answer than this one.

"She will. I know almost everything there is to know about her. She has a curious mind and she likes challenges." He said the word with satisfaction. *"Like her brother."*

"Yes, sir."

"Did you tell her . . . I was sick?"

"Yes."

"Then she'll come," Merritta said, though Nate thought he detected just a tremor of uncertainty in his voice.

"What do you want us to do now?"

"Take care of her. Watch her. Make sure she's safe."

The phone went dead.

"Maybe it's true," Gray said as he leaned forward and turned off the tape. "Maybe he is dying."

Nate snorted.

"You think the daughter's for real?"

Nate shrugged. "I'm just wondering why in the hell he would let us know about it."

"He might think we don't have his newest cell number," Gray ventured. "And he's taking the usual precautions. No names. No places."

"He's a devious son of a bitch. He has something in mind," Nate said. "I don't think he's suddenly got religion or wants to become a papa again."

"Who is she?" Gray asked. "I thought the only daughter had been killed years ago."

"So did I," Nate said thoughtfully. "Thirty-four to be

exact. Both she and her mother in a car crash. Burned beyond recognition, but the mother was identified by dental records."

Gray raised an eyebrow. "A crash. That's convenient."

"Paul Merritta was out of the country at the time, but flew back immediately. Every other member of the family had an alibi. There was no indication of foul play and some evidence that she drank a lot." He didn't add that he'd looked into the deaths years ago, hoping to develop a murder case. He'd talked to investigating officers and the federal agents who'd worked the case. He'd wanted to talk to the medical examiner, but the man had died in an accident himself two years later. Nate had thought it an unlikely coincidence but hadn't had enough evidence to proceed. Not after so many years had passed.

Gray shook his head. "Is there anything you don't know about the Merrittas?"

There wasn't much. Nate probably knew more about the Merritta family than anyone in the Bureau. But his partner — the closest thing he had to a friend — had no idea that the name of Merritta was like a burning brand in his gut, that Nate existed to take that family down. Most kids wanted to be a basketball or football pro. His only ambition as a foster kid had been to send members of the Merritta family to the electric chair. Today, a lethal injection would do.

But he *hadn't* known the daughter and wife were alive. What the hell had he missed?

And now it appeared that the daughter — and possibly the mother — was being resurrected. Why?

That was the million-dollar question.

Gray was regarding him curiously.

Nate ignored his partner's comment. "Let's hear the end of the tape again."

Gray pushed the rewind, then play buttons.

"Take care of her. Watch her. Make sure she's safe."

Safe with Merritta? Like his mother. He stifled his anger. *Think opportunity. Don't let feelings get in the way. Not this time.*

"Maybe he really does just want to see her before he dies," Gray said.

Nathan gave his partner a disbelieving look. "A benevolent Merritta?"

Gray shrugged. "Maybe, but the conversation falls in line with the other reports we have. Visits to several oncologists. Prescriptions for pain killers, though he has enough links to narcotics to get almost anything he wants unless a particular combination isn't available. And now this sudden desire to see this woman."

"And," Nate said, "risking opening an investigation into two unsolved murders. If his wife and child weren't killed, who was in the car?"

"Merritta must know that. Why open himself up to that unless he has a damn good reason?" Gray paused. "Maybe we're jumping to conclusions. Could it be anyone else? Another child?"

Nate shrugged. "Doesn't seem likely. Camda mentioned a wife. Photos. Birth certificates, and the fact the woman *thought* someone else was her biological father. Merritta already claimed George. He probably would have claimed any other illegitimate child. And he mentioned a smart brother. That has to be Nicholas."

"There's George," Gray suggested.

Nate snorted. "We know what Merritta thinks of him."

"How do you suppose brother George will take it?"

Nate cheered up. "Not well. Neither will his mother. She's been Merritta's mistress so long she thinks she owns him."

"Poses any number of questions, doesn't it?" Gray said.

"And possibilities," Nate said. "We've never been able to get anyone inside the family. Maybe this is our opportunity."

"A civilian?"

"An informant," he corrected. "It's worth trying. She shouldn't have any great fondness for Paul Merritta, especially if her mother ran from him."

"Barker would never approve it," Gray said, referring to their superior.

"No sense in mentioning it if we don't get her agreement," Nate said. "You know Barker has his own snitch inside the family, and I suspect that's why some of our investigations have bummed out. Someone told the Merrittas what we were doing."

They looked at each other. They both knew agents who used snitches—and protected them to the extent of overlooking such offenses as murder or permitting another agent's investigation to go bust—to advance their own careers. Barker was a cowboy, a man who would do anything to climb the Bureau ladder.

A daughter, by God. Someone must have put two other bodies in the car that had gone into a ravine and burst into flames thirty-four years ago. That could be murder, and there was no statute of limitations on murder.

If Merritta was ill, as reports had it, he might not live long enough to be tried and convicted, but members of his family might.

Opportunities.

"Then the next step is to get a handle on the former Mrs. Merritta and her daughter," Gray said. "Tommy used a cell phone. Our people know the call came from central Colorado, but that's as far as we can pinpoint it. We don't know her name, have nothing to start with."

"Damn it. I can't believe our guys lost Camda," Nate said.

"Merritta's learned to be cautious."

"Yeah, but he slips occasionally. That brother part, for instance."

"Perhaps we should pay Nick another visit," Gray suggested.

"I think it would be better if we can get a tap on his phone."

"They wouldn't grant it last time."

"This time we might have a potential witness at risk," Nate said. "Maybe we can hang an authorization on that."

"Barker will have our hides."

"He's in Washington this week," Nate said.

"Ah, dammit, McLean."

Nate shrugged. In truth, his career in the FBI meant a lot less to him than bringing the Merrittas to justice.

Gray surrendered with a sigh. "What judge?"

"There's McQueen, Cannon, McGuire and Dempsy. They're the most friendly to us. I'll start with McQueen. You take Cannon. If neither of them will sign, we'll go to the other two."

"Do you know anything about the mother? Where she came from?"

Gray couldn't know. Why should he, when it was ancient history? But Nate had gone over every scrap of information ever compiled against Paul Merritta and his father. "If she's who we think she is, her name is Tracy Edwards. She was a poor kid on a scholarship. Married him in Las Vegas. I don't know if she knew who—or what—he was when she married him, but two years later she was dead."

"Or so everyone thought."

"Merritta wouldn't have just let her walk away," Nate said. "He doesn't operate that way. Once something's his, it stays his. She must have had something damaging on him if he left her alone this long." He tapped a pen against his desk, adrenaline charging his thoughts. Maybe this woman *was* his ticket to a long-delayed justice. He tried to tamp his rising hope. He'd been disappointed too many times.

"What if the daughter doesn't come?" Gray said. "If her mother told her only a little about Merritta, she should run like hell."

"She'll come. Out of curiosity or greed. Merritta wants

it, and he usually gets what he wants. But maybe we'll get a break and get to her first."

"Then what?"

"We'll try the forthright be-a-good-citizen approach, but if that doesn't work, we should have some leverage with her mother. Tracy Edwards must know something. She might even have had something to do with the 'accident,' if it meant her freedom."

Gray nodded. "I'll start the paperwork for the judge."

Once Gray left, Nate stretched back in his chair. It would be ironic if cancer took Paul Merritta before he could. But there were other members of the family. Nate wouldn't rest until every one of them was taken down.

Introducing a prodigal daughter to the mix could stir up some dust. He might finally get the evidence he needed against the Merritta family, including Nick Merritt. Even if he broke all the rules to do it.

For a moment, the all too familiar image flashed in his mind. His mother holding his hand on the walk to school.

A speeding car. His mother turning. Shots. His mother falling. A sharp pain in his side. Then he was kneeling next to her, his fingers covered with blood as they followed the stitch work of bullet holes in her body . . .

Maybe, at last, his mother might rest in peace.

And he might obtain some peace of his own.

To Sam's surprise, her two visitors from the previous day were not at the gallery when she opened it an hour late. Nor did they appear during the rest of the morning.

Every time the little bell on the door rang, electricity shot through her despite a dullness from lack of sleep. It was all she could do be pleasant to the potential customers who wandered in to the shop.

Terri appeared at lunchtime. She took one look at Sam and blinked. "You look awful."

"I didn't get much sleep," Sam said in one of the world's greatest understatements.

"Why don't you go home? I'll watch the shop."

Sam desperately wished she could do that. But what if the two men returned?

Terri noticed her hesitation. "What's going on, Sam?"

Sam wanted to confide in Terri, but again she didn't feel she could tell even her until she knew the truth. She did tell Terri about the break-in, though. One of Terri's friends was with the police department, and she would find out anyway.

Terri stared at her with concern. "Have you been to a doctor?"

"No, I just have a little bump."

Terri's gaze didn't leave her. "Could it have anything to do with those two men yesterday?"

Sam shook her head. "I don't think so."

Terri gave her a dubious look but didn't press the point. "You should have that injury checked. You know any head wound could be dangerous."

"I'm fine," Sam insisted.

"I'll go with you," Terri persisted.

"I'm all right, really I am, and we can't both be gone."

"If you start feeling bad . . ."

"I'll let you know."

"I can stay here with you."

"Not necessary and there's some errands you can run for me. Some paintings need to be packaged and shipped." She didn't want Terri here when — or if — the men returned. She didn't want questions asked she couldn't answer. She had lied to the police. She didn't want to lie to her best friend.

The moment Terri left with wrapped paintings in hand, the two men appeared.

Sam was at her desk this time when they entered. She didn't rise and didn't intend to. Nor would she be intimidated this time. By God, this was *her* gallery, in *her* town. They had invaded it, and possibly had invaded her home. She barely suppressed her rage, but she wanted some answers. Anger might not get them.

The older man held out another envelope.

She made no attempt to take it. "What is it this time?"

"A round-trip plane ticket to Boston. First class." The last was obviously meant to impress her.

It didn't. "I won't do anything until I talk to my mother," she said.

"She'll lie," the man said flatly, letting the envelope fall on her desk.

"Why?"

"She abandoned her husband and son. No decent woman would do that."

"And the man you claim is my father *is* decent?"

The older man looked surprised. "People lie about him."

"Really?" she said. "And what's your name?"

"Tommy."

"Tommy what?"

"Just Tommy. I'm a friend of your father's."

"A soldier?"

He blinked, then shrugged. "An associate," he corrected. The younger man coughed.

She looked at the envelope he'd dropped on her desk. "I don't want it. If I decide to go, I'll pay my own way."

A flash of annoyance flickered in his eyes. "Stubborn. Like your brother."

She couldn't resist the question. "How?"

"Come to Boston and you'll find out."

"Does he know about me?"

Satisfaction flickered across his face. She'd indicated curiosity and he obviously thought his mission had succeeded. Well, it hadn't. She wanted more information. That was all.

"No," he said.

"Why not?"

He shrugged, and she knew he was not going to say more.

She gave in to her curiosity. "How long has . . . Paul Merritta known about me?"

"He's been searching for you for years, ever since the . . . ever since your mother disappeared. He just recently found you."

"How can someone just disappear?"

"You might ask your ma that."

"Then how did he find me?"

He looked uncomfortable. "It's easier to find people today."

It sounded logical. She knew that computerized advances had made the world much smaller. And why would Paul Merritta choose to contact her now, if he'd known where she was for years?

"You can have your answer in the morning," she said.

"The ticket is for this afternoon."

"Too bad you wasted your money."

He hesitated. "My boss isn't happy that your mother kept him from you all these years." There was an odd note in his voice. Odd, and even malevolent.

A threat. And aimed at her mother.

But he wasn't going to see her flinch. She wouldn't show fear. Not in front of them. "You can call me in the morning."

She did not bother to offer her phone number. It was obvious he knew a lot more about her than she did about him, or the Merrittas. It was equally obvious he was not going to say anything more unless she agreed to go.

And if she didn't? She would not put it past them to take her by force.

She thought again of the articles that reported the activities of crime families. To her, they meant murder, narcotics, prostitution, gambling, and God knew what else.

If true, did she want any part of it?

"My house was burglarized this morning," she said, dropping what she hoped was a bomb.

Surprise crossed his face, then anger. It was the first time she had seen him disconcerted.

"When?" he asked.

"While I was jogging. I apparently came home too soon. He . . . struck me."

Something indefinable crossed his face. For a moment, she thought it might be concern.

"Would you know anything about it?" she challenged him.

"No," he said flatly.

For some reason, she believed him. "Then who?"

"I don't know," he said. "I'll try to find out."

Odd, that his reply relieved her even as she wondered why she would believe anything he said. Yet he had been surprised. She would swear to it.

Her world had been turned upside down by these men. Her life had been normal, happy, loving, peaceful. It had been uncomplicated, marred only by the death of her father.

Without another word, the two men left the shop. The older one left the envelope on the table.

For a moment, she felt an odd victory. She had survived the encounter on her terms. But after the door closed, she remembered the satisfaction in his eyes. He'd seen her face when they had referred to her mother. She must have shown some emotion. Fear? Certainly she had tried to hide it.

Now she wasn't sure she had won anything at all.

Instead she felt as if she had just been trumped.

four

The day went all too slowly. Sam's head still ached. And the thought of the looming confrontation with her mother made her nauseous.

She closed the gallery early. Her mother was due home this evening.

Sam would know then if it was all a terrible lie. Or an even more horrendous truth.

Sam decided to go home early and take a nap, but once there, she couldn't sleep, or even rest. She no longer felt safe there. The house she loved so much had been invaded.

Every rustle of a breeze against the window startled her and she found herself wandering listlessly around the house. For the first time, she wondered whether she needed an alarm system and extra locks. She'd never wanted to live in a fortress. Now she didn't want to live in fear.

She fed Sarsy and watered plants, knowing she was avoiding thoughts she didn't want. Giving up any idea of resting, she took her keys and drove over to her mother's condominium.

Once there, she let herself in, poured a glass of red wine and went out to the balcony. The clouds were heavy, ominous, the summer wind heavy with moisture. She hoped her mother arrived before the storm broke.

She went back inside. Her gaze roamed over the family photos that decorated the living area and the grand piano. Her mother was a fine pianist, although she'd never studied music.

Or at least she'd said she never studied.

Sam realized she was now questioning whether anything she thought she knew about her mother was true.

She gazed at all the photos, looking for a secretive glance, a hint somewhere of a life kept concealed. She was tempted to prowl through her mother's drawers, but the thought repelled her.

No clues. At least no obvious ones. Her father had served in the early years of Vietnam. She knew that only from small slips, the odd observation when they'd watched a television show about the war, or she'd talked about a film. Neither of her parents ever talked much about years that were usually important to couples. Early years. Formative years. Dating. Marriage.

"Where did you go to college, Mom?"

"A little college in the Midwest. Your father swept me off my feet and I never finished."

"Maybe I should think about looking at that one."

"Oh, no, honey. You wouldn't like it. It was small. I couldn't afford anything else. Your father and I want the best for you."

And so she had gone to Stanford with a double major in computer science and marketing.

"Oh, Mom, what happened?" she whispered to herself.

She didn't turn on the lights, just watched as the sky grew darker, the clouds more formidable, hoping to hear the key turn in the lock. And dreading it.

Finally she did.

She kept sitting, her purse next to her. In the purse were the photos, and birth certificates.

Her mother turned on the light, then saw her. "Darling, what are you doing sitting here in the dark?"

"Find anything on your trip?"

"Some great paintings. You're going to love them. I took them by the gallery. We'll go over them in the—" She stopped suddenly. "What's wrong? What's happened?"

For a moment Sam couldn't speak. Did she really want to do this? And yet she must. She had to know.

She finally forced the words out. "I had visitors yesterday, and again today. They . . . they said my father . . . my biological father . . . is alive but dying and wants to see me."

All the color drained from her mother's face, and in that moment, Sam knew the story was true.

Her mother's purse dropped, and she reached for the arm of a chair to steady herself. "No," she whispered. "No."

"They said I have a brother. A twin brother."

Her mother slumped into the chair.

Sam noticed the bracelet she always wore. Her good luck charm, her mother said. Sam had thought David had given it to her. Now she wondered. It did not look like something her father would buy. And it never left her wrist.

"I told them they were wrong. That David Carroll was my father."

"He . . . *was*."

"My biological father?"

A long, painful silence. Every muscle in her mother's face seemed frozen.

"Were you married to Paul Merritta?" Sam felt like a bully now. She wanted to stop as she watched her mother crumple, but she couldn't. She had to know now before her courage failed her.

"Yes." The word was little more than a whimper.

"He's my father?"

"No! *David's* your father."

"But not my biological father."

"In every way that was important." Her face twisted with grief.

A clap of thunder rocked the condo. Lightning streaked the sky. Rain fell in torrents, beating against the balcony doors, the windows.

"So it's . . . true," Sam said in a half whisper.

"He swore . . ."

"He swore what?" Sam asked.

"That he would never try to find you." A tear wandered down her mother's cheek. "And David took precautions." She stopped. "Oh, my God, what did I do?"

Sam felt as if the floor had fallen away under her, that she was falling down into Alice's rabbit hole.

Until now, she hadn't realized that she'd really believed everything was a lie. She had been waiting for her mother to deny everything. A terrible mistake. Doctored photos. Doctored documents. *Something.* Some explanation.

"Samantha . . ."

But Sam couldn't answer.

Her safe, sane, comfortable world had just exploded.

Sam didn't know how much time passed before she could speak again.

Her mother looked stricken. She was sitting stiff and pale as a statue, tears puddling in her eyes.

Her own face was probably every bit as pale through the tan. Sam felt as though she herself might shatter.

"David took precautions?" she repeated. "And what did . . . you do?"

"My sister. I contacted my sister. I believed that so many years had gone . . . we were safe."

Sister? More lies. Her mother always said she had no family. But that was a small lie compared to the big one being confirmed by her mother's face, her words.

A brother she had never known. A biological father

whose existence had been hidden from her. Lies and more lies.

"They left photos." Barely suppressing her outrage, Sam placed the family photo on the coffee table in front of her mother, then the one of Nick Merritt.

Her mother stared at the latter one for a long time, touched it in an unmistakable caress, then put it down, a hopeless look in her face. "There were reasons."

"I'm thirty-five. There's been time to explain. For God's sake, I always wanted a brother . . ." Sam's voice trailed off, as her mother kept glancing at the photo, as if she couldn't see enough.

"I know," her mother said, her voice cracking. "It broke my heart."

"Did it?" Sam said coldly, fury and confusion ruling her now.

"Yes," her mother said. "You said he—Paul—wants to see you?"

"My father," Sam corrected. The word was like a huge cold stone in her gut.

Her mother winced. "You have his blood, yes. But you have nothing else in common with him. Don't go," she pleaded. "Don't have anything to do with him." Again, her mother's gaze returned to the photo of Nicholas, seemingly riveted to it.

"I haven't decided," Sam said, knowing it wasn't true. She had to find out about her brother. If only her biological father was the issue, she doubted she would consider it. Apparently he had let her go. But Nicholas . . .

Nicholas!

"My name was Nicole?"

"I wanted you to have similar names," her mother said with a sad whisper of a smile. "I always liked Nicole."

"It's . . . pretty."

"You were a beautiful baby, but I've told you that."

"And my brother? Was he a beautiful baby, too?"

"Yes." Her voice sounded strangled. "Samantha—"

"Did we like each other?" Sam asked, ignoring the plea in her mother's voice, hating herself for pressing. But she couldn't stop. "Did we play with each other?"

"Yes." A sigh. Resigned.

"How could you do it? How could you abandon a child?"

"I could save only one," her mother said. "He would have killed both of us to keep the boy."

"The boy? Is that how you justified leaving him? Save one? Throw away the other?"

Her mother's tears were coming faster now. Sam felt she was drowning in her mother's pain. In her own bewilderment. *The boy*. Not *Nicholas*. Not *my son*. Her mother's way of coping, her defense? Sam wanted to rip that defense away from her.

"I'm going to see him," she said.

"Paul Merritta?" Horror was in her mother's voice.

"My brother. Maybe Mr. . . . Merritta." She couldn't say *father* again. Despite what she'd said earlier, that title still belonged to David Carroll.

"No!"

"Why?"

"They'll destroy you."

Sam met her mother's gaze. "Did they destroy *you*?"

"They tried to."

"And yet you left my brother there?" She tried to keep her voice steady. "How old was I when . . . you left?"

Her mother's head drooped. "Eight months."

"I have a birth certificate with Daddy's name on it," Sam said, suddenly seizing on something that might still deny what she now knew was true.

"David arranged for it," her mother said.

"My father, the ex-soldier. I always knew he was a man of many talents. I didn't know it included forgery."

Her mother's head shot up. "Whatever you think of me,

he was the best thing that could possibly have happened to both of us."

Sam wanted to strike out at something. Everything she thought was solid and right and true was sinking under the weight of what she was hearing.

"Why didn't you tell me?"

"That your biological father was a murderer, a crime lord? Would you have wanted to know that?"

"Perhaps not when I was young, but later . . . I had a right to know. What if there was something hereditary? What if I had children?"

"Then perhaps I would have said something. But you haven't shown any interest in marriage yet and . . ."

"And my brother?" Sam's voice broke. *My brother.* Strange how naturally the words came to her tongue. "You thought it was right not to let me know—"

"He's lost," her mother interrupted in an emotionless voice. "Anyone raised in that family is corrupted."

Disbelieving, Sam stared at her. "You must have seen something in my father. How could you . . ." Her voice trailed off.

"Marry a criminal?" her mother said bitterly. "I was young. Poor. I was on a scholarship at the University of Chicago. Paul was a last-year law student. Older than most. I met him in the library, and he was everything I thought I ever wanted. He was charismatic. He treated me like a princess."

Her hand clenched in a fist. "I fell in love. I didn't know who he was. Or what he was. We eloped to Las Vegas immediately when we graduated. I never questioned why he didn't want a formal wedding. Why I didn't meet his family first. He kept saying he was afraid I would change my mind. I thought he feared his family wouldn't think I was good enough for him, but I thought love would conquer everything."

Her fingers twisted together. "We took a long honeymoon. He had a lot of money, and he bought me clothes and jewelry. He was kind and gentle. Then he took me home, and the nightmare started.

"We moved in with his family. I was the outsider from the beginning. It was obvious everyone disapproved of his choice. They were Italian. I was Anglo-Saxon and a Protestant. But I loved Paul and I tried to please his family. That meant not asking questions.

"I wanted to teach music or art. They were my double majors in college. But he said no. I was pregnant then, and I foolishly thought he was being protective. But that wasn't it. He didn't want me to hear the rumors. I became a prisoner under the guise of my health.

"It didn't take long to discover I'd married into a crime family. Paul always swore he wasn't involved. I wanted to believe him. Then I overheard a conversation . . .

"My blood ran cold, but by then I was very, very pregnant with two babies. I didn't have any place to go. I had a sister who'd raised me after my mother died, but she had two children and no money. I was afraid I might put them in danger."

She stood and walked unsteadily toward the balcony. "I didn't want you to grow up in that way."

Sam tried to absorb it all. She couldn't. It was something out of a novel. Her mother married to a crime lord?

"Does . . . Nicholas know about us?" Her mother's voice broke the tense silence.

"They said not."

A visible shiver ran through her mother's body. "You can't go," she said again. "You have no idea what they are like. What they do."

Sam didn't say anything. To be lied to as a child for one's sake was one thing. To continue the deception was something else. She wondered whether she would ever totally trust her mother again.

And yet as she looked at her, Sam felt an equal amount

of love and even compassion. She'd always respected her
mother's values, her sense of right and wrong. But now she
also remembered how watchful she'd been. Until Sam was
sixteen and had her own car, her mother or father drove her
to school every day and picked her up. She never walked
like other kids in the neighborhood despite her many pleas.

She'd also been drilled to keep the door locked, even at
home, and their house was the first in the area to have a security system. She'd been warned repeatedly never to talk
to a stranger, and to tell either parent if anyone tried to approach her. Her father had told her to run like hell if anyone did.

And their cabin.

She'd hadn't ever been allowed to take friends there, or
even speak of it. *"Our secret place,"* her father had said.
"Our Shangri-la." The image had been pure magic for her,
and she'd never said anything, not even to Terri. Now the
secret took on other dimensions.

Now she knew why her mother was always so cautious,
why they didn't tell anyone about their lake cabin.

"Why did you call your sister?" Sam asked.

"It's been more than three decades since I. . left
Boston," her mother said. "David had been with Special
Forces. He'd had other jobs with the government. He knew
how to get lost, how to create new identities. He told me
never to contact anyone I ever knew. But when he died, I
wanted to see my sister again. I wrote her last month. I visited her three weeks ago. So much time. I can't believe . . ."

"The weekend trip with friends?" Sam had been mildly
surprised that her mother had left three weekends ago. To
visit friends, she'd said. But it had been the first time her
mother had left Steamboat without David or on anything
but short business trips to buy art.

Tears spilled over and ran down her mother's cheeks.

Not just one, but many. They were quiet tears, the kind that held anguish. "I truly thought we were safe."

Another shock ran through Sam. Someone had lain in wait for more than thirty years to find Mother. And her.

Her mother's eyes pleaded with her to understand. "Don't go," she whispered. "We can leave tonight. We can go to Mexico or—"

"Run away?" Sam said. "What about the gallery? Our homes? Friends?"

"You don't understand, Samantha."

"No," Sam agreed. "I don't. I only know I have a twin brother and a life that's been a lie."

"We thought it best."

"You and David thought it best," Sam said. "How did you meet him?"

She watched her mother swallow. "I . . . hired him. I had escaped with you but I knew Paul or his family would come after us. My sister knew someone who had just retired from the military. We fell in love."

Sam had no doubt they had. She remembered how they looked at each other. They'd been in love until the day David Carroll died.

How lonely her mother must have been, to conquer fear and contact her sister.

Sam felt the hot rush of guilt. Perhaps if she had been more attentive, had recognized that her mother had not adjusted to David's death as well as she'd thought . . .

"Tell me more about Paul Merritta," Sam said.

"I've tried not to think about him for the past thirty-four years."

"And . . . my brother? Have you thought about him?"

"All the time." Her mother uttered the three words so quietly, in such an unnaturally tense voice, that Sam could only guess at the pain her mother hid behind her struggle for calm.

"Then how could you have left him?"

"It was the only way I could save you." She had said the words before, but Sam had barely grasped them. It was almost a litany—a painful, frequently repeated litany.

She stiffened. "At his expense?"

Her mother knotted her hands together until the knuckles were white. "I could save only one." The litany again. Sam could imagine the justification being said over and over again, but never quite believed.

Sam was struck with pity that reached through her anger. Her mother had always seemed so controlled, so self-contained, but now Sam knew it was a facade hiding a devastating secret. "Maybe Nicholas didn't need saving," she said gently. "He has your genes as well as his . . . our . . . father's." The "our" was chilling. What kind of nightmare had her mother lived through to drive her to such a choice? "When did you marry Daddy?" she asked, needing time to regroup.

"You were a year old. We moved out here. David changed all our names. We bought this business."

Sam felt she should have known—somehow—that she had not belonged to David, at least in the biological sense. Yet they'd shared many of the same physical characteristics. They'd both been tall, had a certain angular body, the same interest in the outdoors and sports. They were both fairly laid back, while her mother had been more high-strung, a perfectionist.

"David wanted me to tell you," her mother said. "He thought they would come after you some day." She paused. "Please, no matter what you think of my decision, don't go to Boston."

"Paul Merritta has nothing against me," Sam said. She thought of the implied threat against her mother from her two recent visitors. She couldn't mention it. Not now. "They said he'd been searching for me all these years. What about you and Daddy? Did you try to find out about Nicholas? Or did Daddy know anything about him?"

"He knew," her mother said softly. Her hands separated and fingers of one hand touched the bracelet on the other arm.

Sam felt a tug on her heart. Secrets. So many secrets. "I want to meet my brother. And find out why Paul Merritta wants to meet me." She hesitated. "And if he's dying, it might be my only chance to . . ." To do what? She didn't know.

"I'll go with you."

Sam heard fear in her voice. "No," Sam said. "It's something I have to do alone. But I want you to go to the cabin. No one knows about that."

"The gallery—"

"Helen and Terri can look after it. Terri has another three weeks before she reports back to school."

"I won't run and hide now. Not without you."

"Why?" Sam said. "Why did you run then?"

"There were reasons. Believe that, Samantha. Reasons I can't discuss now. Not yet."

Her mother's tight lips told Sam nothing she could do would force any more answers.

Her mother tried once more. "Don't go, Samantha. Stay here among friends. People who love you. And . . ."

"And?" Sam asked as her mother hesitated.

"Nothing," her mother said.

But there was something, and Sam knew it. Her mother had never been a good liar. Or perhaps she had been, after all. Maybe it was the small lies that were difficult.

"Do you think he would harm me?"

He. They were talking about *he.* Paul Merritta. Boston attorney. Reputed mob boss. Father.

"He's capable of anything," her mother said quietly.

"If he meant either of us harm, he could have done it. He knows where we are, where you are. Perhaps if I talk to him, you won't worry about him ever again."

"It doesn't work that way with the Merrittas," her

mother said. Then she stood. "I'll fix some tea." Tea had always been her answer to any problem. But this one was much too huge for tea.

Sam followed. "Will you go to the cabin while I'm gone?" she said. "I don't want anyone trying to use you to get to me." Sam thought that possibility might convince her mother more than any argument for her mother's own safety.

"I won't hide while you walk into that—"

Sam broke in. "They made it clear they aren't going away. I wouldn't be safer here than in Boston, and I'm not going to hide the rest of my life."

As soon as the words left her mouth, she realized what she had said. Her mother's face seemed to collapse.

"I'm sorry, baby. I never meant you to be touched by this. Never."

It was the first time in many years since her mother had called her that. Sam opened her arms and her mother moved into them. Her mother stepped away first.

"You're right. Once he makes up his mind . . ." Then her head snapped back up. "We can go to the cabin together."

"What about the gallery? Our homes? He's found you now. He can find you—us—again. But perhaps I can just meet him and that will be the end of it."

Indecision was written all over her mother's face.

"Was your name really Tracy?" Sam asked, trying to break the tension. "That was the name on the birth certificates."

Her mother bit her lip.

"And your maiden name is Edwards?"

"It's been a long time since I've heard that, but yes."

"You mentioned a sister. Is any more of your family still alive? Or were you really an orphan?" She could not keep a wry note from her voice.

"There's only Susan," Patsy Carroll said. "She's eight

years older than I am. When our mother died, she was more mother than sister."

"And you haven't seen her in all these years?"

"Not until three weeks ago."

Some of Sam's anger faded. How much had her mother given up to make her safe? She felt as if she were walking on quicksand, that her reality had been nothing but an elaborate facade, like those western towns in old movies. Cardboard fronts with nothing behind them.

Her mother's reply did not answer all that Sam wanted to know, but her mother looked so tired Sam didn't have the heart to continue what had turned into an interrogation. Later. Maybe later. But she would eventually get answers.

"Will you go to the cabin?" she asked again. The cabin, she knew, was in the name of an obscure company. She'd never known why her father—David—had purchased it that way. She did know the tax bills went to the address of a local attorney who paid the expenses. She'd thought it one of her father's whims, a part of his need for privacy.

"How much did Daddy know?" she asked suddenly.

"Everything," her mother said with a catch in the word. She stared at Sam for a long moment. "When do you plan to go?" It was a surrender. A weary, resigned surrender.

"In two days. It will take that long to finish a few things at the gallery."

"I'll call Helen and ask her to fill in at the gallery then," her mother said. "I'll take Sarsy with me."

"I want you to go tomorrow," Sam said.

Her mother nodded. Sam had won. But there was no sense of victory. All the pleasure over the success of her business trip had drained from her mother's face. She looked ten years older than when she'd walked in.

She looked defeated.

"Maybe we should call the police," Sam said, throwing out another alternative.

Her mother's face paled to chalky white. "No!"

Sam stared at her. So much had been unreal until now. But the fear on her mother's face was real enough.

"It would destroy us," her mother finally said. "It would destroy Wonders. And if the family . . ." She stopped. "Not unless it's absolutely necessary," she said.

Sam swallowed hard at the way her mother said "the family," as if she weren't speaking of relatives but of something far more sinister. Sam wished she was sure she was doing the right thing.

But she had a twin she didn't know, a biological father who was dying and wanted to see her. Even without the threat, she would go. She had no choice.

five

"I'm going with you," Terri announced.

"No," Sam said. "This is something I have to do alone."

"I've never been to Boston," Terri said, ignoring her friend. "And I've always wanted to go, but there was never anyone to go with." She paused. "You said you planned to stay in a hotel, not with . . . them. At least you'll have a friend nearby."

Sam had debated telling Terri what had happened. Although outwardly gregarious, inside Sam was a private person, always holding her thoughts and fears, even ambitions, close. If she were to fail, she did not want anyone to know it. If she were to succeed, well, that too was occasion for private celebration.

But Terri knew her better than anyone.

After they'd shared their twice-weekly run, they went to their favorite restaurant for breakfast. Once seated, Sam found it disturbingly easy to talk about it, the core of the emotional volcano spewing out. They had always trusted each other completely. She knew none of what she revealed would go further. Not unless something happened to her.

Still, she told only part of the tale, that her mother had

been married before, that Sam had been contacted by her biological father in Boston, that her mother feared him. Sam also said she might—or might not—have a brother. She was going to Boston to meet the latter.

She said nothing about the Merrittas—or crime—but she gave Terri a CD with an account of the past few days as she knew them, along with the news stories she'd pulled from the Internet. "Keep it safe," she said.

"Now you're scaring me," Terri said.

Sam smiled. "You know I can be melodramatic. Too many movies."

Terri didn't smile back. "If you need anything . . ."

"Just keep that in a safe place," Sam replied.

Terri shook her head. "I always wondered why your mother was so much more protective than the other mothers. Of course, mine knew my brothers would look out for me."

"I always envied you so," Sam said. "Three brothers."

"Except none of them really looked after me. I was their 'burden.'"

"I don't think so. They just wanted you to think that. I'm told that's the way brothers think." Sam heard the longing in her own voice.

Terri picked up the photo of Nick Merritt. "He's good-looking. He has your dark coloring."

"Or I have his. He's the oldest."

"I should go with you," Terri persisted. "You're my only boss at the moment, and we're caught up with the paperwork."

The offer was enticing. But the burglary was still too much in Sam's mind. So was the subtle threat against her mother. She didn't want to put anyone else in danger.

"This has upset my mother, and she's going to take a few days off and visit friends. I really need your help at Wonders." It was the one argument she thought would work. Terri was a natural-born caretaker. She believed everyone, trusted everyone and would give a stranger her right arm if so requested. It often frustrated Sam, but she also appreciated it.

"You don't think your mother might be in danger?"

"No, but I want her out of town. I'm sure she hasn't told anyone what has happened." She hesitated, then added, "That's one reason I told you. Someone needed to know." She gave her friend a quick grin. "And you have Jake."

Jake was a captain with the sheriff's department, and he'd been asking Terri out.

"I don't *have* Jake."

"But you like him."

"Yep, but I don't love him and I don't think he loves me. He's still trying to get over Shirley. We both feel snakebit, thanks to our ex-significant others."

Sam knew that feeling. She had been waiting for her knight for the last fifteen years and had been disappointed several times. She was beginning to believe that knights were out of fashion, a long-lost relic in today's hectic society.

And if she was honest, she wasn't looking that hard. If someone came along—someone who wanted a partner as well as a wife—she would be happy. If not, she wasn't going to settle for anything less.

"Hellooo," Terri said, passing her hand in front of Sam's face.

Sam shook off thoughts of what might be in favor of more immediate concerns. "I really don't think anyone will hurt Mom now. After all, he—they—must know where she lives now, and no one has tried to hurt her." She was trying to convince herself. "But still I would feel better if someone was nearby for her to call."

"Anyone but your mother . . ." Terri shook her head.

"I know. I'm still trying to rearrange thoughts, impressions, in my head." Sam agreed. "But my mother's afraid, and she's not easily scared."

"Maybe she's just terrified of losing you to him."

"She could never lose me."

"She might not know that," Terri said.

"I tried to tell her."

Terri's gaze met hers directly. "Any hint of danger, come home."

"I plan to," Sam said.

"I know you. You like to take chances."

"Only when I know the odds are on my side," Sam replied. "I'm smart enough to know a mountain and a bad guy aren't the same thing."

Terri did not look reassured.

"I'll keep in touch," Sam promised.

"I'll call the cavalry if you don't."

Sam left her and returned to her house. It was eight in the morning. She suspected the visitors would be waiting for her.

They were sitting in a car in her driveway.

"Not a good thing to do," she told the one named Tommy. "Our police department checks suspicious-looking vehicles with suspicious-looking people in them."

"We knew you would set things straight," Tommy said with a hint of a smile.

"I wouldn't bet on it."

Tommy ignored that. "You coming?"

"Not now. Friday. And I'll pay my own way," she said.

He didn't argue. "What flight? I'll pick you up at the airport."

"No. I'll be staying at a hotel. I'll get myself to . . . Mr. Merritta's house Saturday."

"Mr. Merritta won't like that."

"Those are the terms. If you don't like them, I will still go and make my own arrangements to see my . . . see Nicholas."

"What about your mother?"

"My mother has nothing to do with this. Leave her

alone, or I will never see any of them. If I hear that anything, anything at all, has happened to her, I'll tell the police exactly where to look."

"Your mother is safe enough. Now."

Sam's truculence broke under the implied threat. "I mean it," she whispered.

"She lied to you, didn't she? She made Mr. Merritta's life hell. He's always wanted his little girl."

"I'm not his little girl. I'm no one's little girl," she said.

The man shrugged. "I'll write down the address."

"No need. I found it on the Internet. That and a lot more."

"Sassy, aren't you?" Tommy said. "I'll see you Saturday. Otherwise, we'll be back."

"She's coming," Nate said. "Friday." A rare surge of excitement gripped him. At last a chance to get inside the family.

"We definitely have a wild card in the game," Gray said.

"Some game. Four—maybe five—factions ready to take over when Merritta dies, and willing to do anything to achieve that. Now a long-lost daughter."

"I feel sorry for her."

Nate tapped his fingers on the desk. "She has to know Merritta's involved in organized crime unless she's been in a convent all these years. So if she's coming, she's either greedy or not too smart. Either way, we might be able to use her."

"You're a cynic, Nate, particularly where the Merritta family is concerned. You know about him, but you've been hunting him all these years. There's no reason someone in Colorado would know. Besides, she just discovered she has a brother. Wouldn't it be normal to want to meet him?"

Nate shrugged. "She's a Merritta. Like her brother."

Gray steepled his fingers. "We still don't know Nicholas Merritt is involved in the family business."

"I do. His company with its foreign sales is perfect for money laundering. He grew up in that family. I haven't seen him walk away, go someplace where it wouldn't follow him. No one else could have gotten the loans to start a company that he did at such favorable rates." Nate sat back in his chair. "Or he could be the witness someone in the Bureau is protecting." He could barely suppress a growl. He hated the Bureau practice of protecting criminals to catch other criminals. It often ended up with catching little guys to make arrest records look good. The real bad guys went free.

"If he is, our superiors won't let us touch him."

"Unless it becomes too hairy for them."

"Don't even think about it, Nate. Nailing Merritta isn't worth our careers."

"It's worth mine."

"I doubt there's anything there, anyway. You've been trying to get something on him for years."

"He's smarter than the rest. Doesn't mean he's any more honest."

Gray shook his head. "How do we find this newest member before they get to her?"

"We know she's coming in from Colorado Friday. We could check out all Denver flights. Maybe even start tonight."

"And look for whom? We don't have the manpower, not unless you want to let a few more people in on this."

"No," Nate said sharply. "I don't. No one else is monitoring these conversations, so we can keep it between us for now." He hesitated. He went to his computer and checked on Denver to Boston flights and printed out the schedule. "Only two nonstops daily. One is coming in tonight, two tomorrow."

Gray looked over his shoulder. "And a bunch of connections."

"Let's concentrate on the nonstops," Nate said. "And she has to drive from wherever she is, or catch a commuter to Denver."

"You're assuming a lot. Maybe she's closer to another airport."

"We've been able to pinpoint the cell phone calls to north central Colorado. Denver's the only thing that makes sense."

"Anyway, how will we recognize her?"

"Maybe she looks like Merritta. Or her twin. Or maybe some of Merritta's men will be there."

"I'll take the afternoon flight tomorrow," Gray said, giving up.

"I'll take the evening flight." Nate tapped his printout of flight schedules. "I'll start tonight, just in case."

"And what do I do if I think I've located her?" Gray said. "She hasn't done anything wrong."

"If you find her, call me. Maybe we can convince her to cooperate."

Gray raised an eyebrow. "Right . . . with your charm."

"Go to hell," Nate said with good nature. It was well known he had no charm. He was direct and argumentative and offended nearly everyone, particularly his superiors with his bluntness and unwillingness to play political head games. He was not, he was told repeatedly, a team player.

But he was damn good with numbers, and he had the tenacity of a bulldog. And he closed more than his share of cases. That had saved him.

"If we miss her?" Gray asked.

"Then I'll keep an eye on Merritta's house," Nate said.

"Do you really think she'll cooperate?"

"If she's an honest citizen, she'll help."

"Come on, Nate. How many honest citizens spy on their families?"

Nate shrugged. "I can try."

"Even if she's stupid or greedy?" Gray mocked.

"Either of those qualities can be used to our advantage," Nate said.

"And we don't tell the boss yet?"

"No," Nate said. "I want to get this woman first."

"He isn't going to like it."

Nate shrugged. "We don't know anything for sure yet. We're just exercising initiative."

Gray grinned. "You're going to get me fired, Nate, ole buddy."

"You're as frustrated at our lack of progress as I am."

"Yep, but it doesn't keep me up at nights like it does you."

Nate didn't answer. There was no answer. He would *never* sleep well until the last Merritta was in prison.

"Another IRS audit," Cal White told Nick Merritt when he entered the office. "They've taken over the office."

"McLean?"

"He's probably behind it. They say it's routine."

"Like it's been routine each of the last five years." Nick tried to hold his temper. "I'm sorry, Cal."

"Don't be. You warned me."

"We should have set up shop someplace else."

"We never would have gotten the financing if we had."

Nick laughed bitterly. "I thought we had gotten it on our own."

"We paid it back. That's what's important. We're on our own now."

"If the feds would leave us alone. This audit will close us down for several weeks."

Cal settled into a chair, his long gangly form slowly sinking into the cushions. He stretched out his legs and hiked them up on the desk. "They won't find anything."

"I wouldn't put it past McLean to plant something."

"Neither would I," Cal said. He'd had his own encounters with Nathan McLean, who'd appeared in their offices several times, once after a Mafia-related killing, and again several weeks ago for no apparent reason. They both knew McLean had been unsuccessful at obtaining telephone taps on company phones.

"It's because of my father," Nick said. "There's so many damn rumors now. I'm even getting queries as to who I'll support to take his place. As if it would make any difference."

Cal's brows furrowed. "You didn't tell me that."

"My aunt asked me to go to lunch this week. It's the first time she's called in five years. Uncle Vic called yesterday. Wants a meeting."

"Are you going?"

"And give the feds more ammunition? To hell with them. Maybe I should take a vacation. Say to the South Seas."

"And leave me with the audit?"

Nick knew he couldn't do that. Cal was the inventor, the idea man and the general nerd in their partnership. He stuttered when he met a stranger. Authority figures intimidated him.

They had met in the service. It had been Nick's rebellion and Cal's only way to an education. Both had been trained as medics. Nick was older, having attended two years of college and nearing the end of his service when the Gulf War broke out. They had been on duty when an Iraqi rocket hit a barracks in Saudi Arabia.

During the harrowing aftermath, he and Cal had become friends and attended the same university on veteran programs. Cal had majored in engineering and Nick in business. Cal had talked about ideas he had for several medical devices he thought would help those suffering traumatic wounds, and the two had decided to start a small firm together.

Boston, with all its medical facilities, seemed the logical place to locate the business. It would be easier to get financing there, as well as professional consultants. Nick had hesitated, knowing that his name might be a detriment, but he didn't like the idea of running away from it, either. And he loved Boston. He loved the waterfront, the row houses, the history and vitality, the sea and his small sailboat. He wasn't going to give it up because of his family. He'd thought Boston would be big enough for all of them—him, the family, the FBI. Then there were times, like now, when he wasn't sure the planet was big enough for all of them.

The phone rang. He picked it up, balancing it on his shoulder.

"Merritt," he said

"Nick?"

He tensed. "Yes."

"Join us for supper Saturday night."

"I can't. I have other plans."

"It's important, Nick. I have a surprise."

"I'm too old for surprises. Are you calling from home?"

"I'm calling my son. I can do that, can't I?"

Yes, he could, and the feds would be listening on the tap they no doubt had on his father's phone. Nick swore under his breath. The only way to end the call was to agree. "What time?"

"Around six?"

"All right," he said. "Good-bye."

"Your father?" Cal asked.

Nick shrugged. "The monthly duty visit. Hell, Cal, he's dying."

"I didn't say anything."

"You never say anything. You're a saint."

"Tell Janet that."

"She already knows that." Nick envied Cal his wife. Janet would never be called beautiful, but she had a warmth that drew people to her. She was funny and realistic and smart and, next to Cal, had the biggest heart of anyone Nick knew.

He stood. "We'd better tell Russell about the audit. It will make his day."

The plane was late taking off from Denver. Sam had taken a puddle jumper to the Denver airport, then had a long wait for her flight. She wouldn't reach Boston until eleven tonight, but it was the only nonstop, and she didn't want to make connections. Too many delays these days; too many airports closing down for some security reason.

She kept glancing around at people in the terminal, then on the plane. She knew she was overreacting but better to err on the side of caution.

Her mother's philosophy. How many times had she heard those words? Now they held new meaning.

Sam sat back and closed her eyes as the plane took off. Ten minutes later, when the expected announcement came about passengers being able to use electronic devices, she turned on her notebook computer and went to her Merritta file again, lingering for a moment on a news photo of her father. She compared that with the one she carried, the photo given her by the "messengers." He wore a proud smile as he loomed above his wife and children. He was handsome and confident-looking and had a possessive hand on her mother's shoulder. The later news photo showed a man putting on weight, his face not as sharply handsome but still possessing magnetic eyes.

She wished she had pushed her mother for more information. Had she been physically abused? She hadn't said so. But would she? Her mother was a proud woman.

What had scared her so badly that she had left a child behind?

Why was she — Samantha — so determined to open Pandora's box?

She usually didn't question her decisions. She learned that didn't help anything. But now she did question.

Was she making a terrible mistake?

Should she have contacted the police? The FBI? Anyone?

And tell them what? That a father wanted to see his daughter?

She swallowed hard. She'd come this far. She couldn't turn around now. She would meet her father, ask him to leave her mother in peace. Surely if he cared enough to want to see his daughter, he would agree to her one request of him.

And perhaps her brother would agree to meet their mother. Sam knew that would mean everything to her mother.

Sam tried to still her spasms of apprehension. And prayed she wasn't opening a door that would plunge both her and her mother into something neither could control.

six

As Sam deplaned at Boston's Logan Airport, she looked around for what she thought of as wiseguys for want of a better description. Then she remembered that nonpassengers were no longer allowed on the concourse.

She was still wary. Her Boston visitors had said they had nothing to do with the burglary of her home. Then who had? The coincidence was too hard to believe, though she'd tried.

The thought of another party involved haunted her.

There were a few loiterers in the gate area. She supposed they had departed the plane before she did or were waiting for a flight.

Her attention focused on a tall, lanky man who stood next to an airline customer-service representative. Since it was past eleven at night, most airport personnel—if not all—were headed toward the exit and home.

The stranger's gaze had lingered on several passengers—all women—who preceded her. She'd noticed with wry resignation—men always scoped out the female of the species, just as he was doing now.

He was lean to the point of thinness, but there was an aura of strength about him. Strength and barely controlled energy. His sandy blond hair looked as if it had been combed by fingers, if at all. His face was all angles. Not handsome, but arresting. She saw battles in his face—in the firm line of his mouth, the wariness in his eyes. The straightness of his bearing suggested he was guarding something and would never surrender it.

Himself, perhaps?

Their gazes met and she felt an odd sense of recognition, of attraction, a quickening of her senses. Her breath stopped for a moment, then came a bit too fast. Something about him touched her—the utter stillness that overtook him as he stared back at her, the starkness in his gaze.

The utter sense of aloneness of it.

She forcibly shook off the spell as he seemed to take in a choppy breath. Her hands trembled as she leaned over to rearrange her carry-on and purse. When she straightened, he had turned away from her, only his profile visible as he smiled at the customer service agent.

Again she shook her head, this time at her odd lapse into imagination. She must really be desperate for diversion from worry and fear to let herself be distracted by a face in a near-empty airport.

"Hey, pretty lady," someone said in a low voice behind her.

She spun around. A fellow passenger. Tall. Good-looking. Nonthreatening. He'd sat in the seat in front of her and had offered to help her with her carry-on bag.

She tried a brief impersonal smile that usually put off unwanted Romeos.

He apparently didn't get the message. "You looked as if you were looking for someone," he continued in the same low, intimate voice. "If someone isn't meeting you, perhaps we could share a cab if you're going downtown. It's late, and you shouldn't be alone." He put an arm around her.

She realized he was a little drunk.

Sam knew her smile was fading. "No, thank you," she said as she released the handle of her wheeled carry-on and faced him, instincts developed in self-defense class kicking in. "I've made arrangements."

It was a lie, but he seemed to accept it. "I'll walk with you down to baggage claim, then."

She turned toward the stranger with the interesting face, but his attention had wandered from her to another woman deplaning.

What had attracted her attention, anyway? He was probably just a pilot or a businessman who spent too many hours settling for a few casual words with acquaintances rather than conversation with friends or family. She'd met men like him when she'd done a lot of business traveling for her former employers. They made their living in the cockpits of airplanes or in first-class seats, and spent much of their time in hotels.

Several of her coworkers used to speculate about people in airports, but she never had. But she'd never before been going to meet a mobster father and brother she'd never known existed.

Any diversion was welcome. Even a drunken stranger.

She started down the concourse, only too aware of the persistent man striding beside her. She didn't want a scene, but she would stop in the next rest room and get rid of her unwanted companion.

Staring straight ahead, she missed a foot in her way and stumbled. She caught herself, but in doing so, she stopped and glanced backward. The man who had so unexpectedly interested her was still there, one hand resting on the counter, the other holding a cell phone to his ear. And for a moment, he seemed to slump—just a little—as if he'd suffered a momentary lapse into weariness.

His gray-green tweed sports coat was unbuttoned and

had fallen open, his gray slacks and white shirt were rumpled and the knot of his tie had been pulled loose.

What struck her, though, was the intensity of his vivid green eyes and the energy radiating from his body as he spoke into the phone. His foot tapped; his hand moved as he talked. His eyes, she thought, didn't seem to miss anything, and now they seemed fastened on her.

She turned back to see her companion charging ahead without her, evidently finally getting the message.

She relaxed, realizing only then that her body had become stiff with tension. It wasn't exactly fear she felt but something more like wariness. Caution.

Was this how her mother had lived—never allowing herself an unguarded moment, always having to watch and suspect everything? Would she feel that way every time she encountered a stranger? She turned back to the concourse, her pace quickening as she passed closed stores and a bar with one lonely-looking patron.

But as fast as she walked, others were keeping pace. Most people at this time of night were on automatic pilot, going their own way. She followed the signs leading to the baggage area and transportation. She would grab a cab there.

As she reached the luggage area and saw all the people waiting in front of empty conveyors, she was grateful she had managed to get everything into her carry-on. She didn't plan to stay long. She had a life to return to.

Something made her turn. She caught a glimpse of the man who had been talking to the airline employee. He was coming toward her, not stopping at luggage claim, all that energy she'd sensed now concentrated on her.

Then she saw two other men approaching her. They had no luggage. No briefcases. Their gaze was focused on her, too, and they had the same look as the men who had entered her shop days ago and turned her world upside down.

Only neither one was Tommy, and she sensed malevolence in their movements.

She looked toward the door. People out there were waiting for pickups or for buses. Where was the taxi line? There shouldn't be much of a line at this time of night. For a split second she searched for the first man . . . the tired one with the arresting eyes. She caught sight of him again and had the strongest urge to run toward him, to ask for help.

But he was taking a diagonal path in front of the other two men, as if to cut them off. As if he'd known she needed help.

Her imagination again. Whatever the reason, she sent him a silent thank-you he could neither hear nor see and continued toward the door . . . and escape.

She spurted forward, no longer rolling her luggage but holding it, ready to use it as a weapon. She looked for police, for someone in uniform. There was no one. She could yell at tired passengers waiting for luggage, but she had no proof of impending trouble.

Just the feeling of being stalked and hunted.

Fear had never ruled her before. Now it did.

She heard a shout. "Stop!"

Then she pushed the door open and rushed outside. With a quick glance back, she saw the sandy-haired man cut off one of the two men who had so disquieted her, blocking his way. The other one was looking around, then homed in on her and headed in her direction. There was no mistaking his intent now.

She bumped someone. A policeman.

Thank God.

He looked down at her. "Is there a problem, miss?"

She didn't know what to say. *I belong to the Merritta family and I think someone is chasing me.* Not likely. What if the men had been sent to protect her? What if news got

out and destroyed her mother? What if no one was following her at all? Maybe she had just become paranoid.

"I thought someone was following me," she said, looking back now that she felt safer.

A shout from inside made the officer look that way, then
at her. She saw a line of taxicabs just ahead and nearly
crumpled with relief. She had to get away from here. "I'm
all right," she assured the policeman. "It's been a long
day." Smiling, she backed away and stepped toward the
nearest cab, all but lunging inside.

"I have to wait—" the driver said.

She reached in her purse and grabbed a fifty, handing it
to him. "Please."

He turned to look at her for a moment that seemed an
eternity. Then he pulled away from the curb and sped off.

Nathan McLean swore long and hard.

He shouldn't have waited. But he hadn't been sure that
the tall, dark-haired woman was the one he sought, especially not after another passenger put his arm around her.
They had looked as if they were traveling together, the
man following her off the plane.

Then her companion had leaned over and whispered in
her ear and she'd stalked off.

Despite that odd second of attraction that flashed between them, he had no interest in getting involved in a
lovers' spat. He studied the other passengers. At least he
had the passenger manifest and phone numbers where passengers could be reached in case of flight changes.

He damned his inability to obtain a photo. He'd had
several people working on the case, going back and checking all the information they had on Tracy Merritta. They'd
located one relative—a sister—but she'd been out of
town. Calls to her children only elicited the fact they all
believed their aunt to be dead.

If he'd had more time . . .

But how to find a needle in a haystack, when all they had was a quick cell call from Colorado? All the conversations had been too brief to track the location any closer. No names. No descriptions. No leads.

If Tracy Merritta was indeed alive, she had dropped off the face of the earth, and to do that, he knew, she'd needed professional help. . . .

The woman who'd so distracted him had blue eyes and dark hair. She started across the gate area, the man beside her. Nate studied her again. Her eyes were blue, and her hair not quite as dark as Nick Merritt's, but there was something about her . . .

Then another woman deplaned alone. She had the same basic coloring, and he stepped up to her, only to discover she was a physician returning to Boston. There were no other likely prospects.

A fool's errand, he thought to himself. It had been a long shot from the beginning. He started to use his cell phone to call Gray when he saw the first woman stumble. Their eyes met again, and the man who had been accompanying her left her.

Adrenaline suddenly flowed through him. Perhaps he'd hesitated earlier because of the intense gaze they'd exchanged. It had hit him like a sledgehammer. He'd quickly dismissed any thought she could be Merritta's daughter. No way. None at all.

But now . .

She was alone. She had Nick Merritta's coloring, even his tall, slim figure.

Damn it.

He mumbled something to Gray on the cell phone, turning to go after her, when the airline employee blocked him, saying all passengers had debarked. When he looked up again, she was gone. He trotted down the concourse looking for her, even as he swore all the way.

He saw her just as she entered the baggage area, and he

increased his pace. Almost as if she knew he was there, he saw her turn, a startled expression on her face. Then she paled as two men walked toward her. He knew one of them. A paid killer. A freelancer.

They moved toward her, nothing welcoming or protective about them. He acted instinctively, cutting one of them off, giving the woman a chance to get away.

Through the corner of his left eye, he saw she was aware of the danger, and she started running. He wanted to go after her, but the man he'd blocked had a knife in his hand. Someone shouted, and people started running for doors.

He ducked then swiveled to avoid the blade. The other thug tripped him and shouted something to his companion. They took off and a uniformed guard stood over him, a gun in his hand.

It took several minutes for her panic to subside as the cab maneuvered out of the terminal area.

"Where to, lady?" the cabbie said.

She had no idea. She certainly wasn't going to the hotel where she'd made a reservation.

That was the only thing she knew. She didn't know who those two men were. Or why they had filled her with such a sense of being menaced. Nor did she know why the first man she'd seen at the gate had not provoked that same sense of imminent danger. In his own way, he'd looked as hard as the other two men. But not threatening.

Go to the police, her mind shouted. But she couldn't stop remembering her mother's face when Sam had proposed that very thing. No. The answer had been unequivocal.

Her mother feared the law as much as she feared her former husband's family. But why?

Sam looked at her watch. Nearly midnight. It was only ten in Colorado, but she felt emotionally and physically drained. Who was the sandy-haired man with all his intensity? And what did he want with her?

And who were the other two men? Paul Merritta's employees?

"Lady, where to?" the cabbie asked again in an impatient voice.

"Know of a good reasonable hotel?"

"No reservation?"

She hesitated long enough to draw another glance in the rearview mirror.

"No," she said.

He made a turn, then another. They were in downtown Boston. She suddenly wondered whether she was wise to entrust her safety to a perfect stranger. She looked at the identification card on the back of the front seat. A name she couldn't decipher.

He drove up to the front of a large hotel. She recognized the chain name. She dug in her pocketbook for the fare, adding it to the fifty she had already given him. "Thank you," she said. She jumped out of the cab and went inside.

The lobby was nearly empty. She went directly to an elevator, rode it up to the tenth floor, then came back down in the other bank of elevators. She went out a side entrance. She'd seen the technique used in a movie. It made sense.

Paranoid. The word was echoing in her head again. *You've seen too many of those movies.*

She walked quickly across the parking lot and down several streets. She passed two hotels before settling on a third. It wasn't as elegant as the first but the desk clerk was understanding when she explained that her wallet with all its credit cards had just been stolen but that she always hid cash in a separate place. She paid cash for a night and left a fifty-dollar deposit for "extras." Her name was given as Alice Carter.

She reached her room, secured the locks and ran water

in the bath as she unpacked her clothes. One dress and several pantsuits. She searched the room for a minibar but didn't find one.

She wanted to call her mother, but not from here. Nor did she wish to frighten her out of hiding. Maybe she'd misconstrued everything, she told herself.

Instead of phoning, she sank into the tub full of hot water and sighed as the tension in her body melted into exhaustion.

Unfortunately, her mind refused to stop working. What in the hell was going on? The question played over and over again.

If her biological—and that was the only way she could even consider the relationship—father had sent for her, why would he wish her harm? And why would anyone try to hurt the supposed daughter of one of the most feared men in Boston?

Questions. So many questions.

She stayed in the bathtub for a long time, continually adding hot water. She wanted to wash away that feeling of fear, of being vulnerable. Of being a victim. She'd never allowed herself to be one. She didn't plan to start now.

"What now, Sherlock?"

If Nate didn't like Gray as much as he did, he would have punched him. Mainly because he couldn't hit himself.

He'd lost her. It had taken him several precious seconds to show the airport police his credentials. While he'd convinced them he was who he said he was, she'd already taken off in a cab.

But at least he knew she'd gotten away. They'd located the cabbie, and he'd told them he'd taken her to a hotel. Problem was no one of her description was registered there.

He'd called Gray from the airport and asked him to meet him at the office.

"They weren't Merritta's men," Nate said now. "I know them all. Carver is a freelancer."

"So all we have to find out is who hired him," Gray said. "But after assaulting a federal officer, he's probably on a plane to Mexico or points south."

"The first shot in a new war?" Nate said, ignoring the comment. "I can't believe even Merritta would send goons after his daughter after inviting her here."

Gray sobered. "God knows what's at play. We have to find her."

"At least we have her brother's phone tapped now. I'll bet my next paycheck she tries to contact him."

"Thank God for McGuire."

McGuire had been the third federal judge they'd approached. He'd been down on the list because he was up for an appellate appointment and Nate knew his record would be scrutinized. Yet he was an ex-cop who had become a prosecutor, and he was generally friendly to the FBI.

And they knew her name now. Nate had checked out every woman on the airline manifest. Only one fit what they now knew. Samantha Carroll. Thirty-five. Half owner of an art gallery in Steamboat Springs. Central Colorado. The age fit. The location fit.

"Photo?" Gray asked.

"I'm trying to get one from motor vehicles in Colorado."

But Nate saw her in his mind's eye. He could give a description to one of their artists. Dark-haired with serious dark blue eyes. He remembered those dark blue eyes that had widened when she'd seen him. She'd been dressed casually in a blue shirt and black slacks. She wore a silver and turquoise bracelet, a silver necklace. She had an elegant walk and confident posture.

"Let's check all the hotels in the downtown area for a

Samantha Carroll," Nate said. "If we don't find her, then we start looking for anyone who paid cash."

"It's just you and me, buddy, and there are a lot of hotels."

"If we don't find her by morning, I'll follow Nicholas Merritt. She's going to dinner at Merritta's Saturday. She must have come early for a reason. Maybe that reason is Merritt."

"That means they'll get to her first," Gray said morosely.

"At least Nicholas Merritt will," Nate agreed. "But by then we'll know more about her. What buttons to push." His voice was purposely cold. He'd acted entirely contrary to form at the airport. He didn't intend to let that happen again.

Sam woke at dawn. She'd slept restlessly even for the few hours she'd been able to shut out thoughts.

She dressed hurriedly and checked out, just in case anyone was looking for someone who had paid cash. That was, she knew, unusual in today's world of plastic.

She checked her bag with the bellman, knowing from extensive experience at hotels that the only record was a numbered claim ticket. She'd taken her personal identification tag off. She'd wandered out, looking first for breakfast, then for a pay telephone.

She read the paper at the coffee shop, first anxiously skimming headlines for anything to do with Merrittas, or crime, or an incident at the airport. Finding nothing, she forced herself to read it as she usually did. She'd always been a newspaper addict, but now it was as much about consuming time as natural curiosity. Nine was when most offices opened. Nine was when she might be able to reach Nicholas Merritt.

Reading the paper, she realized, was an attempt to bring normalcy into a life that had become anything but normal.

She checked her watch again. Eight-thirty. She paid the bill and left the shop and headed three blocks to a large office complex. It would have telephones in the lobby. She reached it a few minutes later and found the pay telephones. Taking a long breath, she dialed the number she'd looked up the night before.

To her surprise, a real voice answered. She'd been ready for a long, involved menu.

"Mr. Merritt, please."

"I'll put you through to his office."

Then a second voice came on the phone. "Mr. Merritt's office."

"Is Mr. Merritt in?"

"May I tell him who is calling?"

Sam willed away the queasiness in her stomach. "Samantha Carroll."

"And may I tell him what this is regarding?"

"It's personal. A family matter."

There was a short silence. Then a deep, wary voice said, "This is Merritt."

"Nicholas Merritt?" Her knees were rubbery, and she could barely keep from stuttering.

"Yes," he said abruptly. "You mentioned a family matter?"

"Have you ever heard of Tracy Edwards?"

A long pause, then a harsh reply. "Why in the hell are you calling and what do you want?"

She took a deep breath. "My name is Samantha. Tracy Edwards is my mother and, I believe, yours." She continued quickly. "I was born on August 15, 1967, in Boston."

"I don't know what you want, or what this is about, but my mother died a long time ago." His voice grew rougher. "If this is some scam—"

"No," she said quickly. "Please listen. I don't want anything from you. But Paul Merritta sent someone to tell me that he . . . was my father and you were my brother. My twin brother. They said he was dying."

A long silence. At least he hadn't hung up.

She hurried on. "One of the men showed me birth certificates. Photos. He asked me to come to Boston. I have an . . . appointment with Mr. Merritta tomorrow. I wanted to meet you first."

"My mother and sister are dead," he said flatly.

"No," she said, not sure how hard she should push. She knew he wanted to slam the phone down. It was exactly what she would have wanted to do.

"No?" he said with a sarcastic edge in his voice. "If this is some sick joke or another scheme of my father's . . ."

He was about to hang up. She knew by the anger and impatience in his voice that she had only a few seconds to convince him.

"Please. Just take a look at the documents I was given. Then tell me whether they could be real." She was speaking rapidly to keep him from hanging up.

"Look, Miss . . . what in the hell did you say your name was?"

"Samantha Carroll, but now I've been told I was born Nicole Merritta. I live in Colorado. I know how you must feel. When I was told . . . well, I was in shock. I'm still in shock. But at least *I* want to know the truth." Her carefully rehearsed speech had gone down the tubes. She knew she was about to lose him.

There was another momentary silence. Then, "Someone is playing a very nasty trick on you."

"Do *you* know someone named Tommy? About fifty? Bulky? Rolex watch? He was one of the men who visited me, who said he was sent by Paul Merritta."

She heard a muttered oath, then, "What do you want?"

"The truth. Nothing else. I have a career. A life. I'm content. But I have to know if I have a brother."

A silence.

"A *twin* brother," she emphasized.

"My sister's dead," he insisted again. "She died with my mother in an accident."

Her heart quickened. So he knew about a twin sister. She knew what he must be feeling. Doubt, and a lot of it. The anger came later. She hurried on. "I know how you feel. I felt the same way. I *still* feel that way. But it was your father who contacted me."

"If this is a con . . ." he started, then stopped abruptly. "Where do you want to meet?"

She'd noticed a small seafood restaurant down the street. "The Chowder House?" she asked. "It's on—"

"I know where it is," he said. "At two? It won't be so crowded. How will I know you?"

"I'll know you," she said. "I have a photo."

"I'll be just inside the door," he said. "Don't show up if you're not who you say you are."

The phone went dead. She held the receiver for a moment, then placed it gently in its cradle. She looked at her watch. Five hours before she would meet him.

And five hours avoiding whoever wanted to find her. The image of the sandy-haired man from last night sprang back into her mind, followed by those of the two larger men who'd approached her at the airport. She remembered the fear that had run down her spine.

Had the first man deliberately headed the others off, as she'd thought? Or had it been one of those coincidences that seemed to come straight from the Twilight Zone?

Maybe Nicholas Merritt would know who they were. And why someone might be tracking her.

If he even acknowledged her.

seven

Sam took one last look at herself in an office building rest room.

She had tramped around Boston for hours and was in the same clothes she'd worn this morning. A pair of slacks, a coral blouse with long sleeves and a matching scarf. Black sandals.

Fine for Steamboat Springs. Not so fine for Boston. Or for the first meeting with a brother she hadn't known existed until a few days ago.

But her dress was in her luggage back at the hotel, and acting on an excess of caution, she hadn't wanted to chance a meeting with someone who might be looking for her. Maybe later.

Paranoia again. She knew it, yet she couldn't dismiss the events of the past few days. Paranoia might be a good thing.

A look at her watch. One-forty.

She checked her purse, making sure the birth certificates and photos were there. Then she took a deep breath and left the relative safety of the rest room.

The streets were busy with people in a rush. Returning from lunch. Shopping. Going to business appointments.

She felt very alone in the crowd. Stomach churning, she forced herself to walk to the restaurant.

He was just inside the door. Even if she hadn't seen the photo, she would have known him. His eyes were a deeper blue than her own. Almost black, in fact. Or maybe it was the lighting. His hair was also darker than her own and it had a reddish tint that hers had never had.

Her breath caught in her throat as their eyes met, and she knew her pulse was racing. Her brother. It hadn't really been real until this moment, but now she saw herself in him, and a jab of familiarity made her reach for a wall to steady herself.

His eyes sharpened and his body stiffened as he saw her, and his hand grasped her elbow to catch her. Just as quickly he withdrew it. His gaze traveled over her, lingering on her eyes. "Miss Carroll?"

She nodded. She knew she was looking at him with the same intensity that radiated from him.

He shook his head as if he couldn't believe what he was seeing. Then he seemed to jerk out of the daze and looked for the maître d'. Almost immediately they had a table, although there were people waiting.

Nick Merritt remained standing as the maître d' pulled out the chair for her. Then he sat down across from her.

He studied her carefully. "There are similarities," he finally admitted. "But blue eyes and dark hair are not uncommon. Easy for them to find."

"Them?"

His lips turned upward, but the expression couldn't be called a smile. "The family," he said with a shrug.

His hand, though, looked white as it clasped a water glass, and she knew he felt far more than he wanted to show. Anger was in the tilt of his head, the strain of a muscle in his throat.

"I was angry, too," she said, swallowing hard and shaking her head. "Those first unbelievable words. Disbelief.

Then the feeling of loss and betrayal. I still—" Again she swallowed. She reached for her water glass, then drew her hand back. It was trembling. She forced it to still. "I didn't believe it, either," she said again.

"Then why are you here?"

"My mother confirmed it. Unwillingly. With the kind of grief I hadn't seen either before or after my father died."

He stared at her, his dark eyes unblinking.

She realized what she had said. "My mother married him after she . . . left . . ." She was suddenly aware she had taken a napkin and was folding and refolding it. She put it back on the table.

"After she left my father and me," he finished grimly. "That's what you meant, isn't it? I think I prefer my version."

"What is your version?"

"My mother and sister were killed in an automobile accident."

She bit her lip. It was a cold, even cruel statement, but she couldn't fault him for it. She could only guess what he felt upon being told that he'd been abandoned by a mother he thought he'd lost in an entirely different way.

"I'm sorry," she said.

"Why?" he asked coolly. "You had nothing to do with it. *If* it happened."

She didn't have an answer for that.

"What explanation did she give *you*?" he asked in a detached voice.

"That I was born a twin, that she was married to Paul Merritta, and that she had to leave him to save—" She stopped.

But he finished for her. "Us? You? I guess we know which one she chose," he said ironically. "*If* what you claim is true."

That *if* again. But she understood. "It took me several days to accept the possibility that it was. But now I know

it's true, or my mother never would have confirmed it."
She took out the photos and the birth certificates and put
them on the table, pushing them over to him.

His face didn't change as he perused them.

"It'll take *me* longer," he said. "I want a blood test."

His face was set in hard lines. It was a handsome face.
But now his mouth was grim, his eyes cold. She understood. She'd had three days to get used to the idea of having a brother, of being fathered by a reputed mobster. He
hadn't had any time to get used to the idea of having a sister and a mother who had apparently deserted him.

She nodded. "I don't think Mother had a choice about
whom to take with her," she said, trying to mitigate the
hurt she would have felt had she been him. "If she had, she
never would have—"

"I'll arrange the test for tomorrow morning," he said,
cutting her off.

"That's fine," she said. "I need that proof, too. That's
one reason I came." She *was* sure now, but she knew the
agonizing steps she'd taken to reach that truth. He had to
take his own journey.

She reached for the documents and photos.

His hand flattened on them. "I want to keep them. At
least for a while."

She was reluctant to let them go. But she'd had them
several days and had made copies of everything. She expected him to do the same. They probably shared an overabundance of caution.

The waiter appeared, and she ordered grouper and he a
steak. Nicholas chose a bottle of wine with an ease she'd
never mastered. She suspected it would be expensive.

"Where do we go from here?" she asked.

"I have no idea," he said flatly as his hand scooped up
the photos and placed them on his right-hand side. "Why
did *you* come? You know what my father is?"

"I read the news accounts I found on the Internet. Articles in the Boston papers." She caught his gaze, held it. "I wanted to meet you. I have always felt that something was missing. I wanted to know if that something was you."

Some emotion flickered in his eyes, but she couldn't define it. She wondered whether he had ever felt the same. She didn't ask, though. It would be asking for a commitment, and he wasn't ready for that.

"Is he?" she asked instead. "Is he a mobster, a criminal, a crime boss, a don, whatever it's called?"

He raised one dark eyebrow. "The papers say so. The feds say so."

"I don't believe everything in the papers."

"That's wise." He gave her another long look. "I can't help but wonder, though," he said, "if you're here because you think you might inherit when he dies." The words were coldly and meanly said.

"I'm not rich, Mr. Merritt, but neither am I poor. I'm part owner of a growing business I love. I don't need money, particularly dirty money. I don't want it. I wouldn't take it if it were offered."

"Then you're the only one," he said.

"Who else?"

"Two uncles, an aunt, cousins, my half brother."

"Half brother?" She didn't miss the "my" that preceded it.

"George—Georgio, as he prefers. He's the son of my father's mistress. I always wondered why he didn't marry her. Maybe he didn't want to commit bigamy." That enigmatic smile passed his lips again.

"Bigamy?"

"If my father knew his wife was still alive, maybe he feared she . . . might just reappear someday. He wouldn't want to be charged with bigamy. The feds would love that. They couldn't get him on racketeering, but they bust him for bigamy." He looked amused at the thought.

"If my father knew his wife was still alive . . ." Not "my

mother." Still, it was the first sign that he thought their relationship might be a possibility.

Sam closed her eyes. She had assumed her mother had divorced Paul Merritta. If she hadn't . . .

Slowly she opened them again and saw Nicholas's gaze intent on her, watching every emotion. He had reached the same damning conclusion, obviously. Why couldn't she be as expressionless as he? But it wouldn't make the earthquake impact on him as it did on her. He didn't know Patsy Carroll. He didn't know the woman who had stressed honesty and honor and law all her life.

She tried to change the subject. "George? I didn't read anything about him."

"He goes by his mother's name. My father has always protected his privacy. To hell with mine."

"Do you see him often?"

"My father? Not any more than necessary."

"I promised I would see him tomorrow. Will you go with me?"

He looked startled. "Tommy isn't picking you up?"

"I told him I would go on my own on Saturday. I want to be able to leave when I wish."

A glimmer of admiration lit eyes that had shown precious little emotion. "A taxi?"

"No, for then I would still be dependent. I planned to rent a car."

"Planned?"

He was quick. "Plan," she corrected herself.

"Where are you staying?" he asked suddenly.

She paused.

"Or is it a secret?" he asked.

It was. Even to her. She had no idea where she was spending the night. "Will you go with me?" she asked again.

"My father won't like it."

"I think his invitation should include whomever I wish to bring."

"You don't know my father. He sets the rules."

"Not this time," Sam said. "He wanted me to leave several days ago on a flight he paid for. I refused. I wanted to pay my own way."

Merritt lifted his glass. "One for you."

Sarcasm? Approval? He was impossible to read. She did not know what she had expected, but it wasn't this cool, almost indifferent demeanor. He acted as if he were an observer. But occasionally she would see a muscle flex in his cheek, and she wondered whether he'd just mastered supreme control.

Her fist knotted under the table. She wanted some emotion, dammit. She wanted it in herself, and she wanted it in him. She'd felt a momentary sense of familiarity, but his responses had been cold, distant.

This was a mistake. A terrible mistake. They had been apart thirty-four years. They were strangers. Yet she had expected . . .

She didn't know what she expected. She just knew bitter disappointment. Still, she struggled not to show it. "You were in the army?"

"You read all about me, too," he said with that wry twist of his lips.

"What I could find," she said honestly.

"Aren't you afraid of me?"

"Should I be?"

"You should run like hell back to Colorado."

"That's not an answer."

He shrugged. "There's no reason to fear me. The family's a far different story."

She couldn't tell whether it was a warning, a threat or a statement. His voice had not changed at all.

She absorbed that. "Tell me about Paul Merritta."

"He'll charm you. He's sick and he's under investigation by the feds, but he'll charm you anyway." He paused. "You should know that once you see him, you'll be on the FBI radar, if you're not already."

"What do you mean?"

"I mean that they will turn your life upside down and keep it that way."

"Have they done that to you?"

He laughed, but there was no humor in it. "If you don't want to explore the possibility, take the next plane back to wherever you came from."

"Steamboat Springs," she reminded him.

"You see, you never should have told me that."

"Why? Those two men who visited me knew where I was."

"When you are a Merritta, you don't give out information for free."

"Not even to a Merritta?" she asked before she could think better of it. The very good food in her stomach turned sour, and the knot in her chest tightened. *The family. FBI radar . . .* She hadn't considered what being a Merritta would mean to her business, to her life—

He was studying her carefully. "Having second thoughts?"

She closed her fist around her napkin, suddenly tired of watching every word, every movement, tired of examining every emotion she felt in herself or observed in others. "I was approached by two men in our gallery and told about my father and my brother without ceremony—without any of the consideration I've shown you. They issued veiled threats when I didn't go along with them. My house was broken into and I was attacked." She stopped for a moment, catching her breath, then started again before he could interrupt her. "I was accosted at the airport by two men who chased me out of the terminal. I gave a false name at the hotel. All day I've walked around looking for thugs or assassins or whatever that might be following me.

I'm suddenly conducting my life as if I were on the run and trying to hide."

She pinned him with a glare she'd perfected on board members and men with more machismo than manners. "I came because I wanted to meet my brother. And I came because I'm angry and outraged and want to let Mr. Merritta know that I will not run around on his leash." Her hands were clenched so tightly they were numb.

He stared at her. "Someone attacked you at the airport? Describe them."

"First there was a man alone. He was standing at the gate when I arrived. He watched every move I made. Then he was behind me when two other men started coming toward me."

"The first man—what did he look like?" Nicholas demanded, cutting her off.

"Tall, lean. Probably about twenty pounds less than you. Sandy hair."

"Green eyes?"

She nodded. "Do you know who—"

"Turn around."

She did as he asked.

Vivid green eyes met hers. He was sitting at the bar. He wore the same tweed coat despite the summer warmth. He gave her a brief smile and a salute.

For a moment, she couldn't move. Then reluctantly she turned back to Nick.

"He came in just minutes after you did," Nick said. "He apparently followed me. Or you."

"Who is he?"

"A bastard," Nick said bitterly. "A real bastard." It was the first real emotion she'd heard from him. The anger curdled her blood.

"Why?"

"You're now on the FBI radar," he said. "His name is McLean, and he's a fed. He's been after the Merrittas for at least five years. He's tried to destroy my business. He'll do the same to you. Stay away from him."

The stab of disappointment was deep, more painful than she would have thought possible. "I think he . . . saved me last night. The two men . . . he intercepted them."

"It was probably one of his games," Nick said. "I don't agree with my father on much, but if he invited you here, you're safe from his people. And from any other family. He has his own kind of honor. No one would dare violate it."

"What about my home in Colorado, the one that was burglarized? Would that be included in his honor?" she asked sarcastically.

"I don't know. I'm not privy to what he does. I don't want to be privy to it. And if you're smart, you won't want to be, either."

Sam had to force herself not to look back at the bar, at the man who had so attracted her last night. The man she hadn't been able to get out of her thoughts.

And then he was there. At the table. Looming over them.

"Want to introduce me?" he asked Nick.

"No."

The intensity in him was as strong as, if not stronger than, it had been the night before. There was a light in those green eyes as if his fondest desire in life was to torment the man across from her.

He leaned over and held out his hand. "I'm Nathan McLean," he said in a surprisingly gentle voice. "I'm sorry I missed you last night."

Her hand tingled in his. Heat spread from his hand into hers and jolted up her arm and through her. His eyes flickered slightly and he looked surprised, as if he might have been affected as well.

"You're not welcome at this table," Nick said in a low

voice as he rose from his seat. "I think there is something called harassment."

"I didn't hear the lady ask me to leave."

Sam heard the enmity between the two men. It was poisonous.

She knew that if she didn't retreat from McLean's hold, she might lose her brother forever.

She jerked her hand away. "Please leave," she said.

"We can give you protection."

"I don't need protection."

He looked at her brother. "No? Then who tried to get to you last night?"

"That's enough," Nick said. "Perhaps it was another one of your games, like telling all my customers they might be subpoenaed even though you have no evidence of anything wrong."

"That's what happens when you take mob money," McLean said. He took out a card and held it out to her. "It was no game, Miss Carroll. One of those men was a hired gun. If you need anything . . ."

Dazed by the bitter hostility between the two men, she barely registered what he'd said.

He dropped the card on the table next to her hand. "You're in dangerous company, Miss Carroll. Don't wait to call us." He left and returned to the bar.

Nick's face was impassive but she saw the anger in his eyes. "I'm sorry for that," he said. "But I warned you."

The very good grouper was rebelling in her stomach. Being the law-abiding citizen she was, she'd always thought well of the FBI and other law enforcement agencies. She had good friends on the Steamboat Springs police force.

For the first time, the enormity of what was happening struck her. It was one thing to read about a mobster. It was another to learn he could be—was—her father. And to become an adversary of an agency she'd always held in high esteem.

"Don't trust him," her brother said. "He'll do anything to bring down the family."

"Why?"

"Damned if I know. But he's made the family his life work."

"How do you know that?"

"The family does have sources inside the FBI."

"How do you know that if you're not part of it?" she asked in a low voice.

"I was raised within the family, groomed by the family to take part in the business. I still see my father occasionally. I have supper there. I hear things."

She was silent. Nothing was as it seemed. Her life had been a lie, and now she was being told by an FBI agent that her family might be dangerous for her, and told by a brother she'd just met that the FBI indulged in personal vendettas. She had no idea who to believe.

"Stay away from him," Nick Merritt said again.

"Are you trying to scare me off?"

"I don't think you scare that easily. Maybe I underestimated you. You might give the feds a run for their money."

She sat back and absorbed what he was saying and the way he continued to say it. Occasionally with a touch of anger or bitterness. But mostly as an observer.

Had she really expected him to hold open his arms?

A hired shooter. She believed the agent, and she didn't want to. No one wanted to believe someone would hire a professional to kill her. It implied unreasoning hatred. Or cold-blooded calculation.

She tried to shake the lingering effects of the FBI agent's intrusion. The attraction she'd felt, the heat, then the chill from his warning. Whom to trust?

She wanted to trust the man across from her. "You

haven't answered me. Will you go with me to your father's?"

"Will you turn around and go home if I don't?"

"No."

"Have to open Pandora's box, do you?"

"And all the evil in the world exploded. Is that what you think will happen?"

"The evil is already out," he said.

"Is my father evil?"

He played with his glass of wine, but didn't answer. "You'll have to make up your own mind . . . if you proceed."

Another warning. She was receiving less information, less help, less sympathy than she had imagined. She had expected doubt because she'd had doubt. She had expected anger at the breakup of the family and his abandonment by his mother. She had expected anything but the icy, analytical composure.

And the intrusion of Agent McLean. His warnings kept rumbling in her mind. She wondered whether he was still at the bar, but she wasn't going to turn and look.

Nick apparently saw the thought, maybe in the flicker of her eyes. "He just left," he said. "Probably waiting outside to follow you. Or me."

She heard the resignation in his voice. The truth.

He had warned her. Her mother had warned her.

The chill in her spread. She felt she'd just entered a gathering of shifting, twisting shadows.

eight

"Go home, Samantha. You don't belong here."

Nicholas's comment brought her back to the moment.

"It's tempting," she admitted. "I have a very nice business in Colorado. I like being in the woods. Hiking, skiing, riding. It's honest. Everything is what it appears to be. The shadows are all benign."

"Then go!"

"I'm afraid the shadows would follow me," she said. "Home is no longer safe because your father invaded it."

"So it's *my* father now?" Nicholas said. *"You* made this journey of discovery. Now you have to live with the consequences." Once again, his tone had hardened.

Because he'd sensed she wanted to look behind her and see if the FBI agent was still there? Had he noticed that hesitancy from her? Had he guessed that she'd wanted the assurance of the man sitting at the bar? Or was it her imagination?

"That Pandora's box you mentioned. I didn't open it. I didn't ask anyone to come to Steamboat Springs. I didn't ask for someone to burglarize my home and assault me. I came to put an end to it as well as meet you and see whether—"

"We had a connection?" he asked. He shrugged, dismissing the notion. "Even if you are my sister, it's been thirty-four years since we've seen each other. We have nothing in common. They say environment has more influence than genes, and our environments have been very different. If you're smart, you'll go back and forget all this."

"Will they let me?"

"I don't know, but it's better than staying here and making yourself a target."

"A target for whom?"

"The FBI. Members of the family who don't want competition. Other families who are lusting over the Merritta turf, now that Pop is —"

"If it's so bad, why do you stay here?"

"Damn good question," he said. "I've asked that a hundred times, but I wasn't going to be run out of a city I love."

She grinned. "Stubborn, huh?"

His lips twitched. "Sometimes. I don't have to ask about you."

It was the first time he'd let down his guard, even a little.

"Tell me more about the . . . family."

"Literally or figuratively?"

She had to smile at that. Gallows humor. "Literally, at the moment."

"I told you about George," Nicholas said. "He hopes to be Pop's successor."

"Pop?"

"My compromise in what to call him," he said.

It sounded homey. Affectionate. Yet there was a coldness in Merritt's eyes.

"What about 'Father'?"

He raised one eyebrow. But said nothing. She sensed it was a subject he was not going to pursue further.

"The others?"

"Anna, my cousin. She lives at the house, has since her father was killed. She's vice president of the Merritta Trust. She gives away money to redeem the family's image," he said cynically. "Then there's her mother, Rosa, and two uncles and their wives. Victor and Maria, and Rich and Caroline."

"That's it?"

"*If* you stay, they are the ones you will probably meet. There are others who are related one way or another, but those are the ones who matter."

"To whom?"

"To Pop. To the family."

"Are you important to him? To the family?"

"You should have been a detective." The observation was obviously not a compliment.

"My mother says that, too." His face tightened, and she suddenly realized what she had said. "I'm sorry."

"Don't be," he said. "You didn't do anything. Yet."

"Yet?"

"You'll be stirring up a pot. If I didn't know about you, then neither did most of the others. I don't think they will be happy."

"I can't be a threat. I don't want anything. I wouldn't take anything."

His gaze locked on hers. "Why do you think they will believe you?"

"Do you?"

"I don't know," he said. "How could I? I don't know you. I don't know the woman who raised you."

She swallowed hard at the detachment in his voice. She hesitated, wondering whether she should tell him about the threat to her mother. Would he even care? It seemed doubtful.

"And," he added, "you came, didn't you?" Accusation dripped all over his words.

"I told you why. I wanted to meet my twin brother."

For a moment his expression seemed to soften, then his face went blank again. He was very good at that. "We're strangers," he said again. "I'm sorry. I don't feel anything." But for just a fraction of a second, his eyes seemed to say something else. The emotion—or whatever it was—was gone as fast as it had come.

Or maybe she was mistaken. Maybe she just wanted to see it. A wave of loneliness washed over her. Despite all she knew about the family, she'd harbored hope that she and Nick would find something. Perhaps instinctive familiarity. She wanted the brother she had lost.

She wouldn't get it by pushing. She changed the subject. "Why do you think he wants to see me?"

"God knows. Some kind of game. Pop loves them. Playing people against people. It's his way of discovering who is worthy and who isn't."

She stared at him silently, giving herself time to comprehend the feelings brewing inside her since meeting him. There had been few indications from him of human emotion, and yet she liked him. She felt comfortable with him.

He was the first to break the silence. "I'll take you tomorrow," he said, "but first I want to go by a doctor's office for blood samples."

She nodded. "All right."

"You really believe it, don't you?"

"Yes, though I understand why you don't."

"Not in anything my father's engineered. He's been trying to involve me in the business since I left college to join the army. He'd sent me to military schools to 'toughen' me up. He just never expected I would carry it that far. He tried his damnedest to get me out, but I was tired of being manipulated. Now he might well be trying to use you to do it for him."

"How?"

"Damned if I know, but I'm sure he has a plan."

She wanted him to ask something about her mother—anything to show a hint of interest—but he did not. He avoided the subject as if one question would plunge him off a cliff. Well, she'd had her own fall.

But hers couldn't be as bad as the one he'd just had. She'd had a good childhood, parents she'd loved, a peaceful yet adventurous life. What had he had? A gangster father. No mother. Military school.

And yet he looked successful. Self-assured. Comfortable in his own skin.

"You've never married?"

"With my family? No nice girl—or woman—could tolerate my family, and I found I really didn't want the other kind." He looked at her ring finger.

"Nope," she said cheerfully. "Always wanted a white knight. Never found him."

"You won't find him here," he said.

She finished her glass of wine. She had been right. It had been a very good bottle of wine. "Is there anything else you would like to know?"

He looked steadily at her. "Not until I see the results of the blood test."

"Fair enough. Thank you for meeting me."

"Can I walk you to your hotel?"

She hesitated. "I don't have a hotel at the moment."

He stared at her. "Why?"

"After last night at the airport, I didn't want anyone to find me. I used a false name last night and checked out this morning. My bag is still there in checked luggage."

He looked at her in amazement, then smiled slowly. "Why didn't you call Pop?"

"I wanted to meet you first."

"Why?"

"I hoped you would tell me the truth."

"What truth did you think you would find? That Pop is an ordinary businessman? That I would welcome you into my life? That thirty-four years would disappear because you want them to? Did you ever think you might not like what you found?"

"Oh, I thought it," she said. "I thought about it very hard."

"And your mother? What did she think about this adventure?"

"She didn't want me to come."

"A book better closed," he said with a trace of bitterness. "You should have listened to her."

Perhaps she should have.

"Back to the problem of a hotel," he said. "I know of one where I often place customers. It's small and personal, and they'll take care of you. The reservation would be in my partner's name. You'll be Miss Connor."

She looked at him for a long moment. Part of her wanted to refuse and make her own way as she insisted earlier, but she was beyond her depth and she knew it. And for some reason, she trusted Nicholas Merritt. "Thank you," she said. "I accept."

He really smiled for the first time. "That easy?"

"If you had the kind of day I had yesterday and again this morning, you would understand."

He took a cell phone from his belt and spoke softly into it. She couldn't hear what he said. When he was finished, he turned it off and turned back to her. "You said some men approached you. Describe them."

"Large. Sturdy. One had very light hair and pale blue eyes. The other was dark. Could your father—"

"No. He invited you. Your safety would be important. Maybe they were sent to protect you."

"They didn't look like they wanted to protect anyone."

He held out his hand. "Give me the claim check for your luggage. I'll have it picked up and delivered to the hotel. I'll make sure no one follows."

"And me? How will you get me there?"

"In ten minutes, someone will drive up to the back of this restaurant. He'll take you there. He knows how to avoid a tail."

She bit her lip at the final comment.

He paid the bill with a credit card, and they waited in silence another few moments until the waiter returned. "I hope everything was satisfactory, sir."

"It was," he said as he wrote down a tip, then his name. He turned back to her. "I would advise you to stay at the hotel. Boston isn't Steamboat Springs."

She didn't want him to leave. "Have you ever been there?"

"Once. On a ski trip."

"I like skiing, too."

"Most people do," he said, bursting that personal bubble. "Why don't you go powder your nose," he said. "The back door is next to the powder room."

She didn't ask how he knew that, or whether he was accustomed to slipping in and out of back doors.

She stood, and he rose too, with old-fashioned gallantry. But his face was shuttered.

She'd been dismissed.

The hotel was small, exclusive and comfortable. A kind of European-style establishment with a staff that was unusually attentive and a doorman who seemed more than the average doorman.

"Miss Connor. We have your reservation ready," said a Mr. Bennett who met her inside the door. He had MANAGER on his name badge. He apparently didn't think it was unusual that she had no baggage.

She started to rummage in her purse for her wallet as they reached the desk. The manager shook his head. "Everything has been taken care of," he said.

"What if I don't want everything taken care of?" she

asked, even as she realized her cash was disappearing quickly.

He looked distressed.

She vowed silently to repay Nick Merritt. "It's all right," she said gently.

He beamed a smile and rang a bell. She didn't think anyone really did that anymore. But immediately there was someone next to her, and the manager handed over the key.

"If you need anything at all, call us," the manager said. "We have room service twenty-four hours a day, and if you forgot any personal items . . ."

She nodded and followed the bellman to the elevator and up to the third floor. A small lounge area was just off the elevator. He led the way down the hall, inserted the card key and opened the door.

The room was really a small suite comprised of a sitting room with desk and a large bedroom furnished with what looked like antiques and a king-size bed. The bellman showed her a minibar and a small refrigerator. She was asked about ice, and said yes. In seconds, he reappeared with a full bucket. He gave her a slight bow as he exited, a sizable tip in hand.

She went to the windows and looked at a fine view of a park. For the first time in days, she felt she could relax.

A bath. And a glass of wine. Room service. Safety.

It all sounded very inviting, but she had a phone call to make first. She hesitated about using her cell phone to call her mother's cell phone, then decided it should be safe enough.

Her mother picked up on the first ring, and Sam knew she had been sitting next to the phone. For how long?

Pleasantries were exchanged, the usual "How are you?" but now there was an intensity to the question.

Sam lied. "I'm fine. You?"

Her mother was fine, too, though Sam knew neither of

them was fine at all. She heard the worry in her mother's voice.

"I met Nicholas," Sam said. "I like him."

"Did he . . . ask about me?"

Sam closed her eyes. She should have anticipated this question, but she hadn't. At least, not quite this soon.

"Samantha? Are you still there?" Stark fear came through the wire, jerking Sam from her preoccupation.

"Yes, I'm still here. He doesn't accept the fact that I might be his sister and that his mother is alive," she said carefully. "He believed we were both killed in an accident when he was a baby. He wants a blood test."

"What's he like?" Her mother was obviously hungry for information.

"He's smart. Cautious. Droll sense of humor. As I said, I like him. I'm not sure he feels the same about me."

"Do you trust him?"

Sam hesitated at that. She did. To a point. She wondered though if she would ever trust anyone completely again. "Yes," she said finally.

"You haven't seen *him* yet." Her mother didn't have to spell out who *him* was. Her mother's former husband. Sam's biological father.

"No," she said.

"Don't let him manipulate you," her mother said.

"Why did you leave Nicholas behind?" Sam asked.

"I told you. I didn't have a choice."

"I don't think you can convince him with that explanation." *Or me.* The unspoken words hung in the air.

A long silence. "I can't expect either of you to understand." Her mother's voice wavered. "Does he look like the photo?"

"Yes. He's tall. Six two or so. Dark hair. Dark blue eyes. He says he has nothing to do with his . . . father's business."

A long pause. "Do you think . . . he will see me?"

"Not right away," Sam said gently. "He has to have time to get used to the idea, just as I did."

"But you're willing to see Paul."

"I've had more time to get used to the idea."

"Did Nicholas have a . . . mother?"

"No," Sam said.

A long silence. Then, "Where can I reach you?"

Sam was hesitant to name the hotel. "My cell phone," she said. "I'll keep it on."

"Be careful, Samantha. Please be careful."

"You, too. Are you where you said you would be?"

"Yes."

"I'll call you tomorrow."

"Samantha?"

"Yes?"

"I love you." Her mother tried to sound normal, but Sam heard the break in her voice.

"I love you, too," Sam said, and signed off, then went to the window and looked out. The park was alive with people.

She'd been born here. She and Nicholas.

Her mother had lived here in Boston with her father. They had loved each other once.

Then her thoughts returned to the FBI agent. McLean. She could see him leaning easily on the bar, his eyes angry when he studied her brother, softening when they turned to her.

She was still startled by the intensity of her reaction to him.

But he'd been identified as the enemy.

If she denied that, she would be denying any trust in her brother.

She felt very alone.

Nick poured a straight scotch and went to the window of his town house.

The night was hot, humid.

A sister, by God. A twin sister. How could he not know she was alive? He should have. Somehow he should have.

If she was his sister.

She was convinced. He knew that. He knew people. He could read them. It was a talent he'd had to develop. Too many people wanted too much from him.

He saw a car down the street. Christ. Did the feds know how obvious they were? McLean had obviously followed him to the restaurant, but he'd made damn sure they wouldn't follow Samantha Carroll. He didn't want McLean or any of his fellow agents anywhere around Samantha. She would be safe enough, though, at the hotel. It had been Cal's find, and because they often recommended it to their customers, they received special consideration. The feds might know about it, but he doubted it. As far as he knew, no one had been questioned there.

Dammit, he'd liked her. He hadn't wanted to. He had more than enough family. And he certainly didn't want a mother after all these years, particularly one who had abandoned him and disappeared.

The thought made him sick inside. He'd had his battles with the old man, but at least his father hadn't dumped him like unwanted garbage.

He'd really believed she'd been killed when he was a toddler. He'd asked a lot of questions, but his father had always turned them away. It was, he'd been told, too painful. No one else would talk about her, either. Let the dead rest, they all said.

He wanted to hit something. He wished he was in the gym and had a punching bag available. Instead he balled up his right fist and slammed it down on his left hand, leaving it stinging.

No question that Samantha would stir up a hornets' nest, and Paul Merritta knew it. George would be livid. So would Victor. They'd already planned to divide up the

Merritta empire between them. Anna wanted a piece, too, but she was a woman. Women didn't have much value in his family.

So why the hell did Pop want to resurrect a daughter who supposedly died more than three decades ago?

He had to applaud Samantha's guts. Would he have done the same thing? If he'd been told he had a sister he'd never known about and a mother still alive, would he have sought them out or would he have done what he had done so many times before—burrow deeper into his hole?

He'd not been able to warn her off. Or scare her off. Maybe he hadn't really tried hard enough.

Why hadn't Pop told him he had invited her?

"I don't think Mother had a choice about whom to take with her . . ."

Maybe that was true. But in all the years since, she'd made no effort to see him, to contact him. Surely if she'd cared anything about him, she would have found a way.

He took another sip of scotch, heard the phone ring and listened as the answering machine replied. "I'm out. Leave a message."

"Don't forget about dinner tomorrow night." His father's voice issuing an order.

Wouldn't Pop like to know he had already met her?

For once, he might have the upper hand in the game.

nine

Sam leaned against the leather seat of the car and looked at Nick Merritt.

She relished the moment. It meant time with him—time to explore, to seek information. Any small nugget was welcome.

He wasn't any warmer than he had been yesterday. In fact, he seemed even more on guard than before. He'd still not asked any questions about her mother, while if their positions had been reversed, she would have been peppering him with questions.

But then her mother had left him, not her. And Paul Merritta? Had he tried to keep her? She had been deserted by him as much as Nick had been deserted by their mother.

Nick obviously hadn't accepted that yet.

He'd had someone pick her up at the hotel, then he'd met her at a doctor's office where blood samples were taken. Then he'd taken her to a late breakfast.

If she'd expected any more warmth than yesterday, she'd been badly mistaken. Nicholas had been taciturn the whole time. She wondered, in fact, whether he had any feelings at all.

She was surprised then when he turned to her at a stop

light. "You should probably know. Pop called me and asked me for dinner. I think he plans to spring you on me then."

"You didn't tell him I'd contacted you?"

"Nope," he said.

She stared at him. "Why?"

"Let's say I didn't want to be manipulated. By anyone." The admonition was quite clear.

She was silent for a moment, then shrugged. "I didn't come to see him anyway."

"I should warn you. He won't be happy. He doesn't like his plans being spoiled."

"I don't really care what he wants," she said.

Nick's mouth twitched, yet he gave away nothing more than that.

She didn't ask any more questions, merely looked around at the neighborhoods he drove through. The homes became more and more elaborate until they reached a long, tall wrought-iron fence that seemed to go on forever. He finally turned into a drive, halting the car when he came to the gates.

A uniformed man in the gatehouse stepped out, apparently recognized Nick and went back inside without a word. The gates glided open.

It wasn't a house. It was an estate. The large and imposing English manor-style mansion sat among huge oak trees. Carefully tended flower plots dotted the rich green lawn, yet there were no bushes along the fence.

No place to hide.

The thought unsettled her. Heck, she was scared out of her wits. Until now, the Merritta family had been a collection of shadows. Now she was seeing reality. Power. Probably evil.

It was all she could do to maintain her composure, not to let the fear show. She'd been operating on adrenaline until now, on anger, on curiosity, on sheer determination.

Now she wondered whether she hadn't ventured way beyond her depth.

The trick was not to let it show.

Nick didn't say anything as he drove up to a rounded drive and parked. Instantly a man appeared from the front door. He stopped when he saw Nick stepping from the car.

"Mr. Merritta, we weren't expecting you." The puzzlement in his voice was audible to Sam.

Mr. Merritta. Not Merritt. It was obvious that his abbreviation of the family name had not been accepted.

"Miss Carroll invited me," he replied easily, going around the other side of the car and opening the door. He offered Sam his hand, and Sam couldn't help but wonder if he was doing it out of courtesy or as a challenge to those who were watching. His face certainly didn't give anything way. He turned to Sam. "Meet Reggie. He runs the house."

Reggie didn't look like a man who ran a gangster's house. He was small and slender and tended not to meet her gaze. He even had a little bit of a British accent. He was, in truth, a cliché.

He led the way inside to a marble hallway and then into a room that was obviously a parlor. He hesitated a moment, as if reluctant to go and impart unpleasant news to his employer. His gaze rested warily on Nick before he backed out the door and disappeared.

"You don't seem entirely welcome," she noted.

"As I told you, my father isn't fond of surprises. I expect he wanted to spring you on me, then take credit for presenting me with a gift."

"Am I a gift?"

"I don't think it's a gift for you." As before, he avoided answering the question.

She walked around the room, unable to sit. There were bookcases, but they were mostly filled with photos, rather than books.

There were some photos of a young Nick, some of another boy. A pretty young girl. Groupings of men.

She stopped at the photo of the girl. "Who is she?"

"Anna, my cousin."

It was still "my" not "our," she noticed. "And the boy must be George."

"Yes," he said shortly.

"Will they be here today?"

"I don't know."

His usually clipped replies had become even more curt since they'd entered the house.

A muscle throbbed in his cheek and jaw, and for the first time she realized how hard this might be on him.

Reggie appeared again. "He will see you," he said.

"He" was said in capital letters, like God. Suddenly she had second thoughts. A lot of them. She'd been carried along this far on pure obsession. An obsession without real thought of consequences.

She turned to Nick. "Come with me."

"He said alone," Reggie emphasized.

"Then I will leave without seeing him."

Reggie shook his head in dismay.

"Losing your courage?" Nick asked.

The question was biting.

"No," she said, then turned back to Reggie. "All right."

She followed him up a curving staircase, along a wide hallway and into a large room.

Reggie backed out, gently closing the door behind him.

She was alone with the man who had given her life.

He was sitting in an armchair to the side of a large desk, a shadow of the man she'd seen in pictures. His hair was gray and thin. Yet his eyes were the same dark blue color as hers, and they seemed to burn with life, or maybe it was the embers of life.

"Nicole?"

"Samantha," she corrected.

"Your mother wanted to name you that," he said. "But I thought twins should have similar names." He paused. "So she finally won that battle."

"Is that what you had with her? A war?"

"Sit down," he commanded her.

She sat. Not because he told her to, but because her legs felt like rubber.

Sam studied him just as he was studying her. "Why did your people contact me after all these years?"

He suddenly smiled, and she saw the charisma that her mother must have seen at one time.

"Direct, aren't you?"

"What else should I be?"

"Why did you call Nicholas before seeing me?"

"I was told he didn't know about me. I thought he had as much right to know about me as I did to know he existed."

"And . . . ?"

"He's not ready to believe it yet. He wanted a blood test."

His smile disappeared. "He would."

"Why?"

"He doesn't trust me." He shook his head. "It's a hard thing to know your son distrusts you."

"Does he have reason?"

His eyes didn't blink. "No, but I should have told him about you long ago."

"How could you when I was supposed to be dead?"

He gave her a thin smile. "So you learned about that?"

"Did you think I wouldn't?" The air was thick between them, charged with emotion that wasn't evident in the calmly spoken words. Every word he spoke was a quiet challenge. And she couldn't help but reciprocate.

"Did Nick tell you?" he asked.

She was silent.

"Loyalty is a fine quality. So is being discreet."

She'd always thought so. But not in the way he meant it.

"Who died to provide you with bodies to use in place of ours?" she asked bluntly.

"Tommy told me you were gutsy," he replied in a satisfied voice. "Don't worry your head about it. They were already dead, and their people received compensation for the use of their bodies."

"But why?"

"If some acquaintances, even members of my family, learned that Tracy had run away, they would have gone after her."

It was still difficult for her to think of her mother as Tracy. "So you were protecting her?" She couldn't keep a wry skepticism from her voice.

"Yes," he said. "She and I made a bargain all those years ago. A devil's bargain. I didn't like it. But she was determined to leave."

"Why?"

"She wasn't comfortable with us."

"With crime, you mean?"

He gave her a chiding look. "My father was head of the family at the time. I've been changing our direction since then."

"What kind of businesses are you in?"

"We broker sanitation equipment, for one. We also have janitorial services, uniform rental and cleaning, real estate . . ." He stopped and a look of agony crossed his face. His hand clutched the arm of his chair.

She stood. "Can I help?"

"Yes. Pills. In a bottle on the desk. And water."

She quickly found the bottle of pills, along with a pitcher and glass. She poured water into the glass and handed both the bottle of pills and water to him. He took out two of the pills, gulped them, then drained the glass of water. In a moment, his face started to relax.

"Thank you," he said finally.

"Are you all right? Should I call someone?"

"No. I want to talk to you."

"Why?" she asked bluntly.

"I've wondered about you all these years," he said. "No matter what your mother told you, I didn't want to let you go."

"But you did let me go. You bargained with my mother. You took one, she took the other." Anger surged through her body, her veins, flushing her face.

"Is that what she told you?"

"Only that she could 'save' only one."

"Does Nick seem mistreated?"

She didn't have an opinion on that yet, so she changed the subject. "How long have you known where I was?"

"I just found out," he said, looking at her steadily through weary eyes.

She wasn't sure she believed him. "How?"

He shrugged. "Your mother's sister."

So her mother had been right. That was how he had found them. "Why did you want to see me now?"

"You're my daughter. I'm sick," he said matter-of-factly. "You're unfinished business."

"No hugs . . . kisses," she said sarcastically. "Just unfinished business."

"We don't know each other. I didn't think you would—"

"You were right," she said coolly, trying desperately to rein in her emotions. Anger, regret. Even confusion.

"I'm not asking you for anything. I wanted to see you. It's as simple as that. I wanted you and your brother to know each other."

"For sentimental reasons?"

"I have only a few months. Maybe not that long. I have a large estate. It's important that you participate in it."

"I don't want it."

"Still, a part of it is yours. Your birthright. And the

money was earned honestly," he added quickly, apparently seeing the rejection in her face.

"But originally—?"

"The fruit of ill-gotten gains?" he said. "That's the problem, is it?"

"That and my mother. Your messenger threatened her."

He sat straighter in the chair. "He wasn't authorized to do that."

"I want your word that my mother will be safe."

"I have no reason to harm her," he said.

It wasn't a direct answer.

"I want a promise," she said, hiding the hand that slightly trembled under the other.

"Would you believe me if I made that promise?"

She regarded him steadily. "I don't know."

"One honest person in the family," he said. "But for what it's worth, I swear I will do nothing to harm your mother if she does nothing to harm me."

She was bargaining with the devil. Her father. She kept trying to tell herself that but everything was surreal. The house. The fading old man. She felt no connection with him, and oddly enough she wanted to.

"If she does nothing to harm me." The phrase was like a knife. Her mother must have some means of hurting him. After thirty years? Was that why he wanted to see her? To see if she knew what it was?

Something froze inside her.

"He likes to play games." She remembered Nick's words only too clearly.

But maybe she was reading too much into her brother's words. They could have another meaning. Her mother hadn't been hurt. Her . . . father had never been convicted of a crime. Maybe he *had* turned the family legitimate amid lingering suspicions. She wanted to believe that.

He continued. "I did love your mother. She's the one—"

He suddenly winced, and his mouth turned grim. "You can leave now. Tell Reggie . . ."

She hesitated, her natural sympathy for anything hurt making her want to reach out to him.

"Dinner," he said through clenched teeth. "I want you to meet the rest of the family at six."

She hesitated, torn between sympathy toward him, uncertainty about why she was even here. She needed to know so much more. She was being sliced by the sharp edges of so many emotions, anger the keenest of all. Anger at her mother. Against the man who had just implied that her mother had lied again.

"You will stay?"

It was both order and plea. She didn't want to stay. She wanted to go back to the hotel and take a hot bath and rerun everything that had happened today. She wanted to weigh it, to judge it.

She looked back at him, saw the pain overtaking the arrogance. She wondered if he was using that pain to manipulate her. Both her mother and Nick had warned her against his charm, and she'd seen more than a few flashes of it. Yet there had also been no sign of affection, no real warmth. More, she thought, a claim of possession.

She got up on legs that barely held her. They were rubbery from the tense exchange, from the expectations that had been dashed, the questions unanswered, the unexpected need unmet. Until this moment, she hadn't known how much she'd wanted a gesture of some kind, just as she had wanted it from Nick.

And she had more questions now than when she'd walked into the room.

ten

Nick watched as Samantha entered the parlor. She was tense, but he saw fire in her eyes.

He wondered what his father had thought he was getting: a mild-mannered woman who could be manipulated?

If so, he'd certainly been wrong.

Nick had few doubts now that the woman really was his sister. She was too sure of it herself.

But then she'd grown up happy and safe, and entirely too trusting.

For a moment, he was envious. Nothing had been easy for him. He'd never trusted easily. Still didn't.

"Want to go?" he asked, trying to give her another easy out.

"I promised to stay for dinner."

Anna walked in then. She looked at him, then regarded Samantha curiously. Obviously she had not been apprised of the new relative, either.

"My sister," he said to Anna, and watched as astonishment flashed across her face. "Samantha, this is Anna. Our cousin."

He paid little heed to Samantha's own look of surprise at his words *my sister*, at his evident surrender.

"No," Anna said. "It's impossible."

"I thought so, too," he said. "Pop says it's true, and there's no reason for him to lie. Samantha—or Nicole—is my twin sister."

All the color fled from Anna's face. "It can't be. She died years ago."

"No. Someone else died. God knows who."

"What does she want?" Anna asked, as if Samantha wasn't even there.

He smiled mirthlessly. "To my surprise, it seems damned little."

He watched as Anna reassessed the visitor, both as a competitor for an inheritance and as a competitor for male attention. Anna, who had lustrous dark brown hair and dark brown eyes, was extremely pretty as well as damn smart. And ambitious. She had a MBA from Harvard and was vice president of one of his father's legitimate corporations. In his name, she'd also established a charitable foundation.

She and Nick's half brother were always in competition for his father's approval.

Her own father had been killed when she was eleven. Pop had taken her in, raised her as the daughter he hadn't had.

Christ, this newest . . . twist hurt. It wasn't a small secret. An oversight. A half-truth. He thought about how many times as a boy he'd longed for a mother. He'd even visited the grave where he'd thought she was buried. It had been bad enough to lose a mother to death. To know, instead, that he'd not only been abandoned as a baby but also lied to his entire life was something that would take a long time for him to accept. Much less forgive. For either parent's part.

Samantha was something else. Another innocent party. A lot more innocent, in fact, than he.

His sister.

How could he keep her from probing any more? The deeper she probed, the more she would be tainted, even endangered. She had no idea of the cesspool bubbling just beneath the civilized trappings of their lives.

He had gone with the flow this past day, not quite believing her, not quite accepting this scenario that came out of the worst of bad novels. At some point—perhaps because of his father's call, perhaps because she believed it so thoroughly—he had come to believe everything she'd said.

And he'd tried to rein in the rage that swamped him in a way he'd never experienced before. Samantha obviously loved her mother and was loved in return. He'd had a succession of nannies and his father's girlfriends. He'd grown up lonely and isolated. His small physical hurts had been a matter of frantic finger-pointing between those looking after him and, as a result, military school had not been much of a hardship. For a moment, he knew grief for what could have been, but never was.

He found himself wanting to protect the woman he was reluctantly recognizing as his sister, while realizing his protection might well put her in more danger. It could, in fact, destroy her.

As for her mother, he had no interest in seeing her. Not now. Not ever.

Anna turned to Samantha, her lips suddenly curving into a charming smile. "Welcome to the family." It was as if her earlier comment about Samantha—and what she wanted—had never been made.

Samantha regarded her warily. "Thank you, but I don't exactly think I'm a member of the family."

"Pop obviously intends for you to be," Anna said.

Nick watched Samantha's face as she caught the easily said "Pop." A flicker of surprise disappeared quickly. She shrugged. "I really don't intend—or want—to be a part of the family. My life is in Colorado. I wanted only to meet my brother."

Anna looked surprised. "Not your father?"

"He made a decision years ago that he wanted Nick, not me," she said.

So she didn't really believe that her father had been looking for her all this time. Wise girl. And wouldn't she feel the same abandonment by his father as he did by her mother? That hadn't occurred to him until now.

Anna shrugged. "Well, welcome anyway. I have to get back to the office for a few hours. Nick, walk me to the car."

She walked to the ornate front door, obviously expecting him to follow. He didn't like being manipulated by her any more than he did by his father, but Samantha had turned away, her gaze wandering over the photos in the room.

He escorted his cousin out to her sports car. "Do you really believe her?" Anna asked. "That she really doesn't want anything?"

"I'm reserving judgment," he said blandly.

"It's a trick. Probably a look-alike that Georgie found."

"To what purpose?"

"To keep the bulk of Pop's estate. He could have an agreement to buy her share if she inherits, then he could take over."

"That's a big if, Anna."

"You've talked to her. What do you think?"

"I think she's exactly what she appears to be, an unsuspecting pawn in someone's game. I'm just not sure whose yet." He raised an eyebrow in question.

"I'm not that devious," Anna said.

"What does Pop have to gain from this?"

Anna sighed. "I don't know. I know he doesn't entirely trust George. And I'm a female and thus not fit to become head of the family. It has to have something to do with you."

Nick secretly agreed. It could well be another one of his father's plots to publicly bring him into his organization. The other crime groups would tear George apart, and Anna was right: Her father would see the organization crumble before putting it in the hands of a woman. "She'll be gone soon. She says she has no interest in Pop or the business, and I believe her."

"I don't," Anna said. "Surely she must know he's worth millions."

"I researched her last night," he said. "She has a successful business and a good reputation. If anything, this relationship is going to do more damage to her than good."

"You're the last person I expected to be naive," she said.

He shrugged. "Believe what you will. But I don't want any harm coming to her."

Her astonishment was plain. "You *really* do believe her."

"Yes, and I'm going to do everything I can to send her back to Colorado."

She put a finger on his cheek. "I'm still not sure about you, Nick. Are you really that indifferent to the family? Or are you just sneaky enough to make us think so?"

"You, my dear cousin, can make up your own mind. I'll see you later." He turned back toward the house. He heard the purr of her engine, then a roar and the spinning of gravel beneath expensive tires as she sped down the drive.

Samantha watched them from a window.

She saw Anna press her finger against Nicholas's cheek. It was more the gesture of a lover than a cousin.

She turned away. She hated this house. It was pretentious, the artwork hanging on the walls modern. She recognized the names. They were popular in the art world, though she didn't care for them. She felt the sudden need to leave, to run and never look back. Everything here was superficial; everything in Steamboat Springs substantive.

"I was wrong to come," she whispered to herself. And yet she knew she would have wondered her entire life if she had not made this personal pilgrimage.

She would see the dinner through tonight. Then she would return to her old life, happy in what and who she was.

"Once you see him, you'll be on the FBI radar."

That brought her thoughts back to McLean and his offer. She hadn't taken his card, but a call to the FBI would probably locate him. The intensity that seemed so uniquely his remained clear in her memory, as did the questioning gaze of striking green eyes.

Then she heard the door open, and Nicholas was back. "Learn anything from Pop?"

"No. He didn't say why he wanted to see me, other than I'm 'unfinished business.' He didn't seem very moved at seeing me."

"He isn't moved by much," Nicholas said. "Maybe we'll learn something at dinner."

Sam shivered slightly. Her gaze traveled around the richly furnished room. It seemed even colder, more inhospitable than before. Everything in this house seemed purchased for show.

"Would you like to see the gardens?" he asked.

"Yes," she replied. She hoped he didn't hear the gratitude in her voice.

He led her through what seemed an endless hall to the back. Formal gardens lay in perfect symmetry. He led her down a path edged by manicured shrubs and stopped at a clearing dominated by a white gazebo. Roses climbed the columns.

"It's—"

"Perfect." He finished the sentence.

They looked at each other and grinned simultaneously.

Perfection lacked spontaneity. Passion. Creativity.

His smile faded. She wanted to bring that expression back. For a moment they'd shared feelings. Something very nice had moved between them.

Too soon, that mask had slipped over his face again.

"Tell me about you," she said. "What do you like? What sports? What books? Where did you go to college? How did you start your business? I feel like I've missed so much."

"There wasn't much to miss." He moved away from her, putting both physical and emotional distance between them. "I went to military school, then to college where I bombed out and finally the military. After my tour, I went back to college and started a business with a friend."

"And who's the friend?"

"Cal White."

"I would like to meet him."

He shrugged. "I thought you would be leaving."

"Is that what you want, Nicholas?"

"Nick. Everyone calls me Nick, and yes, it would be better for you, for both of us. You'll stir up trouble. Perhaps if you leave now, the FBI might forget about you."

She remembered McLean's eyes. She didn't think so. Neither, she guessed, did Nick.

Sam turned away, tortured by doubts again. The house and the garden were illusions of perfection. Was Nick's concern also an illusion?

"He's really dying, isn't he?"

"His doctors say so."

"You don't sound convinced."

"I've learned never to trust anything to do with my father. That wisdom was made only too clear when you appeared. I recall his crocodile tears when I asked about my mother. A saint she was, he said." Sarcasm rippled through his words.

She studied him. "Are you sorry I appeared?"

"No. But I worry about you. You still don't know what you've gotten into. I want you to leave. In the morning."

"I haven't learned what I wanted to."

"You probably won't. He's playing games with you. A clue here, a clue there, until he has you enmeshed in a web."

"What could he want?"

"He could use you to get to your mother. My father never lets anyone go. Not without a battle. Your mother must have something he fears. Or wants. You could be the leverage to getting it."

Uncertainty tugged at her again. And fear, but not for herself. Despite her continued anger toward her mother, she didn't want to be the instrument of pain. Or betrayal.

She nodded. "Will you keep in contact with me?"

"Samantha . . . you don't know what you are asking."

"Sam," she said. "My friends call me Sam."

"I'm not your friend," he said.

"Not yet. I hope you will be."

"You don't take rejection readily, do you?"

"No." She smiled. "Particularly when it seems to be motivated by concern for me."

He sighed. "Is your mother as stubborn as you?"

"She's your mother, too."

"No. She'll never be that."

"She's a good person," she said. "It was hell for her to leave you behind, but—"

"Don't go there," he said, a muscle throbbing in his cheek. He had accused her of not taking rejection readily. Apparently he couldn't take it, either. Not where their mother was concerned. It gave her hope. If he was wounded by all this, then it meant he cared.

She wondered what it had been like for him growing up in Boston, knowing much of what was said about his father, his family. It must have been hard. Bewildering to a child. Had he really been able to throw all the baggage away?

Her mother had warned her. Something had frightened her badly. Was she—Sam—a fool for not listening?

They sat in the gazebo. A silence grew between them. Too many questions, too many guarded emotions. She wanted their relationship to be more. But did he?

"Go home," he said, "and be grateful for what you had and still have."

"How can I when you—?"

"I have what I want now," he said. "I have never believed in playing 'what if' games. They're useless. You deal with reality and choose your own path."

"I want *you* on my path."

"No," he said simply.

She looked at him. His eyes were uncannily like her own, except there was a secretiveness in his she didn't think hers had ever had.

She turned away from him, her body stiff and tense and defiant.

"Go," he said softly. "Go for your mother's sake, if not your own."

She whirled around on him. "What do you mean?"

"I suspect you're meant to be the instrument of her destruction. It's the only answer that makes sense."

Dinner was a nightmare.

Nicholas's words continued to ring in her head. *"The instrument of her destruction."* And why did he keep urging her to leave and never look back?

A fortune?

A well-meaning warning?

"You're in dangerous company . . . Don't wait to call us." Should she take heed of the FBI agent's warning?

Again Sam wondered why she had ever agreed to come, then to stay. Several members of the party had been thoroughly rude. Paul Merritta had been watchful, Nick silent. Only Anna, who had re-appeared, had tried to keep the conversation going.

Her aunt and her uncles and their wives were cold, looking at her as if she had come to rob them. Paul Merritta had been no help. He had introduced her as his daughter, then apparently decided to sit back as the lions tried to rip her apart.

Or perhaps nothing as noble as lions. They were more like jackals.

"I remember Tracy," Victor said dismissively. "Flighty. Ungrateful little—"

"That's enough," Paul Merritta finally interceded.

Victor—like Paul—might have been a handsome man once, but where Paul Merritta's illness had apparently drained life from him, his brother had allowed life to coarsen him. His face was red veined, probably from drinking too much, and his body was bloated. He had the blue eyes common in the family, except his were dull. They didn't carry the spark, the emotion that she saw in Nick's eyes, or even the embers that remained in her father's eyes.

"You look nothing like her," Uncle Ricardo—Rich, everyone called him—added after a pause. The implication that she was a fraud was clear.

"Actually," she said, "I do." She stuck her chin out. "I also look like my brother," she said.

Paul Merritta grimaced at that, or perhaps it was his attempt at a smile. He had limped in on the arm of Reggie, each step obviously painful. His face was pale from the effort, his eyes glazed over, probably by painkillers.

"I understand you have a little shop," George said. She kept reminding herself that he was a half brother, but he had none of Nick's charm.

"It's more than a little shop," she said with forced calm. "We have customers throughout the world."

"Western art," someone said contemptuously. "That's not art at all."

She looked around the table at the hostile faces and paused first on Nick, then on Paul Merritta, still watchful. To see what she was made of?

She shrugged. "We make a good living."

"You can always use more money," one of the aunts said. Her meaning was clear. Everyone at the table thought she was a scavenger.

"That depends on how and where it comes from," she replied evenly.

Her father chuckled. "There's no doubt that she's my daughter and your niece," he said. "She's a member of this family and nothing more will be said about it."

Silence fell around the table.

Her gaze lowered to the glass of wine that was continually refilled even if she'd taken only a few sips.

"We seem to like many of the same things," Nick said, unexpectedly coming to her defense. "Skiing, for instance. And business."

The latter provoked alarmed expressions. It was, she decided, akin to a shot across the bow. One of the games Nick had mentioned? Did he participate in those? She had thought not earlier, but now she wondered.

What was he playing at?

She felt like an alien in a world she didn't understand, a world where every word had a different meaning than the ones she understood, where danger lurked behind every shadow. The room was filled with twisted shadows.

Except for meeting Nick, the visit was a disaster, and even reuniting with her brother had not been very promising. Despite Paul Merritta's words, she'd felt no affection from him, and there was hostility from everyone else.

But she would never regret coming.

Perhaps now she could return home, to her own life. The image of her mother's pale face crept into her consciousness. Sam was beginning to understand just a small piece of her mother's fear. Why she had tried to escape this family. But how could she have left her son? Sam knew if she were a mother, nothing short of death would convince her to relinquish her son.

Had that been the choice her mother faced all those years ago—to leave or to die?

Paul Merritta suddenly stiffened—just as he had earlier—and clutched the table. Anna was the first up. She whispered in his ear, then held out her arm as he struggled to his feet.

He resisted for a moment and turned to Sam. "Tomorrow," he said. "Tomorrow we will have a long talk."

"I planned to go home tomorrow," she said.

"I want to talk to you further," he insisted. "There are things . . ." Agony crossed his face, then he stumbled from the room, leaving an emptiness and silence behind him.

Giving up on any pretense of having an appetite for the rich dessert in front of her, she put down her spoon. "I should go. Nick, are you ready?"

He stood. "Always at your command."

It was stylishly said, though he didn't smile. The others became visibly anxious, as if worried about a possible new alliance.

Nick seemed to enjoy their collective concern. He walked over to her, pulled out the chair as she rose.

George stood and blocked their way. George, as impeccably groomed as the gardens, glared at her. "I don't know what you want or what you're doing here, but I'm warning you: You won't get what we worked so hard for."

She stared at her half brother, seeing only contempt in his face. She was angry, angrier than she had been with her mother. It was as if a gaping wound had been torn open, one she hadn't known existed until a week ago. "I don't want anything from you. I don't want anything from this family. I wouldn't take it if it were gift-wrapped. I came because I was asked. I wanted the truth about my . . . heritage. Now I know and I wish to hell I didn't. I don't like it. I don't like you. And I'm going home."

Tears of frustration, maybe even regret, threatened.

Her brother didn't want her here. Her biological father was obviously playing one family member against the other.

The instrument of her mother's destruction. Was that what she was?

All she was?

eleven

"Good girl," Nicholas said as he gunned the car and drove toward the gate. For a moment, she thought it wouldn't open and she would be trapped here forever. But then the gates slowly yielded, and she relaxed.

"Why?"

"You held your own with them. My father respects guts. He may say otherwise and rant and rave, but it is the only thing he really does respect."

"I don't care if he does or not," she retorted. "I loved my father. At least he was my father in every important way. Paul Merritta doesn't compare with David Carroll. Not in any way—"

She caught herself. She was talking about his father. The only one he knew.

Nicholas shrugged. "Then forget the Merrittas. You seemed to have had a television-family childhood. Why spoil it?"

"I'm sorry, Nick."

"Don't be." His voice was hard.

She tried to change the subject. "He must respect you. You have a successful business. . . ."

Nick looked at her quickly, then shrugged. "Who knows?"

"Do you care?"

"I stopped caring a long time ago," he said.

"But you still keep contact."

"He's still my father, whether or not I approve of him." He turned his gaze from the road and looked at her for a split second before turning back.

Sam looked ahead at the four lane road that wound through a neighborhood of fine homes. Dusk was falling. Traffic was light and everyone was moving fast, probably all exceeding the posted forty-five mile per hour speed limit. Nick was going fifty to fifty-five, and other cars were passing them.

She tried not to worry. Her law-and-order compulsion was working overtime. All she needed was to be arrested in a car belonging to a member of a crime family. Then she realized *she* was a member of the family, too.

He turned on the headlights, and she sat back and relaxed. Oddly enough she was comfortable with him. She didn't feel the need to chatter any longer, or even ask questions.

She wondered if he felt the same.

Then she became aware of his glancing into the rearview mirror. More, she thought, than necessary. She looked over her shoulder.

There seemed to be nothing other than the normal traffic.

For a moment, her mind went back to the burglary of her house.

She decided to mention it. "I told you I was burglarized before coming here."

He nodded, his eyes intent on the road ahead.

"I thought it might be a coincidence."

"There are damned few coincidences in this family," he said. "What did they take?"

"Nothing valuable. I came home from a run and apparently surprised whomever it was."

His gaze left the road again. It was only for an instant but she saw surprise, and something else there. "You said nothing valuable was taken? Was *anything* taken?"

"An address book."

She heard him swear softly.

"Do you know something I should?" she asked.

"Only that I'm not surprised."

"Why would my father . . . ?"

"*Your* father now," he asked. "How quickly we come to accept."

"I've had more time."

"And no evidence."

"My mother's word."

"Oh, yes, your mother's word. Sorry, I can't place much faith in that." He looked in the rearview mirror again. His face tensed. Then he turned onto another road, one lined with commercial activity.

"You still don't believe?"

"Oh, I believe all right, though I wouldn't believe my father if he swore on a stack of Bibles. He uses people, Samantha. And people who believe him die. Remember that."

"He said my mother's not in danger. Can I believe that?"

"No," he said flatly.

Even as he issued the damning word, Sam saw him look at the rearview mirror again. She turned and squinted at the headlights behind them. They were close. Too close. No more than two or three feet from their car.

Nick made one left turn and then another onto an overpass. The car lights behind them receded, then closed the distance again. Instinctively she grasped the armrest.

The other car bumped them from behind.

Her gaze shot to Nick as he sped up, his gaze glued to the road, his mouth tight.

She looked at the speedometer. Eighty miles an hour, and still the needle moved forward.

She looked back at the car gaining on them, its headlights looking like the eyes of a predator intent on making a kill.

The vehicle hit their car again, harder. If she had not fastened her seat belt, her head would have struck the window.

"What are they doing?" she asked through suddenly dry lips.

Nicholas's face tensed as he struggled with the wheel. They were being pushed headlong into oncoming traffic.

She braced for impact as he twisted the wheel to the far right.

Their wheels caught the shoulder. The car that had trailed them hit the left rear of their car, knocking it toward the edge of the road and the forbidding blackness of a drop.

She couldn't scream, couldn't stop lurching against the seat belt. She heard a loud whooshing sound as the airbag exploded, and suddenly she could see nothing as her body was shoved backward, all her breath pushed out of her lungs.

She couldn't move her arms or legs as she struggled for air. Her chest hurt as if an anvil had been thrown against it.

Pain spread from one part of her body to another as she tried to see Nick through the darkness. The horn on the car was blaring, pressed down by his weight once the airbag deflated.

Then she saw him move.

"Are you all right?" Nick asked. His voice was thick.

She turned to look through shattered windows, aware of tiny cuts caused by pieces of glass now scattered over her clothing and seat. "I think—" Her voice abruptly left her at the sight of a figure next to the window. For a split second, she felt relief, then she saw a ski mask and a gun raised and aimed at her.

Nick leaned in front of her. A soft burst of sound, like a wheezing gasp, seemed to fill every corner of her awareness.

Nick slammed backward and slumped.

She cried out, wanting to reach for him, yet unable to move for the shock, paralyzing her. All she could do was stare at the figure . . . at the gun.

Then both were gone, the figure fading into darkness.

"Nick," she said.

"It's . . . all right," he said. "Just . . ." His voice turned into a groan.

A plume of smoke rose from the smashed front of the car. Heart jumping in her chest, she fumbled with her seat belt. The nylon webbing released her suddenly and she all but fell to the side, reaching for Nick.

She forced her fingers to probe gently. The wound was not his chest . . . not his stomach. He groaned again when she touched his arm. She felt something warm and wet on her hands.

"Nick? Can you move?"

"I think so."

Despite the pain in her chest from the airbag that had now disintegrated, she managed to unbuckle his seat belt.

"We have to get out," Nick said, his voice hoarse.

Smoke was creeping inside the car through the shattered windows and the fresh air vent near the floor.

She leaned forward over him to open the door on his side. Her own was pinned against a culvert.

His door was stuck fast.

He tried to help her force open the door. It wouldn't budge.

"Get out," he said. "Go over me."

Ignoring the pain stabbing at her ribs, she wriggled over him, trying to avoid his arm that hung at an odd angle. She tumbled out the smashed window, sprawling on the ground.

A flicker of flame became visible. Nicholas. Dear God, she hadn't just met him to lose him.

"Run," Nick said, pushing against the door.

Instead she started pulling at the door, even as she saw the flame move toward the gas tank.

"The window," she said. "Climb out."

He tried, angling his body as blood poured from his wound. "Go," he ordered again.

She grabbed his shoulders, pulling as he tried to push. He fell out, taking her down with him.

She felt the heat from the car. In seconds it would explode.

She tried to lift him up, but he fell back. "Nick, help me."

But he was dead weight. *Unconscious.*

Her heart pounded till it almost burst from her chest. She knew she couldn't move him alone.

Not in time.

Still, she grabbed one of his arms.

And prayed.

twelve

Nate cursed as the car ahead of him sped up and bumped Merritt's car.

He'd known the second car was tailing Merritt. It hadn't occurred to him that actual harm was the intent.

It should have. Samantha Carroll was a threat to virtually every branch of the Merritta family as well as to opposing factions. Organized crime was just that—organized and carefully controlled. Unknown elements rarely were controllable and therefore were to be eliminated.

The car following Merritt accelerated, and Nate realized he wouldn't be able to close the distance between them in time. Not if the driver of the second car was serious about doing damage.

It was. The car rammed into Merritt's again, this time leaving no room for doubt that this was more than a friendly little warning.

Neither Merritt nor the driver of the car following him seemed to notice that Nate was gaining on them. He was in his personal car—a 1990 BMW he'd bought cheap in a government sale—which he'd thought would be less obvious in this neighborhood. Now he regretted the fact he didn't have a radio.

He'd known from the phone tap on Merritt's home that she would be at Paul Merritta's. He'd lost her earlier, and that had irritated him no end. He didn't intend to lose her again.

Merritt took a turn leading to the Boston Post Road, obviously hoping to outrun whoever was following him.

Nate checked the road ahead and behind, and floored the gas pedal, his gut twisting at the thought of Samantha Carroll in the car ahead.

He thought of everything they'd discovered about her in the past few days. Samantha Carroll of Steamboat Springs, Colorado. Model citizen, pillar of the business community of her town, excellent credit rating, member in the local Better Business Bureau and active in the Chamber of Commerce. Master's degree in business from Stanford. One speeding ticket that he could find.

And then there was Samantha Carroll—daughter of crime boss, twin sister of suspected accomplice, if not mastermind, of money laundering operations and heir to the reins of the "family." Samantha Carroll—obvious target of opposing factions.

And someone was after her. But who? Opposing families? Or members of her own newly discovered family?

Maybe both.

She'd looked more promising than he'd ever imagined. She was a respected member of the community, a role she would probably like to keep both for herself and for her mother.

If she didn't cooperate voluntarily, he might have a weapon there.

He pushed away the twinge of guilt he felt. Putting away the Merrittas justified a hell of a lot of personal reservations about his methods. Paul Merritta had never had any reservations about murder. Nate's stomach tightened at the thought, at the memory that never left him.

But now her life was in jeopardy and he found he didn't give a damn about using her.

The car ahead was closing in on Merritt's car again. Merritt, he knew, had a sports car, but tonight he drove a dark sedan that was no match for the large car on its tail.

Nate noted the make, model and license number of the tailing car. Like his own, the car was expensive. Unlike his, the windows were tinted.

Nate saw a stop sign and a car turning into the road. He hit the brakes to avoid striking it. His car skidded several feet, almost hitting a fence. He backed up, but then another car had cut in front.

He swore as he tried to maneuver around the two cars that blocked him. He leaned on the horn but that only got him a finger in the air from the car ahead. The traffic in the other lane was steady and he couldn't get around them. Then they hit a light, and he was neatly pinned in. Blocked.

Merritt's car and the one following it disappeared.

Hell with this. He edged onto the shoulder that was far too close to a fence. Hearing the crunch as the side of his car hit the fence, he managed to get around one car, then the other. He speeded up and turned onto the main road.

He almost passed it. Would have if he hadn't seen the car parked on the edge of the road, its lights off. He slowed, stopped, just as he saw a man dressed in black slip inside the car. The car screeched off, leaving a trail of gravel and dust behind it.

He wanted to go after it. Instead he looked down and saw the passenger side of a car smashed against a culvert.

He parked his car, called 911 on his cell phone, then left the BMW, half sliding, half running down the hill.

Samantha Carroll was trying to tug a large body away from the wrecked vehicle. He saw the smoke, smelled the gas.

"Get the hell out of here," he said.

"No," she said. "He's unconscious."

"Damn it, I'll get him." He leaned down and put an arm under Merritt's. He half lifted him. Samantha disobeyed and put her arm under the other one. Together they dragged, half carried him. A loud *whoosh* followed by an explosion filled the air as they stumbled away from the car.

The three of them fell forward, flattened to the ground by the blast and the wave of heat. A wail of sirens joined in the hellish chorus.

Merritt was unconscious, either from a head wound or loss of blood. Nate rolled him over and tore Merritt's shirt open. Blood poured from a neat hole in his arm. He was also bleeding from a number of cuts inflicted by shattered glass. So was Samantha Carroll.

Merritt's wound was obviously more pressing.

"Help him," Samantha whispered as she struggled to sit. "Please."

Silently Nate tore a piece from his shirt and pressed it down on the wound. Samantha held Merritt's head. "Help's coming, Nick," she said. She made her voice low, soothing, steady, startling Nate with her presence of mind.

She turned to him. "Thank you."

He wanted to take credit, which might put her in debt to him. But oddly enough he couldn't quite do it. Not when she had risked her own life to save her brother.

"You did most of it," he said honestly. "What happened?"

"Someone forced us off the road, and then a man in a ski mask came down and . . ."

"And?"

"He pointed a gun at me. Nick leaned in front of me. He was hit with a bullet meant for me."

A police car roared to a stop above them, then an ambulance, followed by another police car. Emergency techs came sliding down the bank.

He stood and held out a hand to her, helping her to her feet. Perhaps he would have a few moments to earn her confidence.

But that hope was dashed when he recognized one of the police officers. The man had been burned recently by the FBI, his bust ruined when the Bureau took the suspect in as an informant.

The officer took one look at him, then at Nick Merritt. "What in the hell."

"Someone forced him off the road," Nate said.

"And you were just behind him? A coincidence, I suppose."

"No, I was following him."

He saw Samantha stiffen, a momentary suspicion cross her face.

"And how did he get shot?"

Samantha broke in. "We were forced off the road, then someone—wearing a ski mask—came down and shot at me."

"But Merritt was hit?" The officer's voice was full of disbelief. "And a mystery man in a ski mask just disappeared?" He looked back and forth between both of them. "We'll need statements from all of you."

An EMT finished putting a pressure bandage on Merritt. Another was bandaging one of Samantha's cuts. "That will have to wait," said the first as he looked up from where he was kneeling next to Merritt. "They're both going to the hospital."

"I'll go with them," Nate said.

"No way," said the officer, putting his hand on his holster. "That's Nicholas Merritt. We had a call someone was forcing another car off the road. You stay here until my sergeant comes. We do this by the book."

Nate had no choice but to watch her climb the hill with the help of an officer as two EMTs carried Merritt up on a stretcher.

She looked back toward him, then continued her climb to the road.

Then she was gone.

The family gathered in the sunroom. They were all there, everyone but Paul Merritta. He had gone to bed, sedated and watched over by a nurse.

Victor poured them all a glass of wine. "What's he up to?"

George gulped down his drink. "Did anyone know about this disaster?"

"You're with the family's law firm," Rich said wryly. "If you don't know, how would we?"

"Someone had to know she was alive. I know the background. I know about the accident. I also know Papa was out of town then. One of you had to help identify the bodies."

No one said anything.

George glared around the room. "It had to be Victor or Rich."

"Not necessarily," Anna said. "Pop also had enough friends to see to it."

Victor gave her a grateful look. "I swear it was as much a surprise to me tonight as to anyone. Don't you think my interests lie in maintaining the status quo?"

"But why?" George said. "Why bring her here?"

"We all know he wants Nick to succeed him. Maybe she's some kind of leverage."

"And do any of us know what Nick wants?"

"Nick says she was attacked the night before last," Victor said. "Maybe my brother thought she was in danger and believed she would be safer here. Or that Nick could protect her."

"We all believed she died thirty-four years ago," Rich said. "Who would—?"

He stopped in midsentence at the look on Victor's face. "You know, don't you, Victor?"

But Victor's face had gone blank.

"I still think it's because of Nick," George said. "He's just been biding his time, building that goddamn company as a front," he said bitterly. "You know Papa. You do what he wants and he walks all over you. He only respects those who stand up to him. Nick's no fool."

"But what does the woman have to do with that?" Anna broke in.

"I don't know, but I see Nick's hand in it," George said.

"However she came here, it's a disaster," Rich said. "If she participates equally in our part of the estate, then Nick might be able to take control of everything. As the will's written now, he gets a third of everything if he agrees to take over the businesses. If Paul adds her, and she sides with Nick . . . they can control all the businesses."

"I've seen his will," Victor said. "She's not included."

"Could he have changed it?" Anna asked.

"Damned if I know," George said.

"You're the family lawyer."

"He's never talked to me about the will. Pembroke still handles his personal business."

"Can you talk to him?"

George shook his head. "He's never liked me. I took away the bulk of his business. I wanted to cut his retainer."

Victor turned to Anna. "Talk to Reggie. You can twist

him around your finger. Find out whether Pembroke has been in to see Paul."

Anna frowned. "Even if he hasn't, it's only a matter of time. You must have seen the way he looked at her. And she apparently has Nick's protection."

"How long do you think Nick's known about her?" Victor asked.

"He met with her yesterday," Anna said.

Victor looked at her. "How did you know that?"

"No great secret. Nick told me."

"He didn't say anything else? He believes she's really his sister?"

"He didn't, at first. I think he does now."

"An imposter?" George said hopefully.

"With that hair and eyes? I don't think so," Anna said. "And Pop would know. He would be sure with something this important. His body might be failing, but his mind isn't."

"There's another question," Victor said.

They all looked at him.

"Someone tried to kidnap her. Or worse." Victor looked around the room.

"Don't look at me," George said. "I didn't know about her until today."

"None of us did," Anna added.

"Someone did," Victor said.

"Maybe they can take care of our problem," George said with a small smile.

"Pop will kill anyone who harms her, particularly since he sent for her," Anna pointed out.

"That begs the question as to why." George said. "Why try to see her after all these years?"

"An act of contrition?" Anna asked.

No one believed that for a moment.

"He's dying," Victor said. "He's not thinking right."

A silence settled around the table.

George met Victor's eyes, then nodded.

Victor rose. "It's been a long evening. Let's see what we can find out and resume this conversation tomorrow."

One by one, they left the room.

thirteen

McLean was waiting outside Nick's room.

Sam knew he was there. A nurse had informed her an hour ago.

She looked at her watch. Four hours since the accident. Nick had undergone surgery to repair a small artery and remove a bone splinter.

Her multiple cuts from the glass had been tended. There were none on her face, thank God.

She'd waited until Nick had been taken to a room, then sat with him. She'd been surprised that the FBI agent had not barged in.

She hadn't wanted to think about him or about those few moments when he'd helped her — or she had helped him — carry Nick to safety. She'd been so grateful.

She was still grateful. But she was also wary of the feelings he sparked in her. She'd caught the nuance, even the accusation, in the officer's words. Why *had* he been following them? Could he have prevented what had happened? It was a measure of the distrust that Nick had planted in her that she now weighed every word, every act, and wondered about the motives behind them.

Agent McLean had saved Nick's life. And probably her own.

So how could she have even the slightest doubts about his integrity?

Because Nick had taken a bullet for her. Because he didn't trust McLean. Loyalties pulled at her like riptides.

When Nick emerged from the anesthesia, his first question was about her. "Samantha . . . are you . . ."

"I'm fine," she replied. "Thanks to you."

His gaze roamed over her bandages.

"None are serious," she tried to assure him. "That agent—McLean—was following us. He probably saved both of our lives by dragging you away."

His eyes closed for a moment, then opened again. "Don't trust him," he murmured. He tried to reach for a phone but his arm fell back. "The phone," he said. "Can you dial a number and hand it to me?"

She saw the determination and did as he asked. She couldn't help listening to his slurred words. "Cal . . . there's been an accident. No, I'm not hurt badly but I'm in the hospital for tonight. Will you send Kelley over here? I want him to stay with Samantha."

Apparently Cal was fully aware of who she was.

"Good," Nick said, then gave the receiver back to her to set back into the cradle. "Wait here for a man named Kelley. He'll take care of you. I don't want you alone." He moved, winced, then closed his eyes again. In minutes, he was lost in a drug-induced sleep.

"Don't trust him."

She hadn't known what to expect, but not that. It showed the depth of the antipathy between the two men.

Then why had McLean saved him? Wouldn't it have been better to ignore the accident? It would have likely meant one less Merritta to worry about.

Or had he waited until the very last moment, when she

was at risk, too? Nick had warned her he wanted to use her against the family.

Could it be . . . ?

Could a law enforcement officer be that devious, that cold-blooded?

Yet she couldn't forget the sudden relief she'd felt when he'd appeared seconds before the car exploded. She'd known then she would be safe. As would Nick.

Could her perceptions be that skewed?

But she recalled the pain in her brother's eyes, remembered how he had leaned into the bullet for her, and she would do anything for him in turn. Believe anything. Or at least try to.

She wondered whether she should call his family, then decided that should be his decision. She knew she didn't want to talk to any of them. She and Nick had been followed from Paul Merritta's house. It had to be one of *them* who'd chased them off the road.

She stepped outside the door. McLean was there, just as she knew he would be.

Their gazes met. Her legs felt spindly, but she told herself it was only because of the events of the past few days.

"How is he?" he asked.

"He's asleep," she said shortly, wishing he didn't look as attractive as he did. *He* didn't look like a mummy. Rather, he looked very much in control.

"Can I take you back to your hotel? I still want to talk to you."

"I don't think so. I'm tired and I hurt in places I didn't even think could hurt."

He grinned, and it went straight to her traitorous heart. "I've felt that way myself. All the more reason to give you a ride."

"Thank you," she said, "and thank you for doing what you did back there, but I need to have some time alone."

"Do you really think that's a good idea?"

"I don't know the definition of a good idea any longer," she said. "I just know I need some rest. You are not restful."

He gave her a quizzical look. "You're probably entitled to anything you want at this point. But the police want a statement. I was able to delay it until tomorrow morning. I told them you would pay them a visit."

"Why? I was the victim. I didn't see anything."

"Because your brother was involved," he said. "It's that simple."

"And he's a Merritta?"

"Yes," he said simply. "Did Merritt tell you not to talk to me?"

She didn't say anything, but she was sure her expression gave her away.

"You really shouldn't be alone, Miss Carroll. Or is it Miss Merritta?" There was something about the way he said the last word. The slightest tinge of challenge. Why? Did he feel the same jagged edges of attraction that she did, and was he trying to dull them with animosity, just as she was?

"I appreciate what you did but I really don't want to talk to you," she said, surprising even herself with the comment, she who had always respected the police, who'd always even been a little in awe of them and the risks they took for what was little more than survival wages. But she also felt fiercely protective of Nick at the moment.

He raised an eyebrow. "I checked you out."

"You found the long list of offenses," she retorted.

He grinned, and it was unexpectedly disarming. He had a rough charm. His eyes were a clear green, almost emerald, and their sharpness and intensity belied his rumpled clothes and hair.

"Found nothing," he admitted wryly. "Not in Steamboat Springs."

"How did you know it was Steamboat Springs?"

"All we need is a name, Miss Carroll. From there, we can write a biography on you."

"How did you know I would be on that plane?"

"A guess." He grinned again. "That's not exactly accurate. I met every plane from Denver."

"And how did you know I was coming?"

"Do you really want to know?"

"A bug?"

His silence confirmed it.

"And Nicholas. Do you have one on him, too?"

He shrugged.

"And you have people following him?"

"It's a damn good thing I did."

She suddenly felt foolish. She thought of all the precautions she had taken, but all they'd needed was her name on an airline manifest. They probably knew more about her now than she did.

Despite the attraction that sparked between them, she resented his intrusion into her life. Whom had he asked? The police department back home? Did the officers there now know she was related to an infamous family? She and her mother?

The gratitude she'd felt earlier faded, the words of her brother still haunting her.

"Are you sure I can't give you a ride?"

She shook her head.

"Then I'll wait and talk to him," he said. The challenge was there. She wondered whether he knew about her hotel, whether anyone other than Nick knew about it. But she didn't want McLean here, either. Nick was in no condition to see him.

"The medical staff said 'family only,' " she said.

His crooked smile told her he knew she was bluffing. But of course he would. He was FBI and used to elbowing his way into places where he was unwanted.

He started for the door, and unable to stop him, she followed him in.

Nick's eyes were closed but he opened them when McLean approached. He grimaced.

"Just came in to see if you were still alive," McLean said.

"I hear you helped drag me out of a car. Going soft, McLean? Or did you have another motive?"

"It was the only way to get your sister out of danger. She wouldn't leave without you. Something else on your conscience."

"Leave her alone, McLean."

"She's not the one we want."

"The one *you* want," her brother corrected. His words weren't as slurred now, though the pain etched lines in his face.

"Someone else apparently does, too. We can offer both of you protection."

"I've seen what happens to people you protect," her brother said. "A lot of them end up dead. You can leave now unless you have a warrant."

"A crime's been committed tonight."

"I was the victim. I think even you would have a hard time dreaming up a federal charge."

"The time will come. Why get Miss Carroll involved?"

"If you want to talk to her, then talk to *her*."

"He has," she interrupted.

Nick looked surprised and glanced at the door, apparently noticing her for the first time. She'd been standing there, unseen, she thought, since the two men were so intent on their own personal agenda.

McLean didn't move. She wondered whether he'd known she had been there, listening. "She's as close-mouthed as you," he said. "I don't think she understands how dangerous that can be. How dangerous being with your family can be."

Nick said nothing.

She stepped inside the dark room. Only the light from the bathroom cast any illumination. "I think you should go," she said to McLean.

The agent's eyes glittered as he turned to her, then back to her brother. "Who was the shooter?"

"I don't know," Nick said.

"You must have suspicions."

"*You* always have suspicions, McLean. That doesn't seem to help you."

McLean shrugged and turned back to her. "Will you reconsider a ride to your hotel? And protection?"

"No," Nick said. "Someone is coming here for her."

"One of your soldiers?"

"Go to hell," Nick said.

Hostility vibrated in the room.

Emotions warred inside her. She was protecting someone the FBI obviously thought was a bad guy. She recalled her mother's strained face, the fear in her eyes, and she felt as if her world tipped upside down. She'd always felt safe before, safe and loved. She'd always trusted people, trusted her instincts. Now she didn't know whether she could trust anyone again.

Yet the man in bed had protected her, taking a bullet meant for her. He was the brother she'd always wanted. She didn't want to believe he was involved in his father's business.

There it was again. *His* father. *Her* mother. Neither of them had entirely accepted the new family dynamics except perhaps for each other. In the past twenty-four hours she felt they had started building something together.

She tried to tell herself it didn't matter what he did, or what he was. He had protected her at risk to himself and that meant everything to her.

Events had happened so quickly, she thought part of her must be in shock, which was why she still didn't quite know what she was doing, or why, or what the ramifications would be. For someone who had always been so methodical in her life, she felt she was on a runaway roller coaster, holding on to Nick for dear life.

She realized the FBI agent had not moved, but was watching her carefully. "I'm going to get some coffee," she said as she turned to the door. She stepped outside and let the door close slowly behind her.

Nick had called for someone to come and stay with her, but how long would that take? And how could she trust even that person? She hadn't been safe in Nick's car. Maybe . . .

So many maybes were flying through her head. She needed to call her mother, reassure herself that Patsy was safe. But how? Her pocketbook with most of her money was in the car that had gone up in flames. So, she realized, had her cell phone.

She could ask McLean for a couple of quarters and call collect, but then there would be a record. A call from the hospital room had the same problem.

"Damn," she said. She needed to get back to the hotel room where she'd left both money and two credit cards in a safe. It was always a precaution she took when traveling after a thief had snatched her wallet on one of her business trips.

She knew one thing. She didn't want to talk to McLean again. She was too tired. Too uncertain. Too vulnerable.

She had no idea how long it would take for the man her brother had sent for to arrive.

She would do some exploring, then return up here. Perhaps McLean would be gone then, and her brother would fall asleep.

She walked down to the nurses' station and waited patiently. There was only one person there and she looked swamped. Another nurse was going into a room down the hall.

Finally the woman looked up. Her name tag said SUSAN.

"I'm going to get some coffee," Sam said. "By the way, my brother needs some rest. There's a gentleman there . . ."

She walked swiftly down the hall to the elevator, turning to see a nurse head toward her brother's room. She got in the elevator, thankful that the doors had opened almost immediately. It never did that. An angel was with her.

Or a devil.

She took the elevator to the second floor and wandered down the hall, stopping at a rest room. She entered the small room and locked the door behind her. Then she leaned against the wall and took a deep breath.

Everything had always been easy for her. No big problems. No big decisions. No one had ever betrayed her. She'd never lost a friend, or at least didn't think she had. Distrust was something she'd never really experienced. Fear was part thrill as she skied down a steep slope.

Now she was in a different world, and she didn't know the rules, or whom to trust. She had never believed she would be terrified to go out on a street. Now an empty lobby raised the hackles on the back of her neck.

She never should have come. She knew that now. She might have put her mother in jeopardy, both physically and emotionally. And yet she'd always thought she could control things, control her life, because she'd always been able to. She had blithely believed she had made some ground rules and everyone would honorably respect them, simply because a long-lost father had wanted to meet her.

Her rules were obviously not *their* rules. And she couldn't even be sure—not if she was entirely honest—whether her rules were Nick's rules.

She'd always hated stupid heroines in books and movies. Now she felt like one.

The question was how to repair the damage she might

have caused by her curiosity, by her need to discover what had happened so many years ago.

Or even how *not* to make things worse.

She went to the mirror and faced herself. She was pale, haggard looking. No lipstick, and no purse in which to find lipstick. Her silk shirt was splotched with blood. She looked as if she'd staggered in from a war zone.

She rinsed her face with water and did her best to comb her hair with her fingers. Without her purse, it was the best she could do. There was nothing to be done about her clothes. They were ruined.

What to do now?

She could go back to Nick's room, but Agent McLean might still be there, and she was too tired to fence with him. And too wary.

And Nick's bodyguard? He probably wouldn't be there yet.

She could hide here.

Dear God, she was emotionally drained.

She decided to go down to the lobby. Surely there would be people there. She had never believed the movie world's myth of empty hospital corridors. She wished she had a sweater to cover her stained clothes, but blood shouldn't be out of place at a hospital.

She returned to the elevator and pushed the Down button. When the doors opened, a technician of some kind stood inside. Safe and normal.

Sane.

Her throat felt as if it had a boulder in it. But she was free for a few moments. Free of the hatred that had vibrated between the two men upstairs, of the accusations each had made of the other.

When she reached the first floor, she turned toward the lobby.

She'd always thought a hospital lobby would be occupied, if not busy. This one wasn't. She didn't see another soul. She did see the front door, an information desk that was empty. Lord, but she needed a breath of fresh air, a relief from the antiseptic odor. From being trapped.

She looked first, then stepped outside and glanced around, trying to figure out where she might be. A street name. A cross street. The air wasn't refreshing as she'd hoped. It was hot, stuffy, cloying. A large medical office building across the street looked mainly empty, and a parking lot was only a quarter filled. Several cars were parked along the street, all in places that said "No Parking."

She thought she saw movement in one car, and she edged back toward the door. Then she heard the sounds of a siren and saw an ambulance hurtling around a corner and turning into the hospital. A police car followed.

There was something particularly lonely about a siren in deep night. She fought a wave of quiet despair. She could call Paul Merritta and ask for help. But where had the car come from earlier if not from one of the Merrittas?

In truth, she had no place to turn except to the man her brother had called earlier. If only she had her purse, if only she could get to the hotel, then she would have resources of her own.

She peered at the cars parked in the "No Parking" place again, and wondered whether the police would make them leave. Then she saw one man get out. He walked toward the steps, toward the hospital, toward her.

She turned back into the hospital. The halls were as empty as before.

She looked at the bank of elevators down the hall, but what if she had to wait? She turned down the hall. The waiting room. It was at the other end of a very long corridor, but there would be people there.

Something told her to hurry. She glanced around. One man had entered and was moving toward her. He was large—not fat, but big.

Then he increased his pace. She could hear his steps behind her. She followed the arrows toward the emergency section. God, there had to be someone cleaning. But there wasn't. The only sound was that of footsteps echoing in the hall.

fourteen

Panic raising, Sam turned a corner and ran into a body. A very solid body. Arms wrapped around her and kept her from falling.

"Whoa," said a voice.

She knew that voice.

"What is it?" McLean asked.

"Someone . . . I thought someone was behind me." She glanced over her shoulder.

He steadied her, then let go and strode to the corner. "No one there now," he said.

"It was probably nothing," she said. Someone going on duty. Someone making a late visit to a critically ill patient. It was a measure of what had happened these past few days that she'd assumed it was all about her.

She straightened. She had felt safe for a moment, safe and something else. Somehow, it hadn't surprised her that he was the one there to reassure her. Her arms burned where he'd touched her. But the warmth cooled when he returned and she remembered the exchange in Nicholas's room. She steeled herself against wanting the solidness of his body, that momentary safety she'd felt. "What are you doing here?"

"I was looking for you. The nurse said you would be back. I didn't think you should be alone, so I decided to try the emergency waiting room."

"You wanted to ask more questions."

"I would be lying if I said no."

"Nick doesn't trust you. He said you used people, that you wanted to use me."

She tried to hold back tears. For a while earlier in the evening McLean had been a savior. Even at the airport, she'd sensed safety rather than menace in his presence. Now she didn't know whether he was saint or sinner, at least where she—and her brother—were concerned.

"We go back a way."

"How?"

"He has the kind of business that's the perfect front for money laundering. Foreign sales. Clients worldwide, including in Switzerland."

"Do you have any proof of money laundering?"

"No," he admitted. "But . . ."

"He's a Merritta?" she said. "So am I. Does that make me a criminal?"

"Did your father finance your business?"

"No." At least she didn't think so. Could Merritta have had something to do with the business? Perhaps even secretly? He said he hadn't known where they were, but was that the truth? The shadows were thick again, filling her mind with suspicion and doubts. Nothing was real and whole and honest.

She felt chilled.

"What did you see just now?" he asked.

"Probably no more than someone going to work or to see a patient." She tried a small laugh. "I'm a little spooked."

"That's understandable," he said. "Someone tried to run you off the road and shoved a pistol in your face. Anyone would be."

Anyone might be, but she'd always conquered fear before. She'd always thought she could handle almost anything, and now she was fleeing through hospital corridors like a ninny. She didn't like the image at all, or that this man had witnessed it.

"I'm fine now," she finally said.

"Let me take you somewhere safe," he said.

She was surprised at how much a part of her wanted to accept that offer. He still carried the aura of authority and safety. And he attracted her as few men did.

But he wanted something from her. He wanted her biological father. Her brother. Perhaps so much that he would destroy her mother to accomplish it.

"I'm sorry, but I really have to get back to his room."

"Don't trust him, Miss Carroll."

"He said the same thing about you." She looked at his face, at the eyes that had always attracted her, that had remained painted in her mind. They went through subtle changes in color. Perhaps that's why they fascinated her so. That and his restless energy and the intensity of emotions she sensed in him. It was almost like watching the approach of a hurricane.

Attraction rippled between them again, strong and vibrant and so alive and heated that she forced back a gasp.

Nick saved your life. He doesn't trust this man. How can you?

"Don't trust him." McLean's words.

The problem was that she was inclined to trust both of them. What did that say about her instincts or lack of them? One was a man she'd just met. The other was a brother she barely knew. The former had been in the right place. Three times now. That alone was suspicious.

She stiffened her spine. "I really have to get back to my brother's room."

"I'll go with you."

"As far as the elevator," she said.

One side of his mouth turned up in a half smile. "All right."

He stayed at her side as she walked back through the empty corridor. No bogeyman. No sign of the figure she'd seen earlier. They reached the elevator and he pushed the Up button.

She rested against the wall, waiting. He was inches away. Too close.

"Would it be so bad to lean on someone else for a while?" he asked softly, distractedly, as if he couldn't help himself.

An almost palpable desire leaped between them, filling her with a hungering need. The air seemed to thicken with it. She closed her eyes and swayed. How easy it would be to lean against him, to put her problems, her fears, in his hands . . .

She felt the back of his fingers stroke her cheek, then curl around her neck, easing the tension, cupping the tight muscles, drawing her toward him. His breath brushed her mouth, then his lips followed. Lightly at first, as if testing the waters.

Lightning struck and flashed through her body. She found herself standing on tiptoes to draw even closer. Her body took over her mind as he found her willingness and deepened the kiss.

Every bell rang. Nerve endings erupted. She found herself leaning into him as his fingers tangled in her hair.

She was barely aware of the elevator bell, but then the doors opened. Her legs were rubbery. She hoped it was not entirely because of the kiss. But she'd never responded to a kiss like this before. Her body had never sung like this before.

"Let it go," he whispered into her ear.

She wanted to.

"He'll use you."

The mental reminder was a splash of cold water. What was she doing?

She moved away, but it was too late. The doors had closed again. His hand caught hers, keeping her with him. Then their lips met again and he pressed the kiss, his tongue finding its way inside her mouth, ravishing and seducing in turn until she felt a warm puddling inside. She pressed against him as if their bodies were made for each other and clothes were no obstacle. All the attraction between them exploded into something that went beyond reason.

Reason. The elevator bell rang again and the door opened once more. She jerked away and ducked inside, her legs nearly buckling beneath her. He stood in the corridor, looking stunned as the doors closed. He started to reach out, but it was too late. She forced herself not to push the Open button, forced herself to lean back against the wall of the elevator and take a deep breath. She had never been kissed so spontaneously before, nor had she felt such an impact from a kiss. She tingled all over. She still tasted his lips, felt the warmth of his body.

"Damn," she said softly, though she rarely swore. But there was no other word that really expressed what she felt at this particular moment.

She looked at the numbers lighting up. In her hurry to get inside, she'd pressed the sixth-floor button, passing the floor where she wanted to go.

She looked at her mussed clothes, her shaking hands. Why did she react to him as she did?

The doors opened again, and a man in a white coat stepped in. An intern or resident from his age. She was grateful for his presence.

She reached over and pressed the third-floor button.

"That's mine, too," he said.

She felt an immediate gratitude. A fellow human being who didn't know her, didn't want anything from her.

They both left the elevator. No sign of McLean.

She made her way to the nurse's station.

"Miss Carroll? Someone's looking for you. He's in Mr. Merritt's room." The nurse's eyes sparkled just a little as she said Sam's brother's name.

"Thank you," Sam said.

She went down past two doors, then came to Nick's. The door was open, a light on inside.

Sam hesitated outside, wondering whether the kiss had branded her. She knew her face must be flushed. Her lips felt bruised. Were they swollen, too? She ran her tongue over them before knocking lightly, then entering.

A man sprawled in a chair next to Nick; he stood quickly when she came in. He was thick but not fat, and over six feet tall. Sam noticed that despite his size, he had a quickness about him.

He stuck out a hand to her. "I'm Dan Kelley. Mr. Merritt's security chief sent me to look after you."

She nodded, then looked accusingly at Nick. "You are supposed to be resting."

"Have you ever tried to rest in a hospital? It's a revolving door," Nick said lightly, though is face was strained. "Where did you go?"

"Just for a little walk. I thought it might take some time for someone to get here."

He searched her face. She wondered whether she was still flushed from the kiss. But if he noticed it, he didn't say anything. Instead he turned to Dan Kelley. "I want you to stay with her until she leaves Boston."

"Any special problems?"

"Someone tried to shoot her tonight."

Kelley didn't look surprised. "Anything I need to know?"

"Only that they seem to be professionals."

It was almost as if they were talking about someone

else. He said the words so easily. They were normal for him.

Would they ever be normal for her?

"Any idea who the shooter might be?"

"Someone hired by either my family or an opposing one," Nick said.

The man didn't blink an eye. Sam wondered exactly what he had done for Nick in the past.

"Shouldn't you have someone, too?" Sam asked Nick.

"They aimed at you, Samantha. Not me."

"Sam," she insisted. "My friends and family call me Sam." He was both now.

He grimaced. "Pop never will."

It was time to go. He needed rest, and he was still in an area heavily staffed. He would be safe.

"Good-bye," she said. "I'll be by in the morning."

"Hopefully, I'll be gone."

She hesitated. "I'll call first." She wanted to go over and hug him. But she didn't think he was ready for that.

And maybe she wasn't, either. He was her brother. He had saved her life. But there were still too many questions lurking in her mind.

Nick knew Kelley, who had worked for him before, was competent and honest. He was, in fact, an ex-cop.

Samantha should be safe with him, but how in the hell was he going to get her to leave Boston?

He didn't want her here. She would simply get in his way, and he couldn't afford that. He had plans that couldn't be sidetracked.

He reached for the phone despite the pain in his shoulder. He knew he wasn't going to spend another day here, no matter what the doctors said.

He looked at the clock. Four in the morning. He dialed.

"Hey, Pop . . ."

*   *   *

The private detective—or whatever he was—had his car with him, and Sam wearily allowed him to open the door for her. It was all beginning to hit her now. Someone had actually tried to kill her.

Someone had shot her twin brother.

And she had no idea why.

She'd been invited here. Although she'd known in the back of her mind that it might not be the wisest thing to come, she'd not for one moment envisioned that someone would try to do her harm. She'd meant to meet her brother, find out why her father had wanted to see her and return home.

Nothing had prepared her for her father, the car being forced off the road, or the gunman.

And she certainly hadn't been prepared for McLean.

She glanced around the street. At this hour of the morning, traffic was light, but she still saw a few pedestrians as they traveled down a commercial strip. Steamboat Springs would be sleeping.

She suddenly longed for her home, her town. For the peace she always felt there. Until two men had wandered into her shop.

She turned and looked behind them.

"No one's following us," Dan Kelley said. "I've been watching."

Of course he had. That was what he did for a living. But it wasn't what she did for a living, and she wondered if she could ever accept someone doing it for her. Even after last night.

She wondered whether she would feel the same when she returned to Steamboat Springs. Could she ever get her old life back?

Paul Merritta had found her. Despite her words, she had no idea how long he'd known where his former wife and daughter lived. She might never know. But he—or his henchmen—had obviously known Patsy Carroll would be out of town last week. Someone had been watching both of them for days. Possibly months.

Years?

A now familiar chill returned.

Kelley drove the car to the front of the hotel and asked for valet service. Sam knew how much that cost. Almost as much as her room.

The doorman opened the door and she stepped out just as Dan walked around the car. He tipped the doorman, then took her arm. "Don't do that again," he said.

She looked up at him. "Do what?"

"Get out like that. Wait for me to come around to the door."

The simple warning was a stark reminder.

She walked with him through the doors of the hotel. The lobby was empty except for two lone people at the desk. She waited while Kelley talked to them and got a room key, then he led the way into an elevator and pushed the button for her floor.

Exhaustion hit her. Too much had happened in too short a time. She leaned against the side of the elevator, closed her eyes and tried not to think as the elevator started its upward journey.

She opened them when it stopped. No other stops this time, not at this hour.

Kelley looked at her with sympathy. "Where're you from?"

"Colorado."

All of a sudden, she remembered his conversation with Nick. Nothing had been said about her being Nick's sister. Kelley must think . . .

She knew she shouldn't care but for some reason she did. "Nick's my brother," she explained.

"I know," he said simply.

"I just . . . found out about him." She was babbling family secrets to a stranger, and yet she couldn't seem to help herself.

She felt his hand on her arm, steadying her. "It's all right."

"No," she said. "It isn't. I don't usually . . ."

"You're entitled," he said. "You're doing a hell of a lot better than most people who have just seen a shooting, much less been shot at."

"Where are you going to stay?"

"A room next to yours has been arranged," he said. "There's a connecting door."

She wondered how that had happened so quickly. But she knew by now how efficient her brother was.

Her brother. It was beginning to sound natural. A brother who hated the man who had just kissed her in a way no other man ever had before. "And if they hadn't had one?"

"Mr. Merritt doesn't leave things to chance," the man said.

"You've worked for him before, then?"

"Yep."

Doing what?

She wasn't sure she wanted the answers. She was numb now. Too much had happened in too short of a time. She was unspeakably lonely. She didn't feel that she could call her mother, who would immediately know something was wrong and worry more than she probably already was doing. Terri would be in bed. There was no one else.

Just as Kelley used her key to open the door, a bellman suddenly appeared and unlocked the door between the two rooms. Kelley tipped him, then double locked the doors in each room that led to the corridor.

"I'll leave the door between us open a slit," he said. "Call me if there's anything out of the ordinary."

She almost laughed at the statement. Everything was

out of the ordinary. In fact, she wondered whether anything would be ordinary again.

She took her blood-stained blouse and slacks off, dumping them on a chair. She slipped into the overlarge nightshirt she always wore and crawled inside the bedcovers, but she knew she wouldn't be able to sleep. Too many questions pounded at her. Who? Why? And might they try again?

She found the remote and turned on the television, though it was nearly five in the morning. But she didn't really hear or see anything. She just needed the noise. She needed to feel not quite so alone.

So out of control.

Secrets and shadows. They were drowning her.

fifteen

Sam awakened to see light filtering into the room. She glanced at the clock. Nine.

Four hours' sleep. She was surprised she had slept even that long.

She heard nothing from the other room. Was Kelley asleep?

She lay there for a moment. She'd had difficulty sleeping. Every time she turned, another part of her body hurt, ached or stung. Her ribs still felt the impact of the airbag, and the cuts were raw. All of them brought back the horror of last night.

She finally rolled over to the edge of the bed, rose, and went to the window. People scurried down below, going to work or shopping or doing ordinary things. She still didn't know exactly what had happened last night with Paul Merritta. She had no more idea now why he wanted to see her than she had yesterday morning.

She only knew she didn't want to stay any longer. If Paul Merritta had wanted to tell her something, he could have done it last night. Since leaving him, the car she'd been in had been run off the road, she'd been shot at and her brother had taken the bullet meant for her.

If she returned home, perhaps she would no longer be considered a problem to someone.

Problem? That was one way of putting it, she supposed.

Perhaps her mother might have answers she hadn't divulged before. Sam suspected she wouldn't get them over the phone.

She walked to the door that separated the two rooms and peered inside. Kelley was sitting in a chair, reading a newspaper. He looked up.

"You haven't slept?" she asked.

"No," he said. "But I often go without sleep for a day or two."

She sat down on his bed, running her hand through her hair, aware for the first time that she was wearing only an overlarge shirt and panties, and hadn't given a thought to her hair.

"I'm going to make plane reservations," she said.

He nodded.

"Have you been a private detective long?"

"Eight years. Before that, I was in the Boston P.D."

"Then Merritta is not a name unknown to you?"

His eyes met hers. "No."

"Does that bother you, that I'm Paul Merritta's daughter?"

"No. I never believed in damnation by association."

"What do you know about Nick Merritt?" she asked.

"Only that he's paying the bill," Kelley said.

A diplomatic answer, but she looked at his face and knew she would not get a better one.

He apparently had a certain set of ethics, even if it did include working for a family connected to crime.

"Do you think someone will try again?"

"No," he said. "Not immediately."

"Why?"

"They had surprise on their side last night. Now they

don't. Now they know Mr. Merritt will be expecting something and be prepared."

"Now?" she said. "What about next week or next month?"

His expression told her she was right, that she might well be in danger beyond "now." Her head hurt from the possibilities.

"How long are you going to stay with me?" she asked.

"Until you leave Boston. Mr. Merritt might want someone to meet you on the other end."

"I can't go through life with a bodyguard."

Once more, his expression said clearly what he didn't put into words. She might not have a life without one.

She returned to her room and went into the bathroom. Unfortunately, she glanced in the mirror. Her eyes were shadowed, her usually tanned face drawn and pale, and her hair limp and straggly.

She put her fingers to her lips. She could still feel McLean's kiss. The way it had ignited feelings that were so explosive.

She'd been tired and frightened, she told herself. That was why she'd reacted that way. Still, she couldn't forget his image nor the passion in his eyes as he'd kissed her, or the way her body had reacted.

After a quick—and painful—shower, she brushed her hair dry, annoyed that her hand trembled slightly. She thought she had conquered her fear last night, but now she knew it lingered deep inside. Someone had actually tried to kill her. She also kept remembering Nick's warning about her mother yesterday, that she could lead to her mother's destruction.

Why?

She willed her hand to still. She had to contact her mother, but how? She'd lost her cell phone and her purse in the explosion. She could buy a new one, but then she would have to charge the batteries. She couldn't call her mother from here. The call could be too easily tracked.

Kelley might have a cell phone. But he worked for her brother. He might well be able to retrieve the number and her mother's location at the cabin.

She had to get to a pay phone, and she wanted to do it without Kelley. Otherwise, he or someone else might get access to her mother's number.

She had closed the connecting door but had not locked it. She couldn't do that now without alerting Kelley.

Instead she dressed quickly, took her credit card and money from the room safe and stuffed them in her pocket. Then she turned on the shower again. She took one look at the connecting door, then left the room, closing the hall door quietly behind her.

She avoided the elevator and took the exit steps downstairs, going out the back entrance.

Sam walked several blocks and finally found a pay phone in a coffee shop. Then she dialed her mother's cell phone.

Her mother answered on the first ring. "Samantha? Thank God. I've been worried about you. I tried to reach you but the phone was out of service. You said you would keep it on."

"I know. I'm sorry," she said, trying to decide how much to say without panicking her mother. "There was an accident last night and I lost the phone. I'm not hurt," she added quickly. "Not a mark," she lied. *Not serious ones, anyway.*

"What happened?" Apprehension laced the words.

"Nick was driving me home. Another car came too close and bumped his. He went off the road. Really, it was nothing. I'm untouched."

"And Nicholas?" Fear was evident in her mother's voice.

"A few minor wounds. Nothing serious. He'll be home today."

"Minor?"

"His arm."

She heard the rush of an indrawn breath. "What *about* his arm?"

Sam hated lying, or even being misleading, but she knew her mother's response if she explained exactly what had happened. She would probably be on the next plane. "He's fine, Mother, really he is. So am I."

A brief silence. "Has . . . he changed his mind about seeing me?"

"Not yet. He has to get used to the idea first. He thought you and I were dead. That we had died in an automobile accident."

"I didn't know that." *And she hadn't.* Sam knew that from the stunned tone of her voice. Sam wanted to ask about a divorce, or lack of one, but that was something that had to wait.

"How did you think he would explain your—our—disappearance?" Sam asked.

"I didn't—" Her mother's voice dropped off.

"Didn't think about it?" Sam asked.

Her mother didn't answer. Instead she asked a question of her own. "What does *he* want?"

Sam didn't have to ask who he was. "I still don't know. He said something about unfinished business. But he really is sick. I don't think he has long to live. I said I would see him today, but first I want to see Nick again."

"Has Nicholas asked anything yet . . . about me?" She'd asked the same question yesterday.

"No," Sam said as gently as she could.

"I . . . wanted—" Her mother's voice trailed off. "I could never go near him. Paul told me . . ."

"He told you what?"

"He *warned* me," her mother corrected. "When are you coming home?"

"Soon," Sam said. "Probably tomorrow."

"Maybe I'll return home. The gallery—"

"The gallery is fine, Mother. Terri and Helen can handle things just fine. You should stay where you are."

"Is there any reason—?"

"I don't know," Sam said honestly. "I just think you're safer where you are right now until I get back. Promise me you're staying put."

Sam could feel her mother's reluctance over the phone.

"For another day," her mother finally said. "I won't promise more."

"I'll call you tonight," Sam said, eager to get off the line before her mother changed her mind.

"Nick," her mother said again. "Tell him . . . I would like to see him. Try to explain . . ." The pain in her mother's voice was excruciating.

"I will," Sam promised. She remembered what her mother had said in Steamboat Springs. It was too late for Nick. She evidently hadn't believed that herself, had only wanted to keep Sam from going.

"Be careful."

"I'm always careful," Sam replied.

"No, you're not."

"Then I'm not foolish," Sam said, wondering whether that was an honest statement. Maybe coming here had been foolish. But how could she have not?

She hung up, then called Terri. She needed a friend. She needed sanity.

Terri answered immediately, almost as if she had been waiting next to the phone. The thought warmed Sam.

"Terri?"

"Sam. I didn't expect to hear from you so soon. Are you all right?"

"Yes, but I'm worried about my mother. She's promised

to stay away. I think she will, but if she doesn't, please stay with her. I don't want her alone."

"I will," Terri promised. "Has anything happened?"

"Just a minor accident," Sam said, not wanting to explain everything now. "But I would like you to look after things."

"I will. When will you be back?"

"No later than tomorrow night."

"Can I reach you if necessary?"

"I lost my phone," Sam said. "I'll call you."

"That sounds ominous."

"Not really. I'm just moving around a lot."

"Everything's fine here."

"Good. And thanks."

She hung up, went into the shop and bought two cups of coffee and some donuts, then returned to the hotel. Her gaze kept darting along the street, but nothing seemed out of the ordinary.

When she arrived back at her room, he was pacing the floor. "Where in the hell . . . ?"

She held out the bag.

"There's room service, you know," he said grumpily.

"I know. I had cabin fever."

He gave her a look that said he knew exactly what she'd been doing. "I'm not sure you understand that someone tried to kill you."

The simple, stark statement hit her broadside. Her knees buckled, dropped her onto the bed behind her. She'd been running on automatic pilot. Somehow hearing it said flat out made it more real.

"Let me ask you something," she said.

He nodded.

"Just before I came here, my house was burglarized. I was attacked when I apparently interrupted whoever it was, but they didn't really hurt me. Just knocked me unconscious."

"Mr. Merritt knows about this?"

"Yes. But why would they just hit me then, and try to kill me now?"

"Maybe they didn't have orders to kill you then. Maybe someone just wanted to discover how much you knew. Or frighten you."

She nodded. "Maybe they just wanted to frighten me again last night."

"Maybe," he said. He paused. "As long as I'm watching over you, don't keep anything from me," he warned.

She ignored the detective and picked up the room phone. Sam called the airline, told them that she had an electronic ticket and wanted to book a return flight. In minutes she'd checked on flights and discovered one was available at three today, another at midnight, and several tomorrow. All were available. She decided to wait to make her choice. First, she had to say good-bye to Nick, had to make sure they would keep in touch. She wasn't going to let him go, now that she'd found him.

She called the hospital and asked for his room. He answered.

"Hi," she said. "This is Sam."

There was a silence, then, "I'd hoped you would be flying home by now."

"Have to see you first."

Another silence. Then a sigh. Finally he said, "I'll be leaving here as soon as the doctor comes by."

"I'm on the way," she said.

"With Kelley?"

"With Kelley," she agreed.

A pause. "Did you call the family about last night?"

"No. I thought that should be your decision."

"You show promise." It was the nicest thing he'd said, and despite the last deadly hours, she felt a warm glow replacing some of the chill inside, even though she knew she had to be cautious. For her mother. For herself.

"See you," she said, and hung up.

* * *

Nick was dressed in street clothes and appeared ready to leave when she arrived at his room in the hospital. His arm was in a sling, and he hadn't shaved. He grimaced with each movement, and she knew he shouldn't be leaving the hospital yet. But his face was grim and his lips were tight in a determined line. Another man stood to his side, and she looked at him with curiosity. It must be Nick's partner.

The man was slender and slightly balding, and he had a pleasant face.

Nick's expression didn't change. "This is Cal, my partner," he said. "Cal, this is . . . Samantha Carroll."

Sam had thought for a fraction of a second that he was going to say *my sister.* She wondered whether he was still fighting that truth.

"Where are you going?" she asked Nick.

"Home."

It was a strangely stiff conversation, completely lacking any of the fleeting warmth from last night. They were strangers again, and he seemed intent on keeping it that way.

She wasn't going to allow him to do that. "Will you keep in touch with me?" she asked.

"Why?"

"Because you're my brother."

He looked out the window. "That's an accident of birth, nothing more."

Frustration filled her. Every time she thought she might be building a relationship with him, he kicked it away.

"Ah . . . both of you." The voice came from the doorway, and she spun around. Nathan McLean stood there along with another man dressed in a suit and tie.

The FBI agent's gaze went from her to Nick, then to Cal before finally resting on her. "You saved me a trip, Miss

Carroll," he said formally. There was no hint of the explosive intimacy they'd shared yesterday. Or maybe it had been only lust to him. Or technique.

Nick stepped between them. "What do you want now?"

"You haven't heard?"

Nick's eyebrows drew together. "Heard what?"

"Your father's dead."

sixteen

Her father.

Shock stunned Sam.

He had been that only a few days. How do you find a father—even a not very likeable one—one day and lose him a few days later?

She was grateful she'd at least met him. Now it wouldn't be an open sore. But she would never know what he had meant by "unfinished business." She swallowed, surprised at the lump in her throat.

She looked at Nick. After all, Paul Merritta had been his father since birth.

His expression didn't change. It was like a mask—but it usually was.

He didn't ask why or how.

Nick stared at the FBI agent. "Is there anything else you want?"

"Only to tell you we're requesting an autopsy." His gaze met hers. "Miss Carroll, meet my partner Gray Evans. Gray, this is Samantha Carroll. She was with Mr. Merritt last night."

His fellow agent studied her. She felt uncomfortable under his scrutiny until he smiled. Warm and disarming.

"Not much of a welcome," he said. "I'm sorry for your loss." How many times had she heard those same words in some police series on television? It was, apparently, the condolence of choice.

She should feel something. Instead she was just numb. Numb from the news, numb from the stillness and the hostility of the man who stood stiffly across from her. It was difficult to imagine how he had kissed her last night—or had it been this morning? He clearly regretted it now.

"I don't understand why there's a need for an autopsy," Sam said. "He was very sick."

"You don't often drop dead suddenly of cancer," McLean replied.

"Any signs of violence?" Kelley interceded.

McLean gave him a look of contempt. "Going to the dark side, Kelley?"

"I won't dignify that," Kelley said. "Were there any signs that it was anything but a natural death?" he persisted.

"Not outward ones," McLean said, "but we find it strange that he died the same night someone was trying to kill you two." His gaze pinned Nick. "You called him last night. Would you like to tell me what you talked about?"

"No," Nicholas said. "I wouldn't."

"Why?"

"It's none of your business, unless you think I shot myself, and Miss Carroll here is lying and you didn't see what you saw."

"Want me to list how many times your family and others like it have gone to extremes just to establish an alibi? It might be worth a bullet in the arm and a totaled car to keep a will from being changed."

Sam saw Nicholas's eyes darken. Then it was as if a curtain had dropped over them, for all the emotion they showed. She shivered as the FBI agent's implication sank in.

He thought Nick had staged the accident and had had Paul Merritta killed to keep her from inheriting?

"He wouldn't . . . He knows I don't want . . ." She shook her head, cleared her throat. It was more than she could take in all at once. Only one thing seemed real.

Dead. Paul Merritta—her biological father—was dead.

And she *did* feel grief, she realized. Or was it regret? Not solely for the man she'd never known, but for all she hadn't learned and now probably never would. Why had Paul Merritta let her go? Why had her mother let Nick go?

Nick's eyes lowered just a bit, a crease between his brows. Pain. Yet it didn't seem to be physical pain. He, too, was feeling the loss. And his was by far the greater loss. She realized how much luckier she'd been than Nick. She'd had a mother and father, both of whom had loved her.

She wanted to touch Nick, to share the loss, not only the immediate one but the loss that had been created more than thirty years earlier, but he was even more unapproachable than before. But for that one small betrayal of emotion, it was as if he'd turned to stone.

Then he turned away from McLean. "You've delivered your news. You're not wanted here."

Neither agent made any move to leave. Instead McLean leaned against the wall, looking fresh and relaxed—and irresistibly attractive—even though she knew he hadn't had much, if any, sleep last night.

She felt warm again even though the emotional temperature in the room had grown decidedly chilly.

McLean studied first Sam, then Nicholas. "No one told you about your father's death?"

"You did," Nick said flatly.

McLean's mouth moved, as if he muttered a curse beneath his breath, yet he showed no other sign of remorse or regret for the way Nick had learned of his father's death.

Sam felt the same palpable tension between the two men as she had last night. If anything, it was stronger. She had the instant impression of animals staring one another down, each refusing to show weakness. Or fear.

McLean's gaze dueled with Nick's for a moment. "I find that strange. Just like I find it strange that none of your family is here."

"I imagine they were busy enough with my father," Nick said.

"What time did he die?" Sam asked.

"He was found around seven this morning," the other FBI agent said. "We came to ask him some questions about last evening, and the maid checked on him. He'd been dead perhaps an hour. I expected that someone would have contacted you."

"I doubt anyone knew where I was," Nick said.

McLean turned to her, his eyes cool. "And you? What did you and Merritta talk about last night?"

She shot a look at Nick, then her gaze went back to McLean. "Very little. He said I was unfinished business. I hoped he would say more, but he had an attack of some kind. And that's all *I* know."

She was angry now. Angry at his veiled accusations concerning her brother, at the icy way he regarded both of them.

His gaze met hers. Held it. Probing. She remembered that she'd promised to talk to some officers today about the accident, but there hadn't been time. "Nothing about what he expected from you?" McLean asked. "No questions about your mother?"

Then she remembered. *"I swear I will do nothing to harm your mother if she does nothing to harm me."*

The reminder must have shown in her face.

"Miss Carroll?" McLean tried again.

"Nothing. He just asked about her."

She saw in his face that he knew she was lying. She wished she were a better liar. That was another first.

"My brother has an alibi. He can't be a suspect."

"He wouldn't have to do it himself."

Nick was watching them, a curious smile on his face. It sent a chill down her back. "My sister and I appreciate your giving us the news. Now, if you don't have a warrant, you can get the hell out of here."

"No gratitude for saving your life?" McLean said.

His partner looked surprised.

"We both know why you did that." Nick didn't elaborate.

"Why?" she asked.

"Can you think of a better way of getting your help?" Nick said. "And there would have been questions if he hadn't. His people know how he feels about the Merrittas."

Sam looked at her watch. It was hours after Paul Merritta had been found. Long enough for someone in the family to have found Nick and told him. She looked at him again and saw him give an almost imperceptible shake of his head. He was telling her not to pursue it.

She looked down and saw that her right hand had balled into a fist. She forced herself to open it before the FBI agent saw it and seized upon the gesture as weakness. Loneliness washed over her.

She fastened her gaze on the window. She needed someone who was objective. But there was only herself and her instincts, and those seemed to have gone into hibernation.

She swallowed hard. She wished she could talk to McLean. There had been a moment last night when she'd felt she could confide in him, when a moment of magic seemed to wrap around them, shutting out everything else. When she'd felt safe, when she'd felt complete trust. She still felt the tingling of her body, the taste of his lips.

But his face had warmth in it. No remembrances for him, apparently. She had to remind herself he was Nick's declared enemy.

"You've delivered your news," Nick said.

McLean ignored his suggestion. "His death makes you the heir," he said.

"Does it? Then you know more than I do."

"What are your plans now, Merritt?" McLean asked.

"None of your business." They were bristling like two junkyard dogs.

"Don't go out of town, Merritt," the other agent said softly.

"You can't keep me here. You have no cause."

The other agent stepped forward. "The attack last night is under investigation. You and Miss . . . Carroll are material witnesses."

"My attorney won't think so," Nick said.

"I was planning on leaving soon," she said.

McLean's attention shot to her. "Not staying for the funeral?"

Funeral. She hadn't thought about that. She was speeding down a roller coaster that had no end.

"That's her business," Nick said.

McLean's gaze remained on her. "We can help you, Miss Carroll," he said coolly. "After last night, we thought you might change your mind. We can give you protection. Just say the word."

Sam thought briefly about staying for the funeral. She'd just met the man. A cold chill ran through her as she realized he'd died just hours after she'd met him.

But staying would be a fraud. She hadn't particularly liked him. She didn't want any of what he had.

Because of him, her life had become the stuff of nightmares. She suspected it would remain a nightmare for a long time.

She suddenly knew she had to get home, had to ask more questions of her mother. Perhaps then she could return. But now she wanted her life back. The nice sane life that she'd loved. She longed to sip a glass of wine while watching a sunset over the mountains, to see people without wondering whether they wanted to kill her.

"I plan to leave in the morning." She challenged the FBI agent with her eyes. She couldn't take his offer even if she wanted to. He had pretended an attraction and sympathy when all he'd wanted was to use her to destroy her brother. "Unless you have a charge . . ."

He studied her as if she were a butterfly on a pin, and that hurt more than she thought possible. So much for that brief intimacy, for the safety she'd felt when he'd caught her in his arms.

"We'll want to talk to you again," he said. "Let us know where you will be staying."

"As I told you, I met Paul Merritta for the first time yesterday. I know nothing about his business and I really don't care to know anything."

"You could be one of his heirs," he said. "If so, you would have an interest in his death."

"Since he showed little interest in me yesterday, I doubt he left me anything," she said.

McLean looked skeptical. "Your brother called his father early this morning," he said. "Probably not long before he died."

She swiveled around to stare at Nick. She'd been under the impression that he seldom saw, or talked to, his father. He gave her a bland stare, and she turned back to McLean. "How do you know?" she asked.

"We checked with the phone company," he said.

"He has a tap on all the phones at the house," Nick corrected with a slight half smile.

Sam looked at McLean. "You can do that?"

"They can do any damn thing they want," Nick said. "And they do. In fact, I don't suppose you have anything to do with the new IRS audit."

"Different jurisdiction."

"Like hell," Nick muttered. "Just leave Samantha alone," he added. "She has nothing to do with this. She didn't even know we existed until a week or so ago."

That plea cost her brother. Sam felt it to the marrow of her bones. His supposed indifference toward her was a lie.

"*You* could cooperate with us," McLean said.

Nick gave him a look of disbelief. "Peddle your wares someplace else."

McLean shrugged and turned back to Sam. "Do you still have my card?"

She hesitated.

He took one out of his jacket and dropped it in her pocket. "Even from Steamboat Springs," he said.

She wondered whether he knew about her calls to the airline this morning.

Everyone knew more about her than she knew about them.

It was disconcerting . . .

Terrifying.

Nate watched Samantha Carroll carefully. There was no mistaking the shock in her face at the news of Paul Merritta's death. Her brother's face was far less easy to read. Nate had never been able to touch him, and that frustrated him no end.

If Nick Merritt wasn't directly involved in his family's business, particularly laundering money, then he had information. But Nate had always felt deep in his gut that Nicholas Merritt *was* involved more directly. Original seed money for the company came from a bank that also managed most of the Merritta family's accounts.

Coincidence? Nate didn't think so. Despite audits, despite wiretaps, they'd never found a connection between Merritta's family businesses and Nick Merritt's corporation. He would, though. One of these days, he would.

If Merritt survived the next few weeks.

His instincts convinced him that the hit last night had been meant for Nick Merritt, not the woman. A hit on Samantha made no sense, not unless she was in Paul Merritta's will, and he didn't think anyone knew if that was the case yet.

Nate had no illusions about what would happen now. The Merrittas had gradually moved much of the family wealth into legitimate businesses, but the family was still involved in protection and city contracts, both areas the Irish mafia coveted. He also was well aware that some members of the Merritta family wanted to get back into narcotics.

In the past few hours he'd checked further into Samantha Carroll's background. The big puzzle was why—after all these years—Paul Merritta had asked to see her. Most likely, he'd known she existed—and where she lived—for the past thirty-four years.

One interesting fact was her business. Like her brother's firm, Western Wonders had the right dynamics to launder money. It served international clients over the web. But he suspected Paul Merritta's interest went deeper than that.

Paul Merritta had been dying of cancer, but no one had expected his death to come this soon.

That it had sharpened Nate's instincts.

So had his impression that Merritt hadn't heard about his father's death. Merritt had been expressionless, but Nate thought he'd seen a flicker of surprise in his eyes. Had no one called the man who predictably would inherit most of the Merritta empire? They had known where he was. He himself had informed them, waiting to see their reaction. They had shown precious little concern—or even interest—for their relative, but they had been stunned by the old man's death.

Or had they been? Rosa had been crying. Victor had been stoic. George had appeared, looking sleepy. He'd demanded to know why the police and FBI were there when his father obviously had died of natural causes. He'd announced he would fight an autopsy, but Nate knew George couldn't stop it.

Trying to decipher the Merritta clan was like stumbling through a maze. Or quicksand.

And then there was the kiss. He still couldn't fathom how it had happened. Samantha had looked tired and vulnerable and wounded, and there had also been something so damned appealing about her.

It had been impulsive and stupid, but the moment their lips touched, he'd felt explosions inside. God only knew the last time that had happened to him. He couldn't remember ever feeling an overwhelming need such as the one that had seized him early this morning. Especially when her body had started to melt into his, and her lips had been as eager as his own. For a moment he'd lost himself in the magnetism that had bound them together since their gazes had met in the airport.

He'd been dazed, even thunderstruck when the elevator had *ping*ed and opened.

He'd never mixed business with pleasure. Never. And this particular business was the Merrittas, the family that had killed his mother.

"Nate?"

His partner's expression told him to pay attention. How long had he been standing there like a panting fool?

He tried to tell himself he could keep his interest purely professional. There were any number of mysteries evolving around her, and more than anything he wanted to get her away from her brother and just try to talk to her. But he might well have ruined any chance to do that, first with his kiss early this morning and now with the professional coolness he was struggling to maintain. The hostility between Merritt and himself didn't help, either.

And now she would probably want an attorney before talking, an attorney who was associated with the family and who would advise her to say nothing.

He'd watched as she digested the death of Paul Merritta, the emotion that had flashed across her face. A face too expressive for deception. He'd seen shock, regret, fear.

Nate still wondered what had happened years ago. He'd asked for copies of the death certificates of the mother and daughter. Deaths that hadn't happened at all. He wondered exactly who was in the accident that supposedly had claimed the wife and daughter of the heir apparent to Boston's deadliest crime family.

He had someone checking into other disappearances at the time.

What would the mother have to say?

That would have to be his next move. He had to get to Patsy Carroll before either Samantha or Nick did.

Patsy would have a story to tell. No one left a crime family and lived to tell about it. It followed that she just might have something on them all. Something that had given her a passport to the rest of her life. And she would have no love for or loyalty to a man she'd likely had to blackmail into granting her freedom, particularly now that he was dead.

She might even want Nate's protection if Merritta had been all that stood between her and the rest of his family.

He looked at his watch, then at Samantha Carroll. Her dark eyes caught his, and a frisson of heat ran down his spine. He didn't know when he'd last experienced anything like it, and God knew it had never happened to him with someone who was—or might be—involved in a case.

He dismissed the thought. He'd always been able to control his libido. He could damn well do it now.

He could do it better without distraction in the form of a dark-haired, dark-eyed woman with more guts than sense.

Despite her lack of cooperation, he sensed she was an innocent. She had walked into something she couldn't possibly be prepared for.

He'd like to get someone in to watch over her, someone unconnected to either side. Nick Merritt had beat him to it. And regardless of his theories on who was guilty and who wasn't, he knew Kelley to be a good man. Hell, he might have chosen him for the job if Merritt hadn't already done it.

"I'll be talking to you," he said, directing the comment to Nick Merritt as he headed for the door. If he didn't get out of here soon, he'd start believing that Merritt was as innocent as his sister just because it would make her happy.

Sam stared at the door as it closed behind the two agents, then looked at Nick. "Did you know about your father's death?" she asked.

"Yes. Reggie called."

"You didn't tell me."

"No."

"Why?" She was getting more and more angry.

"I wanted you to go home. It's dangerous here. Someone might think you plan to claim part of the estate."

"Do you have any idea who that might be?"

"No."

"You would tell me if you did?" It was a ridiculous plea, and she knew it the moment the words came out of her mouth. If he really was hiding something, of course he wouldn't tell her.

But she so badly wanted one person—just one person—she could trust.

His gaze didn't quite meet hers. "I can't promise that."

"You know more than you're telling me," she accused.

"No, Samantha, I don't. I can only imagine it has something to do with Pop's businesses. My family is not one to . . . share."

He stepped over to her and pulled her into a surprisingly protective embrace. "I'm sorry you walked into this," he said. "You would have been far better off never knowing about the Merrittas."

Sam knew she was being foolish. Paul Merritta was nothing to her. David Carroll had been her father in every way.

Yet, now she had unfinished business, too.

"Go home," he said. "There's nothing here but trouble."

"Will you go back with me? Meet our mother?"

"No," he said flatly. He stepped away, his eyes going completely cold again. "I believed she was dead all these years. She still is to me."

She felt defeated. "I'll go to the hotel until I leave."

Nick shook his head. "No hotel. Kelley told me you left the hotel for a while." His tone was accusing. "I think you will be safer with me."

She looked pointedly at his arm.

He gave her a sheepish look. "I didn't expect it then. And Kelley will be with us. But I know the family and I know McLean. If they don't know about the hotel now, they soon will."

"All right," she said. Another day and she would know more about him, their father, and possibly about herself. And she could convince him to see, if not forgive, their mother.

She turned toward the silent partner, Cal. "Thank you for sending Kelley."

"You are very welcome," he said. "Anything you need . . ."

She needed a great deal, but nothing, she feared, that he could provide.

She needed her brother. She needed McLean.

Dammit.

seventeen

Nate had three notes on his desk when he and Gray returned to their offices, each demanding that Nate contact their superior.

Nate groaned. Robert Barker was not one of Nate's favorite people.

Barker had only recently been promoted to Assistant Agent in Charge. Before that, he had worked in organized crime, along with Nate and Gray. Barker had been uniquely successful, bagging more arrests and convictions than others on the task force; all convictions had been in families other than the Merrittas, except for a few minor exceptions. He'd specialized in the Irish mafia, while Nate and Gray concentrated on the Merrittas.

Barker had never worked well with others, withholding information from fellow agents and in one instance destroying a case Nate was developing by approving a premature raid that netted nothing. Since that investigation had involved the Merrittas, Nate held a grudge.

Still, Barker had compiled a record that had brought him to the attention of his superiors. Nate had always tried to avoid that same attention. He'd shared his arrests. The job had been important to him, not the credit.

Gray looked up at the ceiling and sighed.

"You're not included in the invitation," Nate said.

"I'm probably next on his list."

"I'll keep you out of it."

"Hell, it's our case."

"Maybe it's nothing to do with the case."

"And maybe pigs fly," Gray said morosely.

Gray was right.

The lecture began the moment he entered his superior's office. "How nice of you to drop in the office for a change," Barker said.

"I've been here," Nate said. "You haven't."

"I've had reports," Barker shot back.

Nate knew the worse thing he could do was remain silent. Barker hated that. Yet he wasn't ready to tell Barker what he wanted to do. And definitely not about Samantha Carroll. He was aware now of what damage he could do to both her and her mother.

It had been a long time since he had considered the implications of the actions he took. He'd always thought much was justified in the name of justice. He still did, particularly in the case of a family that had repeatedly gotten away with murder. But something made him hold back this time.

"I had a complaint from the Boston police. You apparently were reluctant to explain why you suddenly appeared at a crime scene."

"I was working the Merritta case. The old man was dying, and I was following the son."

"Why?"

"Someone's going to take over the family business. The obvious choice is Nicholas."

"What about this woman? This purported daughter?"

Damn it. He'd thought he would have more time before Barker caught up with the information about Samantha.

He wondered whether Barker had gotten copies of the

tapes from Merritta's home. Or whether someone from the Merritta family had reported to him. Nate had long suspected Barker had an informant in the family.

Barker looked down on the desk. "And a tap on Nick Merritt's phone? I don't remember authorizing it."

"You weren't here. You left the authority in Dick's hands and he said if we could get a judge to okay it, it was fine with him. We've been trying to get one for months."

"You purposely waited until I was gone," Barker accused.

"No, sir," Nate said. Damn, he hated the "sir," but he knew just how hard he could push Barker. "We didn't know anything about this woman until after you'd left. We certainly didn't know she would be the target of a hit team. She needed protection, and we didn't know whether Merritt was involved."

"Do you now?"

"No," he answered honestly.

"I understand he was shot, too. Doesn't sound logical he would be part of an attempt to harm her."

Nate shrugged. He wasn't ready to let go yet. How better to gain absolute trust than to take a bullet for her?

"Damn it, McLean. No reports. No updates. You're wasting your time on the Merrittas now that Paul Merritta is dead." He stared at Nate. "It's gotten too personal with you. I'm assigning you and Evans to another case. We're establishing a task force on Medicare fraud. You're on it."

Nate stood there, stunned, though he should have known it was coming. Barker had never liked him.

Until Barker's promotion, Nate and Gray had had a lot of freedom. They'd been on the organized task force for several years, along with Barker, and had produced some good cases, but Barker had trumped them in number if not in quality.

Nate knew one thing. He wasn't going on a Medicare

fraud case. Not now. Not when the Merritta family was ready to implode.

Not as long as the newest known member could be in danger.

He was immediately struck with the realization that the latter thought was far more important than the former.

"If I'm switching cases, I think I'll take the leave I've accumulated," he said amiably.

Barker frowned, his eyes reflecting surprise, then suspicion. It was obvious he'd expected protests and perhaps even wanted them so he could enjoy denying them. "Put in your request," he replied gruffly.

"I'll need you to sign off on it. I'm owed nearly two months," Nate said. "This looks like a good time; I wouldn't be in the middle of a case." He paused, then played his trump card. "I think Woodward would agree." Woodward was the Agent in Charge; he hated piled-up leave time.

Barker paused. "You want to take the entire two months?"

"Let's say two weeks to start."

"Where are you going?"

"I'm not sure. Maybe the mountains. Away from phones."

Barker stared at him for a long moment, then frowned. "Send Gray Evans in."

Sam knew she had to call her mother again and tell her about Paul Merritta's death.

She dreaded it. She didn't know what her mother's reaction would be to the death of Paul Merritta. But Sam did know her mother would ask again about Nick and whether he would talk to her. Hope would be in her mother's heart, just as it had been in her own when she went to meet Nick. Hope and apprehension. Fear of rejection. Fear of what they might find.

She was moving again. Nick had invited her to stay at his house, most likely, she thought, to keep her away from the FBI. She, on the other hand, had her own motives. She could help Nick, whose arm was now in a sling, and she wanted to learn more about him. And the family. Kelley was going to pick up her luggage, then go home and get some sleep.

Nick's partner drove them to Nick's home, an expensive town house near the harbor, then drove off. Nick clumsily unlocked the door with his left hand and held it open for her to enter first.

His home was everything the Merrittas' home wasn't. The furniture was leather. Tasteful. Comfortable. And yet the room was devoid of photographs, of a sense of being lived in, shared.

Nick sat down heavily in a chair. The gesture was unlike him. He usually moved decisively. She knew he hadn't taken the narcotic that had been prescribed for him and purchased on the way to his home. His mouth was a tight grimace and his eyes looked red.

"I should call Mom," she said. "I have to tell her about Paul Merritta's death. And tell her the FBI knows about her. They might try to find her."

A muscle moved in his cheek. "Do you have a cell phone?"

"Not now. Mine was burned in the car. I was going to get one today."

"I have one you can use. It's clean," he said.

She hesitated. *Clean?*

"You're suspicious. Good. Stay that way. You can erase the number when you finish, and take the phone with you if you like. I have no interest in where she is."

She still hesitated, then agreed. She would call her mother's cell phone.

"Is your home phone tapped?"

"Probably," he said.

"Can they do that even when you haven't been accused of anything?"

He gave her a look that told her how naive he thought she was. "Anything involving organized crime gives them more powers than they usually have. Say 'conspiracy' and a judge signs on the dotted line. Be careful, Samantha. Don't trust McLean, or any fed. They'll use you, then throw you away."

"Did that happen to you?"

"I didn't let it happen to me, but it's not for lack of trying on their part. My company is audited every year. They visit our customers and warn them about doing business with us. They follow us on occasion."

As McLean had, the night of the accident.

"How do you stay in business?"

"A lot of our sales are with foreign companies who could care less about the FBI. The others . . . well, we have good products, good prices and great service."

She wanted to ask more questions, but he simply looked at her. "Use the study. It's down the hall on the left."

"Will you talk to her?" she asked again.

"No."

She wanted to argue, but he looked too tired, too drawn.

Sam went down the hall and found the study. His desk was completely clear, the opposite of her own, which she always termed as organized chaos. She looked at the computer and thought about turning it on.

A touch of a few keys might supply a clue.

But just as she couldn't invade her mother's privacy, neither could she do it to Nick's.

Instead she used the cell phone he had given her and dialed.

Her mother picked up immediately. She must have had the phone next to her.

"Is everything all right?" her mother asked. Almost as if she knew it was not.

"My *father* . . . Paul Merritta died this morning." She didn't know why she used the word *father,* except possibly to evoke a reaction. As much as she deplored it, a residue of resentment, of loss, of anger still lingered deep inside.

"He *wasn't* your father. David was." Her mother's voice broke slightly.

Sam regretted that flash of anger. "I know. David will always be my dad."

"Your brother . . . Nick. How is he?"

"He's all right." Sam paused, then added, "He came home from the hospital today. I'm staying with him." She didn't think it was the time to tell her mother what had really happened, that someone had actually taken a shot at her. She just prayed there wouldn't be any news coverage.

"Are you still planning to return tomorrow?"

Sam wavered. In the last few hours, she'd considered—briefly—staying for the funeral. If it was within the next two or three days. Maybe it would be a closure. But could you have closure, when you never had opening?

"I want to see you," her mother said. "There are things I can tell you, that I have to tell you."

"Tomorrow," she promised.

"Don't let them drag you into their web," her mother warned. "Victor . . . the others . . ."

"I won't."

A pause. She knew her mother didn't want to let her go, probably wanted to ask a dozen questions about Nick, but she had always been a very private, very proud woman. The fact that she had not asked to talk to him said volumes.

There was a hopelessness in the sigh that came over the line.

Then Sam said what she hated to say. "The FBI knows about you. Why don't you stay where you are?" She was careful not to say where. It was a unique experience, weighing every question, every answer, every comment.

"I knew it was coming," her mother said, resignation softening her voice into a mere whisper.

But Sam had not, and now she felt wracked with guilt. She had been so consumed with meeting her brother that she'd not considered the cost to her mother, the fact that a life she'd so carefully constructed might collapse.

"I'm sorry," she said.

"Don't be," her mother said. "It was going to happen sooner or later. Secrets have a way of leaking out."

"It could hurt you."

"*You've* already been hurt. That's what grieves me," her mother said.

"I'm safe here," Sam said. She wanted to assure her mother that she should be, too, now that Paul Merritta was dead. She was struck by the irony of feeling grief for a father she'd never known, while being relieved that the threat to her mother had probably died with Paul Merritta. "Why don't you stay where you are until I come home? Then we can spend a few days together before . . ."

"Before all hell breaks loose?" her mother said.

It was an uncharacteristic comment from her mother. "Yes," Sam said.

"Be careful of Nicholas. He was raised by them."

Sam winced at the strain in her mother's voice and wondered what it had cost her to say that about her own son. "That wasn't his fault."

"No, but it's fact."

Sam knew that. The seed of doubt that McLean had planted hadn't entirely faded. Nor had the finger of fear. It was just that the emotional need to get to know Nick was stronger. That didn't mean she wouldn't be careful.

"I'll see you tomorrow," she said.

She heard a relieved sigh.

"Will you call Terri and tell her?" Sam said. She didn't want to go over the explanations again with her friend.

"Of course."

"I'll try to reach you," Sam said. She didn't want to give her Nick's number. She shuddered at the idea of some stranger listening in on a conversation between them.

"I love you, Samantha," her mother said.

"I love you, too," Sam said, and turned the phone off. God knew it was true. She was angry, even furious at her mother for hiding the truth so many years. And yet she couldn't deny thirty-five years of love, or caring. It was as much a part of her as her heart. Or maybe it *was* her heart.

And what would happen to Western Wonders when rumors started flying that the Carrolls might be connected to organized crime? How could her mother lose that, too?

Sam sat down in a comfortable chair and looked about the office. It was much neater than her own, the product of an organized mind. How organized? How compartmentalized? How much did she really know about him?

She heard the faint sound of a voice. She hadn't heard a phone ring, but then she probably wouldn't hear a cell phone. She stood and went over to the door, but was able to hear only a word now and then.

She did hear the word "Pop," and she thought he would probably only use it with a member of the family. She opened the door and walked in.

"I'll talk to you later," Nick said into the phone, then replaced it in his pocket.

"You didn't have to stop talking for my sake," she said, wondering why he felt she shouldn't hear any of the conversation. That wriggle of doubt ran down her spine again.

"I was through. By the way, Kelley brought over your luggage. He also checked the safe and retrieved what you left there. They're in your room upstairs."

She felt a tug of annoyance. It had probably been easy enough for Kelley to open the safe since he was an ex-officer, and then there were the adjoining rooms. Still, she felt choices being taken away from her. "How did he open the safe?"

He shrugged. "Did you use your birthday?"

Feeling somewhat simple, she nodded.

"That's probably it, then."

He peered at her as if aware of her disquieting feelings. "Hungry?"

"Starving."

"Can you cook?" he asked. "I have bacon and eggs."

She nodded. "I enjoy cooking."

"Good. I can make the toast," he offered.

He seemed more relaxed than at any time since she'd met him. She wondered whether it was real or a pose.

There were so many things she didn't understand about him.

She followed him into a spacious kitchen that was as tidy—and pristine—as the rest of the house.

She got the bacon and eggs from the fridge and, at his instructions, found the frying pan in the cabinet. He took a stool and watched her as she started frying the bacon.

"Mother asked about you."

"Thirty-four years late," he said abruptly.

She was becoming accustomed to his broad Boston accent and short answers.

She sighed. "Her life is turned upside down, too."

He didn't reply.

What was she doing here? He obviously didn't want her. Her mother probably needed her. Her mother *would* need her once she was assaulted by federal officers and the resulting publicity.

"Was that someone with the family?" she asked about the phone call he'd just ended.

"Yes."

"Who?" she asked with exasperation.

"Victor."

The one her mother warned her about. "Did he say anything about what happened last night?"

"Says he doesn't know anything about the attempt on

your life. About Pop, only that the maid discovered him this morning. He wanted me to know that's why no one showed up at the hospital. They were all detained."

"Could the two be a coincidence? The attempt on my life? His death?"

He gave her a sharp look. "His death was apparently natural."

She was struck by his coolness, by his concern for food rather than going to the Merritta house and sharing grief over a lost loved one. "Are you going over there?"

"Later."

"I want to go."

"Glutton for punishment, aren't you?"

She turned over the bacon and put down the long fork with more emphasis than she'd intended. "Don't you care?"

He gave her a long, level look. "Not that it's your business, but yes, I care," he said through clenched teeth. "But I didn't intend to show it in front of McLean, and I don't care to share it with Victor or George or the others." He waited a minute, then said softly, "Or with you. You didn't know him. You don't know me."

His icy disdain chilled her from her toes to the top of her head, stunning her.

She thought him capable of anything at that moment. Had she been wrong to trust him? To come here? What did she really know about him, other than they shared the same blood?

"Can you tell me anything about him? And the business?"

"I only know that he's been trying to steer the family toward legitimate businesses. He saw the handwriting on the wall. Every family in the northeast has been decimated by the feds. There's damn little loyalty any longer. People turn on a dime."

"Did everyone agree on the new direction?"

"No," he said flatly.

"Who didn't?"

His eyes grew hard again. "Don't get into it, Samantha. Don't even think about it."

"I still don't know why he asked me to come."

"You probably never will. Just as I won't. If you go home and disappear, you'll probably be safe. You and your mother. But butt into this, and all bets are off. Whoever forced us off the road last night wasn't playing games."

Her blood ran cold. *"You and your mother."* He'd mentioned her mother several times. Why? What had happened more than thirty years ago couldn't possibly threaten anyone today . . . could it? Maybe someone thought she might take some tiny part of an inheritance. But why her mother?

Something nagged at her. It was more than apprehension. It was foreboding.

"*Was* his death natural?" she asked.

"I have no reason to believe otherwise. You saw him."

"Yes, I saw him. He looked sick but not as if he would die in a few hours."

"And you're a doctor?"

The sarcasm hurt. "Agent McLean seems to think it wasn't natural." She wanted to ruffle him. She was tired of his cool demeanor, his seeming indifference to his father's death, his lack of curiosity about his mother. Or perhaps, she thought, it was his defense. Hers had been charging forward. His might be retreating.

But at the mention of the FBI agent's name, he became silent, building a wall too high for her to breach. She put the food on the table while he rummaged with his one good hand for silverware.

They ate in silence. He'd closed up like a clam, apparently unwillingly to let her inside whatever walls he'd built. She wished Terri were here. She would have had him talking in a moment. But Sam couldn't do that. There were too many secrets between them, too much pain, too much time.

"When do you plan to fly home?" he asked as they finished the meal.

"Tomorrow. When is the funeral?"

His face tightened. "It'll be at least five days away. There will be an autopsy, thanks to the police, and a lot of people will want to attend. It will take some time to arrange that." He scowled at her. "You aren't thinking of coming back?"

"Eager to get rid of me?"

"That's not what I meant. I just think you will be safer in Colorado. Why in the hell do you want to go to the funeral, anyway? He meant nothing to you. You didn't even know he existed until a few days ago. Why pretend differently?"

She felt violated. Insulted by his judgment of her. She wasn't pretending. She really didn't feel anything toward the man whose seed had created her. But she wanted closure on this, and somehow she felt the funeral would do that. It was obvious from his voice that he didn't want her here. The thought hurt more than she believed possible.

"I'll make reservations now."

"Are there people there who can watch out for you?"

"Yes," she said sharply, angry with him for his lack of interest in her mother and, for that matter, in her. He was making token queries, nothing more.

"I'll have Kelley take you to the airport and wait there until the plane leaves."

"Thank you," she said, hoping her voice held the same frigid indifference as his had.

He stood and carried his plate to the sink. She did the same. Then she retreated to the bedroom he'd showed her. She found the airline number and dialed.

In minutes, she had booked a flight for the next afternoon. It would put her in Denver at seven.

She remembered the FBI agent's words. *"We don't want you to leave town."*

But she knew enough law to know she could go any-place she wished unless she'd been charged. Thus far, she'd only been a victim, and she was damn tired of being manipulated by everyone who had a dog in this fight.

Her mother had lied to her, as had her father. The brother she'd always wanted was cool, indifferent. Her biological father had shown not the faintest paternal inter-est. An FBI agent had tried to convince her to betray a family she'd just found. And she had, she thought. She'd betrayed them by kissing the enemy. A kiss she couldn't forget.

She felt as if she were wandering in an alien landscape. She wanted to escape it, and all its land mines, even as she realized she could never really go home again. That, too, would be changed. Nothing would be as it had been a week ago. That knowledge left a huge hole inside her.

She returned to the living room. "I have a flight tomor-row."

Nick simply stood there. "I'm sorry you didn't find what you wanted," he finally said.

"It would mean a lot to Mother if you would contact her."

"I can't do that."

"I'll tell her about you."

"What? That I'm on the FBI's most favorite target list? Or that I've managed very well without her?" He paused. "I'm going to work in my office. Consider the rest of the house yours. There's books, an entertainment room. Stay inside until Kelley's people arrive." He started for the door, then turned. "I'll have someone meet you in Den-ver."

"It's not necessary," she said. "That's my home turf."

He strode over to her. He took her chin with his good

hand and forced her gaze to meet his. A muscle throbbed in his throat.

"It's not going away, Sam. That's not the way this family works."

"You said I would be safe back home."

"Safer, at least," he corrected. "But you still should take precautions until everything shakes out."

"You mean against your family?"

"I like the way you choose when it's my family and when it's yours," he said with a slight shadow of a smile. "I honestly don't know who's responsible for last night or why. I do intend to find out." He paused, then added, "My father was able to keep peace while he was alive. Now . . ."

"But why me? No one knew about me. I'm not a threat to anyone."

"Maybe Pop's will has something to do with it."

"Will?" She knew she must be looking stupid. "But why? He never even knew where I was until a few days ago."

"You think so?"

"That's what he said."

Nick shrugged. "Then it must be true." He said it with such sarcasm that she took a step backward.

She was tired of being treated as a simple child. She was even more tired of riddles no one wished to explain. "I need some fresh air."

Before he could stop her, she found the door. She opened it and stood outside, looking around at the stately town homes. The street was bumper to bumper with parked cars. She longed to take a run. She thought she could smell the sea from here. Instead she leaned against the wall.

Nick came out. "You shouldn't be out here," he said.

She turned to him, even as she became aware of a car pulling out of a parking place. Nothing unusual about that.

Nick jerked her down and fell on her as she heard the car speed up. She was conscious of his weight, then everything was blotted out by shots shattering the summer day, thudding against the heavy wood of the door and spraying the pavement below.

eighteen

Sam could hardly breathe from the pressure of Nick's body. She felt numb, then a burning pain in her arm.

She heard a yell, more gunshots, then the roar of an engine and the screeching of tires.

Silence. A deadly, still silence.

Heavy breathing above her. A curse. The weight left her.

"Nick," she whispered.

"I'm all right," he said.

She struggled to sit. Her entire body was sore from the impact on concrete. He was bleeding again, but she saw it was from the earlier injury. Then she looked down at her arm. A large wooden splinter protruded.

She looked at it, her mind in turmoil, her senses still ringing with noise and dulled by the smell and sight of blood.

"Are you all right?"

A voice. Not Nick's. She looked up. Nathan McLean stood there, a gun in his hand.

"I'm not sure," she said, ashamed that her voice seemed to waver.

She watched as Nick stood unsteadily. The bandage and sling were bright red, as was her blouse.

"Nick?" she asked. "Were you hit?"

"No major harm done," he said. "Just opened up the wound." He ignored McLean and pulled out the splinter, then pressed a handkerchief against her arm.

McLean appeared to be doing a quick visual survey of the area. The car with the shooters was long gone. His gaze stopped at the door.

"The bullets were high," he said. "And low. You were lucky they were such bad shots. If," he said, "they were."

He took the handkerchief from her arm and looked at the gash. "It'll need stitches. I'll drive you to the hospital."

Nick shook his head. "It will take too long. I'll call my doctor. He's a block away. How did you happen to be here?"

"I thought she might need a little more protection than you could provide." Nate paused. "I hit their windshield. Maybe more."

"You appear at very convenient times," Nick observed. "Perhaps you think that this could scare my sister into helping you."

She heard what both were saying. The FBI agent had noted the attackers were poor shots, obviously implying that it was staged. Her brother was likewise accusing Nate of having some kind of involvement, perhaps setting up the attack so that she would want protection.

They both claimed they were protecting her.

Nick was right. McLean always was conveniently close.

She stepped away from both of them. The pain in her arm was intensifying and she knew she needed those stitches.

She also knew she had to get the hell out of Dodge before one—or both—of these two men destroyed her. Her purse was upstairs, and her luggage. Her credit cards.

She heard the sirens. Someone must have heard the shots, or McLean himself had called it in.

She didn't stay. She whirled around, ran inside and grabbed her credit cards and money, stuffing them in pockets. Not wanting to deal with either man right now, she grabbed a towel and escaped through the back way. She had to leave before the police tried to detain her.

She wanted home.

She wanted familiarity.

She wanted to feel safe again.

Foolish, maybe, but at the moment she felt safer on her own than with either of the men at the front of the house.

She hurried to the walkway between the backs of the houses, turned right, away from the road. Two more turns, each taking her farther from the house. She looked around but didn't see anyone.

Another turn and she was on a main road. She saw a cab and hailed it.

She would take the first train to Washington, then take a plane from there. Thank God she had a credit card with a photo on it.

She would go to the cabin, and both she and her mother would disappear for a few days. She would hear the whole story, then together they could decide what to do.

It was nearly two in the morning when Sam reached Steamboat Springs in the car she'd rented at the Denver Airport. Thank God, she had a gold card, which expedited the procedure, and she didn't need a driver's license. There had been no commuter flights until the next day.

She was dead tired, and her arm burned like the furies, though she'd had the taxi drop her at a small emergency care office in Boston before she'd gone to the train station. Her arm had required ten stitches, but it had stopped bleeding.

She'd had precious little sleep during the past few days, and her eyes wanted to close despite the wide but winding interstate with its sharp turns and shoulders that plunged hundreds of feet down.

She continued to glance in the rearview mirror window to see whether or not someone was following her. She hadn't relaxed since she'd first sat in the driver's seat of the rental car, though she usually enjoyed driving.

She'd planned to drive up to the cabin, but she desperately needed some fresh clothes and sleep and she didn't know if she could last that long. Better to stop at home, get a change of clothes, then stay at a hotel tonight. She didn't want to stay in her own house. Not after those shots last night and this afternoon.

Yet, Boston was the dangerous place. Not Steamboat Springs. Still, she meant to take a few precautions. She was aware now.

She circled her neighborhood twice before parking several streets away and moving stealthily through the shadows and trees to the back of her house.

She hesitated. Suddenly she wasn't sure she wanted to go inside. She kept remembering what had happened there just a few days ago. But, dammit, she wasn't going through the rest of her life in hiding.

She would purchase a gun in the morning before going to the cabin. Her father—David Carroll—had taught her how to shoot when she was sixteen. She'd practiced occasionally since then, but her pistol had been stolen from her car in Washington. She'd never bought a new one. Why supply criminals?

Another reason she'd never replaced it was her mother's dislike of guns and her disapproval when David Carroll had insisted their daughter learn. Now that aversion took on new dimensions. Had she hated guns because of the Merritta family's fondness for them?

Sam found the extra key she kept beneath a stone and unlocked the back door. She hesitated, letting her eyes get used to the darkness. She took off her shoes so she wouldn't make any sound, then padded to her room and quickly packed a suitcase. She wanted a cup of coffee, but she didn't want to stay here that long.

Her answering machine light blinked. She went over to

it. The readout indicated eight messages. The first six were all business oriented. The seventh was from her mother. "Now that Paul is dead, I don't think there's any reason to stay at the cabin. Call me at home when you get here, sweetie. We need to talk."

Sam's thumb slipped off the play button. Why hadn't she told her mother about the shootings? Because she hadn't wanted to worry her. She had thought her mother would stay at the cabin. Now . . .

She quickly dialed her mother's house. No answer. She should have been there. Her mother did not wander at night, particularly when she expected to see Sam. Fear rippled down her spine.

Sam grabbed her extra set of keys from a drawer and ran back to her own car, fumbling the key into the ignition. Her mother's house was just a few moments away.

Be there. Be all right, she prayed.

The house was dark, the driveway empty. She used her key to open the door, wishing she had that gun.

The house was neat as always. No sign of her mother, or of an intruder. Nothing was out of place.

As she had at her own house, she moved through her mother's condominium carefully. She paused occasionally to listen for a sound. Any sound.

No one downstairs. She went up to her mother's bedroom. The bed was made. The bathroom looked unused. Not a drop of water in the sink or bath.

She went to the kitchen and froze. A note was attached to the fridge by a magnet. Sam read it slowly, measuring every word.

> *Dear Samantha . . .*
>   *I'm sorry to leave when you planned to return home, but once I arrived, I noticed that someone had been in the house. I didn't think I should stay here and I was afraid to go back to our place. I*

*also need time before I talk to the FBI. Time to put
things in order. I contacted a friend who found a
safe place for me to go. He'll be looking out for
you, too. I couldn't reach Terri, but I know she can
take care of the gallery while I'm gone and until
you return.*

I hope you found what you needed to find.

*Don't worry about me. I'll be back in a few
days.*

In the meantime, you have my lasting love.
Mom

It didn't make sense. She used her mother's phone to
call her mother's cell phone and received an "out of service" message. The fingers of fear became a fist in her heart.

"Meow." The low keening preceded the feel of fur rubbing against her.

Sam leaned down and picked up the cat, examining her.

Her mother would never have left without Sarsy, not
without knowing she was all right, not without being absolutely sure that there would be someone to care for her.
Or maybe she knew Sam would be home.

Sam checked the water dish. Full. So was the food dish.
There was enough for several days.

One question answered.

But it was still unlike her mother.

Call the police.

And tell them what?

Would she betray her mother by doing so? She read the
note again. It was in her mother's handwriting. She was
sure of that. No waver. No hint that anything was wrong.
If she had been forced, wouldn't her mother have left a
clue? Called her Sam, for instance, rather than Samantha.
Her mother never used her nickname. That was something
no one would know.

Sam felt deep in her heart that her absence wasn't forced.

But it was so unlike her.

And who was the friend? Her mother's friends were all businesswomen who would no more know how to hide someone than Sarsy would.

How much did she really know about her mother? Sam had begun to realize how much she didn't know. Her mother had married a man she barely knew, then fled from him, making what had to be an agonizing choice.

Yet nothing in her life had indicated anything but normality. Yes, she had been protective. But every other part of Sam's life had seemed normal. Her mother had laughed and smiled and had seemed fulfilled.

How could she have been fulfilled when she'd left a son behind?

Sam still didn't understand that. Could never understand that.

Call the police. But they were still unaware of the Carrolls' connection to an infamous family. Did she have the right to make this decision?

Bigamy. An ugly word. But if everything she'd been told was correct, her mother's second marriage had been bigamy.

Feeling more alone than she ever had in her life, Sam checked the house once more, turning out all the lights except those in the kitchen.

Then she sat down at the kitchen table. It was the large oak table they'd had when she was a child, when they lived in a larger home on the edge of the town. Her mother's kitchen had always been a welcoming place filled with good smells.

But now that she thought about it, the kitchen had always been empty except for the three of them. She'd had few friends because her mother kept her close and never invited other children there. It wasn't until she had gone to college that her mother had widened her range of friends, almost as if . . .

As if she no longer had anything to worry about.

A sickness settled in her stomach. How much fear had her mother known? How much heartbreak?

Could she really open the whole pail of snakes for the entire town of Steamboat Springs to see?

But she would do it in a second if she thought that was what her mother wanted, or if she thought it would save her mother's life.

Her mother left for reasons of her own, reasons she couldn't explain. The note made it clear that she expected Sam to respect her wishes . . . to trust her.

Oddly, in spite of everything, Sam did trust her.

What had happened in the last few hours to make her mother flee? Had it been Sam's mention of the FBI on the phone? Her mother seemed to have taken it in stride. Had she had second thoughts? Had she considered the implications for herself and Sam, for the gallery, and decided to delay any meeting with law enforcement officers as long as possible?

She could believe that. Exposure could be terribly damaging to all of them—and the gallery—particularly if her mother had committed bigamy. She doubted whether her mother could be prosecuted—it must be far outside the statute of limitations—but the bad publicity could be deadly.

She wouldn't have left Sam alone to deal with it.

Sam was at a complete loss as to whether to take the note to the police. But then she would have to tell the complete story, for no law enforcement officer would start a search on the basis of that note.

And if there was foul play involved, would she put her mother in more danger if she approached the local police? The FBI?

She had to trust someone. She thought about Nick, recalled his disdain for the woman who had given him birth, and turned to the only other alternative.

Nathan McLean.

Despite her brother's accusations, McLean had helped her three times. Maybe he had ulterior motives, but he also knew the Merritta family. She thought he was wrong about Nick, but he knew other members of the family far better than she.

She dug in her pocket for a number she had thought she would never call. Praying she wasn't making a terrible mistake, she punched in the number.

What in the hell did she want?

The question haunted Nate as he drove through the mountains to Steamboat Springs. When he'd left the FBI offices after finally winning a week of leave, he'd turned off his cell phone. He didn't want Barker finding him. It was only a matter of time before Barker would learn about the shooting in front of Nick Merritt's home.

He hadn't even bothered to check messages until he arrived in Denver and rented a car. Then he scanned the numbers.

Gray's number. Two numbers he knew came from the Bureau. Then a number he recognized. He'd obtained it from the search he'd conducted just hours ago. It belonged to Samantha Carroll's mother. He had memorized both her mother's number and Samantha's. He called the number displayed and got an answering machine. He hung up.

Then he called Gray. "What's up?"

"Barker's livid," Gray said.

"Did he say why?"

"Nope. He called me in to find out where you were. I said you went fishing. Didn't say exactly where. You didn't say, did you?"

"Nope. I keep my private fishing hole secret."

"Good. I wouldn't want to lie to the boss."

"You haven't," he reassured Gray. Then he asked, "No one's called you, have they?"

"Who do you mean?"

"There's a number on my cell phone. It's Patsy Carroll's home phone number. When I returned the call, I got an answering machine. I thought she might have called the office."

"Not that I know of, but if I didn't answer your phone, it might have gone to Barker."

Nate swore.

"Well, keep me posted," Gray said, "and I'll keep Barker off your trail."

"Done."

He switched off the call, debating whether or not to keep the phone on. Barker wouldn't give up. He was like a bulldog, and if Nate answered the phone, Barker could trace the location. He turned it off. He could always say he lost the damn thing.

His heart pounded harder. What if the call *was* from Samantha Carroll rather than her mother? Only a handful of people had his private cell number. She was one of them.

He tried to shift his thoughts to the hours ahead as he drove through the mountains. He was told it was a three-hour drive. It seemed a hundred.

He'd been stunned when he discovered Samantha Carroll had left Merritt's home. So, apparently, had Merritt.

By unspoken consent—and, Nate thought, their own personal reasons—neither of them had mentioned Samantha to the police. Nate had told the beat police that he'd witnessed the drive-by shooting after arriving to interview Nick Merritt. He and Merritt were at the door when a car sped by, and both of them hit the deck.

Nate knew he could be suspended. He'd disobeyed a direct order. But he might be able to justify this one last visit to Nick, saying he was merely wrapping up a few details from the previous night's accident.

He wasn't ready to lose his job or take a suspension. Not as long as there were killers sniffing around Samantha Carroll. He might not be "official," but he could still ask for professional courtesy from local police departments.

Truthfully, he thought she was safer anywhere but Boston.

He'd not broached the offer of protection with his boss, because she'd already made it clear she would refuse it. This last shooting episode might have changed things . . . if she'd stuck around long enough for him to find out. He also suspected that Samantha might be in even more danger if she came to the attention of his superiors. Perhaps because some of his own informants had been killed when their names drifted up the ladder.

That he'd been so abruptly taken off the case needled his suspicions even more. He'd been assigned to the organized crime unit for years. He'd been moderately successful. There was no reason, at least none he could see, that would justify his removal.

Perhaps it had been that suspicion that had raised hackles along his spine, and he'd decided to drive out to Merritt's house and keep an eye on it. He had not expected the drive-by shooting. For a moment he had to decide whether to follow the car or to give her assistance.

It wasn't much of a conflict, not when he saw her under Merritt, blood pouring from her arm.

But then she had disappeared, and it hadn't taken him long to figure out she was returning to Denver. He didn't blame her after what had happened yesterday.

He wouldn't trust anyone, either, if he were she.

There should have been something he could have done to convince her she was in way over her head. Now she was probably as suspicious of him as she was of the family. Perhaps he should have better explained the Bureau's suspicions concerning Nick Merritt. But that's all they were. Suspicions.

Now the only hope he had was to reach Patsy Carroll and get her to cooperate. As Paul Merritta's wife, she would know things. If she had stayed alive this long, then she must have a kind of insurance that included evidence.

Perhaps she would help him if she thought her daughter was in danger.

The only thing he *did* know was that the unexpected appearance of Samantha Carroll had changed the dynamics of the family as much as the death of Paul Merritta had. He wondered whether it had even brought about the don's murder. The forensics people still hadn't finished the testing yet.

All those questions had bombarded him these past twenty-four hours, along with the strong feeling that Samantha Carroll was on a collision course with disaster.

Her image hadn't left him. If she had been anyone else, he might have given a thought to asking her out. Her seemingly sincere, though misguided, defense of Nick Merritt oddly appealed to him. So had her understated looks. Her hairstyle was easy, her makeup just enough, and her clothes simple but stylish. He liked her confident manner, the way her eyebrows furrowed when she was thinking. He admired her loyalty and tenacity, though he thought it misplaced.

Quite simply, it had been difficult—impossible—to keep that reaction in check. He'd had no business kissing her. He wasn't even sure where it came from. But he still felt it. Still tasted her in his memory.

He would have to rein in his libido. He had been after the Merritta family for far too long to fail now. Gray had called it an obsession, but Nate knew that even his partner had been infected with the need to prosecute the one family in Boston that had been nearly untouchable.

Nothing would get in Nate's way. *Nothing.* Not even a dark-haired woman who stirred something he thought had died with his wife five years ago.

Reaching Steamboat Springs, he stopped at the city's tourist office to locate the address he had. He also asked for directions to Western Wonders, the Carrolls' gallery. He could have gone to the police department, but he didn't want to do that. Not yet. If he turned to the local police, he might lose his best bargaining tool: privacy. Probably he would lose his job as well.

If he had been there for any other reason, he would have taken pleasure in the area. The drive from Denver had been scenic, and the town, nestled in a green valley, was picturesque. He knew that Olympic-caliber skiers practiced here.

He turned his thoughts back to the supposedly long-dead Mrs. Merritta.

Had her daughter told her what had happened in Boston? That Samantha had been nearly killed? Or that Patsy Carroll was now a widow twice over? The odd thing was that he'd discovered precious little about the man she had called her husband; his history began about the time the two moved to Steamboat Springs more than thirty years ago.

A coincidence?

The whole scenario stank like a week-old fish.

He risked trying to call Patsy Carroll's number again.

Still the machine answered.

Something must have happened.

He had both addresses. The mother's and Samantha's. According to the map, they were fairly close together. He'd meant to try the mother first, since he'd expected Samantha not to be very cooperative. Now he changed his mind.

He looked at the map again, then made several turns

and drove up in front of a house made of logs. Roses climbed up the posts of the front porch. The house looked natural in its setting. And inviting.

He'd barely pulled up when the door opened and Samantha stepped out, her lips starting to form an anxious smile. It faded when she saw him. Disappointment stabbed through him at that emotional retreat even as his heart suddenly lurched at the sight of her. She wore jeans and a T-shirt and looked younger in casual clothes. Her arm was bandaged. But she was as appealing to him as she had been in Boston, perhaps even more so.

As he walked up the drive, he saw that her face was drawn, her eyes tired. Some of the joy of life he'd seen there before was gone.

"Miss Carroll?"

She leaned against the doorjamb.

"Mr. McLean," she acknowledged in a voice heavy with disappointment.

"You were expecting someone else?"

She didn't say anything. Neither did she invite him in. She stood there, stiff and unyielding.

"You called?" he tried, wondering now whether she really had been the one who called.

She nodded.

So it had been her. "The number was on my cell phone. I recognized it as belonging to your mother." His voice softened.

"My mother's?" she asked, suspicion in her voice.

"It wasn't difficult to find," he said. "I had both numbers—yours and your mother's."

He wanted to touch her. To soothe away the agony he saw in her face. He had to will himself not to reach out and take her in his arms. "Is something wrong?" he asked gently.

"Yes," she admitted in a broken voice.

"What?"

"My mother's disappeared."

The words, though, didn't half convey the agony he saw on her face. Nor, he knew, the frustration he suddenly felt.

Almost without thinking, he held his arms open, and she walked straight into them.

nineteen

She walked into his arms.

She needed their warmth. She'd been so cold since she'd discovered her mother's absence.

She'd lost control of her life. She knew she shouldn't be here in the house, but it was the only place her mother could find her. And she was exhausted, both mentally and physically. Hoping against hope, she'd driven up to the cabin early this morning after finding the note. She'd hoped to find some explanation there.

The cabin had looked as it always did when they—as a family—arrived and left. Dishes put away. Bed made. Door locked. No sign of habitation. No hidden message. Nothing. Once she found the cabin empty, she'd turned around and returned home, watching her rearview mirror.

Her body was exhausted but her mind kept her awake as she drove back to her own house and collapsed in the chair next to the phone. She didn't wake until she heard a car drive up. She'd run to the door and thrown it open. She was so sure . . .

And he stood there.

Tall, with that relaxed lean strength and a shadow of a

smile. Confident. Assured. Dear God, how she needed some of that assurance.

She'd called him during a moment of sheer desperation. She hadn't really expected him to show. She hadn't really known if she wanted him to or not.

Now she felt enormous relief and yet . . .

"I called your office, too," she said.

His brows furrowed together. "Do you know whom you spoke with?"

She should have taken the name. She always did that on a business call. She wanted to know who to hold responsible if something went wrong. But in her panic this morning, she hadn't.

"I don't remember. A man. I just asked that he tell you to call Sam. I didn't think anyone would know who Sam was but you."

Then she remembered she'd made both calls from her mother's phone. How would he have known the phone call had been from her? Had he had that number handy because he had come to see her mother, not her?

She backed out of his arms, and the warmth she'd just felt faded in the cool early morning air. Not friends, she told herself. Not anything. Just as the Merrittas obviously wanted something from her, now he wanted something from her, too.

They stood there like strangers. Probably because they were. Yet there had always been some kind of electric recognition between them. She still remembered the magic of a kiss that had lasted such a brief time and yet had had such a lasting impact. She didn't understand how the awareness between them could still be as strong as it had been that night.

She'd been exhausted then, too. Exhausted and scared. She'd hoped that had been all there was. Now she knew that wasn't true. The awareness was still alive, still as vibrant. And she was still as wary.

But she wanted to trust him. She needed guidance as to

what to do in a world she didn't understand. She was tired of being the vulnerable victim.

Hesitancy. Fear. Need. And, dammit, attraction. They all radiated between them.

She swallowed hard, trying to regain the sea legs of reason.

"Tell me what happened," he said softly.

She opened the door wider to let him in.

"You're not staying alone, are you?" he asked.

"I just got home a little while ago," she replied. She wasn't going to tell him about the cabin. Not yet.

"Can I have a cup of coffee?"

She nodded. She needed one, too. Perhaps then she could sort out her wayward feelings.

It seemed everyone told her not to trust anyone else. And yet she had to trust someone. Her world had spun out of control.

He *was* FBI. He was supposed to be one of the good guys. Instinctively, she knew he was. To her knowledge he was the only one who hadn't lied to her or kept secrets from her.

She led the way to the kitchen.

"Can I make it for you?" he asked, his gaze touching the bandage on her arm.

"It's nothing," she said. "A few stitches."

"Does anything daunt you?" he asked.

"A great deal bothers me, but in the grand scheme of the past few days, a splinter ranks about a fourth of a point on a ten-point scale."

"What ranks tenth?"

"My mother."

"I'm sorry," he said. "I should have known that."

"No, you shouldn't. You don't know me," she said more sharply than she intended because of her mixed feelings. She wanted him here, yet out of loyalty to Nick, she shouldn't. But she knew she was in over her head and McLean was all she had at the moment.

"I'll make the coffee," he offered.

"I know where everything is," she said. "I'll make it."

But it was more than knowing where everything was. She needed to keep busy. She needed to keep her hands moving.

Even if she hadn't known he was right behind her, she would have felt his presence. Odd that even the air seemed to hum with expectation when he was near. She filled the filter and plugged in the pot, her movements calculated to avoid brushing against him . . . touching him.

He was silent, too, as the coffee started to drip.

She didn't look at him as she took two cups from the cupboard. Nor when she went to the fridge and found some milk.

Finally she had to turn back to where he leaned against one of the counters, waiting silently for her to accept his presence . . . to acknowledge she needed him. Did he ever sit? There was a natural restlessness about him. Watchfulness.

And also patience. It was the patience that was disconcerting.

God knew he was trying to practice patience as he watched her make the coffee with quietly determined movements. Her exhaustion was obvious, yet he held back, waiting for her to admit it. Something told him she would resent it if he forced the admission on her. If he tried to take control of her.

Patience was an art he'd never quite conquered, but she was as skittish—and wary—as a mistreated dog. And well she had the right to be.

He knew a cornered animal when he saw one. The last thing he wanted was to add to her anxiety right now. There were enough hunters after her. He was supposed to be the embodiment of a safe haven to her.

The bandage on her arm was a sign of his failure thus far. Somehow he should have prevented that shooting.

"The coffee smells good," he said after several moments. "It's been a long drive."

She didn't say anything. He wanted to ask about her mother, but it was obvious she wasn't ready to talk about it yet. Wait, he warned himself. She was like a volcano ready to erupt. He tried to curb his questions by evaluating the house and its furnishings. Surroundings often told him much about a person.

The hallway had been lined with western art. The spacious kitchen was uniquely welcoming with tiles painted with Indian designs and a huge brick fireplace that stretched across an entire wall. Copper pots and pans hung from hooks over a cooking island.

As he stood against the counter, relieved to stretch legs stiff from hours on the highway, a cat walked in, its tail waving high in the air.

McLean stooped and held out his hand.

"That's Sarsy," Samantha told him. "She doesn't like strangers."

He was quiet. Didn't move his hand. After several seconds, Sarsy approached him, purring as she butted her head against his hand. He'd always liked animals, and they'd always seemed to like him. Perhaps because he didn't demand anything from them.

Samantha looked startled and then thoughtful.

He thought that undemanding tactic might work best with Samantha Carroll, too.

He drank in the smell of the coffee and watched as she poured a healthy amount into a large mug. No delicate cup with three swallows here.

"Would you like anything in it?"

"No." He took the cup and sat on a stool next to the island. "Thank you."

She poured coffee into another cup and sipped it. Her hand shook slightly.

His gaze met hers. The uncanny attraction between

them seemed to intensify with every passing moment. He wanted to lean over and take her hand. He forced himself to resist the temptation. He needed to keep his distance, to allow her to come to him . . . like the cat. "Tell me about your mother," he said softly.

"I don't know if anything's wrong," she blurted. "She left a note saying not to worry."

"But you do?" he probed gently.

"She's been asking me to come home. She had something to tell me. Yet she left a few hours before I was to return. It doesn't make sense."

"Can I see the note?"

She hesitated.

"I'm not your enemy," he said.

"I know. You just want to help me even as you try to hurt my brother." Her voice was slightly edged with sarcasm.

"Not if he's innocent," he countered, surprising himself. "Don't let the Merrittas influence you," he said. "They're not worth it."

It was exactly the wrong thing to say, and he knew it immediately from the curtain that fell over her face. But he had never been tactful, and he honestly wanted to make her aware of the pitfalls of being allied in any way with the Merrittas.

He tried again. "The note?"

He saw her swallow, struggle with the decision. Then her shoulders slumped. "I'll get it."

She left the room, but he didn't follow. He knew he couldn't push.

She brought it back, and he skimmed over it first, then read it more carefully, looking for nuances. But he didn't know Patsy Carroll, formerly Tracy Edwards Merritta. He could not judge whether she had been forced or not, not without knowing more about her.

"You said there was nothing unusual about the note. She usually called you Samantha?"

"Yes," she said. "There's nothing there. I've been over it a dozen times."

"She mentioned a friend. Do you have any idea who that might be?"

"No," she said in a small voice. "She had friends, but I don't think she had any close ones. My father was her best friend. I thought it was just natural reticence but now I think it might have been fear of exposure."

"No family?"

A look flitted across her face. A sudden memory? Revelation?

"No," she said, but this time he didn't believe her. There was something she wasn't saying.

He read the note once again. "Have the local police been called?"

"No. She said she didn't want to talk to you yet. Bringing in the local police would just raise questions." Her gaze met his, challenged him.

He took another sip of coffee. "You're not going to be able to keep this quiet. Not now. Too many people know."

"I realize that," she said with quiet desperation. "But I can't be the cause."

He said nothing, just continued to watch her.

"I *am*, aren't I?" she said. "If I hadn't gone to Boston—"

"It wouldn't have made a difference," he said gently. "Merritta's man, Camda, had made calls to him. We recorded them. We knew there was a daughter. We would have found you . . . and so would whoever is taking shots at you."

"Why?"

"Because she might have information we need."

"But it was thirty years ago." Her eyes pleaded with him.

"It's too late," he said. He sipped the coffee. It was strong and very good. The kitchen seemed to become smaller. Warmer. Damn, but he liked her.

More than liked her.

Restrain your libido, he told himself again. He longed to reach over and touch her. But he remembered what happened at the hospital. Too much proximity and combustion happened.

She seemed caught in the moment, too. She looked dazed, but then that might well be plain exhaustion.

She shook her head, as if trying to chase away a thought. "Do you think someone might have taken her?" Her words broke the momentary spell. "I *know* her. I just don't think she would leave like that." She paused. "At least, I *thought* I knew her."

The coffee was working. Or perhaps it was the fact she could no longer conceal her fear. Whatever the reason, he knew he had to be very careful. She and her mother could be the key to dismantling the Merritta family. Someone obviously considered them a threat.

Reason dictated that Patsy Carroll, aka Tracy Merritta, had something on the family. Nothing else explained why she was still alive after her defection from the family. What possibly could hang like the sword of Damocles over the Merrittas for thirty years? That's what he needed to know.

Or did he? Did he want to risk the fragile shell of intimacy weaving around them?

You've been working toward this for more than twenty years. He sought the image that had sustained him through those years. The shot, the blood. His mother's face. Scared. Then empty.

It could happen to Samantha. He suspected that she knew she was far beyond her depth. He could exploit that, but he didn't want to use her. He wanted to protect her. Hell, he *would* protect her.

Keep her talking. Questions. Gentle questions. And keep lustful thoughts at bay. "When exactly did you find out about your connection to the Merrittas?" He knew, or thought he knew, but good interviews always went back to the beginning, putting together different sources and clues, then finding the common string.

She looked at him suspiciously, but then shrugged. "Last week. Two men sent by Paul Merritta came by the gallery. They showed me a family photo of Nick and myself as babies with my mother and . . . Paul Merritta. They said he was dying and wanted to see me."

He leaned forward. "You had no inkling before that? None?"

"No. I thought David Carroll was my birth father." She hesitated.

"What did your mother say?"

Her gaze met his. Solemn and honest and full of pain. He knew he was plumbing that vulnerability.

He brushed aside his reservations. He couldn't help her without knowing as much as possible. "Do you know how unusual it is for someone to leave the family?" he asked. "Alive?"

He saw in her face that she knew exactly what he meant. She had a quick mind.

"Maybe they just couldn't find her. Maybe they went on with their lives and didn't care." Her voice was defensive again. Just as it had been when she'd asked if perhaps her father hadn't searched for them because he cared about her mother.

He didn't say anything.

Then a slight smile. "That dumb, huh?"

The smile went straight to his heart. Still, he had to tell her the truth. The more she knew, the more she could protect herself. "If they want to find someone, they can do it. The Merrittas have a lot of connections." Some, in fact, in the Boston police department and possibly one in his own office. "I don't buy for a moment that you were just located. Not just before his death. I don't believe in coincidences."

"Do you think someone from the family might have taken my mother?"

"I don't know," he admitted.

"How could she hurt Paul Merritta now that he's dead?"

"Perhaps she had Merritta's protection, and that's gone now that he's dead. Maybe others were involved. I'm betting they want to make sure the secret stays secret. Aside from that, they might not want any more claimants to Merritta's fortune. If they weren't divorced, she could be his widow now. That makes her—and you—a complication, and the Merrittas do not like complications."

Her face paled.

He continued. "She was able to bury herself very well. She had to have had help. Which brings up another question. David Carroll has no background. Not prior to the time he married your mother. None." He searched her face. "Maybe he had some friends—relatives—who might help her." He wanted to know a great deal more about the mysterious David Carroll who didn't exist before his marriage to Samantha's mother.

She shook her head. "He didn't have any family, and his life was my mother and me."

"Do you know where he was born? Raised?"

"His parents died when he was young. He grew up in a Catholic home and then went into the army," she said. "He died two years ago."

"Is there any place he or your mother might have kept important documents? Like a safe deposit box?" He held his breath as she seemed to consider the question.

"The insurance you mentioned?"

"Yes."

"There is one where they kept their wills and deeds. I went through it with mother."

"Could there be another?" He couldn't keep the urgency from his voice.

"Not that I know about." Another flicker in her eyes. She was lying, or perhaps just remembering something.

"Think about it."

"I will."

"It's important, Samantha."

"To me? Or to you?"

Every time he thought she was on the edge of trusting him, she stepped back. "It's important to both of you," he said flatly. "It might save your life, and your mother's life."

"And you?"

"Hell, I'm not even supposed to be here," he admitted. "The Bureau didn't send me. I've taken vacation time."

"Why?"

"Because you're in over your head," he said bluntly.

She tilted her head, studying his expression. "Anything else you want to confess?" she asked wryly.

Should he tell her the rest of it? Or would that scare her off? He decided to compromise.

"I won't lie to you about wanting to take down the Merrittas," he said. "I know what they do to people. How they use—then discard—them. I don't want to see you hurt. So I do have a personal interest."

"Why do you care?"

"I know you've been thrown into something that's not of your making."

"Are you sure of that?" Her eyes were bleak.

"Yes." And he was now. He hadn't been in the beginning, but the more he'd learned about her background, her life, the more he had seen her struggle between loyalty to a brother she didn't know and a mother she did, he *knew*. He knew something else now: she was terrified something had happened to her mother.

And so was he.

twenty

She wanted to believe him. She wanted to believe that he was everything he seemed to be.

A nagging doubt kept her from accepting it. She decided to challenge him directly. "Nick said that destroying the Merritta family is your life's work."

He hesitated, seeming to weigh his words. "Paul Merritta slipped through our fingers time and time again. Witnesses recant or end up dead. Undercover agents disappear. And now there will be a battle for succession. There's a lot at stake."

"My brother thinks it's personal. You make it sound personal. Why?"

"It happens," he said. "When we're on a case for a long time . . ."

"But now you said you're here on your own."

"Yes."

"Because you were worried about me?"

"Yes."

"You didn't intend to see my mother?"

"You were my first concern. But I won't lie to you. I also want to know what your mother knows."

"Is this where you insert a nugget of truth to conceal the vein of subterfuge?"

He gave her a quick grin. "I like that. I'll have to remember it."

"That's not an answer."

"I'll give you the best answer I can," he said. "I want the Merrittas. They've caused untold misery. They've killed with impunity. They corrupt officials."

"Don't sugarcoat it," she said.

"I didn't think you would want me to."

"No," she agreed. She trusted him more because of those words. "But it's more personal between you and Nick. Why?"

"Because I believe he's gotten away with money laundering all these years."

"Why?" she asked again. "What proof do you have?"

"He says he's distanced himself from his father, but he's met with him on a regular basis, often in out-of-the-way places where they didn't think they could be traced."

"Maybe he didn't want to be tarred with the same brush."

"His company was financed by a loan institution connected to Merritta."

"Is that Nicholas's fault?"

"It has a branch in Switzerland."

"They do a lot of foreign business, partly because they are hounded by the government here."

He raised an eyebrow.

"He says you've driven off business, harassed customers. . . ."

He shrugged. "If he's an honest businessman . . ."

It wasn't an honest answer, and her heart dipped. They had been dueling. With words, with their eyes, even with their bodies. Feint and parry.

She moved away.

"I'm sorry," he said. "But you wanted me to be honest."

"Somehow I don't quite think you're doing that," she said.

"I'm trying," he said simply.

She *did* believe that. She believed he was being as honest as he felt he could be. She was doing the same. There were things she couldn't say, either.

She decided to change the subject. "Did you grow up in Boston?"

He nodded.

"You have family there?"

His face closed. "No."

"Never been married?"

"Yes," he said shortly.

Her heart slowed. For some reason, she'd thought . . .

No, not for some reason. It had been the kiss.

"Oh," she said, feeling not too bright and even a little betrayed. She wasn't fond of married men who kissed other women passionately. "Do you have kids?"

"No," he said flatly. "There was a miscarriage, then the doctor said she couldn't have children. She died a few years ago."

She wanted to ask more, but his lips had narrowed into a thin line, and shadows had fallen across his eyes.

She tried again. "Mother? Father?"

"My mother died when I was a kid. I never knew my father."

"Then . . ."

"Foster families," he said. "I played football and won a scholarship to a small college. I wasn't Big Ten material."

Sam was impressed. She knew about foster families, how difficult it was for most kids to fight their way out of the trap.

Their gazes met again. Intimacy had spun a web around them again. Those few exchanges had only added to his appeal. The air grew dense, electric.

His hand reached out toward her, then stilled. She leaned forward as if a piece of metal drawn to a magnet.

Stop it, she told herself. *Your mother is missing. Someone is trying to kill you. And you're acting like a dog in heat. . . .*

He suddenly stood, consciously breaking the invisible ties. "Back to your mother . . . Does she have a cell phone?"

"She has one. It's out of service."

"Wouldn't she call you? Make sure you wouldn't worry?"

"She might have thought the note was enough," she replied, but without any real conviction.

"Tell me about her."

She looked at him suspiciously, wondering for a moment if he would use whatever she said against her and her mother. Or Nicholas. But then she shrugged. She would tell him nothing he couldn't discover on his own. "She's a private person. I always thought it was a natural reticence."

"And now you're not so sure?"

"No," she said. "I think she was probably afraid that a slip might reveal her past."

"No grandparents?"

"No. She always said she was an orphan."

He shook his head. "Didn't you ever think it strange they were both orphans?"

"No, I always thought that was what drew them together, why they were so close, so . . . dependent on each other." She knew she sounded defensive now.

"It must be hard," he said softly, "to be told that everything you believed may not be entirely true."

"That was diplomatically said," she said. "I feel like I'm lost in the woods. There are no paths, only dense forest. I thought I knew everything there was to know about my father and mother, and now I find out I know nothing. Not even who their friends were." She shivered.

Sympathy replaced the shadows in his eyes. She thought of him—of a boy who'd lost his mother and was then given to strangers. His world must have been full of uncertainty, just as hers was now.

"Do you want me to ask the local police to try to find her?" he said. "I could just say she is missing. Nothing more."

"You said you were here on your own," she said.

"I am. I could make it a favor. A professional courtesy."

"Wouldn't they check with your superior?"

He shrugged. "Maybe. You might think about telling the local authorities about your other family," he said.

"You won't?"

"No," he said. "But if you don't hear from her by tomorrow," he said, "I think you should tell them."

"It could destroy her," Samantha said bleakly.

He didn't say anything, but he held out his hand to her, and this time he didn't take it away.

His hand was strong and warm, and her fingers wove with his. He raised his other hand to her face, and skimmed the back of his knuckles along her cheekbone. Her skin tingled from his touch. And burned.

His hand lingered for a moment at the corner of her lips, and then he bent down and touched his lips to hers with a lightness, a tenderness, that sapped all her caution. She responded with reckless abandon, with a longing so strong, she couldn't harness it. She was drawing strength from a man who had so much of it, and knew a lessening of the panic that had been bubbling up inside her.

His kiss deepened, and the heat between them was like the fiercest part of a flame. Shudders ran through her body, and she felt the slightest tremor in his.

His lips moved to her ear, and the shudders turned

into hot spasms. She struggled against them, finally moving slightly until his lips left the ear he had been nuzzling.

They were like match and kindling together, she thought. *No. Like fire and dynamite.*

She felt the tiny explosions throughout her body as his lips played along her cheekbone and then the nape of her neck before returning once more to her lips and plundering them with violent delicacy—two incongruent words, but oddly enough they fit.

There was need between them, and gentleness, rough passion and tenderness. There was reluctance and eagerness.

She was so attracted to him, and yet so reluctant to give him any part of her. She still didn't entirely trust his motives, but she was irresistibly drawn to him. She was aware of the dichotomy of her emotions, and yet, the mixture fueled the fire.

Nate mentally surrendered. He didn't know what had happened thirty-four years ago, what kind of arrangement Samantha's mother had made with her husband. At the moment, he didn't care.

He only cared about Samantha Carroll and the desire in her eyes. Desire for him. Need for him. He'd forgotten what it was like to be needed.

But then he saw a flash of fear in her eyes and realized part of her fear was of him. Of what she thought he could—or might—do. Of kisses she was afraid to believe meant anything other than a way of gaining her cooperation.

He saw it in every expression, in every movement, in everything she didn't say. She was trying to stay calm. She was trying to lose herself in the moment, trying to believe there was more than fear in her world.

She was as gallant a woman as he'd ever met. An innocent thrown in a pit of wolves and doing her best—which was pretty damn good—to survive. He reached over and touched her shoulder, half expecting her to shy away. She hadn't done that the evening he'd kissed her, but tension—even anger—had vibrated between them. She knew he wanted something from her.

He did. But now it was more than a deposition or eyewitness testimony. Or even evidence to put away a Merritta.

Her gaze held his for a long moment. Emotions ran amok in him.

He liked her strength. He liked her. He more than liked her.

And that was dangerous.

Yet he didn't move his hand from her shoulder, and his fingers—almost of their own accord—moved against her skin at the back of her neck. Her dark hair curled around them and she leaned toward him . . .

Need. She needed something to hold on to. Nothing more. He would be kidding himself to think otherwise.

He was astonished at the intensity of his feelings, feelings he had thought dead. He wanted her, and he wanted her more than he had thought it was possible to want a woman.

He also wanted to erase the fear and the bewilderment and the abandonment he saw in her eyes.

Their lips met. Explored. The electricity between them intensified. It sparked, then caught, and roared into flames. Even their clothes didn't protect them from the heat that flared between them.

His mouth played with hers, feeling her lips open to his, and his tongue reached greedily for hers. To his surprise, she responded with an equal quest, her tongue meeting his and engaging in a dance that sent all his senses reeling.

Her passion met his, and that was an aphrodisiac that put any lingering reservations to rest.

His lips caressed with a possessiveness that jolted him at the same time her body pressed against his. God, how he wanted her. How he wanted something warm and alive in his life rather than the constant frost of hatred.

Once again his mind warned him. He knew this meant disaster. How would she feel when she knew why he had been pursuing the Merrittas? But at this particular moment, he didn't care. His heart seemed to beat outside his chest, and tenderness was an aching thing growing inside him. He realized he'd been waiting for this for a long time. This caring. This gentle, yearning link to another person.

He'd believed these feelings beyond him, that they came only to someone with a heart, but now he knew that his heart was not as dead as he'd thought it was. Something had become more important than the Merrittas. Than his job. Than his childish vow that had become a man's obsession.

He looked in Samantha's eyes and saw the question there. Then it was replaced by a kind of desperation. He couldn't even begin to comprehend what she had gone through these past few days. He could, though, comprehend the loss of a mother.

The thought should have made him back away. Instead he tightened his arms around her with a compelling need of his own. Merritta wasn't going to take someone else from him. Even dead, Merritta seemed to have power. No longer, dammit. No longer.

Somehow Nate was going to free them both from him.

He felt her hand on his face, exploring the angles. Then it moved to the back of his neck, stroking the sensitive skin, plunging him into waves of sensation.

He was no longer aware of anything but her. His hands instinctively went to her T-shirt and reluctantly he forced his lips away long enough to slip the shirt over her head, then her bra.

Damn, but she was beautiful. The spirit was back. Her eyes glistened, and her body responded to his as if they'd both been made for each other. He leaned down, and his tongue ran lightly over one of her breasts, then the other.

She gasped. Her fingers fumbled with the buttons of his shirt, then madness overtook both of them and they were pulling off the other's clothes even as they stood and moved toward the hall and, he suspected, her bedroom.

He knew it would change the dynamics between them forever. The complications could ruin everything he'd worked for. But he couldn't stop. The expression in her face had been too raw, too anguished.

He cared only about easing the fear he saw in her eyes. Not fear for herself but for someone she loved. He longed to erase that fear. He longed to touch her and be touched by her. She lit the darkness that had invaded his life until nearly everything decent in him had begun to shrivel.

Samantha closed her eyes. He felt as if he belonged with her. She'd known attraction. She'd even thought herself in love. But it had never felt so natural before. As if it was meant to be.

Sam knew what she was doing would cause even more complications in her life, yet she couldn't stop. She wanted him so badly, she ached.

Her arm had hurt all day, but now she barely felt it as they reached the bedroom and she undid his belt while he pulled down the zipper of her jeans. Their lips met again as they wrested the last of their clothes off each other, and flesh met flesh.

His hands moved up and down her body, igniting fires. Her world had always been full of colors, but never had she felt this kind of physical intensity when a touch made her ache and a breath against her skin made her quiver with delicious sensations.

All the weariness of the past few days faded in the magic of his kiss. His mouth held her, his arms squeezing her so tightly to him that she felt they were already one. Her body was consumed with him, with the need of him.

He slid his mouth down her body, teasing, making it glow. She heard herself murmur little sighs of pleasure.

He touched the small of her back, turning her and guiding her down on the bed. He sank down with her, their lips meeting in a maelstrom of need, of expectation that had been building since he'd first walked into the house. Even when she'd thought she'd been in love before, she'd never felt this physical yearning, this exquisite need.

He rose above her, his body teasing hers until she arched upward to meet him. He entered her with tantalizing slowness. She responded, moving her body in concert with his in a primitive, sensuous dance that sent ripples of sensation through her until she thought she would go mad with wanting.

The tempo of his movement quickened, and she felt as if she were disintegrating into white-hot heat and bellowing waves of pleasure. Their bodies arched together and seemed to burst in a fireball of sensations. Convulsive spasms rocked both of them.

Then he cradled her as they both fell back to earth, their bodies still rippling from the aftershocks of lovemaking.

Neither of them spoke as their bodies remained connected in the most intimate of ways as an occasional spasm continued to echo the wonder she'd just experienced.

twenty-one

Nate woke first, content to lie quietly and watch her sleep. Dark lashes shielded her eyes, her hair was a mop of short curls and a slight smile made her face look relaxed. She'd been both emotionally and physically exhausted. God only knew when she'd last slept.

He couldn't remember the last time he'd been still like this, without the restlessness that charged him. He enjoyed watching her, even as he agonized over the conflict between job and crusade and the woman who filled a need he hadn't known existed in him until now.

She was a woman who valued truth and honesty. He had not been honest with her, not completely. She deserved to know the whole story. How could he expect her to be completely candid with him when he hadn't been candid with her?

If she knew her father's family had killed his mother, would she lie in his arms so peacefully? If she knew the Merrittas had been his burning obsession since the day he'd watched his mother bleed to death on Boston streets, would she trust him to help her, or would she always wonder if he tarred her with the same brush as the Merrittas?

Would she understand how he'd felt at the death of his wife?

The phone rang, and she woke with a lazy sensuality that made him ache all over again. Then alarm widened her blue eyes, and she grabbed the phone. Her face didn't change as she snagged a shirt and carried the phone into another room.

He wanted to follow. To listen. If he were caught eavesdropping, he could well lose more than he gained. Instead he made a mental note to get the phone records.

He went to the bathroom and rinsed his face and smoothed back his hair, then pulled on his slacks that had been dumped next to the bed. Coffee! He needed it after the past hours. He started toward the kitchen, then gave up any pretense at being honorable. He stepped quietly into the hallway, hoping to hear her in the living room. She wasn't there.

He wondered whether she was talking to her brother or her mother. He eyed a phone in the living room.

Sometimes he hated the restraints on his work, both judicial and those set by his own conscience. The latter had lessened over the years. Results had often become more important than observing the niceties of his profession. He was a maverick, had been for a long time, but he knew how far he could stretch the rules.

He had an instinct for that.

He couldn't force himself to pick up that phone.

He sat in a chair and waited, wondering what she would tell him. How much she trusted him.

How much he trusted himself.

Sam shook as she gently replaced the phone in its cradle.

It hadn't been her mother.

It had been a voice with a Boston accent, noting the fact that there was an FBI agent with her and warning her to get rid of him.

Or what? The threat hovered unsaid over the line.

Then the phone went dead.

He hadn't said he had her mother. Just that he knew where she was.

Which was a great deal more than she knew.

The idea that her mother disappeared voluntarily kept prickling.

She thought she knew how to find out.

The last gift her father had given her mother had been a silver brush and comb. She never went on a trip without it. If they sat on the dresser, Sam would know something was wrong. If they were gone, then her mother had probably left on her own, just as she said in the note.

And the voice? He'd presented no proof he had her mother or knew where she was. Maybe the call was made to tempt her into leading him to her mother.

She had to get to her mother's house.

She mentally went over the note again, still finding no clues that her mother had left under duress.

Had she ever really known her mother? Or her father whom she now knew had no past?

And now someone was watching her house. How else could he have known Nate was here?

Once again, she felt both fear and real anger. Not just fear. Terror mixed with disbelief. It clung to her like the remnants of a bad nightmare. What was happening was light-years from her previous life, a nightmare from which she couldn't awaken. Or a bad suspense novel. But those novels never really answered one question. How do you melt the ice that fear forms in your soul?

For a short while, she'd been warmed. She'd allowed herself to get lost in Nathan McLean's arms. She'd been consumed by their joint conflagration.

But now the icy fingers of fear ran through her again.

For a few moments, she wanted to run back to his arms. *"Get rid of him."*

She was too aware that McLean was probably waiting impatiently for her. What should she tell him? Was his interest more in striking at the Boston Merrittas than protecting her mother? Did it matter as long as the same result was achieved? She stared out of the window. She saw no out-of-place cars or trucks or other vehicles. Had someone trailed her from Boston, or had they already been here?

Had someone taken her mother? Dear God, was she even still alive?

She brushed her hair and dressed. Added a trace of lipstick. Her hand trembled slightly.

She wanted to ask help from McLean but she couldn't completely forget Nick's warnings. Now there was the warning from whoever was on the phone. If she talked to McLean, would she be signing her mother's death warrant?

The longer she stayed up here, the more he would wonder.

She needed to return to her mother's house to see whether her mother's silver brush was in its usual place on the dresser. She should have checked it last night, but she'd been so tired, so frantic. Instead she'd checked the obvious things. Suitcase? Gone. Favorite sweater? Gone. Travel cosmetic bag? Gone.

But she hadn't checked to see whether the brush, comb and mirror set remained.

If not . . .

Tell McLean about your mother.

A week ago, she wouldn't have considered withholding information from the FBI. She'd always been immensely critical of television shows and movies when the heroine did something really stupid, like trying to defeat the villain on her own instead of calling the police.

Now she understood that sometimes there were circumstances. . . .

Someone's watching. Someone will know. And that someone may well kill my mother.

Nick. Patsy Carroll was his mother, too, even if he didn't want to admit it.

She would try him first.

She steeled herself, tried a smile, then went down the hall, down the stairs. Damn, she'd never been good at being led, or being subtle.

Nate McLean stood at the window. She glanced toward the phone, but knew she would have heard a click if he'd picked up the receiver.

He'd dressed and combed his hair. Even then, a shock fell over his forehead. She'd always thought FBI agents were supposed to be well groomed, but he had a casualness about him that was almost western. His tie was always untied, his sleeves usually rolled up, his hair falling over his forehead. But it was the steady green eyes that affected her in ways she knew she shouldn't, couldn't, feel.

"No need to worry," she said. "My mother is safe."

"Where is she?"

"She didn't tell me. She just said she was safe."

He didn't say anything but she saw the questions in his eyes. Was she really that poor a liar?

"If you want to know where she is, I can get the phone records."

"No."

"Samantha . . ." Concern reflected in his eyes.

"Get rid of him," she'd been warned by the voice on the telephone. An "or else" dangled after the warning like an ax, ready to strike.

She was suddenly aware that her fingernails were biting into her palms. She had to concentrate to relax her fists, to stand at ease, as if all were right with the world.

She wanted to hold her hand out to him and tell him she didn't know where her mother was, only that she was in terrible danger. She wanted to ask his help.

She didn't want to be alone.

But she *was* alone, and had to be alone, or risk her mother's life.

He didn't leave. Instead his green eyes darkened, drawing her into his spell, offering a respite from the evil that had invaded into her life.

Tell him, an inner voice prompted.

His hand rose and touched a lock of hair, his fingers brushing her cheek. It was exactly what she wanted. And feared. Everything in her reacted to him in a way she'd never before experienced. Her legs felt rubbery, her nerves tingled. The touch was all tenderness. A longing that matched hers.

How much was real? She trusted him, yet she wondered if she could trust his feelings. She didn't even know what they were.

She stepped back. "Part of FBI procedure?" she asked, desperate now to keep a distance between them.

The intensity in his eyes faded. The side of his mouth crooked in a small smile. "No, I think the Bureau would disapprove."

The wry look on his face disarmed her. As much as she could be disarmed at the moment. She didn't want to get rid of Nate McLean, but she knew she must.

"I have to get to the gallery," she said.

"I'll come with you."

That was the last thing she needed. "No thanks."

"It's not negotiable."

She stared at him. The gentleness was gone.

"You're still in danger," he said. "As is your mother."

She shivered. He hadn't believed her. He suspected— or knew— her mother was in trouble. She swallowed hard, steered the conversation away from what she dared not discuss. "This morning was a mistake."

"Was it?"

"I don't want you here!"

"I want to help."

"You want to send Merrittas to prison."

"Some, yes, and I want to protect another Merritta," he admitted, disarming her again. She hadn't expected that.

"Please." Her voice started to break.

"You can't stay here alone. Not after the attempts on your life."

"I won't be alone. I'll be at the gallery, then stay with a friend. She has a bunch of big brothers."

He didn't move. "I won't leave you alone," he said. "You're too important to me and not because you are a Merritta, dammit."

The admission disconcerted her. It sounded protective and loving. She needed that, needed it now more than she needed air to breathe.

But she had to go, and she had to go alone. "Can you make coffee?" she said. "I have a few calls to make."

He nodded stiffly.

She watched as he turned toward the kitchen. She went to the desk drawer where she kept the keys to her mother's house, then grabbed her rental car keys. She glanced around for his, but couldn't find them.

She wanted to look in the kitchen, but she knew he would sense her presence. Just as she had sensed his so many times. He'd evidently believed she would do as he said. He was probably used to being obeyed.

She took a sharp letter opener from her desk. *"Get rid of him."* The words kept echoing in her mind.

The moment he heard the engine, he would be out the door. She had to slow him down, so he couldn't follow.

She stepped outside and around to the other side of his

car and kneeled. After several jabs, she knew the tire had been punctured.

She went to her rental car, unlocked it and got in. She started it and backed out of the driveway, looking back to see him running out the door. She put her foot on the gas pedal and speeded up.

Three blocks later, she lost him.

Her mother's home was exactly the way she'd left it earlier. She studied every car on the street, every person, even every bush as she drove up. She wondered whether she would always do that now.

Suddenly she hated Paul Merritta for what he had done to her life, to her mother's life. He'd plunged them both into terror.

For what? To prove that he could?

She didn't see anyone, but she hadn't seen anyone at her house the night of the burglary, either.

Invisible eyes again.

Or had her house been bugged? Had her mother's? The idea of her privacy being so invaded enraged her more than the actual attempts on her life. Her stomach churning, she paused at the doorstep before inserting the key.

She wished she had a gun. Dammit, she just hadn't had time to purchase one. She would remedy that today. She wasn't going to feel vulnerable any longer.

She turned the key in the lock and stepped cautiously inside. She had been there very early this morning, but she hadn't felt the air of abandonment she did now. No Sarsy rubbing her legs to take off the edge of aloneness.

She listened for a moment, heard complete stillness, then climbed the stairs to her mother's bedroom. She went to the dresser.

The silver comb and brush were gone.

She heard the sound of running water. She entered the bathroom.

A steady stream of water was coming from the sink faucet.

It hadn't been this morning.

twenty-two

Someone had been in the house since she'd left it early this morning.

Sam wanted to run out the door and never stop.

She wished she hadn't punctured McLean's tire.

She forced herself to look through each room before leaving. No other trace of a presence.

She thought about looking through her mother's desk, but she wouldn't know if anything was missing. Like an address book. Like her own address book that had gone missing a week ago.

Was someone looking for family friends?

Sam left the house and drove away, watching carefully through her rearview mirror.

Her next stop was the local gun store. She braced herself. The owner, Ed Greene, was an old friend of her father's. He'd been a Green Beret, and retired warriors always seemed to recognize each other.

He gave her a bear hug. "Going to start target shooting again?" he asked. "You were good. Your dad was always proud of you."

"You know the way my mother felt about guns," she said. "I never got a new one when my pistol was stolen."

"I figured that. Got interested again, huh? Good thing. Woman alone needs protection these days. Both my girls carry guns."

"I do a lot of driving at night," she agreed.

He gave her a searching look. She was wearing a long sleeve shirt and slacks, so he couldn't see all her wounds, but she had scratches on the back of one hand and a cut from windshield glass along her neck. "You okay?"

"An accident," she said.

He apparently accepted that. "Haven't seen much of Patsy," he said.

Ed was a widower and had indicated an interest in Patsy a year after her husband's death, but her mother hadn't been interested.

"She's been busy," Sam said, then changed the subject. "What weapon would you suggest?"

"Protection or target practice?"

She hesitated a moment, then said, "Both."

He took out a .38 Police Special and handed it to her. The revolver fit well in her hands.

She bought the gun and several packages of ammunition after he made the mandatory background check via phone.

"Thanks, Ed."

"Any time. I miss your father."

"Me, too," she said. She wondered whether he would approve of what she was doing. She was trying to protect her mother, as he apparently had done, but she had no idea whether she was doing the right thing. He obviously hadn't gone to the authorities. Instead he'd changed names, changed histories. He hadn't trusted the legal system.

"You need anything, you just call me," Ed said.

"There is something. Can I use your phone? I lost my cell phone in the accident. That's next on my list."

"Say, I have one you can borrow," he said. "Never use the damn thing anyway. Why don't you use it until you get a new one charged? Woman alone shouldn't be without one. Number is taped on the top. Never can remember the damn thing myself."

"Woman alone" seemed to be a mantra with him.

"Thank you," she said. "You send any bill to me."

"I look forward to you being a steady customer now," he said. He fumbled with the cell phone on his belt and gave it to her. "My girls are the only ones who have the number," he said. "But they also have the number at the shop and home. If they want me, they can get me. But a woman alone . . ."

She took the phone and put it in her purse, then paid him for the revolver.

"You might want to try the gun range," he reminded her.

"I'll do that," she said, anxious now to get to her next errand.

Warn Terri.

She got to her car, looking around for McLean's vehicle. The gun shop was three blocks away from Western Wonders, which was, she thought, where McLean would go first.

She closed her eyes as she remembered the way he had looked when she woke. Impossibly attractive. Impossibly safe.

Should she have told him about the call?

"Get rid of him." The words from a disembodied voice echoed in her ears.

She dialed Western Wonders.

Terri answered. "When did you get back?" she asked as soon as she heard Sam's voice.

"Early this morning. I tried to call you earlier, but you didn't answer."

"Probably running," Terri said. "I've been here most of the day." There was a question in her voice. "Someone is looking for you."

"Is he still there?"

"I didn't say it was a he," Terri said. "But it *was* a he, a very attractive he, and I think he went to your mother's house."

"How did he seem?"

"I don't think he was happy. He's one intense man."

McLean. It was a good description of him.

"He said he was FBI," Terri added. "He showed credentials."

"He is," Sam replied, "except he's here unofficially."

"He didn't say that."

Sam wasn't surprised. She wasn't surprised about anything any longer. McLean wanted information. She knew him well enough by now to know he wouldn't pay attention to technicalities. "Did you tell him anything?"

"Nothing to tell."

"What about my mother? Did he ask about her?"

"Yep. I said I heard from her yesterday afternoon."

"When?"

"About three in the afternoon."

"Did she say anything about leaving town?"

"Leaving?" The surprise was evident in her friend's voice. "She'd just arrived. She couldn't wait to see you."

"She left before I arrived. She left a note saying all was fine, that she just needed to get away for a few days."

"That's odd," Terri said. "She seemed so eager to see . . ." Her voice trailed off.

"Did she seem distracted at all? Nervous?"

"No. I think I would have noticed."

So whatever had frightened her away happened between three and probably midnight.

"Where are you?" Terri asked.

"Not far."

"I want to see you."

Sam wanted to see her, too. She wanted to hear everything that her mother had said, but not in Western Wonders.

"Is Helen there?"

"Yes."

"Take Jupiter to our favorite place. I'll meet you there in an hour. Make sure you're not followed."

A pause. Then, "If someone does, I have some big brothers who will take a gun to them."

The comment reminded Sam about her own brother. Her newly discovered brother. It should be a time of rejoicing. Not of terror. Not filled with this terrible uncertainty.

Was she putting Terri in jeopardy, too?

She started to say she'd changed her mind, but Terri had hung up.

She didn't call back, though. Now all she had to do was leave town without anyone seeing her. Not McLean. Not whoever was watching.

She always thought better outdoors. And she trusted Terri. Terri was the only person who hadn't lied to her— either by commission or omission—or tried to use her. Sam knew she could no longer see the forest for the trees. Maybe Terri could.

She looked at her car. McLean had seen it. Someone else might have seen it, too, and planted some electronic gizmo while she and McLean . . .

She went to the garage where she had much of her mechanical work done. They always gave her a loaner. She left the car around the side and went inside. "There's a noise in the car. It's a rental, and I have to drive it back to Denver. Can you take a look at it?"

"For you, anything," said Harry, the owner, with a grin. "Want the eyesore?"

"Yep," she said. "I have a few errands."

He pulled some keys off a nail and handed them to her.

The loaner didn't look like much, but it was in superb running condition. She'd discovered that long ago.

Praying she wasn't outsmarting herself, she drove the

car through the busy summer traffic of Steamboat. It was getting more and more popular, and the traffic seemed thicker than usual. Suddenly aware she hadn't eaten in the past twelve hours, she stopped at a fast food restaurant and ate a hamburger and fries.

It was time to head out toward Terri's ranch.

Before reaching it, she took a side road, then a dirt road into a heavily forested area. No one was behind her. She was sure of it.

Not the bad guys. Or the good guys.

She was alone.

Berating himself for trusting Samantha, Nate returned to Western Wonders after an unfruitful trip to her mother's home, only to find the gallery empty except for an elderly woman who apparently was in charge. She was talking to a customer.

He was convinced Sam would show up at the gallery sooner or later. He also suspected the pretty woman he'd questioned knew more than she'd said.

He glanced around, searching for Samantha even as he noted the paintings and sculptures situated around the spacious showroom. His gaze roamed over the walls and then the sculptures artfully displayed. He readily recognized a Remington, but not the others. Nate didn't know much about art but he knew these were good. There was an illumination—a play of light and shadows—that lifted most of them out of the ordinary.

He'd been in too much of a hurry earlier to notice.

The customer left and he went over to the older woman who gazed at him with open curiosity.

"I'm looking for Miss Carroll," he said.

"Oh, yes, I saw you earlier. You haven't found her yet?"

"I'm afraid not."

"I'm sorry, but I can't help you. But I think she was just talking to her friend."

"The young lady who was just here?"

The woman nodded. "Terri Faulkner. She and Sam are good friends."

"Sam?"

"Oh, we all call her Sam." The woman paused.

Sam. It didn't seem to fit her. She was too feminine. And yet maybe it did. The independence. The confidence.

Confident enough to elude him and strike out on her own.

She'd outwitted him. She'd been too compliant, and that had not gone along with everything else he'd observed about her. So he should have known better, but he thought there had been a moment or two when he was gaining her trust. Obviously, he'd never been more wrong.

She was in trouble. She'd tried to look unconcerned when she'd come down the stairs, but she'd been tense, the way people were when they'd received bad news. He'd thought he could coax it from her.

Some fool he. She obviously didn't trust anyone now, and he couldn't blame her. "Where does Miss Faulkner live?" he asked.

She gave him directions and he went back to his car.

He could go to the local police, but then he would be jerked back to Boston on the next plane. He would be opening a can of worms that he knew Samantha wasn't ready to deal with.

He headed for the Faulkner ranch.

It was better than sitting on Samantha's front stoop.

Sam felt some of the tension drain from her as she neared the meeting place. The fresh air, the mountains, the blue sky were exactly what she needed to clear her mind.

She had parked the borrowed car about half a mile from a wide spot in a stream that meandered down from the hills. It was a place where she and Terri had picnicked and was the only safe site that had immediately come to mind.

She had to talk to someone whose only loyalty was to her. She had to let Terri know what was happening in the event she disappeared or was killed.

She gave a half laugh at how easily she thought in terms of disappearing or being killed.

It shouldn't be real. It shouldn't be real. But it was.

Sam considered taking the revolver with her, but she'd been in such a hurry she hadn't purchased a holster. Terri wouldn't have brought saddlebags, and Sam really didn't want a pistol tucked in her slacks when she was riding. Besides, this country should be safe enough. They would be on Faulkner land.

She locked it in the glove compartment, then locked the car.

Terri appeared on her horse Pal Joey. She was leading Jupiter, Sam's usual mount when they rode together. Sam mounted the horse and settled into the saddle.

Terri studied her for a moment. "You look terrible."

"Thanks."

"Anything I can do?"

"Keep your distance, my friend. I don't want you hurt."

"You think I might be?"

"I'm not sure whether Mother disappeared of her own free will."

Terri didn't say anything for a few moments. "Have you called the police?"

"I'm not sure she wants me to."

"Oh, Sam."

"My brother was shot in Boston," Sam blurted out.

Terri's usually smiling face became grave.

"The bullet was meant for me. Nick was shielding me."

Sam could hear her friend's gasp. She nudged Jupiter into a walk. Terri followed. They headed toward the pasture area.

"And the FBI agent?" Terri asked.

"He wants to talk to my mother."

"Does he know she's disappeared?"

Sam nodded. "I asked him not to call the police . . . or to pursue it right now."

"Why would he do that? Not contact the police, I mean."

"He wants something from me."

"He seemed like a nice guy."

"He's been after the Merrittas for years. Nick says he would do anything to destroy the family. He might try to use my mother."

Terri halted her mount. "Do you really believe that? For God's sake, Sam, he's FBI." Then her gaze sharpened. "You like him," she said.

Sam knew a rosy flush was spreading over her face.

"I can't accept his help," she said. "He was at my house. I received a call from a man saying he knew the agent was there. He told me to get rid of him or my mother would be hurt. Don't you see? I might be killing my mother. . . ."

"What does he think about your mother's disappearance?"

"I don't know. I can't tell. He's hard to read. I never quite know what he's thinking."

"But you *want* to trust him."

"It's his agenda I worry about. In any case, if I help him or let him help me, I'm betraying my brother. They hate each other. And my brother saved my life. Twice." She hesitated. "But so did the agent."

Terri blinked. "What do your instincts tell *you* about this man?"

Terri had always had a way of getting to the core of things. Sam's instincts said to trust him completely, to put hers and her mother's safety into his hands. But they also said to trust Nick. The two were incompatible.

"He said his name was McLean," Terri said. "What's his first name?"

"Nathan, and he'll be asking you more questions."

"I'm forewarned," Terri said. "What should I tell him?"

Terri's loyalty was that deep, that complete. Sam suddenly realized she had put Terri in an untenable position.

She was enmeshed in a web that had no escape. By going to Boston, she might well have put her mother into danger, and now she was putting Terri in legal and physical jeopardy.

The chill that was becoming all too familiar was intensifying despite the warmth of the afternoon. "Don't lie," she finally said.

Terri looked miserable.

A blast broke the silence. Sam's horse lurched and neighed, then broke into a panicked gallop. A seasoned rider, Sam clenched her legs around the horse's sides and leaned forward, fighting the urge to saw on the reins. It took what seemed an eternity to gain control of the horse's direction.

"The woods," Terri yelled, but Sam had already turned Jupiter in that direction. They would have some protection there. Jupiter crashed through the trees, mindless of the branches whipping both his rider and himself. The ground was rough, full of rotting logs and rabbit holes. She heard Terri right behind her.

Please don't let anything happen to Terri or to the horses.

Jupiter slowed as the underbrush became thicker, but Sam had to duck to keep low branches from knocking her from the saddle.

They reached the stream. Jupiter shied and neighed plaintively. Sam slipped off and looked at him. Terri was there beside her, and both of them saw blood on Sam's horse. "A bullet graze," Sam said. "I don't think it's serious, but we have to get back to the ranch."

Terri looked bewildered. As bewildered as Sam had felt the first time a bullet came close to her.

"Dammit," Sam said. "I didn't mean to put you, or the horses, in danger."

"It's you I'm worried about," Terri said.

"No. Everyone I'm close to seems to be in danger. I didn't think—"

"You think they came all the way out here?" Terri demanded. "Why?"

"I don't know. I don't know why *they* would pursue and attack me anywhere. I thought—"

"They?"

"I don't know who 'they' are," Sam said. "The Merrittas? I don't know who else it could be. But why? I told them I didn't want anything. I thought when I left . . ."

"Did your father leave you anything? Could it be money?"

"I don't think so. The will is to be read later this week. I thought if I came home, let them all know I didn't want anything, that it would all be over."

"What about your brother?"

"He doesn't want anything to do with them, either."

"You believe that."

"Yes." She tried to sound sure of herself. She *was* sure of herself. "Anyway, the less you know, the better off you are."

"Don't start that nonsense," Terri said. "If you and I— and the animals—are in danger, I need to know why."

"It could be a hunting accident," Sam said even as she wondered why she'd make such a stupid remark. Self-denial? Overload? She didn't know. She did know she hadn't fooled Terri. The fact was that once more, someone had tried to kill her.

And instead they'd struck a helpless animal.

She took his reins. "Let's get him back," she said. "Later—"

"We can't go back the way we came," Terri said. "Look, I have a cell phone with me. I'm going to call Dan. He'll get my brothers out here."

"What if—"

"No one could have followed you after that ride," Terri said.

"I'm beginning to wonder whether there's *any* safe place."

Terri stared at her. "How many times have they attacked you?"

"Three. This makes four."

"Either you're very lucky, or they're not trying very hard," Terri said. She paused, then asked, "How much did you tell your mother the last time you talked to her?"

Sam jerked around. She'd always admired Terri's analytical mind. "Very little."

"Maybe they thought you would tell her, scare her into reappearing. Wasn't she in hiding until she heard your father died? Maybe someone wanted to use you to make her do something."

Why had she not thought of that? Had her fear been planted, cultivated, harvested?

Terri was working with the phone. "Blast," she said. "I'm not getting anything."

Another blast echoed through the aspens. The horses shied away.

Sam felt the shock of being hit, then pain.

Terri was wrong. This time they hadn't wanted to miss.

twenty-three

"There's a contract out on Samantha Carroll and her mother," Gray said urgently.

Nate had called after checking his cell phone and finding seven numbers there, four from Barker and three from his partner. Soon, he thought, to be his ex-partner. Especially after today.

"How much?"

"A quarter of a million dollars. Word on the street is it's to take them alive. However, once the buyer gets what he wants . . ."

"Information," Nate said.

"Looks like it. You were right. Merritta's wife must have taken something important when she left, and someone wants it back. I suspect that everything until now has been to frighten her into giving it up."

"Only murder could be that important," Nate said. "It's the only thing that makes sense after thirty years."

"And it wasn't Merritta. My contacts say word didn't get out until after Merritta died."

"Then someone else in the family? Someone who might be worried about what could surface after Merritta's death?"

"That leaves Victor. Or Anna. George. Rich. Even Rosa. A dozen more assorted relatives and associates."

"Or an outsider," Nate mused out loud. "Will you hunt down agents and BPD officers who worked the family? Maybe they would know who was close enough to the family to be involved in their activities thirty years ago."

"I'll do it on my own time," Gray said. "You should know that Barker is apoplectic. He's threatening to fire you."

"I'm on vacation," Nate said innocently.

"He knows about the attack on Samantha Carroll in Boston. You'd better get back here."

"I can't do that, particularly now. I don't trust Barker to take care of her."

"Then take her and get the hell out of there. You know how to hide. Of course, it'll mean the end of your career."

"The career was the means to the end," Nate said. "That's all. I'll talk to you later." He turned off the phone.

He had to find her. He had to tell her someone had been offered a fortune to take her.

Hoping against hope that he could reach her before a paid killer did, Nate knocked on the door of the sprawling ranch house that belonged to the family of Samantha's friend.

His gut twisted with apprehension.

A large, stocky man answered the door. He was dressed in jeans, a plaid shirt and very worn boots. His expression wasn't exactly welcoming.

"Yeah?"

Nate knew instinctively it wouldn't be wise to flash his badge. He suspected that this man would not be impressed.

"I'm looking for Samantha Carroll."

"Any particular reason?"

"She's a friend. That's why she told me about you."

The man studied him for a moment, then thrust out his hand. "I'm Dan Faulkner. You from Boston?"

"Yes," he said, thoroughly nonplussed by the welcome as well as the immediate assessment of his background.

"Terri told us Sam had gone there. Didn't know she'd brought someone back with her."

Nate tried not to look surprised. Sam again. This man talked about her with a familiarity that instantly sparked a flame of jealousy in him. "Have you seen her?"

"Sam? No. But Terri said she was going out to meet her. Took Sam's horse with her."

"I'm not sure it's safe," Nate said.

"She's a good rider."

"That's not what I meant."

Dan Faulkner stiffened. "What *do* you mean?"

"Did you know she was attacked several times in Boston?" He wanted to add that her mother was also missing, but he thought Sam might not forgive him for that. She'd made it clear she didn't want anyone to know. Not yet.

"Hell you say." Faulkner paused, then seemed to relax. "Well, she's back home now." Affection was in his voice, but nothing more.

"The people who attacked her have a long reach."

"Who did you say you were?"

It was time. "Nathan McLean. FBI." He took out his credentials.

"You said you were a friend of Sam's." Accusation tinged the large man's voice. He stepped back inside, and Nate knew he was going for a phone. Probably to call a buddy law enforcement officer.

"I am. She left a few hours ago, and I don't think she knows what kind of danger she might be in."

"You ride?"

"Not well."

"Can't get to where she usually goes on wheels," he said, eyeing him with something close to disdain.

"I'll manage," Nathan said. He'd ridden when a boy. His mother had wanted it for him, and he hadn't realized until years after she had died what she must have sacrificed to give that to him. His stomach knotted just as it always did when his memories, vivid and ageless, returned to that time. He'd lived with the color red and had felt the warm thickness of blood for all these years.

Those memories had kept him alive. The instincts aroused in those terrible minutes had guided him, or he had thought they had.

Until now. Now they were fading, becoming blurred.

He shook off the thought as he followed the other man to the stables. They were at the door when a horse, its mouth foaming, galloped in, reins dangling. Blood dripped from its hindquarters.

"It's Sam's horse," Dan said, moving quickly to the horse and inspecting the wound. "Gunshot," he said.

He moved quicker than Nate thought possible into a back room and returned with a rifle. "You got a firearm?"

Nate nodded.

Dan took the cell phone hooked to his belt and dialed a number. "Something's happened. Get over here. I think Terri and Sam might be in trouble."

Another shot hit a log just an inch from her head.

Sam had no doubt now. This was no mere threat. Someone wanted to kill her.

Shock had been an anesthesia for the first few moments, then the pain struck with the impact of a torch thrust into her thigh. Another shot rang out, and Terri rolled next to her, trying to shield Sam's body with her own.

No. She didn't want that. "Run," she said.

"You want to get me killed?" Terri replied with humor that stunned Sam as much as the bullet had.

"We need help."

"It's a sniper," Terri said. "I don't think he's going to let us go." Then she put a hand on Sam. "Can you move? There's a small ditch behind us. If we can roll into it . . ."

Sam nodded. The burn was spreading. She had to bite her lips to keep from screaming out loud as she willed herself to roll down a slight incline. A bullet spit up earth just inches from her.

She'd been terrified during the earlier incidents, but everything had happened so fast then—and stopped just as swiftly—that the fear hadn't been prolonged. Now her heart slammed against her rib cage. She could barely breathe. The terror was paralyzing.

She was being hunted. And because of her, so was Terri.

She heard the rustling in the woods. To the left. Then she heard another crack from another direction.

Two shooters.

She and Terri looked at each other and with a nod crawled—an inch at a time—several feet away until they were protected by a rotten log. More movement in the woods. She could hear it.

She wanted to lift her head. She wanted to see what was going on, but she knew better than that.

Another shot, a curse. She heard the sound of someone crashing through underbrush. No longer stealthily. They were moving away from them. More gunfire. Farther away.

A ruse? She didn't dare raise her head. She looked at her hand. It was trembling. Fear still pounded through her. She swore she would never, ever leave the revolver behind again.

But even if she had it, she doubted she could do any

good. Whoever was shooting was probably using a rifle. A revolver against a good rifle wasn't much of a match. Still, she wouldn't feel so helpless.

Her thigh burned. She touched her slacks and felt the warm, thick liquid congealing. How long had it been? Each second had stretched into minutes. It seemed like an eternity since the first shot had hit Jupiter.

The pressure of Terri's body next to hers relaxed slightly, but neither of them moved.

Then she heard shouts—Terri's name, and her own.

Dan Faulkner.

And McLean.

Terri audibly exhaled a breath as she moved.

"Over here," Sam called. The voice didn't sound like hers, she thought. Just as her body didn't feel like hers.

Dear God, but she hurt. "Terri?" she said.

"I'm okay," Terri said. "I think."

Through her own haze of pain, she saw that Terri, too, was bleeding.

Terri apparently saw her expression and followed her gaze to a stream of blood flowing down her shirt sleeve. She pulled it up. Blood poured from a ragged wound. She shook her head. "Just a rock, I think."

But guilt was as strong as pain. Sam was turning into a Jonah, a danger to anyone near her.

Then Dan was next to them, stooping beside his sister. A shadow loomed over her. She looked up.

McLean stood there, a gun in his hand. A heavy-looking weapon. Then he was next to her, his hands running over her body until he stopped at her thigh. "This is becoming a bad habit," he said, but his voice was rough, broken.

He took a pocket knife from his pocket, unfolded it and cut the cloth until he saw the wound. He examined it briefly. "It went in and out. Good." He muttered something else to himself, then glanced at Dan. "How is she?"

"A bad cut on her arm."

McLean turned back to Sam, cut a strip of material from her slacks and held it against the wound.

"Know a good doctor?"

"They need to go to the hospital," Dan said. He took out a cell phone and started to dial.

"No," McLean said.

Dan stared at him.

"You can take your sister, but I expect someone will be waiting for Sam there. I'm not going to chance it. I'll find a private doctor."

"Any doctor has to report a gunshot wound."

"I realize that," McLean said patiently, "but by then we'll be gone."

"I can't—"

"You can, unless you want her death on your conscience."

"Dan," Terri said, "there's Doc McIntyre."

McLean cast a quick glance at him.

"He's retired," Dan explained. "He also hates authority. He'll do it."

"I'll take Sam there. You take your sister to the hospital."

"One of my brothers will meet you at the ranch house. He'll make sure you aren't followed."

McLean nodded.

"You sure about this?" Dan asked. "The police chief is a friend. He'll look out for her."

McLean looked at him. "I don't think he can," he said. "Not for long. She needs to disappear."

Dan gave him a long searching glance. "Are you sure *you* can make her disappear?"

"I have the best shot."

"What about witness protection?"

"She's not a witness. And it's more and more difficult to hide people." He looked at Sam. "I don't think she wants to be hidden. It would mean giving up the gallery, her friends—"

"I won't do that," Sam said.

"Let's get them to help first."

Dan slid his arms under his sister and helped her up.

McLean leaned over Sam, put an arm under her shoulder. "It's going to hurt," he said. "Can you make it?"

She nodded. The pain was getting worse, and the amount of blood scared her. His pressure against the bandage had slowed the flow slightly.

When she moved, a small cry escaped. She knew then how Nick had felt days earlier. Still, she tried to rise on her own.

McLean shook his head. "Let me do it. Lean on me." He picked her up as though she weighed no more than a basket of feathers. Her arms closed around his neck, and for the first time since the shooting began, she felt safe. Still, a dozen questions reverberated in her head. How had the snipers found them? Who would know this valley? The woods? She would have sworn that no one had followed her.

The shooters were like ghosts—unseen and deadly.

It was an invasion she'd not expected. She'd been on her guard, yes, but she'd really believed that once she left Boston, she would be safe.

Would she ever be safe anywhere again?

"What happened to the people shooting at us?" she asked although she was feeling weak.

"Damned if I know," he said. "I heard a shot, then another from a different location. We found blood. No body. I think one shot at the other."

"It appears you have another protector," Dan said.

She couldn't comprehend it. None of it. She didn't even want to. Not now. She just wanted to lay her head back and rest. She wanted the pain to go away.

She wanted to erase the nightmare that had become her life.

Sam woke slowly. The room was small, bright. It was very clean but casual with old, comfortable furnishings. For a moment, she wanted to sink back into the feather bed she found herself in.

Memories intruded. Impressions. Flashbacks.

She was in a small cabin. She knew it belonged to Ed McIntyre, a retired doctor who'd been ousted by the local hospital for violating their rules once too often. She'd known him for years—as had Terri and Dan. He'd asked no questions, not even when he saw the gunshot wound. Instead he'd cleaned it and stitched it closed. He'd also given them a prescription for antibiotics.

McLean had sat next to her, held her hand. He'd been there when she'd gone to sleep.

When she asked about going home, he told her in stark terms about a contract.

A contract on her and her mother.

It seemed so impossible. Everything that had happened in the past few weeks was the stuff of the Twilight Zone.

And yet very real.

The one thing neither she nor McLean understood was who the second shooter was.

She suspected she would have died yesterday without his presence.

McLean was sprawled out in a chair beside her. His eyes were closed, his cheek dark with beard, lines etched deeper in his face. She wondered if he had been there all night.

She no longer cared about his agenda or why he was so single-mindedly trying to bring down the Merrittas. She would trust him with her life now, no matter what. She should have all along.

Her mother should know about the contract, but how

could Sam get word to her? Or did her mother already know?

She shifted, and that slight move woke McLean. He blinked, then his eyes flew wide open.

He leaned down and kissed her. So much tenderness in that gesture. So much caring.

She tried to equate that with the cool, deliberate man she'd first seen at the airport, then in her brother's hospital room. She had been struck then by a simmering energy, a barely contained impatience. But now she was struck by his gentleness.

She held out her hand to him and he took it, holding it tightly.

"We'll have to leave soon," he said.

She nodded. She no longer had any defiance in her. "My car?" she asked.

He grinned. "You mean that wreck? You sent me in circles, lady."

"Has Dan learned anything?" she asked. "Someone . . ."

"He called me. He and his brother combed the area after seeing to your friend. Two sets of footprints. Shell casings. No more."

"But how would they know where I was? I was so careful."

"People know you and Terri Faulkner were friends. Who else would you go to?"

"But our place. I never—"

"Would your mother know about it?"

Of course! She realized what had been staring her in the face: If her mother thought that Sam was in danger, she never would have left her alone.

"Mother," she said.

"What?"

"The second man out there was from my mother."

twenty-four

Nick paced his living room. He'd gone to the office, but he couldn't concentrate and had left early.

Where had Samantha gone?

He knew why she had fled two days ago. Hell, she'd lasted longer than he'd thought she would.

He was slowly getting used to the idea of having a sister. He wasn't sure he liked that idea. He'd never had to worry about anyone before. He didn't quite know how to go about it. Should he be protective? Or should he sit back and let her return to her own life?

That would be the best thing for both of them, but especially better for her. She shouldn't come within a million miles of this family. It consumed its young.

The phone rang. He hesitated before going to it. He hadn't left a number at the office, telling his secretary he didn't want to be disturbed.

He listened as his answering machine picked up. "Nick, it's Victor. I know you're there."

The bastard.

Still, he answered the phone. "Victor," he acknowledged.

"The will is to be read on Friday. The attorney wants

you to be there. Along with Samantha Carroll and her mother."

"She left. I'm not going to ask her to return. Not after what happened."

"What about the mother?"

"What *about* the mother?"

"I thought the girl might have said something to you about where she is."

"Nope. I didn't ask. I would have thought your people knew."

A hesitation on the phone. Then, "We need to know." There was an urgency in Victor's voice.

"Hell we do. The will can be read without all the parties there."

"But Tracy . . . your mother should be there."

Nick didn't dignify that with an answer. He was fully aware Victor could care less whether Tracy or Patsy or whoever she was attended the reading of the will.

"Tell me why you really want to know," Nick said.

"She appears to be missing."

"I would be missing, too, after what happened to her daughter."

"I told you before I didn't have anything to do with it."

"Why don't I believe you?"

"Have you considered the possibility that McLean might have tried to turn her against us?"

"I have."

"And . . . ?"

"I'm withholding judgment."

"You wouldn't if you knew the true story," Victor said.

"You've never told me why McLean's hell bent in sending us all to prison," Nick said.

"He's a fed."

"It goes deeper than that, and you know it," Nick said.

"Not over the phone. Meet me for lunch and I'll tell you."

"Outside. The small park." Nick knew Victor would realize where he meant.

"Noon."

"All right," Nick said, and hung up. Victor had been very careful, weighing each word. He obviously knew, as Nick did, that his phone was tapped.

"I told you before we had nothing to do with it."

Nick had made the accusation after the shooting on his doorstep. He'd immediately recognized that the shots were meant to threaten or warn rather than kill. Still, mistakes were possible, and he or Samantha could have been killed. He hadn't been surprised that Samantha had disappeared when she had gone back inside the house.

Victor had thought he would be dealing with a woman who could be cowed and intimidated. That assumption fit his general opinion of the gender. He should have learned from Anna, but he'd always underestimated her, too.

It just so happened—unfortunately for his uncle—that Samantha Carroll/Nicole Merritta was smarter and far more independent than he had ever imagined. She had not been seduced by thoughts of wealth as Victor had believed. In fact, the very thought of inheriting what she considered ill-gotten gains had seemed to affront her.

It was a notion Victor could not comprehend.

Now Nick had no idea what to do. He'd been disconcerted and worried when she'd left the town house. He'd extracted a statement from Victor that he'd not been responsible for the shooting or for Samantha's disappearance. Nick wasn't sure he believed him.

But he wanted her away from Boston. Away from the Merrittas. She appeared to be a catalyst. Whether it was for his family, McLean or someone else, she was pure trouble.

Yet he was drawn to her. Surprisingly, Samantha had begun to fill a void in his life, something no one else had been able to do. His father had tried on and off, but was never able to resist trying to twist him into his own image. Nick hadn't liked that image.

He checked his watch. He wanted to know why Victor was so intent on finding a woman who had been missing for more than thirty years. This time he would discover the truth.

The park was nearly empty except for a few nannies and a dog walker or two. A hot dog stand provided lunch.

His uncle seemed to have aged in the past few days. He was now head of the family, at least for the moment, but he didn't have the surface smoothness that his brother had, or the respect he would need. He'd been second banana too long.

And he was too tired. Nick saw it in his eyes.

Now was the time to ask questions. Some Nick had the answers to. Some he did not. But he had to know what Victor knew. He had to know what part Victor had played in what had happened thirty-four years ago.

But first he had to know about McLean. McLean had followed Samantha. That much was obvious. He'd defied his own bureau to do so.

How much harm could he do?

"You told me you would tell me why McLean is so persistent."

"All feds are persistent."

"Not like him."

Victor's mouth tightened. "You really want to know?"

"No, I'm asking you for the fun of it."

Victor hesitated, then sighed in surrender. "Your grandfather had his mother killed. She was a waitress in the restaurant he frequented, and she overheard a conversation she shouldn't have."

"McLean knows this?"

"Hell, he was with her when it happened." Victor muttered something about the gunmen should have killed the kid, too.

"He knew it was the Merrittas?"

"He knew. She'd apparently told him they were going away, that he had to be very careful of the Merrittas. The kid told the police. He even identified one of the shooters. But there was no other proof. Then he disappeared into the welfare system. We didn't know he was the McLean with the FBI until four years ago."

"Do his superiors know about it?"

"Hell, no. We didn't want that case reopened."

"How old was he?"

Victor shrugged. "Eight. Nine."

"And you didn't see fit to tell me?"

"Your father didn't . . . want you to know."

"It concerned me, Victor. McLean has nearly destroyed my business. If I had known why . . ."

"Do you think your sister knows?" Victor said slyly. "I understand he . . . stayed at her home part of the day yesterday. I wonder whether she would have done that if she'd known her grandfather killed his mother."

Nick swore.

"And my mother?" he asked again. "How did she escape the same fate?"

"Your father made some kind of bargain with her."

"Like he got me, and she took my sister? There had to be more, or he would have taken both of us."

"She took something with her," Victor said reluctantly.

"Something that could have hurt Pop."

"Yes."

"And others?"

Victor was silent.

"Tell me about my mother and why you told me she died all those years ago."

"She couldn't accept our life," Victor said. "She endangered us from the moment she arrived. Papa was afraid she would go to the feds. You were better off thinking she was dead."

"Along with the authorities?"

"Yes."

"From what I know of my grandfather, he wouldn't let go that easily. She must have taken something very important."

Victor was silent.

"What was it, Victor?"

"I don't know."

"Don't give me that. You know everything about the family."

"Not that."

"Okay," Nick said. "Tell me more about my mother."

"Didn't *she* tell you?"

"She? My sister? Yes. I heard her version. Now I want to hear yours."

Victor looked away. "She never fit in. She hated it here. And she was a sneak. She knew too much. Paul should have . . ." He stopped.

"Paul should have what?"

Victor gave him a weak smile. "He shouldn't have let her go. That's all."

"Did you like her?"

"No. She had nothing in common with your father. She didn't understand our life and never could. Paul never should have married her."

"But she tried, didn't she?" Nick said. "She played the piano and was proficient at art, and she was gentle. Pop loved her. Otherwise he wouldn't have defied his family by marrying her."

"Did she tell you that?" Victor said. "Well, she was wrong. Tracy complained from the day she arrived. She saw a meal ticket, that's all, and your father wanted her in bed. Her daughter is no better. Butting into business that doesn't concern her."

"Really?" Nick said. He was tiring of the game. He'd wanted to rattle his uncle into telling him what and how much he knew. He also wanted to know who, other than Victor, wanted Samantha out of the way.

"I asked you before whether you had anything to do with the attempts on Samantha's life. I want you to tell me again."

Victor was silent.

"I could come after you, Victor. You know I can."

"Okay, I ordered the attack at your home. I wanted to scare her. I wanted her out of Boston temporarily. If anything happens to her here, you know we'll be blamed. More investigations, more search warrants. We can't afford that."

"Why did Pop bring Sam here in the first place?"

"I don't know," Victor said. "Paul never mentioned her name until several weeks ago. He told me he'd found her. Found both of them. But I had no idea he'd sent for her."

"A shock to George's ambitions," Nick said dryly.

"Your father would never leave a sizeable part of his empire to a woman."

"Then why was she summoned?"

Victor shook his head. "He told us he wanted to talk to both her and Tracy. He might have been afraid Tracy would come after the estate. I don't know."

"She never divorced my father?"

"As far as I know."

Nick still struggled with the idea of having a live mother. God knew he had wished for one as a boy. No, he'd prayed for one. Nothing happened, though. He was just shipped off to another school. That was when he decided prayer was for normal people. Not for Merrittas.

"I don't want anything to happen to her," Nick said.

"Which one?"

"My sister *and* her mother. I want you to swear on that."

"Tracy deserted you. She deserted your father. It broke his heart."

Nick looked at him skeptically. "What heart?"

"He loved you. More than you'll ever know."

"Then why didn't he let me go?"

"He believed you were the only one who could continue to take the family into respectable businesses."

Nick smiled slowly. "That's what he said. But he never left the protection business, or the loan sharking, or the city contracts."

"We did the city a damn good job on those contracts."

"Yeah, at twice the price."

"We're positioned to go legit."

"Pop said that for the last ten years. It didn't happen."

"The other families wouldn't allow it. You can outsmart them."

"If I'm not dead first," Nick said wryly. "I'm happy as I am."

"You make a fraction of what you could."

"I don't crave power like Pop did. I saw what happened when you did."

"They're going to come after you, boy, whether or not you're in."

Nick was silent for a moment. He knew it was true. Too many people thought he was heir apparent. Maybe part of him had always known it, too. How could you derail destiny?

The family had been his destiny.

"There's no one else, Nick."

"George. And Anna."

"No one will obey a woman."

"Then George . . ."

"He's a fool."

"Pop sent him to law school. He intended—"

"He intended to convince you that the family was your responsibility. He thought you would realize George would lead us into disaster. He wants to get in the drug business."

"He can't do it without approval."

"Approval from whom? He would kill me in a second if he thought I stood in his way."

"And Samantha? What does she have to do with this?"

"Your father thought he would be able to control her, use her to get you back in the family."

"Is George behind the attempts on her life?"

"I don't know. I don't think so. Maury said not."

Maury was the closest thing to an "enforcer" the family had these days. He'd been completely loyal to Paul Merritta. And now that George has expectations, he would have gone to Maury if he wanted anything done.

"I don't want anything to happen to Samantha," Nick repeated.

"There's only one way to do that," Victor said.

The meaning was clear.

"Damn you," he said. "Damn my father."

"It's the family, Nick," Victor said. "It's always been the family."

"The family can go to hell." He turned to leave.

"Nick, bring her back for the memorial service, for the reading of the will."

"I thought you wanted her gone."

"Things have changed in the past two days."

"How?"

Victor shook his head. "We have to talk to the mother," he said. "We didn't think she would pull a disappearing act."

"Maybe you frightened her daughter a little too much."

"The bitch knows she has the upper hand. We can't touch her. But we do want to talk to her."

"You still haven't told me why."

"Someone else was involved in what she knows. That someone wants to make sure she will never talk about it."

"Ah. Finally the truth. You frightened the daughter to get to the mother."

"No one wanted the girl hurt. She's a Merritta."

"What about me? The car crash could have killed me. I won't even talk about the gunshot."

Victor shrugged. "He would have missed. It was unfortunate you decided to play hero."

"Go to hell."

"That was a warning. But now someone wants to kill both of them. The mother and daughter. You're the only one who can stop it."

"Damn it, Victor, stop trying to play me. You're not good at it. You keep lying. You can't even keep the lies straight."

"When Tracy left, she took something valuable with her, something that can ruin a very important figure in this state."

"Why all the interest now?"

"That figure will soon be nationally known. He can't afford loose ends."

"Who?"

"I can't tell you. Not as long as you're outside the family."

Nick stared at him for a long moment. "But I'm not outside the family."

twenty-five

"He's our connection," Sam said. "Whoever is out there is the connection to my mother."

"If you're right," Nathan said, "he's keeping out of sight."

"Why?"

"Damned if I know." He was already fuming at the fact that he'd been a few moments too late yet again. Someone else did what he should have done. Protect Sam.

Some FBI agent he was.

His personal involvement with Sam should not have happened. It had obviously dulled his instincts. How could he have been so careless to let her go alone as she had this morning? Yet she wasn't under arrest. He'd had no reason to detain her.

But it was obvious that she didn't trust him. She'd slept with him. She obviously felt something for him. But she didn't trust him.

That was something that needed to be remedied. Now.

His fingers interlocked with hers. "I'm sorry I wasn't there."

She gave him a wry grin. "That was my doing. Not yours."

"I'm a cop. I should have anticipated—"

"I wanted to see my friend alone. I thought I had taken precautions."

"You took some damn good ones, but don't do it again. Okay?"

"How could they have found me?"

"Research. Who works for your gallery. Who your friends are. Wouldn't take a professional long. A question at the diner, a friendly observation. A global positioning unit on the car."

"But I changed cars."

"Did you take anything from one car to another?"

"My purse."

He was silent.

"There was no way to get something inside my purse. It was in the house, then I left it in the trunk when I met Terri."

"Someone might have been following Terri," he said.

She closed her eyes. How many more people were going to be hurt?

"Where is my purse now?"

"Dan called. He took the car back to the garage. He's bringing your purse and gun here, once he's sure no one's tracking him."

"What do I do now?"

"What do *we* do now," he corrected.

"Because it's your job?"

"I doubt I'll have it long," he said, surprised suddenly at how little he cared. He had made the FBI the focus of his life for years, had taken night courses while working in a law office as a paralegal to meet FBI qualifications. He'd gone into it for the wrong reasons, but nonetheless it had taken over his life. He was FBI to the core. Or had been.

But now he'd found something more important.

"Why?"

"I've been ordered off the case. And away from you."

"Why?"

"I'm too personally involved, I was told," he said.

"Are you?" she asked bluntly.

"It's too convenient," he said. "Gray and I have been working on the Merrittas for four years. There have been other cases, but we were the most knowledgeable. It doesn't make sense that all of a sudden, we're taken off it."

"Are you saying someone in the FBI . . . ?"

"I don't know, Samantha. I don't like to think that. But I do know that they've had an informer inside the family for years. I'm not sure that it doesn't go two ways."

"Sam," she corrected.

His lips cracked into a smile. He was finally being admitted into her world. "You don't look like a Sam."

"I hope not," she said with the smallest shadow of a smile.

"Still, I like it."

The door opened and Dr. McIntyre entered. "Ah, you're awake."

She nodded, moved and winced with pain.

The doctor leaned over, checked the bloody bandage, then unwrapped it and inspected the wound. "It's draining well." He busied himself replacing the bandage.

"Can she leave?" Nate said.

"If she takes the antibiotics and you keep the wound clean."

Nate nodded.

"Where are you going?"

"South," he said shortly.

"Which probably means north," McIntyre said.

"You could get in trouble for this."

"I've always been in trouble," the doctor said.

"Thank you," Sam said.

"I liked your father," McIntyre said.

Nate saw tears gathered in the corners of her eyes. She hadn't cried when he knew she was in great pain. She hadn't wrung her hands over what had happened or complained, as she had every right to do, about his competence as an agent.

But she had shed tears over a father who had died two years ago.

Not Paul Merritta.

His hand tightened on hers. She must feel that everything she knew, thought, believed was being ripped away from her.

His mind raced. He had to get them the hell away from here and keep them moving until he and Gray could figure out who in the hell had put out a contract and why.

It obviously had something to do with her mother and the "insurance" he and Gray had speculated about.

But her mother was spooked now, too—spooked enough to disappear but not spooked enough to leave her daughter unprotected.

So bad guys were following them. And a good guy was not far behind.

McIntyre finished wrapping the bandage.

Nate squeezed her hand. "We need to go."

She nodded. No questions this time. Not even any arguments.

"I'm sorry," she said. "I shouldn't have flattened your tire."

"Nope," he agreed. "You shouldn't have. I haven't changed a tire in years. Besides," he added, "it was embarrassing, particularly driving down the road on that little tire. Thank God the flat only needed a plug."

She gave him a faint grin. "I planned it that way. I could have ripped—"

He gave her a wry look. "I didn't know you had destructive tendencies."

Her eyes brightened. "I won't do it again. I don't think."

"Damn right, you won't."

Her hair was mussed, her face devoid of makeup, but he didn't know when he'd been so attracted to a woman. To what she was, and to who she was.

It was all he could do to make himself behave. He wanted to lean down and kiss her, but now was not the time. The bad guys would know by now that she'd not gone to the hospital and would be looking for someone like McIntyre.

He glanced at the doctor. "Can you take a little vacation yourself?"

McIntyre seemed surprised, then nodded. "I have a little fishing shack."

"Anyone know about it?"

"A few people, but they don't talk much to strangers."

"Have a gun?"

"Yep. And I know how to use it. I was in Korea. That's why I liked Dave Carroll so much. He understood."

Nate smiled. "How much do you know about him?"

"Only that he was in some kind of special services. Seals, Rangers. He never said. But I knew he had special training."

"He never said where he served?"

McIntyre looked at Sam, who nodded. "Vietnam for sure," he said. "Not that he talked much about it. Just a few things slipped now and then."

Nate knew he was wasting too much time, but David Carroll was one of the keys to this puzzle. He came from nowhere. He settled in a small town as a struggling owner of a small art gallery. It might make sense if he had a past.

Had Carroll given up everything for Sam's mother? If her mother was anything like Sam, Nate understood.

Satisfied with McIntyre's answers, he helped Sam sit up. She wore the shirt she'd worn riding. McIntyre had washed what was left of her slacks. They were stained and cut.

She looked down at them.

"We'll buy some new clothes," Nate said. "Let's get going."

Dr. Mac gave her a cane. Sam hadn't thought she would need one, but when she tried to stand, pain ripped through her. She accepted the cane gratefully.

She thanked him and hoped with all her heart she hadn't put him in danger as she had Terri.

She took the purse that Dan had brought from her car, making sure the gun was inside. Then she left with Nathan.

He had his rental car. While she watched, he examined every part of it. He crawled underneath, checked the trunk and the engine area.

She only hoped that their unexpected savior had thrown whoever the killer was off stride. There was no question, Nate said, that the stalker had been injured. Was he the only one? Would someone else come after them?

"Gray is trying to find out who's behind the contract," Nate said.

A contract.

Such a cold, objective word to describe a violent act. A legal word used to commission an illegal act.

Who? Why?

"Do you think it's someone in the family?" she asked.

"I don't know. But if I had to guess, no."

"Why?"

"The suspicion would go straight to them. They can't afford that. Not now."

"Why?"

"The other families would sense a weakness. While the Merrittas were tied up in an investigation, their rivals could take over the protection part of the business. City contracts are another big part of their activity. If they're under a microscope, they will likely lose them all."

He drove onto a secondary road, and she saw the alertness in him, the way his gaze never stopped moving from the road in front to the rearview mirror. "The only thing I can figure is that whatever your mother knows, or has, involves a third party. That's why we need to get to her."

"And Nick?"

She watched him hesitate, then carefully chose his words. "I've been convinced for years that he was involved in his father's business. But I saw his face in the hospital. He didn't like what happened. He hadn't expected it."

"I should . . . call him. Maybe he's in danger, too."

"Believe me, Nicholas Merritt can take care of himself."

She looked over at him. His jaw was set.

"Why do you distrust him so?"

He turned his gaze from the road. "Because he says one thing and does something else. He keeps saying he wants out, but he used his father's money to start the business. He claims he has nothing to do with the family, but he's met with his father several times a week in the past year."

"Maybe because he knew his father was ill."

"Merritta himself didn't know until two months ago."

She stared at him.

"We tapped his phones," he said unapologetically. "We had court orders."

"Then he knew about them."

"I'm sure he did. He kept changing cell phones, though.

He may not have realized we found most — if not all — of them."

"How much can you track?"

"If we have your number, we can get the number you're calling almost immediately. The location takes more time. We tapped Tommy's calls to your father when he found you."

"So if I called my mother . . ."

"If she stayed on long enough, sophisticated equipment could find her, right down to the street address."

"How many people have that kind of equipment?"

"More than you would like to know."

"Do you think Nick knows what my mother . . . might have?"

"I don't know."

"I want to talk to him."

"I'll arrange it so it will be safe."

She nodded. She was going to do it whether he helped her or not. A public telephone someplace. It didn't matter. She had to let him know that violence had followed her. She wanted to hear his response. She wanted to believe him.

"Nick seems to think your . . . diligence goes deeper than your job," she probed.

He was quiet for several moments, but the watchfulness never lessened. She felt wariness in him. Tension. "Your grandfather killed my mother," he said.

The words were another body blow, more painful than the gunshot wound.

She looked at his hands. The knuckles were white where he clutched the steering wheel.

"But why?"

"She was a waitress in a restaurant he and some of his people frequented. He was in a private room when she brought some food. They were talking about assassinating a public official. She dropped a dish and fled."

His voice was emotionless, as if it was a story he'd recited too many times. "She came to the school to pick me up. She was going to take me to a friend's home in Pennsylvania. They found us just as we were exiting the school, and a gunman in a car sprayed bullets at us. She covered me with her body. I watched her bleed to death."

"How did you know who . . . ?" She wanted to believe there was some mistake, that he hadn't really known.

"She told me as we left the school. She said Mr. Merritta was very angry. I knew who he was. I sometimes met her at the restaurant. He was there most days."

"And then?"

"I was sent to foster homes."

"How old were you?"

"Eight," he replied, a muscle flexing in his cheek.

"She had no family?"

"No. My father was killed in Vietnam. At least she said he was. I'm not sure if he was or not, or whether he was just someone who left when she got pregnant. But she didn't give me away. She tried her best to care for me."

Sam had had her own horrors in the past few days, but nothing like this. An eight-year-old boy watching his mother get shot? An eight-year-old boy lying in his mother's blood as she died? She swallowed back the cry rising in her throat, blinked away the tears. "Does Nick know?"

"I don't know," he said.

"Did Paul Merritta?"

He shook his head. "I don't know whether they ever associated an inconvenient waitress with me. She probably wasn't important enough to remember." His words were tinged with bitterness.

"Does your partner know?"

"No. Neither does the Bureau, or I would never have been allowed near the Merrittas."

She turned her gaze away from him, from his striking face, his clear green eyes that probably too often saw the bloody scene repeated over and over. Still, she cherished the trust he'd just handed her.

"I'm sorry."

"Don't be. You had nothing to do with it."

"I'm sorry for that boy."

"That boy grew up."

"But he still feels the pain."

"It faded."

"But the outrage never has."

"No," he said.

"You said you could lose your job."

"Possibly. I'm disobeying orders in a big way."

She angled herself in the seat so she could see him. "Because of me?"

"Because of you," he agreed. "For the first time since I was eight, something else is more important."

She saw a muscle move in his neck, the bunching of muscles in his jaw. She believed him.

He had never lied to her. He hadn't told her the full truth, but he'd never lied. There was a strength, an integrity in him that had shone through the hard facade, his distaste for the Merrittas. They had been there when he helped her save Nick's life, but she'd been assaulted by so many emotions, so many questions, so many possibilities, that she hadn't really believed in them.

"What's the plan?"

"Get you out of here," he said. "Then try to find out who put out the contract. Gray is working on that, and I have some people I can call."

"And find my mother."

"Yes."

"How?"

"Keep trying her cell phone. Then, let whoever is helping her find us."

"If we lost the . . . bad guy, wouldn't we have lost the other, too?"

"Yep. But your protector, whoever he is, has more information about you. Think about it, Samantha. Where might your mother expect you to go?"

The only place that came to mind was the cabin. But she had been there, and her mother was gone.

Still . . .

Sam had sworn she would never tell anyone about it.

Did she trust him or didn't she? And if she didn't, what in the hell was she doing here?

"There's a cabin," she said. "No one knows about it. My mother was staying there when I was in Boston, but she came back to Steamboat for some reason."

"No one knows about it? Not even your friend Terri?"

"No," she said. "Dad always said it would be our special place if no one knew about it. I never suspected there was any other reason."

"And now you do?"

"Of course," she said. "It was meant as a place where we could hide if need be."

"So he knew?"

"I've come to accept that," she said softly.

"His history didn't start until he married your mother," he said carefully.

"He was in Vietnam," Sam said. "I know that."

"Why do you think that?"

"Just odd comments. We would be watching a movie and he would shake his head occasionally as if something was wrong. Things like that."

"Will you tell me where this cabin is?"

"Sixty miles north of here. It's beside a stream. There's two exit roads." She'd been thinking about it a lot lately, about the way it was positioned near two roads going in two different directions.

He turned and looked at her.

"Take the next exit," she said.

She'd made her choice. She only hoped it was the right one.

twenty-six

Nicholas Merritt drove through Steamboat Springs. He'd been here once before and had liked it.

Unlike some Colorado ski towns, it was unpretentious. It still had the feel of a small town where people knew each other.

He passed a restaurant he'd visited, then the condominium where he'd stayed. He immediately saw Western Wonders.

He knew he must have passed it five years ago when he'd been here on a skiing trip. But he didn't remember seeing it.

It was late. He wondered whether it would still be open. He found a parking place and went inside. He scoured the place with his gaze, noting a pretty woman with hair the color of gold and memorable blue eyes. A bandage was wrapped around her arm. His gut twisted as he wondered if she was yet another casualty of his family. He tried not to show it. "Hi."

"Hello," she said in a cool voice, her eyes widening at seeing him.

"Your shop looked interesting," he said inanely.

"It's not mine," she said. "I'm the bookkeeper." She rose, her gaze meeting his directly. "Can I help you?"

He found himself off balance. He'd heard about cornflower blue eyes but had never seen them before. Now he had. "You must be Terri."

She nodded, her eyes wary.

"I'm Nick," he said.

"Samantha's brother," she said.

"So I'm told."

Her face reddened with a flush. "She's not here."

"Can you tell me where she is?"

"No." The flush grew deeper. "I mean that I don't know," she said.

"When did you see her last?"

"Yesterday."

"Was she all right?"

"No. Someone shot at us when we were riding. She was hit."

The twist in his gut knotted and something like fear stuck in his throat. For the first time in his life, he couldn't seem to form words. "How bad?" he finally asked, his voice strained.

"Shot in the thigh."

He inhaled sharply, forcing the air out slowly, and tried again. "She's alive," he stated.

"Yes." Another statement, made in an equally even tone. Terri leaned forward. "Hey," she said. "She's okay."

He looked at her arm.

"She went to the hospital?"

"No, to a private doctor."

"Then where is she?" he asked, his heart thumping against his rib cage.

"She got medical attention. She's fine. Truly, she is." Then she gave him an abashed smile that was appealing. "So is my horse. He was grazed in the hind quarter."

He forced a smile, then averted his gaze. Somehow

Terri's mention of the horse was the last straw. He'd always known what his family was capable of, and even guilty of. Yet never had it struck him as it did now—like a boulder falling squarely on his head without granting him the mercy of unconsciousness. Innocent women and helpless animals.

"You shouldn't be here," he said, unable to look at her.

"Where else would I be? I don't have anything to do with Boston."

"Are you the only person here?"

"There's Helen Peevy. I told her to go home."

"But you stayed. Gutsy lady."

"It's safe enough. Sam had a panic button installed. One push and the whole police department will be here."

"I'm properly warned," he said.

She relaxed and gave him a smile. "She likes you, you know. She's happy to have a brother."

"I'm trouble," he said. "Just like the rest of the family."

"Then why did you come?"

"I was afraid that something would happen. I really need to reach her, Miss Faulkner."

"I can't help you. I wouldn't, even if I could. And I can't."

He forced his gaze from her. She was one of the most attractive women he'd seen recently, the type he liked. Pretty, smart, loyal. But he'd decided long ago not to get involved with that kind of woman. She was definitely not a one-night stand, and she was Samantha's friend.

It was a long time since such distinctions had been important. His business partner was the only person he really cared about or respected. Until Sam.

He took a long breath.

"Can you get a message to her?"

"No."

He raked his hand through his hair in frustration. "Tell me what happened yesterday."

"We were riding. Someone fired at her, hit the horse she was riding. We thought it might be a hunter," she said. "Maybe for a moment," she added with a trace of humor. "But it's not hunting season. At least the legal hunting season."

He couldn't smile back. "And . . . ?"

"Someone kept firing. Obviously aiming for us."

He waited, his blood running cold at the image of two women being hunted.

"My brother and . . . an FBI agent appeared. There was someone else, someone we didn't see, who chased the sniper off. Both disappeared, but we think the sniper was wounded. There was blood." She paused, those blue eyes searching his face.

"Where was Samantha hit?"

"Her leg. My brother said it was a flesh wound. It didn't hit the bone."

"Thank God for that." He felt as if he could breathe again. He hadn't realized how much he had come to care about Sam.

Then his mind turned to the FBI agent. "Was the agent named McLean?"

"Yes." Her gaze hadn't left his face. He wondered how much she knew about his background . . . and McLean's.

"And she's with him now?"

She nodded.

He wondered whether his face was as frozen as it felt. Ever since he heard about McLean's mother, he'd worried about his sister. How far would McLean go to get his revenge, or his idea of justice?

"And you have no idea who chased away the sniper?" he finally asked.

"As I said, he just disappeared." She paused, then asked, "It wasn't you?"

"No." He wished it had been when he saw the light disappear from her face.

"Then it must have been someone Patsy sent. Sam believes that."

Patsy. His mother. He didn't want to talk about Patsy Carroll. It was too late for that. But he did want to continue talking to Terri Faulkner. And he wanted to know more about Sam. And McLean. "Will you have supper with me?"

"My brother is going to pick me up," she said.

"I'll take you home afterward," he offered.

"My brothers might well end up eating at the next table," she said. "They are skittish after what happened."

"I'm glad they are," he said. He told himself he wanted to take her to supper only to learn more. But another voice in his head chided him for lying to himself. He needed her at the moment. Someone who didn't want anything from him. And perhaps he would get to know more about Sam.

And her mother.

He had to admit in the past few days to a curiosity. He didn't want it. No matter the circumstance, she had chosen to abandon him. But she'd also evoked strong loyalty from Sam and even from the husband she'd betrayed and left.

"Okay," she said. "But I have to make a phone call." She paused. "Where will we be going?"

"Your choice."

"There's a good restaurant down the block." She seemed to be holding her breath.

"Sounds good to me."

"Give me a few moments."

She disappeared into the back, and a cat wandered out. A calico. It eyed him with haughty dignity as if she belonged and he didn't.

He smiled. He'd often thought about getting a dog, but it just didn't work with his lifestyle. He traveled overseas too frequently, and spent long days at the office when in Boston. He'd never had a pet. As a boy, he'd longed for one. But he'd been in military schools.

Terri emerged from the back room. He'd come here to warn Samantha but he knew—reluctantly—she was probably in good hands. If McLean didn't let the past get in the way.

She's an adult. She can take care of herself.

He kept telling himself that.

Still, he wanted to find her. Maybe Terri Faulkner *could* help *him*.

Terri turned the OPEN sign on the door to CLOSED.

"Ready," she said.

She didn't say anything else and he didn't ask. He was grateful to have gotten as far as he had.

He touched her arm lightly as they left the gallery and she turned to lock it, then they walked down the street. Several people stopped to speak to her, and she introduced him as a friend from the East.

She had an easy, friendly manner and a quirky sense of humor. He enjoyed being with her more than he should have. He was used to escorting attractive ladies, most of whom were businesswomen climbing the corporate ladder. Sam had told him about Terri, said she was a teacher.

He'd never dated a teacher before.

This wasn't a date, he told himself. He just wanted information.

His mind went to McLean, who'd watched his mother die in the streets, according to Victor. No wonder he was after the Merrittas. Nick wasn't sure he would have had that kind of patience to pursue his enemies within the boundaries of the law.

It was early enough that they were quickly seated. The restaurant was "Old West rustic" with candles on the table. He leaned back and studied his companion. She wore a simple pink blouse and jeans that were just tight enough.

"What's good?"

"Steaks," she said. "Especially if you're hungry."

"I'm hungry," he said.

"Did you fly into Denver?"

He nodded. "Then took a commuter here."

"How long do you plan to stay?"

"I don't know," he replied, and truly didn't. He had planned to come, offer his protection to both Sam and her mother, then return to Boston and finish his business. His and Pop's.

Nate didn't like driving up the driveway of the cabin without anyone watching his back.

He noticed that Sam was tense, too, and well she should be after the past week. She'd taken one of the pills McIntyre had given her for pain, but it hadn't relaxed her.

"You're sure no one knows about this place?"

"I'm not sure of anything any longer," she said, "but the title is in someone else's name. So are the taxes."

"Your mother was here."

"My mother would have been very careful," she said. "She would have warned me in some way if she thought this place was compromised."

He raised an eyebrow. "Compromised?"

"I read books," she said defensively.

He parked the car. "You have the revolver with you?"

"Yes."

"You know how to use it?"

"Yes."

"*Will* you use it?"

"Yes."

He believed her. There was a sureness in her voice. Even a confidence. She was angry now, and the anger had conquered uncertainty.

"Stay here," he said, "and get in the driver's seat. If you see anything, anything at all, drive off. Contact Gray, my partner."

She nodded.

"Keys to the cabin?"

"There's one in the birdhouse," she said.

He gave her a disgusted look.

"It's better than a doormat," she said.

He took his own gun from the holster attached to his belt and got out. He waited until she moved over, then said, "When you leave, keep the car keys with you."

He didn't wait this time to see whether she understood. His gaze searching for anything out of place, he approached the birdhouse and stuck his free hand inside, not entirely sure what he would find. Thankfully, it was only a key.

He strode to the cabin, paused with the .45 pistol still in his hand and opened the door. He went through each room, one at a time, then stood at the door and motioned her inside. She left the car, using the cane to support her leg, and stepped inside.

She was wearing oversized jeans to accommodate the bandage on her thigh, and a shirt, one of the several pieces of clothing he'd purchased at a store along the way. Even in the loose clothes and with her limp, she looked appealing to him. He watched her look around and wondered what she was thinking. Her gaze rested on an overstuffed burgundy chair and a rocker next to the fireplace. Ashes were still in the fireplace.

He walked over to her and took her in his arms. She relaxed against him, and his arms tightened around her. He felt her heart beating, smelled soap and a subtle scent of roses, and relished the feel of her body against his.

"I need to get you in bed," he said, "and see to those bandages."

"Let me look around first," she replied. "I want to make sure I didn't miss anything. She might have left a clue as to where she went."

She limped through the house, pulling open every drawer. He followed, watching as frustration and then disappointment clouded her face.

She returned and plopped down in her mother's chair. "Nothing."

"We'll stay here tonight. Tomorrow I'll get you a phone."

She longingly looked at the one sitting on a table. "Do you think it's safe to try to call Mom's cell phone from here? This one's listed in the name of a corporation," she said. "The bill is paid by that same corporation."

"How?"

"I'm not exactly sure. My mother takes care of it."

"And you never wondered about that?"

"Not until recently. I knew how much my father valued privacy. He always called this his Shangri-la. I didn't know about the financing and utility bills until last year. Mother inherited everything, of course, and she never mentioned how bills were paid. I asked her whether we should keep the phone and power on since we were here so little now, and she said it was all taken care of. Then one day a few months ago, she told me that if anything happened to her, she wanted me to know about the cabin, that everything concerning the cabin was paid by a corporation."

He was quickly reassessing his opinion of her mother. His first opinion had been based on a rather low opinion of anyone who would marry a Merritta. The second on allowing someone to die in her place. The third on abandoning a child.

But there was no mistaking Sam's love for her mother, and he doubted she would love an opportunist.

Patsy Carroll was a woman who lived with fear, with the threat of being discovered, of having to go into hiding again. Yet she had raised an independent daughter, created a sound business, gained the respect of the entire community.

She was also damn good at hiding.

And taking care of her daughter. The mysterious paladin who'd chased off the sniper proved that.

He wanted to be that paladin, that figure of literature who was a paragon of chivalry. Stupid thought, he scolded himself. He felt more like Don Quixote, who tilted at windmills.

He watched as she sagged farther into the chair.

"Another pill?" he asked.

She looked out the shaded windows. The last remnants of sun were dragging away shadows. Not long before night. "No. It dulls my senses."

"Not a bad thing at the moment."

"No," she agreed. "You didn't answer me about whether I can use the phone."

"Did you ever call your mother on this phone?"

"No. I always called her cell phone."

"Do you think she might have called you from this phone?"

"No."

He paced the floor. "It's probably safe, but I wouldn't guarantee it. I don't know if it's the Merrittas who are behind this, but it's obvious whoever is responsible has a lot of power and resources. I wouldn't take anything for granted."

"*You* have a cell phone. That should be safe."

"It's the Bureau's telephone," he said. "I would trust that less than your own."

"Surely . . ." She suddenly stopped, and her gaze met his.

He knew she remembered what he'd said earlier.

"Tomorrow then," she said. "Tomorrow we'll try to call from a pay phone. Will that be okay?"

"Yes," he said gently, admiring her for not arguing out of stubbornness or just to prove she was independent, as some people would do. "If you won't go to bed, will you eat something?"

Her eyes lit up, and he realized they hadn't eaten anything for nearly ten hours. She hadn't complained once.

"Mom was here a few days ago. There's probably bread in the fridge. Milk. There's always a bunch of canned stuff," she said. "And coffee."

"I think coffee is the last thing you need."

"You might need some," she said with an attempt at a smile.

"Good point." He turned toward the kitchen and opened the refrigerator. Several beers were stuck way in the back. A half gallon container of milk that was almost full. Half of a roasted chicken. Some fruit. Bacon. Eggs. Cheese. Butter. Basics.

He didn't dare try the chicken. He looked back at her, gratified that the kitchen wasn't separated by walls from the rest of the house. He wasn't going to let her out of his sight this time.

"Toasted cheese sandwich?" he asked.

She smiled. "The ultimate comfort food. Sounds good."

He made several, then poured each a glass of milk.

"Thank you," she said as he handed her a plate and her glass.

"You're welcome."

"I'm sorry about yesterday."

"I'd almost forgotten how to change a tire."

She gave him a quick smile. It trembled slightly but it was still a smile. "I'm glad I could help hone your skills."

"Nice move," he said, "but don't do it again."

"No. I've learned my lesson. I didn't think they could find me so quickly. I took a roundabout route back."

"They—whoever they are—know Steamboat is your home. It's the first place they would come."

"I thought the trouble was in Boston, that when I left . . ." She stopped. "It was naive, I know, and I'm not usually naive. I think I was hoping life would—could—go back to normal. I wanted to believe it."

"I know," he said softly.

They finished their food in silence.

She curled her feet under her. "Do you think we can have a fire?"

He thought about it. Hell, there was no way to really hide the car, so what difference would a fire make?

He built a fire with logs stacked by the hearth. He sat on the floor next to her as a small blaze caught, then finally flared. Neither of them said anything as it filled the darkening room with a warm glow.

He felt her hand on his shoulder. He didn't move. He just liked the feel of it, as if it belonged there. As if they were simply two people who took pleasure in being together. He reminded himself it wasn't pleasure, but his duty . . . her safety.

Life and death.

He reached out and took her hand in his.

Silence wrapped around them. A companionable silence that needed no words, no justifications. The only light was the fire, the only movement shadows.

Heat from the fire touched them. Or maybe it was just the combustion he always felt with her. He remembered the hours they'd spent together at her house in every agonizing detail. He wanted her, but she'd taken a bad wound.

But if they stayed like this . . .

He turned around and cupped the back of her neck, urging her to lean over, and kissed her lightly, intending nothing more than that. But it quickly became something more. Something deeper. More intense. The flicker of flames threw shadows around the room and brightened the gloom of dusk. The warmth embraced them.

He felt his body tense, react. But she was in no shape to go any further. Not now.

And he couldn't afford to be distracted.

He eased away from her, holding the kiss until distance separated them. "To bed with you," he said.

He stood, leaned down and picked her up. Her arms wrapped around his neck and she rested her head against his shoulder. That simple act of trust undid him. He knew at that moment that he loved her, that he would do anything to keep her safe. Lie. Steal. Cheat. He knew how David Carroll must have felt when he started an entirely new life with the woman he loved.

Had Carroll been as scarred as Nate was? As haunted by memories? Had he found redemption in love?

He lowered her to the bed and turned on the bedside light. She snuggled under a sheet but winced when she moved. Her cheeks appeared a little too red. Probably from the fire, but it worried him. He leaned down and feathered a light kiss on her cheek, then went into the other room and took bottles of pills from her purse, one of an antibiotic and another of a painkiller.

Her eyes were sleepy as she obediently took the pills. "Thank you."

"You're very welcome."

"I do trust you," she said.

"I know."

She closed her eyes.

He turned off the light and settled in the chair near her. It was enough, for the moment, to just be next to her.

twenty-seven

Nate wasn't sure how long he'd watched her when he felt a tingling along his back.

He stood.

She turned toward him, and he wondered whether it was due to his sudden movement, or did she sense something as he did? Her eyes opened.

"Hi," she said in a lazy, very sexy voice.

"Hi," he replied, and put his hand on her shoulder. "Stay put, Sam. I'm just going to take a look around. Do you have a flashlight?"

"There's one in the top drawer of the cabinet closest to the fridge." She sat up. "Did you hear something?"

"Nope. Just an overabundance of caution."

He hoped that was it. That the sudden apprehension was nothing more than realizing he should make a sweep of the area.

He found the flashlight immediately, then went to the door. "Swear you won't move from this spot," he said over his shoulder.

"I won't move from this spot," she agreed with a smile that slammed his heart.

He took his weapon from its holster and went outside.

Smoke twisted upward from the chimney against a dark sky. Heavy clouds blocked out the moon, obscuring the mountain peak behind him. He stopped, listened.

A wind had started blowing. He heard rustling not far away and couldn't tell whether it was from the wind or not. But he'd heard no car, nor did he see one now.

Instinct and years of training told him someone was out here.

He moved into the shadows, released the safety on the .45 and froze, listening for any sound that would indicate an intruder.

An owl hooted. He thought he saw something move among the trees.

He slipped around the side of the cabin, knowing he must have been visible when he'd left the front door. He swore. The back door was locked from the inside. He'd very carefully made sure of that, just as he'd made sure every window was closed and locked.

Could the form he thought he saw have been an animal? He'd made too many mistakes already to take it for granted.

He balanced the flashlight in his left hand, while the pistol remained in his right. He stepped back to the corner of the cabin, letting it shield him. He wanted the intruder—if there was one—to think he was circling the cabin. Instead he stepped out and flashed the light toward where he thought he had seen someone. Nothing. He swept the area. Waist height, then over the ground.

A sudden movement.

"Stop, or I'll shoot," he said.

Then there was nothing, only an unnatural stillness.

He swept the area again, wondering whether to investigate the area or stay near Sam.

It could be a diversion, a ploy to get him away from Sam.

The best spot was inside. He sprinted to the porch and

took the steps two at a time and then was inside, slamming the door behind him.

Sam was standing, her own gun in her hand. She must have heard his shout. She'd moved to the side and behind the door. She didn't look sleepy any longer.

The room was dark except for the embers glowing in the fireplace, but he saw her eyes were wide, her face tense.

"What—?"

"I thought I saw someone out there."

"You're not sure?" She stepped toward him.

"The wind's blowing," he said. "I heard rustling that could have been trees. Do you get many animal visitors?"

"All the time," she said. "There's deer. Coyotes."

"That's probably all it was," he said as he turned the lock in the door.

She didn't believe him.

Neither did he.

A knock sounded at the door. A whine.

He used a finger to direct her back against the wall again.

A heavy knock again.

He went to the window and peered out.

A man stood there, a rifle in his hands, a dog at his side.

The bad guys wouldn't knock, Nate thought. They would lie in wait, or barge on through. Not knock politely.

He heard a noise behind him.

Sam was limping toward him, her weapon in her hand, looking like a slightly battered avenging angel.

"Who?" She mouthed the word.

The knock came again. Not impatient, but determined. Nate debated with himself. God knew he'd made enough mistakes since he'd met Samantha.

He looked outside again. He didn't see anyone other than the man and dog.

Even with a gun in his hand, he didn't like the idea of

the dog out there. Nate knew the dog could lunge at the door, distract him.

He opened the door slightly. "Put the gun down on the ground and tie the dog to the railing."

The man nodded, went down the steps and lay down the shotgun, then whispered something to the dog. He returned to the porch and the dog stayed at the bottom of the stairs. "I don't have a leash with me, and he's a good guard dog. He'll let us know if anyone comes."

Nate opened the door wide enough for the man to step in, then he pushed him toward the wall with one hand, keeping his weapon ready in the other. "Hands against the wall."

The man complied and Nate frisked him. He found a knife in an ankle sheath and a pistol in the small of his back. He took both and backed away, tucking the gun into his belt and handing the knife to Sam. Then he looked at a billfold he'd found in a pocket.

Jack Maddox. Arizona driver's license, Flagstaff address.

"Can I turn around?" Maddox said.

"Slowly. Do everything very, very slowly," Nate said, keeping his weapon pointed at him.

Maddox turned. He was older than Nate had first thought. His hair had been covered by a hunter's cap, but Nate saw the gray on the sides. His face was weathered yet there was a vitality in it and in his steps.

He was obviously a man who spent a lot of time outside. He also handled a rifle with ease.

"Who are you?"

Instead of answering, the man looked over toward Sam. "You're Samantha."

She nodded.

"I'm Jack Maddox, a friend of your father's."

"Which father?" Nate asked.

"Carroll. David Carroll," he said.

Samantha broke in. "You know where my mother is?"

"Yes. She's safe."

Nate watched as Sam blinked and her face dissolved. A tear rolled down her cheek. Only then did he realize the extent of her concern. She'd expressed it, of course, but she'd kept a tight rein on her emotions.

But Nate wasn't as willing to accept his word. "How do we know that?"

"She told me about the cabin. I lost you after you left the Faulkner place."

"You were the one who shot the sniper?"

He winced. "Did a helluva poor job of it, too. Meant to kill the bastard. Shooting a horse, two harmless women. That's damn low."

Nate concurred, but he still wasn't quite ready to accept Maddox. "You alone?"

"There's someone with Patsy," Maddox said, looking at Samantha. "I was sent to look after you. Patsy hoped you wouldn't be a target, that once Merritta was dead, you would be safe. Thought that up to the time she knew someone had prowled through her house and then she heard what happened in Boston. By then we couldn't find you." He looked at her accusingly. "You should have told her what happened in Boston."

"I thought it would worry her."

"You being dead would worry her a lot more," the man said.

Sam's face flushed, then she nodded. "You're right, of course, but I thought what she thought, that when Paul Merritta died and I returned here, that would be the end of it."

Nate interrupted. "Who in the hell are you? Besides your name." He lowered his weapon but kept it in his hand.

"Patsy's husband and I served together in 'Nam. There were two others. One's dead. The other is Simon. He's with Patsy now. When Red—David Carroll—realized he was going to die, he asked us to look after her if she ever needed help."

"Red?" Sam asked. "Why Red? He didn't have red hair."

Maddox looked embarrassed. "Private joke. We all had nicknames. Never used our real ones."

"Vietnam? What did you do?" Nate interrupted. "What branch?"

Maddox looked as if he wasn't going to answer, then shrugged. "The Company."

CIA. That explained a lot. Especially how Sam's mother was able to disappear so completely.

Maddox sat down. "Each of us was approached as we were finishing school. Never knew why we were picked, but we were given a choice. CIA or the army. The four of us stayed in until the war ended. Red and Simon remained in a few more years, until the Company started getting involved in some internal affairs they didn't like. All of us had saved one another's hide in those years, and we kept in touch."

Nate absorbed that. He knew some others who had taken the same track. The legion of ex-CIA spooks was massive and more fraternal than many families. They looked after their own. "Your driver's license says you live in Arizona."

"North of Flagstaff. I'm a white water guide now. Own an outside adventures company."

Nate would take help where he could get it. Ex-CIA was a bonus.

"Where is my mother?" Sam asked.

"Simon has her safe, but she wouldn't leave Steamboat until she knew we had you covered, too. She's a stubborn woman."

"Like her daughter," Nate muttered.

She shot him a look. "What do we do now?"

"Simon's moving your mother around. But it's time to

get you two together. Particularly with McLean. I'll stay with you two and watch your back."

Nate looked at him for a long time. "Do we have a choice?"

"I don't think so. I'm pretty good at picking up trails, and you don't have any backup. Not now. They're ready to fry your ass back in Boston."

"How do you know that?"

"We still have a few friends in strategic places. Unfortunately, we think someone else does, too."

"You don't know who?"

"Patsy's not sure."

"What do you mean?"

"She was a witness years ago when a Boston policeman on the Merritta payroll killed an undercover agent. She never heard the name. She thinks whoever did it might be the one causing you problems."

Nate froze. "What?"

Maddox ignored him. "I think—and it's really just a guess—Paul Merritta protected your mother, at least kept anyone from looking for her by staging her death. Someone else, though, had to be involved. I think the reason he sent for you was to warn you, wrap you in his protection. He died sooner than he thought."

"And you have no idea who is after Sam and her mother?"

"No, but a place to start is the Boston police department, thirty-four years ago. I have the names. I'm trying to get photos. When they arrive, I want Patsy to look at them. Maybe she can identify the killer. I want you to look at them, too. You might know some of them."

"I might," Nate said wryly. An old spook had accomplished more in a few days than he had in years. He comforted himself with the thought he hadn't had Patsy Carroll's input.

Sam limped over to the chair and sat. "Who is Simon? Or is that a nickname, too?"

Maddox looked at her appreciatively. "He lives in Durango. That's one reason Red contacted us. Neither of us were too far away." He looked at the gun in Nate's hand. "Can I sit down? I've been out there for a while."

"Go ahead," Nate said. "Why didn't you knock immediately instead of skulking around?"

"Wanted to make sure no one else was around or following you. I also wanted to make sure you were who you seemed to be. Did some checking on you, McLean. Seems you're in a lot of trouble."

"So are you, after that shooting."

"Didn't see you hanging around for the police. Kind of endeared you to me, you being FBI and all."

Nate lowered the weapon. "Did you know there's a contract out on Mrs. Carroll and her daughter?"

Maddox shook his head. "Doesn't surprise me, though. But we didn't think they would try to kill the girl before they found the mother. We thought they would try to follow her to get to Patsy. That's why your mother tried to let you know she was safe but didn't tell you how to get in touch with her."

"Why? What does she have?"

"Don't know. I just know it must be dynamite to invoke this kind of response. I know Red always feared that someone would come for her someday."

"The Merrittas?"

He shook his head. "I really don't know, though I doubt it."

"What was Red's real name?" Nate asked. The question had been plaguing him for a long time.

"Patsy will have to tell you that."

Nate studied the older man. Late fifties, he decided. He instinctively trusted the man, and he rarely did that. But did he trust him enough to put Sam's life in his hands?

"What do you suggest now?"

"I think we ought to get out of here," Maddox said. "After Patsy told me about this cabin, I did a trace of my own. Wanted to know if it could be done. Red was good, careful. But sometimes you can't be careful enough. It took me time, but I found it. I just needed a general location. I ran a check of ownerships of properties of five acres or more within a hundred-mile radius, searching for corporation ownership. Then I checked out each of the corporations. This one had the oddities I was looking for. It was obviously a blind."

"But you knew one existed," Sam said.

"Yep, but if I really wanted to find you, it's one of the trails I'd pursue. It makes sense that there would be a safe house nearby."

Sam looked at Nate. "What do you think?"

"I think he's right," Nate said. This place had worried him from the beginning. He hadn't liked the utter isolation of it. It might offer solitude, but that very quality also prevented adequate support systems.

"I want to speak to my mother," Sam said.

"Not from here," Nate replied, and Maddox nodded.

Sam looked from one to the other. "How did my father meet my mother?"

It was a question, Nate knew, to answer the last of her doubts.

"He was an investigator, specialized in corporate espionage and crime. He had an office in the Chicago area. Patsy found him there, said she wanted to disappear and needed help.

"He knew all the tricks. We all did. But in the midst of arranging a new identity for her, he fell in love. Never fell out, apparently. Contacted Simon two and a half years ago, said she might be in danger from a mobster and asked him to be there for her if she ever needed anything."

There was a lack of bullshit and minimum of explanation that Nate appreciated. Never volunteer more information than was requested in the first place. Offer less whenever possible. He decided to be quiet as Sam asked the questions.

"What's Simon's last name, and why did he rather than you stay with my mother?"

"He was closer. Has a private plane. When you were first contacted, Patsy called Simon and he flew up here. He'd been waiting to be of service. I don't think either of us doubted something would happen eventually, given the history Red gave us. She didn't call him in, though, until she returned to her house and saw someone had been there. When he arrived, he scouted out the place, saw a van that was suspicious and told her to go out the back door and meet him a block away."

"Why didn't you come directly to my house?"

"I didn't get here until after McLean arrived. I saw two cars. Then you pulled your disappearing act. I saw you puncture his tire and figured you were trying to get away from him, that he was one of the bad guys. But then I followed you. Cute trick with changing the cars, by the way. Your mother told me about Terri Faulkner so I had a damn good idea where you were going." He grimaced. "Then I followed the shooter instead of you. Someone picked him up, and I lost you. Not as sharp as I used to be."

"Sharp enough," Nate said. "I understand there's a contract to grab and snatch both Samantha and her mother."

"Why didn't my mother go to the authorities?" Sam asked.

"It was a policeman who committed murder. She has no idea what happened to him, but she knew the Merrittas had bought off members of the department. She doesn't know how high the corruption goes or who to trust beyond me and Simon."

"And why should I trust *you*?" Sam persisted.

Nate hid a smile at that. Sam should be in the CIA. He

didn't know whether she had always been this suspicious, but she certainly had honed that quality lately.

"Your mother said if you had any doubts, I should mention Ginger."

Nate saw a smile spread over her face. "My stuffed cat when I was growing up," she explained.

Nate grimaced and glanced away from her. His suspicions were as healthy as hers, and he wasn't quite as easily convinced.

Too much had happened. There were too many unexpected characters. He would swear that someone tried to kill her—not snatch and grab. That meant there might be more than one player involved. But he didn't want to say that in front of Sam.

Judging from Maddox's expression when he'd mentioned the snatch and grab, he'd had the same opinion. There were two games in progress simultaneously, one more deadly than the other.

Someone wanted what Patsy Carroll knew—or had in her possession—and someone else just wanted both her and her daughter dead.

twenty-eight

They decided to leave immediately and stop at a motel somewhere along the way.

At her suggestion, Maddox brought in the dog that had been waiting, without sound, at the foot of the steps. He was part shepherd and part unknown. But he was a handsome fellow with good manners.

He tolerated Sam scratching his ears and looked grateful when she offered a bowl of water.

"His name is Jock," Maddox said. "Jock and Jack, everyone says. He goes on all my trips. Keeps the tourists in line." He cracked a smile for the first time.

Sam saw Nathan's face. She'd been astounded at how quickly Sarsy had taken to him, but he was not happy about the dog. And though Jock had approached her with no hesitation, he kept a respectful distance from Nathan.

Sam wasn't sure where they were going. Jack Maddox had been unclear on that. It was better, he said, not to mention locations.

How long to get there?

"A while."

She didn't like the answers, nor she noticed, did Nathan, yet in him she saw understanding. These men spoke the same language. Nate just wasn't used to being on the receiving end.

"I can call my mother?"

"When we get out of here," Nate broke in. "You might want to return, and I don't want a phone call traced back to this location. They may never find this place. I just think there's a possibility that they could."

There wasn't much to pack. Neither of them had salvaged any clothes after the shooting. Nathan had purchased several changes of clothes for both of them, but it was basic jeans and shirts.

"Where's your car?" Nathan asked.

"A half mile from here."

"We'll drive you there."

Maddox shook his head. "You go ahead. There's a restaurant five miles east of here. Saw it coming in. It should be full with the late dinner crowd. I'll meet you there."

He left with the dog and disappeared into the woods.

Nathan packed their few belongings, then regarded her compassionately.

"I'm all right. Really I am," she said. She wasn't, but she wasn't going to tell him. Her thigh hurt unbearably. She felt half-drugged from the pain pill and lack of sleep.

Once in the car, she turned to him. "What do you think?"

"I don't know what to think," he said. "I just know when we get about an hour from here, I'm going to check in with Gray. See what he can find out about Jack Maddox and a Simon who has a private plane near Durango."

"You're not sure that's their real names?"

"I don't know, but I'll find out soon enough."

She leaned against the door so she could face him. His face always gave her confidence.

He started the car, then reached out and took her hand. "I'm sorry."

"I'm the one who's sorry. I might be responsible for getting you fired."

"It's time for me to leave the Bureau," he said. "I was there for all the wrong reasons."

"The Merrittas, you mean?"

"Yes. I grew up reliving that moment every day. I still have flashbacks, but they're less frequent now. I let it consume my life. That doesn't make for a good cop."

"What will you do?"

"I don't know," he said. "Never thought about it. I'll find something."

He turned his attention to the road ahead as she leaned her head back against the seat in thoughtful silence.

Thirty minutes later, they saw a red pickup truck pull into the restaurant parking lot. Sam saw Jack Maddox and Jock, who dominated the passenger seat. Maddox parked next to him. "There's a motel in Fort Collins, the Westerner—"

Sam nodded. "I know it."

"I'll follow you, make sure no one else is," Maddox said. "We'll stay there tonight and drive through tomorrow."

"Through to where?"

"Chicago," Maddox said. "That's where it all started."

He backed up into a parking slot without any more explanation.

Sam watched Nate take one sweeping glance around the parking area, then he drove out of the lot onto the road and turned east.

His expression gave away very little. She wondered whether he was as disconcerted as she was. Maddox had said she could call her mother, but had left before giving the number.

She wanted to trust Maddox, just as she'd wanted to trust Nathan when she first met him.

Too many things kept getting in the way. Why hadn't he

paused long enough to let her call her mother? Was the motel in Fort Collins a trap?

"Tell me about the motel," Nathan said, as if he'd just read her mind.

"It's like a lot of motels," she said. "They have meeting rooms, and I was at a conference there. Nice rooms. Nothing fancy but comfortable. Heated pool."

"A lot of lighting?"

"As far as I remember."

"Large lobby?"

"Medium size. Why?"

"A large lobby usually means more people," he said. "Why do you think he would pick that place?"

"Maybe for that reason," she said, feeling better. "Surely if he meant to set some kind of trap, he would have picked a motel with one person at the desk and rooms swathed in shadows."

"Maybe," he said cautiously.

"He has a dog," she said hopefully. She'd always believed anyone who liked dogs was, at heart, a good person.

"Yes," he said noncommittally.

She heard the skepticism in his voice, and she knew she must sound naive. But she was an optimist at heart, and she was seeking any sign of hope. It was very dark now as he wound around curves. She wished she didn't like looking at him so much, at the way he radiated competency.

She glanced behind them. She didn't see headlights.

"He's keeping a distance," Nathan said. "He knows where we're going."

" 'Where it all started.' " She repeated Maddox's words. "Why didn't it start in Boston?"

"Maybe because Chicago is where your mother met David Carroll, or whoever he is. Maybe that's where she stashed whatever it is that seems to be scaring people so much."

"Mostly me," she said.

He chuckled. "I like a lady with a sense of humor."

"It's that or scream."

Suddenly he swerved onto a dirt road, one shielded by overhanging trees. The car bounced as they moved deeper into the trees, and she winced, swallowing a cry.

He turned out the lights.

They both waited.

A car passed the road, then another. Still he didn't start the car.

"Maybe he has one of those tracing devices," Sam said.

"He might," Nathan said, and Sam knew he'd already thought about that.

"Is there a way of finding one?"

"Oh, yes, with a lot of time and even more light. We'll find out soon enough," he said.

"You have a plan," she said.

"I always have a plan. They don't always work."

"What is it?" she asked.

"I want to arrive well after he does. I want to check automobiles in the parking lot. I want to check security. I also want to give Gray time to check him out."

"Why Gray?"

"He can get to computers with nationwide databases. Police records. Drivers' licenses. I can't," he said. "Not now."

"I still don't know if my mother is safe. . . ."

"No," he said. "But I don't want anyone to use you to get to her, either."

She agreed. She was shaken by the fact that Maddox had not given her a number. It had made her a doubter as well. She watched Nate take out his cell phone. Turn it on. Obviously look at the messages.

He pushed some numbers. She couldn't help but hear his side of the conversation.

"Hi, buddy. You called?"

He frowned as he heard the answer. "I expected as much. And you?"

She heard real distress in his voice. "Damn, I'm sorry, Gray."

A silence on his side, then, "Just fishing, friend. I'll be damned if I come back until then. Let them stew. But you stay out of it, hear. It's just Barker. I haven't done anything wrong, and it'll be straightened out when I get back. Just don't eat too many hot dogs at the ball game."

He hung up. "I have to find a public telephone."

"There's a small town not far away."

"How far?"

"Twenty minutes, maybe."

"Then we'll wait here for a few more minutes."

She looked at him curiously.

"Gray's phone might be tapped and they could possibly trace my cell phone if I'd stayed on any longer."

"And the hot dogs?"

"A bar where we sometimes watch ball games. He'll go there."

"Why did he call you?"

"I'm being suspended. I haven't been keeping in touch. And someone told them I'm in Steamboat Springs in the company of someone I've been told to avoid. There's a hearing next week."

"Who told them?"

"Very good question. I didn't speak to anyone but you and the Faulkners. Somehow I don't think they would call the Boston office."

"You have to go back."

"Hell I do. I'm sticking to my fish story."

"They're going to find out you're with me."

"By then you and your mother will be safe," he said. "Hopefully, we'll have some bad guys. There's no better argument than success."

She felt lost in that dank swamp again. "What if my brother's involved?"

"Then it's better that you know," he said.

"Easy for you to say."

"Not any longer, Sam. I hope like hell—for your sake—that he has nothing to do with this."

"What do *you* think?"

"I saw him throw his body in front of yours at his house, Samantha. I saw the way he looked at you when you were bleeding. No, I don't think he's been involved in anything that has happened to you."

He had narrowed his scope to that, and she recognized it. She knew he had still not completely absolved her brother in his mind.

She looked longingly at the phone. "Can I try my mother's cell phone?"

"I'd rather you didn't. They will have a fix on this number and might be able to pick up her location. You can call on the public phone."

"The FBI is monitoring your phone?"

"Count on it. There were ten messages from my superior on the phone. Gray's been reassigned to review old cases. He wasn't suspended, but there's no doubt his career will suffer because of me."

"Us," she corrected.

"Us," he agreed with a trace of a smile. "But suspension makes it hard to ask for help from any local law. It also means my password won't get me into files any longer."

"But how could they suspend you when you're on vacation?"

"Because I was told quite clearly to drop the Merritta case and they think I'm continuing to work it."

"Continuing to work it?" She didn't like the inference but she was tired of unsaid suspicions. She planned to attack every doubt head-on, from now on.

"I didn't put that very well," he said. "In their eyes, I've disobeyed a direct order. Maybe Barker can't make it stand, but he'll give it one hell of a good try."

"Barker?"

"My boss." His lips thinned, and she knew from his voice and expression that he held his superior in contempt.

She understood now why he pursued the Merrittas. If she had seen her mother gunned down when she was a child, she knew she too would want justice.

The question was: How much was justice, and how much concern for her and her mother? Her mother, after all, apparently knew something that could have hurt the Merrittas years ago. Even before his mother was killed.

If she had gone to federal authorities then, perhaps the Merrittas would have been in jail. Perhaps his mother wouldn't have been in the wrong place at the wrong time.

She sighed. Years ago, their parents made decisions that inevitably affected both of them.

He reached out his hand, placed it over hers on the seat between them. "I want you to believe that the only person I really care about now is you. I want you safe. I want you to have the life you used to have."

"I'll never have that again," she replied. "I'll never look at my mother without knowing what I lost. What you lost. I'll love her. I'll always love her. But I don't know whether I will ever have the same trust."

"I imagine she did what she felt she had to do at the time. Remember how young she was and that she had two children to think about. I imagine she was afraid to do anything with Nick in Paul's hands," he said gently. "You know things now she didn't know. Hindsight isn't fair."

"But your mother might still be alive if she had gone to the FBI."

"And your mother might be dead," he finished. "We can't change history. We can only try to change the future."

His hand squeezed hers, and she knew he meant what he was saying. He was willing—and apparently able—to throw off the past. But could he ever really escape the memories?

She angled around and leaned against him, ignoring the sudden pain in her leg. She had been attracted to him from the first moment she saw him in the airport. She'd carried that image with her, and the attraction had intensified when he'd helped her carry Nick to safety.

Then the kiss.

The kiss that had warmed her down to her toes, and still did every time she thought about it.

He'd said he wasn't good at his job, that he'd let too much happen to her. But he had always been there. He'd helped her at the airport, then when the car had been run off the road. He'd rescued her yet again at the hospital, followed her to Colorado.

So many times.

"Thank you," she said, looking up at the face that so appealed to her.

"Ah, pretty lady. There's nothing to thank me for. We're not done yet and I'm not sure whether I'm leading you into even greater trouble."

"You don't trust Jack Maddox, do you?"

He hesitated, and she knew he was debating what to tell her.

"I want the truth, Nathan."

"I told you there was a contract for a grab and snatch."

She waited for him to continue.

"Whoever commissioned this contract wanted you and your mother alive and, I suspect, together. The better to intimidate her."

She nodded her understanding.

"I don't think that's what your assailant in Steamboat Springs had in mind. I think he meant to kill you."

The implication hung in the air. She didn't want to believe it.

"You mean two different groups . . . ?"

He nodded, his mouth grim. "With two different agendas."

"Why?"

"I can guess," he said. "If your mother never got a divorce, she will probably have a legal right to a significant portion of Paul Merritta's estate. The fact that she was declared dead wouldn't matter if someone else was responsible for the fraud. At the very least, she could tie the estate up in probate for years, which would leave it vulnerable to scrutiny. There are family members who wouldn't like to see that happen. One of them may well want you two to disappear."

She tried a smile and knew she was failing miserably. "Someone in the Merritta family wants me dead so I won't take any of their money, and someone outside wants to kidnap me to get whatever information or evidence my mother might have. Is that it?"

"It might be."

"Wonderful," she said. "And you think Jack Maddox is with which faction?"

"He stopped someone from killing you."

"You're saying my guardian angel could be my ultimate executioner," she said. "Then why would my mother have told him so much about me?"

"I don't know," he said. "He might be exactly who he says he is, but I won't know until I talk to Gray. I just know we need to be careful."

He reached over and touched her cheek. "You must be exhausted."

She was. Adrenaline sufficed only so long. Yet being here with him—even in these circumstances—made her feel warm and oddly content. And safe.

He looked at his watch, then leaned over and touched her lips with his, his fingers tucking a curl behind an ear in a devastatingly intimate way. "One of these days . . ."

"One of these days, what?" she asked lazily after a moment's silence.

But he didn't reply to that question. Instead, he straightened. "We should be going."

She laid her head on his shoulder. She felt an intake of breath. She affected him as he affected her. A comforting thought.

He backed out of the narrow dirt track until they neared the main road, then turned the car around.

"As much as I like you there," he said, "you'd better put on your seat belt."

Reluctantly she did. And thought ahead, wondering whether they were traveling toward her mother.

Or a trap.

They stopped at a gas station. Nate suggested that Sam go inside and pick up several soft drinks and a variety of snacks while he used the pay phone. He knew that bar number intimately. He'd spent a lot of hours there after his wife died.

Gray picked it up on the first ring.

"You weren't followed?"

"Come on, Nate. You know me better than that."

"These are professionals," Nate said. "They must have gotten to Steamboat before Sam did. There was another attack."

"Is she all right?"

"A bullet in the leg. She's one hell of a lady. Tried to protect her friend just as she tried to pull Merritt from a burning car. But I picked up some interesting information, and I need you to check on two men. A Jack Maddox in Flagstaff, Arizona. He says he owns an outdoor adventures company. And someone named Simon—either first or last name—who owns a private plane in Durango, Colorado."

"Why not something hard?" Gray complained.

"I know how you like challenges."

"What else?"

"I need the names and photos of Boston patrolmen who worked in and around Merritta's home and business thirty-four years ago. And whether an undercover agent turned up missing at that time." Nate knew that Maddox said he had obtained a list, but Nate wanted his own, and he knew that if anyone could get the photos, Gray could.

Gray gave a low whistle. "Are you saying what I think you're saying?"

"Just guesses at the moment. And by the way, someone else might be trying to obtain those photos, too, so . . ."

"Be sly," Gray finished. "I can do sly," he added with a chuckle. "It should be easy enough to get the names of those stations, then the names of the men working out of them. Photos might be a bit harder if they left the department more than twenty years ago."

"Concentrate on any names that might ring bells with you," Nate said. "Someone who might have a lot to lose now."

"Okay. How do I reach you?"

"You don't," he said. "I'll call you at Janie's. Ten tomorrow morning?"

"I'll see what I can get."

"Thanks."

He hung up. He owed Gray more than his thanks, but he would take care of that later.

Sam stood next to him with a bag. She also held a T-shirt with an elk on the front. "I got two of them," she said. "I'll wear the cougar. You can have the elk."

He grinned at her. She limped but wasn't using the cane. She apparently had just combed her hair and put on lipstick and she looked gorgeous, especially with the trace of mischief in her eyes.

He handed the phone to her. "I think it's safe enough to make some calls."

She took it and dialed a number. It rang and rang and rang.

He saw the disappointment in her eyes. He felt it, too. He wanted to confirm that her mother was safe with the man called Simon. But if he had been Simon, he would have told Patsy Carroll not to answer the phone.

She clicked the number off, then called a second number.

"Terri?"

He started to move away.

Then he heard Sam say, "Nick?" and moved back closer where he could hear.

"He's staying in town. He's worried about you." Terri's voice was barely audible.

"Where is he?" Sam asked, turning the receiver so he could hear better.

"Your favorite hotel. Call him." Terri rattled off a number.

"Thanks."

"Should I tell him you called me?"

Nate shook his head.

"No," Sam said reluctantly. "I have to think about it."

"I like him, Sam. He took me to supper earlier. I think—"

Nate shook his head. "Cut it off," he mouthed.

She looked rebellious for a moment, then nodded. "I have to go. I'll check back with you later."

He reached over and hung up the receiver.

"Surely there wouldn't be someone tracing her brother's phone."

"It's better not to take chances," he said, starting for the car.

"You don't believe he came because he's worried about me?" she asked.

"I don't know, Sam. I don't think it's a good idea to trust anyone at this point."

He saw her fighting tears, and it was so rare, despite all she had been going through, that his heart ached for her. She was hurting and tired and scared. Hell, he was scared, too. And he realized how much she wanted to trust Nick Merritt. How important it was to her. And now Merritt might have come to help her and he was throwing cold water on the idea.

But Merritt had always been an enigma to Nathan and that's why he'd always suspected him of being involved. Too many inconsistencies. Too many coincidences.

Even if Merritt had noble intentions, Nate didn't want Sam in the cesspool that was organized crime in Boston.

He opened the car door for her and she got in while he filled the tank with gas. Then he got in the driver's seat.

Another thirty minutes and they would be in Fort Collins. Perhaps then they could both get some rest. And some answers the next morning.

He wanted to reach over and touch her again, but she looked so fragile he feared she might break.

"For the record," he said, "I don't think your brother would hurt either you or your mother. But . . ."

But he didn't like Merritt's sudden appearance in Steamboat, either. He didn't like him taking Terri to supper.

Raging inside, he started the car and pulled out on the road.

twenty-nine

Sam guided Nate to the motel. It was, as she said, large and well-lit.

He drove around the parking lot, looking for tags obviously belonging to rental cars.

He noticed several scattered throughout the area. He checked each one of them. Hit men usually kept their cars pristine clean. They wanted no clues, and they didn't take chances that a piece of paper might find its way under the seat, or a map might have a fingerprint.

None of the cars reached that pristine state. Most had maps scattered on the seat, a jacket or some hint of its occupant.

He quickly saw Maddox's truck and wondered whether the dog was also a welcome guest in the hotel.

Then he saw a door open. It was six rooms down from the pickup. Maddox had obviously seen him.

The dog, Jock, stepped out with him. Nate saw no sign of a weapon. Just a manila envelope in Maddox's hand. That didn't mean anything, though.

"I thought you would check out the parking lot before driving in." Maddox said it with satisfaction rather than irritation.

"I'm sure you did the same."

Maddox's expression didn't change. "You purposely lost me."

"There was a stop we had to make."

Through the car window, the two men evaluated each other. Judged.

Maddox nodded. "I rented a room for you two. Mr. and Mrs. Powell. I rather thought you wanted to stay together."

"I'm not sure I want to go into an empty room when you've been holding the key."

"Understandable," Maddox said.

Nate realized then that Maddox had just as many doubts about him as he did about Maddox. He grinned. "Then you won't mind if I get another room."

"Nope. But perhaps you won't feel the need when you look at this." He held up the envelope.

"What's in it?"

"The list of police officers who served in 1968. A few photos. A phone number for Miss Carroll." Maddox glanced around the parking lot again. "Will you come in to talk or are we going to keep dancing around one another?"

Hell, Nate thought, the door was open. He could see nearly the whole room. And Maddox was right. They weren't going to accomplish much if they kept this up. He looked at Sam, who nodded.

He found a parking place and stepped out of the car, putting his hand on his holstered weapon. Maddox opened the passenger door and helped Sam out and led the way into the room, Jock following.

Once inside, Nate checked the bathroom and closet. Nothing unusual. A notebook computer sat open on the desk.

Maddox closed the door, turned the locks, fastened the chain. He handed Nate the envelope.

Nate didn't tell him he was obtaining his own list. They

had different sources. They might get different results, either on purpose or by oversight.

"I want to call my mother," Sam said.

Maddox handed Samantha a cell phone and a piece of paper with a number. "It's clean," he said. "No way anyone can trace that."

Samantha grabbed them like a lifeline and looked around.

"The bathroom," Maddox suggested.

Samantha disappeared inside and closed the door.

Nate turned back to Maddox. "The photos?"

Maddox handed him the envelope.

Nate sat down and opened it. Page after page of names fell out. "There're no precinct numbers."

"No."

Nate took the chair at the desk and took a quick preliminary look at the list. It had been faxed, but he found no telephone number, no way to identify who had sent it.

It was lengthy and, to his eyes, blurry. He wished he'd had more sleep, but he started reviewing the many hundreds of names.

He was only barely aware that Maddox made a pot of coffee from the in-room miniature maker and placed a cup in front of him.

Nate recognized many of the names. Except for a few years with the Florida and Atlanta offices, he'd lived in Boston. He'd been in the FBI Boston office ten years. He knew the history of many of the precincts.

Some on the list were still with the Boston P.D., many of them as captains, lieutenants, even battalion commanders. Some had left, going to surrounding jurisdictions as police chiefs. Some had become private investigators.

He marked several names as he went through the list. Then one caught his attention, because he'd seen the man just a few days ago.

He was the judge who'd approved the tap on Nick Merritt's home. Judge Terrence McGuire.

For a moment, he dismissed the idea. Judge McGuire was legendary among law enforcement officers. A former policeman who had worked his way through college and then law school. He'd been an assistant district attorney before being elected as a state judge, then appointed to a federal judgeship.

Cops loved him. He was a law-and-order judge, the one most of them chose to go to for search warrants, wires and phone taps.

He was also up for a U.S. Court of Appeals judgeship and was already being discussed as a potential Supreme Court justice.

He had one hell of a lot to lose.

Nate was aware of Maddox's gaze on him. He went past McGuire's name without marking it. He would wait until tomorrow morning when he received some information back from Gray.

He continued down the list of names. One was now a deputy police commissioner, another a high-ranking confidant of the mayor. By the time he'd finished, he had marked fifteen names, not including McGuire.

He knew in his gut that the man they were looking for could be McGuire. He fit the profile of someone who had a great deal to lose, particularly now. But Nate didn't want the least suspicion to fall on him unless he was absolutely sure.

Sam dialed the number Maddox had given her. Her hand shook.

It was answered by a man with a deep, gruff voice. "Yes?"

"This is Samantha Carroll," she said.

"Just a moment."

In seconds, her mother's voice came on the phone.

"Samantha, thank God you're safe. I heard about . . . I didn't think you would be hurt. I am so very, very sorry. You're all right, aren't you?" she hurried on. "Jack assured me that you were. That you're with an FBI agent you trust."

Sam took a deep breath. "I'm fine. Truly, I am. But I've been worrying about you. Are you—?"

"Yes. I'm perfectly safe. A friend of David's is looking after me. I wanted to tell you, but my . . . friend didn't want any trail left, and he said my house was wired. I was afraid yours was, too. They said they would take care of you."

Sam heard the tears in her mother's voice. "Don't worry. I'm safe."

"This agent with you? Are you—?"

"Sure of him? Yes. He's saved my life—and Nick's. He's risking his career to help me."

"Jack will bring you to me," her mother said. "Then we can sort things out. I'm so sorry," she said again. "I never thought this would touch you. It had been so long, and . . ."

"I know," Sam said. "But your sister. You said you contacted her. Is she safe?"

"Yes. She and her family have gone on vacation. That's my fault, too. If I hadn't contacted her—"

"Then they would have found you some other way," Sam said. "It needs to end."

"I thought it had. I truly thought it would when Paul died . . ." Her voice trailed off.

Sam wondered how much Simon had told her. She thought her mother should know the whole truth. "Nathan thinks there might be divergent interests after us. That someone in the family feels you or I will complicate the estate, and that someone else believes you can tie an old murder to him."

A silence. "Samantha—"

"Nick's in Steamboat," Sam interrupted. She didn't want any more apologies.

"Why?"

"I don't know. He went to the gallery. He met Terri and took her out to supper. I'm not sure why, but she said he's desperate to get in touch with me."

"But not me?"

"Once he knows you—"

"He could never forgive me. I can't forgive myself. I deserve anything that happens to me. But you don't. Neither does he."

"We'll be there soon. We'll sort it out."

Sam heard a voice in the background. "You'd better cut it off, Patsy."

"I should go," her mother said.

"See you soon."

"I love you."

"I know," Sam said. "I love you, too."

Despite his earlier reservations, Nathan decided he and Sam would take the room Maddox had already rented. He could drive to another motel, but Sam was exhausted and obviously in pain.

And Maddox had had his chances if he'd intended any immediate harm.

Nate looked at the table and the cell phone Maddox had left with them. He didn't know exactly what Sam's mother had said, but Sam was convinced now that her mother was in safe hands and had dropped all her suspicions of Jack Maddox.

Nate knew he would feel better when he had a complete report on Sam's new benefactor; he knew Gray would have something for him in the morning. In the meantime, he intended to be very, very cautious.

The room was only three doors down from Maddox. That meant an extra gun. An additional set of eyes.

The thing to worry about was Chicago. And getting there.

Tomorrow he would exchange rental cars again.

He carried what few things they had into the room, secured all the locks, then for good measure put a chair under the doorknob. Primitive, but useful.

The room contained two double beds, a small refrigerator with ice trays and a large bathroom.

Sam headed for that, and in seconds he heard the sound of a shower.

He filled a glass with ice, then water from a faucet in the room, and he sat back in a chair and tried to keep his mind off the woman in the shower and on the matter at hand. His problem with Maddox and his friend Simon was they were too good to be true. Yet it made sense that David Carroll's precautions wouldn't end with his death. Men like him thought beyond the grave as thoroughly as they saw beyond shadows. And Sam was convinced her mother wasn't under any kind of restraint, that she completely trusted the men who had been friends of her husband.

He heard a voice from inside the bathroom, an off-tune but lilting melody, and smiled. He wanted to go in there. He felt dirty and grungy and frustrated that he'd not been more effective.

He rose and went into the bathroom. Steam drifted up around him and he grabbed a towel just as she stepped from the shower. She looked startled, then her lips curved into a smile that went straight to his heart.

Nate wrapped the towel around her and slowly dried her, massaging her neck and back. Then he used a second towel to dry her hair.

He stood back and stared at her. She looked glorious to him with sleepy eyes and that slight smile on her face.

"You're beautiful," he said.

"Thank you," she said.

He liked that, too. No demurrals. No protestations.

He leaned over and touched her lips with his before stepping back, then he lifted her easily and carried her to one of the double beds. He changed the wet bandage on her thigh. It looked raw and angry to him, but he knew the antibiotics would work their magic. He finished, fetched her a glass of water with pills and watched as she downed them.

Then he sat next to her and massaged her neck again.

"How did you learn to do that?" she said.

"It's a natural talent," he replied. He had learned to do it for his mother when she would return home from waiting tables, barely able to walk. He would make toasted cheese sandwiches for her or heat canned soup and massage her neck.

He'd recognized, even then, how hard she had tried to keep them together. His fingers paused and Sam murmured, her eyes drifting shut.

"Stay with me," she said as he rose.

"I'll be here."

"I mean in bed."

That hadn't been his intention. He meant to stay at the window that overlooked the parking lot.

A few moments . . .

He shucked his shoes and socks. He wanted to shuck the jeans and shirt as well, but that, he knew, wouldn't be wise. Above all, she needed rest, not a horny agent. He lay down next to her, and she snuggled in his arms. He was very aware of her nakedness, of the awareness spreading in his own body.

He couldn't help but reach out with one hand and touch her damp curling hair and trace his fingers down her cheek, relishing the smooth, soft texture.

A purr escaped her, and he knew he was smiling. He wanted her to purr. He wanted her to relax and sleep and feel safe again.

He stayed there, unmoving except for an occasional

touch of wistful yearning. He stayed until he knew she was well asleep, then gently disengaged himself and walked over to the window. He scanned the lit parking lot. There were a few more cars, none of which looked suspicious. He turned out the last light and pulled a chair up to the window, resting his weapon within reach on the bedside table.

His thoughts kept returning to the naked woman sleeping in the bed beside him while his gaze continued to roam the parking lot. Every movement, every new car was scrutinized. He glanced at the clock. Four in the morning.

He would try to catch a few hours' sleep when she woke.

It was going to be a long time before dawn.

Nick had never been so frustrated. He'd barely slept last night after leaving Terri Faulkner.

Thoughts tumbled in his mind. He'd been in Steamboat a day. There was no sign of Sam. Nor of Nathan McLean. He wanted to believe that meant she was safe. Ironically, her best chance of safety could be Nathan McLean, though he hated to admit that, even to himself. The very qualities in McLean that angered Nick were the ones needed to protect Sam.

Still, he wished he knew how far McLean would go to bring down the Merritta family. Especially since he'd heard why McLean had been so relentless in his investigations.

Worse, Nick worried about Sam being hurt emotionally, when he should be worrying that she could be killed. The last thing *he* needed was to allow Sam into his life.

The last thing *she* needed was any kind of personal connection with any member of his family.

Sam, as an heir, had become a very valuable commodity.

So had her mother, though for a different reason.

Whoever made both of them disappear would make a great deal of money. And someone who used them to prosecute the Merritta family would advance his career immeasurably.

Nick wasn't going to let either happen.

He checked his e-mail. That, he'd concluded, was the safest method to talk to Victor.

He'd told Victor through an agreed-upon e-mail address about the shooting and that he didn't want any more incidents involving Samantha.

In his reply, Victor vehemently denied having anything to do with the latest attack and said he'd passed on Nick's message to other members of the family. But then he'd lied to Nick before.

He ran over other possibilities.

Rosa? Anna? According to Terri, she and Samantha both thought the shooter meant to kill. According to the contract on them, the other party involved wanted them alive to retrieve property lost three decades earlier.

He e-mailed Victor back. *Tell the family I'll crush anyone I find involved in the attacks on my sister.*

He signed off and sat back, pondering his next move. Terri either didn't know or wouldn't tell him where Sam was. He suspected it was the first, since McLean appeared to be in charge. But Terri would be in contact with Sam. He knew his sister well enough now to know she would want to make sure Terri Faulkner was safe.

Maybe if he spent enough time with Terri . . .

Dammit, but it wouldn't be hard. He wondered whether he was making up a reason to be with her.

She'd made him relax. She was the least self-conscious person he'd ever met, and it was obvious from everyone who greeted her that she was a much loved person in the town.

She was gentle, funny, bright. She'd made him smile. It had been a long time since that had happened.

He made coffee in the small drip machine, grimacing as he tasted it, then sat back at the desk in his room. He shouldn't be thinking of a woman. Matters were coming to a head. The violence was stepping up. No telling how many people were looking for his sister and his mother.

His sister and his mother. Strange words for him. Uncomfortable ones. New. Even painful.

Terri Faulkner could be the key to finding his sister.

He told himself that again as he picked up the phone and dialed her number.

thirty

"Samantha!"

Nathan's voice was brusque, rousing her.

It had been such a deep sleep that it took her a moment to recognize the urgency. She opened her eyes and sat up.

"Nate?"

"Get dressed," he said.

His tone told her not to question. Her clothes were folded neatly at the end of the bed. She'd left them in the bathroom last night. At least, she thought she had.

He was looking out the window. He was fully dressed, his weapon out of the holster attached to his belt. Something had obviously alerted him.

Sam put on the bra, pulled the T-shirt over her head, then shimmied into her briefs and jeans. Her leg was stiff. It still hurt but not as much as yesterday.

"What is it?" she asked as she reached his side.

"Call Maddox. Room 128. See if he's awake. Then ask him to look outside."

His eyes glinted approval as she followed his instructions, trusting his instincts over her own fears.

Maddox was curt. Sam finished the short conversation and hung up the phone. "He's awake. He says you're right and to give him five minutes, then expect one hell of a disturbance. We should leave then."

"And go where?"

"We have a number to call," she said. "And his cell phone. He insists it's safe."

She saw Nate look at his watch. She looked at her own. Only a few moments had passed between a sound sleep and more fear, more running.

Time crawled. She wanted to go to the window but his body language told her he didn't want her there. Instead she went quietly throughout the room, picked up everything and packed their belongings in one bag. She took her own weapon from her purse, gripping her gun with her right hand and the bag and purse with her left hand.

He motioned for her to go to the door. She dropped the bag while she undid all the locks, then picked up their meager belongings again.

Suddenly she heard a loud crash outside followed by loud angry voices.

Nate had car keys in one hand, his pistol in the other. "Leave the bag," he said, and tossed her the keys. "Go to the car. Unlock it and get in. I'll be right behind you."

She obediently opened the door. A pickup truck had smashed into a black sedan. She saw two men swearing at Maddox. She sprinted the few feet to their car and unlocked it, sliding over to the passenger's side, and leaving the door open on the driver's side.

She glanced back at the wreck Maddox had caused. Jock was growling. Maddox was bristling, loudly telling them that there was no need for hostility. He'd turned away, forcing the two men to do the same. She heard one last complaint from him—it was a simple accident—as she closed the door and ducked down. Sirens wailed, the sound growing louder as official vehicles approached.

Maddox obviously had timed everything to the last second. He'd probably called the police to report the accident just before he'd rammed the car.

Nate got into the driver's seat and steered the car out onto the road just as a police car turned into the parking lot.

He grinned. "Maddox must have been damned good at his job. He has them neatly foxed. He's the righteous citizen who called the police when he'd backed into a car. No need for harsh words. It will take them a few moments to sort things out."

"But they'll know about Maddox then."

"Not really. I imagine they might guess what happened, but they have more important goals now."

"To find us."

"Yes, and we're going to make it hard on them."

She saw his twitching mouth. He was obviously still amused by Maddox and Jock. "How?"

"I need sleep. I can't go much farther without it, and you can't drive with that leg. That leaves plane, train and bus," he explained. "If they know about Chicago, they'll be looking at airports and airline manifests, but buses and trains . . ."

"How did they find us?" she asked.

"Your friend Terri's phone might be tapped. House wired. Next time you talk to her, you might ask whether there have been repairmen at either the gallery or her home. Or we could have a GPU unit secreted someplace in this car. I checked pretty thoroughly but it's basically just a chip. It could be anywhere."

"Then which is it? Bus or train?"

"My preference is a train. Except in the northern corridor, we can purchase a ticket aboard the train. We need a photo identification, but I doubt if anyone will find us soon. Not only that, there's a number of stations near Chicago. We can get off at any one of them."

"We need cash," she said.

"I picked some up before leaving Boston," he replied. "I thought there might be a time I wouldn't want to leave a paper trail."

"Maddox said the phone is safe. Should I call and get a train schedule?"

"I have renewed faith in him," Nate said. "But let's stop at a pay phone."

"I'm a big fan of trains," she said.

He turned slightly to look at her. "When I was a kid, I wanted a train set more than anything in the world. I never got over it. I travel by train whenever I can and never get tired of them."

Another small insight into him. She was beginning to understand the man who had been so distant when she'd first met him. She wondered about the foster homes he'd lived in. She hoped they had been good ones, but she had enough experience in charitable endeavors to know it was unlikely.

"How do we get to Denver?" he asked, interrupting her thoughts.

"There's the interstate or a parallel state road."

"We'll take the state road," he said.

She looked at the map in the car, then gave him directions. She leaned back against the door where she could both view the cars following them as well as glance at his face.

She saw the lines in his face. Obviously he hadn't slept at all. How long could someone go without rest?

Denver was approximately two hours away on the state route, closer on the fast-moving interstate.

They stopped midway at a small café where several trucks and cars were parked. Sam had always heard that truck drivers knew the best places to eat. She hoped that legend was correct because she was hungry.

It was like stepping back in time. A juke box was just inside the entrance and the tables were worn and the vinyl seat fabric torn, but the smell of hamburger curled around her nostrils as if it was a porterhouse steak.

They sat in a booth and read a much-used menu. She ordered ham and eggs; he ordered the eight ninety-nine steak.

"I'll call the train station," she said.

He nodded.

She went to the pay telephone, still wondering how they had been located, still worried about Jack Maddox and his dog. If the rental car did carry a tracing device, they wouldn't be safe until they reached Denver and ditched the car. She dialed information and got an 800 number. She dialed that and learned the Zephyr would leave the Denver Station at 7:45 P.M. and arrive in Chicago late the next afternoon.

She declined the opportunity to make a reservation.

She returned to the booth. Nate was eating a wilted-looking salad as if it were food of the gods.

"The train to Chicago leaves at seven forty-five," she said.

He looked at his watch. "Eight hours from now. Plenty of time to get some clothes."

Their food arrived. She was starving, yet she had trouble eating. She was worried about Maddox and Jock. About her mother and Terri. About the man across from her.

He sat facing the door, his gaze slicing toward it every time someone entered.

"What do we do when we find my mother?" she said.

"Set a trap."

"What kind of trap?"

"We can narrow possibilities to several people," he said. "We will call each one and tell them that we've taken precautions, but want two hundred thousand to keep quiet."

"And we wait to see who bites?"

"Yes."

"And if no one does?"

"We try something else, but he will. He can't afford not to."

"He? You know who it is, don't you?"

He gave her a bland look.

"Does Jack Maddox?"

"I don't think so."

"Who?"

It was clear he didn't want to tell her. "We agreed to be honest," she said. "It's my life. And I"m not going to leave this place without knowing."

He grimaced. "It's only supposition, but you have the right to know. It could be a judge named McGuire. He was a patrolman in 1968. He's a federal judge now, nominated for the federal appeals bench."

Her heart dropped. A federal judge, and all the political connections that went with that.

"How—?"

"He must be very good at burying the past," he said. "Cops love him. They think he's on their side. He's cultivated a law-and-order image. But a federal Appeals judgeship means more scrutiny than for a district judge. Once there, he doesn't only interpret law, but makes it." He paused. "It could be the reason I was taken off the case. One cautionary warning from a federal judge is next to an order."

She looked down at eggs growing cold. She'd lost her appetite completely now, but she forced herself to eat.

After several bites, she knew she couldn't eat any more. "Do you really think we lost them? They seem to be everywhere."

"We will once I get rid of the car," he said. "And no one thinks about trains these days."

"Except you," she said.

"Except me," he agreed.

"I want to call Terri."

"Are you worried about her or Nick?" His voice was cool and she wondered whether she had just lost the ground she'd gained.

"Both."

"Let's wait a while," he said. "We need that cell phone. If they have a trace on the Faulkner phones, we might compromise it. Nor should we call from here. If they pinpoint this telephone, they can find whatever other numbers were called within a few moments."

"And learn that someone called Amtrak," she said.

He paid the bill and they went to the car. He studied every car in the parking lot, but then shook his head. "Won't do any good if they have something planted in my car, and they had the opportunity at your house." He went back into the restaurant; she followed him.

He went straight to the cash register and gave the lady behind it a devastating smile.

"Do you know someone reliable who could give us a ride to the bus station in Denver?" he said. "I don't like the way the car is running, and we're due in Flagstaff for her mother's wedding." He put an arm around Sam. "I'll make it worth his while."

"What about your car?"

"I'll call the rental company and have them pick it up."

"I'll see what I can do," she said.

Ten minutes later they had a ride to Denver for a hundred dollars cash and a full tank of gas.

They caught the train seconds before it pulled out. The tardiness was planned.

The train started moving, and Nate looked for the conductor. Within minutes, they had tickets for a deluxe bedroom.

Nate said a brief prayer of thanks. He was ready to drop. A coach seat had not appealed to him.

The conductor showed them to a compartment. It was tiny with a cushy sofa and armchair and its own private sink, shower and toilet. A decided plus.

An attendant appeared almost immediately and asked whether they wanted their meal in the room or in the café or lounge car. They opted for the room. They ordered steaks and a bottle of wine and sat on the sofa, watching as foothills became prairie and the last glimmers of twilight faded into night.

He hoped he wasn't relaxing too much. But there was no way anyone could find them here, not after all the precautions he'd taken. And he was so damned tired.

He checked his weapon. That was the other reason he wanted to take a train. No one checked for weapons.

As a federal law enforcement officer, he could have declared his weapon on a flight but new security measures probably would mean a check with his office. He hadn't wanted that.

As soon as they ate, he would ask that the beds be prepared. The sofa would magically become a bed and an upper berth pulled down. The clackety clack of wheels beneath them already made a soothing lullaby.

In the interim, he simply enjoyed being with Sam. She leaned against him, and he put his arm around her. Tension drained from him. There was something about a train that always had that effect on him.

He'd picked up the schedule at the station. They'd bought tickets to Chicago, but he planned to leave the train at Naperville and take a second train into the city. Then they would find the elusive Patsy Carroll.

His eyes had almost closed when the attendant arrived to set a table with a linen tablecloth, then returned with steaks, baked potatoes and mixed vegetables.

Nate couldn't take his eyes from Sam as she ate with apprehension. They'd both purchased new clothes and she had a way of making even the most casual slacks and plain shirt look elegant. He continued to watch her rather than eat until she very pointedly looked at his plate.

He nursed one glass of wine while she had a second. He wasn't sure how well that went with the medicine she was taking, but if anyone deserved a few moments of normalcy, it was Samantha. When they finished, he asked the attendant to prepare the beds.

The lower one was wider than the upper berth. Two people could fit on the lower one only if they lay like spoons.

Spoons sounded pretty good.

But sleep sounded even better if not as enjoyable. He needed sleep to maintain an edge.

He looked at his watch. Ten Denver time.

He put out the DO NOT DISTURB sign, secured the door, then backed up the one chair against it.

"You take the shower first," he offered.

She smiled. "What about simultaneously?"

"You haven't seen the shower."

"Where there's a will, there's a way," she said. She lifted up on her toes to brush a kiss across his lips.

"Don't do that to your bodyguard," he scolded.

"A bodyguard is Kelley," she said. "You're—"

"I'm what?" he asked when she stopped.

"A friend."

He flinched at that. He didn't want to be that either.

He skimmed his hand over the shirt they'd purchased for her that afternoon while waiting for the train. Clothes and simple things like a razor and toothbrushes. He stopped at the open vee, and his fingers touched the swelling of her breast.

She trembled, but probably no more than he.

"Damn," he said out loud. *Stupid,* he said under his breath. Yet he bent over her, his lips brushing hers and raining light kisses over her cheek and down her neck.

He kissed his way back up to her mouth, deepening the

kiss. He was exhausted. He was also on fire as he always was when near her. Her eyes, weary a few moments ago, were now glimmering with life. He touched her everywhere, sliding her clothes off, his gaze possessively following the progress of his hands.

She turned toward the window.

"There's no one out there," he said, but he leaned over and pulled down the shade as she unbuttoned his shirt. His skin was alive with wanting, alive with hundreds of writhing nerve ends.

She was as adept at taking off his clothes as he had been at hers. The car lurched and her body impacted with his. His body hardened, trembling with a need that went beyond lust or passion.

There was so little space that they naturally drifted onto the lower berth. He entered her, full and throbbing, but slowly. The urgency between them intensified and he felt her tighten around him. Their bodies reacted to each other with frenzied need and he plunged deeper into her, his strokes growing faster.

She wrapped her good leg around him, bringing him to the core of her. She cried out as the primitive dance turned wild and uncontrollable, reaching beyond familiar feelings and ending in flashes of white-hot splendor.

He kept her next to him, his body still fused to hers. They heard the lonesome call of the train whistle as they approached a crossing. Her body snuggled closer into his and relaxed, and several moments later he realized she was asleep.

Nathan McLean, sworn enemy of the Merrittas, touched her hair as his own eyes closed. He reached over to his clothes, felt the pistol there. Satisfied, he began the slow descent into sleep, knowing he wanted this Merritta with him. Always.

Tomorrow, though, they would be taunting the tiger.

He had to remember that.

thirty-one

Sam woke to the light filtering into the small compartment and the sound of movement outside their room.

Nate's arms were still wrapped around her, probably by necessity due to the narrow berth, but they felt wonderful under any circumstances. She moved slightly and then so did he, and she realized he must have been awake but had not wanted to disturb her.

"Hmmmm," she murmured as she turned and looked at him.

His hair looked more mussed than usual and his cheeks had an overnight beard, but his eyes were as brilliant as ever and he looked incredibly sexy. "They deliver coffee," he said.

"I don't need coffee."

"How is your leg?"

She grinned at him. "What leg?"

He looked toward the door. He had locked it last night and shoved a chair in front of it as an extra precaution, but she knew he felt that they were safe here. Secure.

For a few more hours, anyway. Hours that belonged just to them.

For a fraction of a second, she wondered how Jack

Maddox was making out with the police. And Terri. Was she safe? Then her mind jumped to her newly found brother. *What was he doing in Steamboat Springs?*

"What are you thinking about?"

"You. Jack Maddox. Terri. My . . . brother." She wasn't sure how the latter would affect him. He'd seemed to change in the past few days, but . . .

"You want to call Terri?" He knew it wasn't only Terri she wanted to know about. But Nick Merritt as well. Was he still in Steamboat Springs? Well, he wanted to know that, too.

"Yes."

His arms tightened around her.

"Can we call from the train?"

He looked at his watch. "There's a brief stop in Omaha," he said. "You can call from a pay phone there. I hate to use Maddox's cell phone unless we have to. He says it's safe, but there are always ways with sophisticated equipment."

"How long before we get there?"

"About thirty minutes."

She snuggled into him, hearing his indrawn breath and feeling his body harden again.

"Sam?"

"We have time," she pointed out logically and, hopefully, steadily. Her body was already reacting to his in very sensuous ways.

He didn't require more convincing. He nibbled at her neck until her body felt as if it were on fire. His fingers played with her pubic hair, then touched the most intimate part of her until she was writhing with need.

When he finally entered her, his movements were slow and tantalizing until she was nearly mad with wanting him. She wondered whether this kind of madness remained through the years, the fierce urgency that counterpointed moments of extreme tenderness and wonder. He stopped and leaned over, showering her face and neck and shoulders with light teasing kisses, titillating and tormenting her until she arched her body toward him.

Nate's slow deliberate strokes fanned the blazes inside her. He moved faster until the world swirled with such speed that she thought she would be carried away by some magical force. Shattering explosions rocked every fiber of her being with rolling waves of sensations.

They both sank down to earth, depleted and sated, and she felt a warm, wonderful lassitude that cosseted and enveloped them like a thick feather comforter on a cold winter night. She heard his heartbeat. It seemed in rhythm with the song of the wheels beneath them, and nothing in her life had ever seemed so natural. So right.

The back of her hand rubbed against the bristle on his cheeks. Then her tongue ran over them, then licked the tiny lines that fanned from his eyes.

"Oh, you're heading for trouble, Miss Carroll," he said lazily, even as he rolled away from her and easily sprang to his feet. He leaned down and kissed her lightly before looking at his watch. "You have five minutes before the train stops, then fifteen to find a phone booth outside the station."

Still feeling fuzzy and warm and filled with him, she forced herself to get up, pull on the same clothes she wore yesterday and run a comb through her hair while he took a hurried shower. She rinsed her face and noticed it was glowing. The train whistle blew and the car seemed to slow.

She quickly added a touch of lipstick and then left the tiny bathroom.

Nathan pushed the chair away from the door and unlocked it. He still hadn't shaved, but she liked the way he looked just fine.

They met the attendant. He smiled, and she wondered

whether her face told him exactly what had happened a few minutes ago.

"Would you like coffee and breakfast?" the attendant asked.

"We're going to step inside the station for a few moments," Nate said. "Then we'll go to the dining car."

"As you like, sir, madam. Would you like me to make up your room?"

Nathan nodded.

The train slowed, jerked. Came to a halt.

"We leave in twenty minutes sharp," the attendant said. "We'll be back."

Together they stepped off the train, went through the station and looked around. Nate wanted anything but a train station phone. He saw a café and they hurried over to it. She found a phone and dialed Terri's cell number.

Nate had said they might have four or five minutes before anyone could trace the numbers.

Terri picked up immediately.

"Terri?"

"Yes. Are you all right?"

"It's been quiet," she said.

"Any repairman at your home?"

"I don't think so."

"Is Nicholas still there?"

"Yes. He needs to talk to you. He knows who is behind at least some of the attacks. He says he has to see you."

Sam looked at Nate. He had his eye on his watch. He held up one finger. She covered the mouthpiece. "Nicholas says he knows who is behind what's been happening. He wants to see me."

"Tomorrow," he said. "The Adler Planetarium in Chicago. The Sky Show at eleven a.m."

She stared at him for a moment, then relayed the message to Terri.

"Get off," he mouthed.

"Have to go. I'll talk to you later." She hung up before Terri could say anything else, then turned to him. "How did you know the schedule?"

"I was there three months ago on business." He took the phone and dialed Gray's cell phone.

It took eight rings, then Gray answered. As he'd listened in on her conversation, now she did the same.

"Had to duck out, buddy," the disembodied voice said.

"What did you find out?"

"Very little. Your man Maddox seems on the level. He *is* ex-CIA. Has a company in Flagstaff. He's well liked, well respected."

"And Simon?"

"Not so lucky. Can't find a Simon in Durango. Checked all the local airfields. I have a list of private plane owners but it's extensive, and I have to be careful."

"That's okay," Nate said. "Drop it. You gave me what I needed."

"The photos of those officers will take time," Gray said.

"I need only one," he said.

"Which one?"

"McGuire."

A long silence. Too long.

"You've got to be wrong."

"I might be," Nate said. "But if you can find one of him as a patrolman, e-mail it to me. I'll find a computer some-place."

"Done, but I think you're wrong."

Then Nate took a step away from her, and she knew he wanted a few words in privacy.

She left the telephone and walked to the door. Waited.

In another minute, Nate met her there. "Let's go," he said, grabbing her hand and walking swiftly back through the station and on board the train. They went to the compartment, and it had been transformed back into a sitting room. A newspaper was on the table.

Nate took a quick visual check of the room, then they walked to the dining car as the train started once more. They walked—or lurched—through three cars as the train gathered speed.

A few more hours of peace, then . . . all hell was going to break loose.

Nick picked up the telephone.

"Hi, it's Terri."

Just the sound of her voice brightened his day.

"I have to talk to you," she continued.

"Breakfast?"

"Yes," she replied.

"Where?"

"The coffee shop next to the hotel down the street."

"I'll be there in ten minutes."

"Good."

He shaved hurriedly. He'd already had a cup of coffee and read the national paper that had appeared at his door.

She was seated in a corner table. Her hair was pulled back in a braid, and she wore jeans and a dark blue shirt.

"Sam called," she said.

Relief flooded him. "She's all right?"

"At the moment."

"Where—?"

"I don't know, but she said she would meet you at the Adler Planetarium in Chicago at eleven a.m. tomorrow."

"How did she contact you?"

"I don't know where she called from," Terri said. "But she called me on my cell phone."

"How long was she on it?"

"Just a few minutes."

"Good."

"Do you really think someone's tracking my cell phone?"

"I don't think we can dismiss the idea." He took a sip of coffee. "Is she still with McLean?"

"She didn't mention it, but I think so."

"Good."

"I didn't think you liked him."

"I don't, and I'm still afraid he will try to use her, but he'll do his damnedest to keep her alive."

"You're going to go, then?"

"Yes."

"I want to go with you."

He studied her for a moment. "Why?"

"She's my friend."

"And you're afraid I might hurt her?" An unexpected pain struck him.

"No," she said. "I don't think that. But you might need someone to run interference."

"It's too dangerous."

"I won't stay around except for the meeting," she said. "Please."

"What about the gallery?"

"We can close it for several days."

He shook his head, then ran a finger along her cheekbone. "I would like to have you with me, but you could endanger everyone. If I have to look out for you, I can't look after Samantha."

It was the one argument he thought might work. And it did. Her face fell.

"I'll come back," he said.

Her expression was disbelieving.

"Believe it," he said.

She smiled and looked up straight in his eyes and through to his soul.

And he knew it was one promise he would keep.

*   *   *

Nathan and Sam left the train in Naperville, the station before the Chicago terminal. "Time to use the cell phone," he said.

Sam dialed the number Maddox had given them when they'd arrived in Fort Collins. The same man answered after half a ring.

"Yes."

"This is Samantha."

"We've been worried about you."

"Mr. Maddox?"

"He's fine. He arrived a few hours ago."

"Jock, too?"

"Yep. They used my plane. Where are you now?"

"Is this line safe?"

"I would stake my life on it."

"Naperville."

"How did you get there?"

"Train."

"Paid with cash?"

"Yes."

"Good. Go to the Riverwalk. Be at the foot of Chicago Avenue and Main Street at eight tonight."

"Who do I look for?"

"Don't. I'll find you."

The phone went dead.

Sam and Nathan looked at each other. Five hours to kill and they should have some answers. At last.

The house where Sam was to meet her mother was in an area north of Chicago, in a lake community of large wooded lots and contemporary houses. Simon drove up a long, curving driveway to a stone house. It was shielded from other houses by a stand of trees.

The man in the driver's seat of a plain black sedan had been mostly silent since he'd approached them on Chicago Avenue. A quiet, wiry man who walked soundlessly and

said little, he, like Maddox, had a certain vitality about
him.

He'd merely nodded at them and said, "Follow me."

He wasn't any more talkative as he drove. His mouth
had tightened when he heard about the calls to Terri
Faulkner and the proposed meeting with Nicholas Merritt.

"We don't have to meet him," Nathan said. "But I
wanted him in a place where we can find him if we do need
him. He says he knows who did it."

Sam noticed that Nate didn't add that he knew, too, or
thought he did. He was waiting, she suspected, to see what
the others knew. She also knew he'd checked his weapon
just after they got in to the car and that he'd insisted on the
backseat.

She wondered whether there would ever be a day when
such precautions wouldn't be necessary. But right now, she
felt a thrill of excitement at seeing her mother.

It increased as the driver parked in front of the house.
He opened the door to her side while Nate exited the
other.

The house door opened before they could ring the bell
or knock. Sam saw her mother standing there, a broad
smile on her face. They embraced for a moment, and then
Sam stepped back and studied her face.

It had been only a few days, but it seemed a lifetime.

Patsy Carroll looked different. Older. Yet there was also
an ease about her that hadn't been there before. It was almost like a tremendous weight had been lifted from her
shoulders.

Nathan had entered and stood to the side. Her mother
turned to him. "You must be Nathan McLean."

"Yes, ma'am."

"Thank you."

Nathan didn't say anything, but Sam watched his eyes

evaluate her mother. There was reservation in his voice, in his face, but she was familiar with that.

"Whose house is this?" Sam asked.

"Friends," Simon said. "They're out of the country and friends often stay here when they're gone. The neighbors are used to comings and goings."

He led the way into a kitchen. Sam smelled coffee and knew it would probably be a long evening.

Papers were spread across the table. So were photos.

Nate sat down and looked at the names on the list, then the photos. "Do you have a computer here?"

The man called Simon disappeared and returned with a small laptop, plugged in the modem and turned it on.

He turned to Nate with a question in his face.

"Find McGuire," said Nate. "Terrence McGuire. Boston."

Simon showed surprise for the first time, and his fingers raced over the keyboard. He went to the *Boston Globe* site, then searched on McGuire. Articles and a photo appeared. He turned it around for Patsy to see.

"I don't know," she said. "It was so long ago. . . ."

Simon was reading one of the articles. "Nominated for the Federal Appeals Court. Former police officer, assistant district attorney, then district attorney."

"He's a favorite of ours," Nate said. "He leaned over backward to give us search warrants and other orders."

Simon mumbled something that sounded like a curse.

Patsy looked at the photo again. "It could be. He had dark hair then and was thin. I thought he had a . . . hungry look."

But the photos now were of a well-fed man with gray hair. He looked benign, not hungry.

But then maybe that was because he'd eaten his fill of what he wanted.

"He's Irish," Sam said. "Why would he connect with the Merrittas?"

"Good for both of them," Nathan said. "No one would

suspect him. And he might have had knowledge of the Irish families that Merritta wanted, and vice versa."

"How could he have kept it quiet all these years?"

"I'd guess he quit when he went to law school. People died. And I'm sure he had a lot of insurance of his own."

Nathan's glance turned to Patsy. "What exactly happened?"

She looked at Simon, and he nodded.

Her hands twisted together in front of her. "Lucas Gaberna was a driver and often chauffeured the children and me. I saw him as the only way out. I thought he . . . he liked me, and to my everlasting shame, I used that.

"But his interest, apparently, was not me. He was an undercover federal agent. A police officer had been taking payoffs from my father-in-law and heard there was a snitch in the family. Paul's father and the officer narrowed it down to Lucas.

"They'd bugged the car. They knew what he was and that I had asked him to help me get away. Paul's father was furious. Beyond furious. I had appealed to the enemy. I had betrayed Paul. I would take his children over his dead body."

She paused, swallowed hard. "It was Lucas's body instead. I saw the officer go into the study with my husband and father-in-law. Several minutes later, two men went after Lucas. I knew what was going to happen. I knew it by their faces. And I couldn't do anything about it. Victor and another man dragged me to another room.

"I heard a shot, then a second. I ran out before they could reach me and saw Paul coming out of the room. He brushed past me, as if he didn't see anything at all. He had blood on his clothes.

"Then Paul's father left, carrying a gun wrapped in a handkerchief. There was blood on that, too. I thought then that Paul had killed Lucas.

"I couldn't stand to have him near me after that. His father, who had never liked me because I wasn't Italian or Catholic, became openly threatening.

"I kept expecting a bullet myself, but instead I was isolated. I knew I had to get away, but I also knew I didn't have the resources to escape the family's reach. I had no doubt they would kill me if they found me unless I had something of value to them.

"The only possibility was the safe in Paul's father's study. I'd been in the study once when he'd opened it to give me a family heirloom at Paul's insistence. I knew where it was and that it was a combination lock, and I prayed there would be something in it with which I could bargain.

"I started working on a collection of safe combination possibilities. His birthday. His late wife's birthday; the day of her death; Paul's birthday; Nick's birthday. Anniversaries. Anything I could think of.

"Two weeks went by before I had a chance, then there was a baptism for Anna. Everyone in the family was going but me. I was to stay with the children.

"While everyone was at church, I asked my minder to look after the children while I went down and made formula. I made several bottles, then went into my father-in-law's office. I found the safe and started turning the combination lock. I won't tell you how terrified I was, how my fingers wouldn't work properly, but on the third number—his wedding anniversary—the lock clicked.

"I heard one of the babies screaming, and I knew my minder would be down soon. I looked inside. Money. Then, toward the back, in the shadows, I saw an object wrapped in a handkerchief. It was a pistol wrapped in a bloodstained cloth. I knew it was my one chance to escape. I grabbed it, was able to hide it in a towel."

"Why," Nathan asked, "would he keep the pistol?"

Patsy shook her head. "I've thought about it all these years. I don't think he trusted the police officer. The killing was also staged to keep Paul in line. I think Paul was wavering, that he wanted out, but now he was an accessory to the murder of a federal agent. He could never leave the family."

Sam was stunned. She couldn't even imagine how her mother had survived, much less escaped. "How did you leave?"

"I knew I didn't have much time. They would find the gun was missing. The next day, when Paul and his father were gone, I put heating pads on both your faces. I'd mentioned earlier in the day you were both fretful.

"Then I screamed that you had to go to the doctor. You had unbelievably high temperatures. I think they were afraid not to take me. Paul and his father worshiped Nicholas. He was their heir.

"I won't go into details, but I called a cab from the doctor's office and was able to slip out while the bodyguard was in the waiting room. I reached Chicago before Paul found me. He knew I would go to my sister's for help. I was careful in arranging to meet her, but I underestimated Paul's reach.

"But by then I had put the gun in a safe deposit box. I wanted to take it to federal authorities, but not in Boston. I didn't trust anyone in Boston. My only friend had been killed. To tell you the truth, I didn't know what to do when Paul appeared. He had men with him. He could have taken my children and killed me. He even threatened my sister's children." Tears rolled silently down her face. "He offered me a deal. He would take Nicholas. I would take Nicole. Otherwise his father had ordered me killed, along with my sister's family.

"Paul said he would hunt us all down if I ever tried to contact Nicholas. When I agreed, he promised that my sister would not be touched, or any of her family. He kept that promise."

Pain was in every word. Sam could only imagine having to make that choice. And her biological father was the one who forced that choice.

The man who had called her to Boston.

"The devil's bargain," he had called the arrangement.

But *he* had been the devil.

thirty-two

"That's not enough," Nathan said, a cold clamp on his heart. "It wouldn't be half enough to convict someone of McGuire's standing. No body. No live witness. Only a gun with prints."

Simon nodded. "But questions would certainly derail his nomination."

"He'd still be alive to come after the people who destroyed his dream," Nathan said.

Sam broke in. "Nicholas says he knows who it is, too. Maybe he knows something we don't."

"Or maybe he wants to know exactly what we know," Nate said.

Sam's face fell, and he took her hand. "If it *is* McGuire, he must be desperate."

"I suspect that Paul Merritta assured him that she was either dead or under control. When Paul got sick, McGuire could have learned about you and your mother through FBI tapes of conversations in the Merritta family. He must have had heart palpitations. Especially coming at a time of intense political and media scrutiny."

"In other words . . . my father's timing was very poor."

"I think Paul wanted to see his daughter before he

died," Patsy interjected quietly. "I believe he really thought he could protect you." She hesitated. "I've been thinking about him a lot, remembering little things. I think what he did thirty-four years ago came from his father, that he knew his father would kill me without regret. He used the only weapon he knew to keep me from going to the authorities, and that was my children and my sister's children."

Heads turned toward Sam. "What exactly did Merritta tell you?"

"All he said was that I was unfinished business."

"Nicholas," Patsy said. "He's the key."

Simon looked at the three of them. Patsy Carroll. Sam. And finally Nate. "You know him. What do you think, Nate?"

It was the time to sort out feelings. To discard the prejudice he had against Nick Merritt because he was a Merritta. In his mind's eye, he saw Merritt throw himself in front of Sam when a car speeded by his front step, hearing Sam's words that he leaned into a bullet for her that night his car was run off the road.

If Nate was wrong, he could be signing Samantha's death warrant.

"I think we should talk to him," he said.

Simon nodded. "That was an interesting selection of meeting places."

"It was the only crowded place that came readily to my mind," he admitted. "I don't know Chicago that well, but the planetarium is one of my favorite places. I stop there whenever I come to town. I know its nooks and crannies."

Simon stood. "Jack and I will go early tomorrow and scout it out."

"Where is he?" Sam asked.

"After the little tussle in Fort Collins, we figured he ought to stay away from this place. He's in Chicago, though. He flew in on a private plane."

Nate felt a hell of a lot better. He was beginning to think their small shadow army was a match for the person authorizing contracts, or even his fellow cops. They didn't have to play by the rules.

"We think there's someone else involved, too," Nate told them.

"Jack explained," Simon said. His glance rested a little longer than necessary on Sam's mother.

"There's Victor, George, Anna, Rosa, and a few other assorted characters. My money's on George," said Nate. "He's ambitious and vicious."

"Nicholas Merritt can help us with that. If he will."

Patsy bit her lip. "I don't know why he would. I don't mean anything to him."

"I think Sam does," Nathan said.

Simon poured another cup of coffee. "If Nicholas confirms all this, then we have to set a neat little trap."

"My thoughts exactly," Nathan said.

"McGuire—if it is McGuire—probably doesn't know exactly what Patsy has. A little blackmail threat might do wonders in bringing him out of his hole."

Simon was right. There was no other way. From what Patsy said, the evidence was slim. It might have been more powerful thirty-four years ago. A fresh patrolman wouldn't have the clout of a federal judge.

But he didn't like making Sam—or her mother—a bull's-eye. He didn't want to think that he had planned exactly that a week or ten days ago. Now he would do almost anything to keep it from happening.

It was the only way to keep them safe, to give them back a life.

They left it that way when they left the table, which turned out to be a little awkward. There were three bedrooms. Patsy had one, Simon another.

"Nathan and I will share a bedroom," Sam offered. Her mother raised an eyebrow but said nothing.

Sam turned to Nathan. "I want to talk to my mother for a while."

"We'll check outside," Simon said. Nate went with him out the front door. Nothing unusual, though Nate didn't like the woods around them. Too many hiding places.

"The house has a state-of-the-art security system," Simon said.

They walked around to the back and sat down in lawn chairs.

Simon looked relaxed, but Nate knew he was listening, that every instinct was alert.

"Will McGuire bite?" Simon asked.

"He has to. He has too many loose ends now. Now that we know where to start, we can eventually find out he was the one issuing a contract. There has to be a money trail."

"I found out a lot about you," Simon said.

Nate raised an eyebrow.

"Good cop, bad team player. You hate the Merrittas. How did you get hooked up with the daughter?"

"Lucky, I guess," he said wryly.

"You're willing to lose your job for her?"

"I probably already have."

"No doubt you will if you go along with this."

"I've made my decision," Nate said softly. "She doesn't deserve any of this."

"Neither did her mother."

Nate didn't say anything.

"I saw you look at her when you first came in. How could she abandon a child? David told me it haunted her every day of her life. He said she woke up two or three nights a week with nightmares."

"I'm not judging anyone."

"I just wanted you to know."

"Thanks."

They sat out there a few more moments. Nate wanted to give Sam time with her mother. They needed it.

The silence between him and Simon was companionable. They instinctively trusted each other. "Your name isn't Simon."

"No," Simon said. "But Jack's using his own name. We thought one of us should retain some mystery." He hesitated. "My buddies stuck it on me. Simple Simon, they used to call me, cause I had a real talent for making things simple. I don't believe in bullshit."

Nate smiled. "You and Jack and David Carroll must have been hell on wheels."

"David was the best one of us," Simon said.

"Are either of you married?"

"Both divorced. It's not easy to settle down after the kind of life we had. We're both wanderers." He hesitated then said, "My name is Michael Malone."

They heard a car coming down the street and without a word they both rose and went around the house, keeping to the shadows. A car disappeared down the street.

"People who own this with the government?" Nate asked.

"Yep. I asked around for a safe house."

"Do the other residents know what their neighbor does for a living?"

"Probably don't have a clue. And by the way, it's a she."

They went inside.

Sam wanted to go to the planetarium.

Nathan hesitated. All his protective instincts said no.

"He might not show if he sees only you," Sam said. "Terri said he wanted to see *me*."

"I want to go, too," Patsy said.

"Hell, no," both men said in unison.

"He's my son. I've waited more than thirty-four years to see him." Tears hovered in the corners of her eyes and she played with the bracelet she always wore.

"It *will* happen," Simon said. "But not now."

"She shouldn't be left alone. Neither should Sam," Nate said.

"She won't be," Simon said. "I'll stay. You and Jack and Samantha meet him. Jack was there earlier. He studied every inch of the place. Every exit. Every fire alarm if it comes to that."

So that became the plan. Nathan didn't like it but he knew he was outvoted.

They had cereal, orange juice and toast for breakfast, though Patsy offered to fix a big breakfast. Nathan borrowed a lightweight sports jacket from one of the closets to cover his holstered pistol.

At ten, Nathan and Sam left the house in Simon's rented sedan. They would meet Jack at the door of the planetarium.

When they arrived, children were streaming off school buses. For a moment, Nathan regretted his choice. If there was any shooting, he'd never forgive himself.

They saw Maddox sitting at the top of the steps, wearing dark glasses. Jock was wearing a seeing eye dog harness.

Sam chuckled but passed without a word. Nathan grinned to himself and continued inside, knowing Maddox and Jock would follow.

There was a metal detector that hadn't been there last time he had entered. Sam went through first. He followed, pulling out his credentials and badge, saying there was a confidential investigation and the officer was not to say anything. An awed security guard allowed him in.

Maddox made it through the checkpoint with even more ease after the dog refused to go through the metal detector. "Just go around, sir," the guard said.

Nate watched with amusement as he stopped to replace his credentials. Jock was the model of seeing eye dog behavior. Nate wondered how many times they'd pulled that act before, and why.

He checked his watch. A few moments before the appointed time. They reached the designated place. No Merritt.

Kids were lining up at the doors. Sam looked around anxiously. Maddox sat on a bench nearby.

Eleven came and went. The kids disappeared inside, then Nate saw Merritt striding across the hall. His arm was no longer in a sling but he held it stiffly.

"You're late," Nate said dourly.

"I wanted to make sure you weren't followed."

"I took precautions."

"Let's go somewhere where we can talk."

"There's some classrooms upstairs. We can go up there."

"You still don't trust me."

"I wouldn't trust my own brother right now," Nate replied.

"Nice," Merritt said, and turned to Sam. His expression softened. "I heard about what happened in Steamboat Springs. I'm sorry."

Nate shook his head, then led the way to an escalator. Maddox and the dog followed.

Merritt did a double take, then stared at Maddox's face and glasses. He turned to Nate and gave him a puzzled look. "He's with us," Nate said.

For the first time in their long-standing adversarial relationship, Merritt smiled.

They found an empty room and went inside. Maddox followed, shutting the door behind them. He took off his dark glasses and leaned against it.

"Okay," Nate said. "What do you know?"

"The man behind one of the contracts is Judge McGuire." Nick raised an eyebrow. "You're not surprised."

"Not much. Who else?"

Nick looked stunned that they knew McGuire's name.

"Georgie? Victor?" Nate persisted.

"Not Victor. He doesn't have the guts. George is too cautious."

"Then . . . ?"

Nick shrugged.

"Damn you," Nate said.

"I really *don't* know. I can help you find out."

"Why?"

"Because it's time for the family to stop Pop—" He stopped suddenly.

"How can you help?"

"You have to draw out McGuire first, then whoever in the family wants Samantha dead."

Nate didn't want to trust him. He'd spent too many years trying to put him in jail. But now, reluctantly, he did.

He looked at Maddox. He nodded.

"Okay. What do you propose?"

"That I pretend to find what my mother has been hiding. I'll sell it—and silence—for a hundred thousand dollars." He paused. "I'm a Merritta. He'll believe me. He won't believe you." Bitterness tinged his words.

Sam shook her head. "It's too dangerous. You'll be making yourself a target."

"A target like you?" Nick asked. "*You* didn't do anything."

"Neither did you."

"I tolerated," he said. "I closed my eyes. I never really left."

They decided to stay in Chicago. McGuire had too many contacts in Boston, including, quite possibly, some agents in the Bureau. They would make him come to them. He would have no choice now.

Sam knew Nathan still hesitated to take Nick Merritt to the safe house. But it would be too dangerous for him to stay alone. And she knew Nathan wanted to keep an eye on him. She suspected the next few days wouldn't be easy.

"Mother's there," Sam told Nick.

A muscle moved in his throat. "I suppose it's time."

The three of them left together. Maddox and his ever-present companion went somewhere else. The drive was long and tense. Nick was moody and quiet. Nathan obviously had lingering suspicions. She wondered whether the two would ever be friends.

The atmosphere of tension grew denser as they neared the house. Nathan stopped a mile away and looked at Nick in the backseat. "If anything goes wrong, I'll kill you," he said mildly.

"A great deal could go wrong," Nick replied. "You're not playing with amateurs."

"Just as long as it's not because of you."

He started the car again.

"Fair enough," Nick said, matching Nathan's mild tone.

Sam shivered at the utter ruthlessness with which these two men she loved had to conduct their lives.

They drove into the garage. Sam got out before anyone could help her and knocked on the door. Her mother answered it, then fixed her gaze on the tall, loose-limbed man who climbed out of the backseat.

Her mother swallowed hard and her body tensed. Sam knew it was all she could do to remain motionless, to let Nick come to her.

He ascended the steps at a measured pace. His expression was stiff. Cold.

"Nicholas," Patsy said. "Thank you for coming."

He remained silent for a moment, then, "You look like the photo I have."

She held out her hand to him, and Sam couldn't breathe. *Take it,* she willed him. *Take it.*

After a brief hesitation, he did. Not for long, but it was the first step.

Her mother turned and walked inside, her back unnaturally straight. Nick stood back for Sam to go after her. She gave him a broad smile as she passed him.

A beginning.

Nick called McGuire on Simon's phone. They had the judge's direct line.

"Remember," Simon said, "keep it simple."

Nick nodded. He punched the numbers, asking for Judge McGuire and was told the judge was in the courtroom. "Tell him it's about Tracy Merritta," he said. "I'll call back at five."

Simon approved. He'd had reservations about Nick, too, but they had seemed to fade as they sat around the kitchen table and planned out every word. "That should give him something to think about for the rest of the afternoon," he said with satisfaction.

Strangely enough, Simon and Nick seemed to gravitate toward each other. Sam thought it might be because Simon gave him a shield against Patsy and herself.

She did manage to get him alone for a few moments. "How is Terri?"

His face softened, and she saw something in his eyes she'd not seen before. "She's a good friend," he said cautiously.

"She said you went to supper together," she continued to probe.

"Yes," he replied unhelpfully.

"Will you come and see me in Steamboat?"

"Are you trying to be a matchmaker?"

Her face flushed with heat.

"I like her, Samantha," he said. "Is that what you wanted to hear?"

It was indeed.

*   *   *

Nick waited to call McGuire at five-thirty, thirty minutes late. "Let him sweat," Simon said, handing him a cell phone. "Don't stay on the line more than four minutes. He might have it traced, though I doubt it. He won't want anyone to know about this." McGuire picked the phone up almost immediately.

Minutes later, Simon ran the recorded conversation for the others. If there had been any doubt that McGuire was their man, there was none now.

"Nicholas Merritt," Nick said. "I might have something you lost."

"Can't think of anything," McGuire said cautiously.

"Well then, I can turn it—them—over to the proper authorities in Washington."

Silence. McGuire would most certainly be worried about being taped. "What do you want?"

"A finder's fee."

"Are you speaking for your family?"

"I speak for myself."

"I'm sorry, young man. Whatever you have is of no interest to me."

"Not even a thirty-four-year old pistol?" He allowed that to sink in, then added, "Tomorrow is the weekend. I would take a trip to Chicago if I were you. It's an interesting city." He named a hotel. "There will be something there on your arrival." He hung up.

"Simon will take over a message for him tomorrow," Nate said.

"*If* he comes."

"Oh, he'll come all right. He has to learn how many people know what happened thirty-four years ago, and the location of that gun."

"I've rented a cabin on a lake not far from here," Simon said. "No one else is around. I don't want a shoot-out in this neighborhood, or I'll never get a loaner house again. Patsy, Samantha and Nate will stay here. I don't think he should be involved in what's going on. And he can protect you."

Nate nodded.

"Now we wait," Simon agreed.

The tension in the house was thick. It wasn't only the waiting but awkwardness. Nathan and Nick still reacted like junkyard dogs, bristling when they neared each other. Patsy Carroll tried too hard to act normally, even when her gaze constantly roamed to her son, who treated her with studied politeness.

Nate no longer shared her bed. Nick was given the second bedroom. Simon and Nate decided to share the sofa. One watched from the window while the other slept. Sam wasn't happy with the arrangement. She missed the feel of his body beside her, but she realized it was for the best. There was enough tension without the two of them retiring to bed together.

But the hours crawled at night. She worried about each and every one of them.

Simon left the next morning to deliver a note to the hotel, then to find a pistol identical to the one that killed an undercover agent thirty-four years ago. Nate stayed at her side while Nicholas used a laptop he'd brought with him.

Her mother cooked, something she always did when she was nervous.

The phone rang and Jack Maddox picked it up, listened for a moment, then hung up. "He has the note," he told the others. "Simon says he does not look like a happy man."

"Anyone with him?"

"Not at the hotel."

"Maybe he will try to handle it alone," Nate said. "He used to be a cop. He knows how to use a firearm. He probably doesn't want to bring anyone else in; a federal judge is a big catch. Someone would turn on him in a New York second for a deal."

They had lunch together, then it was time to split.

Nicholas approached her. "I'm glad we met," he said, which she knew was a huge thing for him. She looked at Nate, whose expression didn't change.

They were more alike than they wanted to admit. Both of them had had difficult childhoods. As a result, both had barricaded their hearts. Neither knew how to reach out or commit. She wondered whether they recognized it in each other. Probably not.

Her mother stood there, her face agonized. Everyone in the room knew that the next few hours were going to be very dangerous. McGuire hadn't reached his position without being damned smart.

After a moment that seemed to last forever, Nick stepped over to Patsy Carroll. "We'll get acquainted," he said. There was a sudden gentleness in him that surprised Sam, but he'd surprised her before with it. Like Nate, she thought, his hard shell was there to protect a heart not as hard as he wanted everyone to think.

Then Nick and Simon left.

Her mother made coffee. Nate paced, pausing frequently to look outside, his body still, watchful, alert.

She turned on the television, more for the noise than anything else. Speech was too awkward, and she suspected neither she nor her mother had the attention span for a book. An all-news station didn't help relieve the tension. Death. Civil war. Scandal.

What was unwinding might turn out to be one of the biggest scandals yet.

She turned the television off.

And waited.

Nate knew something was wrong when five o'clock slipped by, then six. A judge would be punctual. Even a crooked one.

The note to McGuire had told him to meet Merritt at the cabin at five. It had instructed him to rent a car and gave directions to a public booth where there would be a phone call and further directions.

Nate called Merritt on the cell phone.

"McGuire answered the call at the service station," Merritt said. "But he hasn't shown up."

"Jack Maddox?"

"He's prowling the woods with Simon. He lost McGuire in the traffic."

That, Nate knew immediately, was where they'd made their mistake. But there hadn't been enough of them to go around.

Nate swore. "McGuire's probably on his way to the airport. Something must have spooked him."

"You're alone?"

"In here, I am."

Nate knew tiny television cameras and recording devices had been planted throughout the house and even outside.

Merritt hesitated. "Could they know about the house where you're staying?"

Nate's worry exactly. "Simon didn't think so. I was damned careful when I brought you back here, and there's no way McGuire could know about Simon."

Or was there? He had asked Gray to check out the two men. Had someone picked up their trail? Someone with better resources than their own?

"Get back here," he said. "If they get Sam and her mother, they can bargain for the gun." He hung up.

The cabin was at least an hour away.

He looked outside again. It seemed peaceful enough. He checked the locks and security system.

He thought about leaving the house, but he suspected that if he was right, they would be surrounded. If they left in a car, they would be even more vulnerable.

They were safer here.

"What is it?" Samantha said.

"Our judge didn't show."

"Then why did he come to Chicago?"

"More communication. More opportunities to find us."

"And you think they have?"

"I think it's possible."

"But Simon was so sure it was safe."

"There's always a way to find someone if you have sophisticated equipment, and I called Gray to check on Maddox and Simon. Someone might have picked up on that and found one or the other." He looked out again. "Get your gun," he said. Then he looked at Patsy Carroll. "Do you have a weapon?" She shook her head.

"Call the police," he said. "Tell them we're using a friend's house and there could be a burglar."

He wasn't going to take any chances this time. To hell with the consequences. She went to the phone in the house and lifted the receiver. "It's dead."

He took Simon's cell phone from his belt. A squealing noise. "Someone's blocking calls." He swore under his breath.

He looked out and saw a shadow among the trees. If he could see one, others were out there.

Suddenly the lights and power went off. It was not yet dusk and he could still see, but no electricity meant the alarm system was off, too.

He blamed himself for being a fool. He should have seen it coming.

Samantha had retrieved her gun.

"Mrs. Carroll, pull out the sofa and get behind it. Samantha, you cover the back."

He turned back to watch from the side of the window. Why in the hell hadn't he kept someone else with him? They had all been so sure they were safe here, that McGuire would go after the most immediate danger: Merritt. Evidently McGuire still considered the Carrolls more angerous. But why? The gun was of no use without a ody.

And the body had disappeared. That was the one part of ne equation that never made sense.

Unless . . . unless that was why Paul Merritta wanted to ee his daughter. To give her the one last piece to safeguard er. The location of a body long missing.

The sound of breaking glass came from a bedroom. He rouldn't make the mistake of going there. The intruder rould have to come through the hallway. He moved to the ide of the window just as the glass broke. A silencer. Then nother muffled sound. They were trying to keep him oc-upied.

He moved quickly in front of the window and fired nree shots at the direction from which the shot had seemed o come. Noise. He needed lots of noise now. Noise to rouse the neighbors and prompt them to call the police.

"Nathan!" Patsy Carroll's voice.

He whirled around and saw someone emerge from the all. He fired and the man went down.

Then another shot from outside the window passed just nches from Patsy Carroll and drove into a wall. She stood here, a butcher knife in her hand. She obviously was as areless of her own safety as her daughter.

Still carrying the knife, she went close to the man lying n the hall. "He looks dead."

A shot came from the back, and another one.

"Sam? Are you all right?" he yelled.

"Yes. He's crawling away."

That made three attackers down at least.

The sound of sirens pierced the air.

Nate saw a shadow disappear within the trees. He went o the back where Sam stood, holding her gun. A man lressed in camouflage was trying to get up from the round.

"Go see about the man in the hallway," he said. "I'll take care of this one."

She nodded.

Nathan went to where the man writhed on the ground. He tried to grab the automatic beside him, but Nathan kicked it away.

"The judge can't help you now," he said.

"What judge?" The man looked totally blank.

"Who sent you?"

The man didn't say anything, just moaned in agony.

Nate pointed his gun at the wounded man, ignoring his gasp of pain and the way he clutched his leg. "No one will know whether or not it was self-defense, if I shoot," Nate said.

"Anna," he said. "Anna Merritta."

thirty-three

Word of Anna Merritta's arrest and the Chicago shoot-out leaked through local law enforcement agencies, and enterprising reporters milked all their sources for information. Sam's and her mother's lives were being dissected across the country. So was every detail about the Merritta family.

Nick had demanded that the funeral be postponed until he and Sam returned to Boston the day after the shooting. At least the publicity would discourage attendance, Sam thought. The feeding frenzy of the local and national media would keep the infamous away in droves.

Not many of Paul Merritta's associates wanted to bear the scrutiny of hordes of federal agents and members of the press after newspaper headlines detailed the arrest of Anna Merritta and the attempted murder of Paul Merritta's wife and daughter, supposedly killed in an accident three decades ago.

Sam didn't want to consider what it would mean to her life, her mother's life and their gallery. Nothing would ever be the same for either of them.

But they were alive. And Sam was determined that they would stay that way.

She also had something she'd thought she would never

have. Even if it never came to anything more, she and Nate had experienced something grand and glorious. She didn't like to think about the future. He was FBI inside and out, despite his protestations. And now she was the notorious daughter of a mobster. That was obviously a career breaker.

After the shooting, her mother had answered the police's questions, then they had been released. Patsy disappeared with Simon—a matter of leverage, Simon and Nate said, with federal officials. They didn't dare play all their cards at once—and in the open—until they knew for sure if there was a leak in the Bureau.

Sam and Nate had gone straight to the FBI offices in Boston. She stared blandly at his immediate supervisor as he tried to take over and patronize her. She had never liked men who automatically treated women like the nearest footstool.

"I'm sorry, Agent Barker," she said evenly, surprising herself as well as Nate. "But I won't talk to anyone but the Agent in Charge. Nate tells me his name is Richard Woodward."

Barker looked at Nate, who shrugged, but Sam would have sworn she saw his mouth twitch as he glanced down at his shoes.

Barker gave her another condescending smile, a sure sign he was going to treat her like a piece of furniture again.

She lifted her chin a notch as she continued to stare at him. "Richard Woodward or no one," she said quietly.

Barker spun on his heel and stiffly walked to the door, ordering his secretary to show them to Woodward's office.

"Did you forget that he is armed?" Nate asked as they entered a larger reception office.

"I try very hard not to think of things like that when I'm being a feminist," she replied. "And I also knew I had you at my side," she added with a quick smile.

A secretary said they would have to wait a moment. In a moment, Agent in Charge Richard Woodward appeared in the doorway. "Nate, I understand you've had a few interesting days."

Nate turned to Sam. "This is Samantha Carroll. She won't talk to anyone but you."

Woodward raised an eyebrow. "And you didn't have anything to do with that?"

"He didn't," Sam confirmed.

He gave her a long, level stare, then grinned. "I like her. Come with me."

Sam felt immense relief that he wasn't holding her demand against either Nate or herself. The man definitely did not fool around.

Once inside, Nick didn't bother with preliminaries. "Listen to this tape first," he said.

He ran the tape of Nick's phone conversation with McGuire and injected their suspicions at strategic points in the dialogue. He also told Woodward he suspected leaks in the Bureau and had for a long time.

"The wounded suspect in Chicago said there had been four of them," Nate said as he punched the off button. "He also said they had expected only two women. He was angry at being lied to and ready to turn against Anna Merritta. In his world, being lied to was obviously a far worse sin than murdering women. Attempted murder will put her away for a long time."

But the judge had remained a problem.

Woodward was skeptical but obviously interested. "Why," he asked, "would McGuire want the gun so damned bad that he would risk going to Chicago and then not even make the meet?"

"I think he meant to make it, and had second thoughts," Nate said. "Either that or he heard from someone in the Bureau or from the family that Anna had also sent out a team of assassins. Maybe he thought the Merrittas would take care of the problem for him. It affected them, too, of course—"

"But if there's no body, there can be no comparison with bullets from the gun registered to or used by McGuire," Woodward protested.

Nate shook his head. "There has to be something. My best guess is a body. We think it's possible that's what Merritta wanted to tell Samantha. He might have thought that knowledge would provide some protection. Now we can only hope that he wrote it down somewhere where she can find it."

"A hell of a long shot," Woodward said. "McGuire never admitted to anything on those tapes. They only cast suspicion toward him. That might destroy his nomination, but we sure as hell won't get an indictment on that."

"We have an eyewitness in Patsy Carroll," Nate reminded him.

"It's not enough in this case and you know it," Woodward shot back. "The defense will paint her as the embittered wife with an ax to grind against the family. But I'm still listening. You have more?"

"No," Nate said reluctantly. "But Merritta wanted to see Miss Carroll for some reason. Anna may know more, too. She had to get information from someone about our being in Chicago, and I suspect that someone was the judge. Maybe through Victor. Maybe through someone here at the Bureau. I'm sure McGuire wouldn't have personally included her. He wouldn't want anyone else to know what happened, but I wouldn't preclude Victor as a conduit of information. If so, she might know more than she thinks she knows and be willing to make a deal."

"If she's not afraid to go against a federal judge," Woodward said. "And we're going to need one hell of a lot of evidence to try to indict a sitting judge, especially one with McGuire's reputation."

Nate nodded. "I'm hoping the will produces something.

If either Sam or Nicholas inherits, we can gain access to all of Merritta's records."

Woodward raised an eyebrow. "Nicholas Merritt?"

Nate looked at Sam, then back at Woodward. "Yeah," he said. "He'll cooperate."

"You've changed your mind about him?"

"He gave us the information about McGuire. It paralleled what we had. I believe him."

Woodward's gaze went from Nate to Sam and back again. "We'll wait to see what's in the will. In the meantime, we'll begin a discreet probe of Judge McGuire. We'll want to talk to your mother, of course."

That had been Sam and Nate's ace in the hole. Simon had taken Patsy to a small Pennsylvania town until Sam and Nate summoned them.

"She'll be here if Mr. McLean stays on the case," Sam said.

Woodward took a sip of coffee from a mug he lifted from his crowded desk, then directed his attention to Nate. "I don't think so. Because of the shooting in Boston, he's on temporary desk duty, and Agent Barker has filed a complaint against him."

"If he doesn't stay with the case, you will never get the gun. Or find my mother. She remained lost for thirty years. She can do it again."

"You and your mother are material witnesses," Woodward said. "We can hold you, if not your mother."

"Then you'll never find the gun. I don't trust anyone but Nate."

Woodward looked irritated, then shrugged. He turned back to Nate. "All right. But stay out of trouble."

Nate grimaced. "I told you we have a leak in the office. We need to keep Sam's location between you, me and agents I pick."

Woodward raised his brows in a way that Sam thought might intimidate a lesser man than Nate. "You choose the detail," he finally agreed. "I want at least two agents with her all the time." He leaned forward in his chair. "When can I see Patsy Carroll?"

"After we know the leak in the Bureau has been eliminated," Nate said.

Woodward gave him a hard look. "There's a murder of a federal agent. Thirty-four years ago or not, we want that case solved."

"I do, too," Nate said simply. "What about Barker?"

Woodward stared down at his desk, then sighed and nodded. "I hope to hell you're wrong about the leak, but we'll keep him out of the loop for now."

Satisfied for the moment, Sam and Nate left for the funeral.

The Merritta family and their retainers crowded into the law offices of Paul Merritta's attorney after his somber funeral mass and burial.

Sam watched as each family member settled into chairs placed around the room for the reading of the will. Her mother was not present. She'd had no desire to see Victor and other members of the family who once had made her life a nightmare.

Feeling oddly detached, Sam wondered if any more of them had deadly intentions. Anna had said nothing since her arrest. Were any of the other family members involved? Either with Judge McGuire or Anna?

None of them looked at her. Among them, only Nicholas acknowledged her. He had given her an encouraging—and sympathetic—smile, and then found a seat in a corner. Nate stood just inside the door, allowed to remain at her request and, surprisingly, at Nicholas's demand. His presence had not helped the temperature in the room. Hostility steamed from Victor Merritta and the others.

As she waited for the attorney to proceed, she thought of the last few hours and the funeral that morning.

Appropriately, it had been a grim and lifeless affair but for the suspicion that rippled through the family in waves. Thankful that she attended the funeral with Nick, she'd walked between her brother and Nate, holding her head high and ignoring reporters' questions. They had not sat with the rest of the family but several pews back. She said her own prayer, wishing she'd had more time with a very flawed man who, nonetheless, had once loved her mother and herself enough to protect them at risk of his own life should anyone have discovered what he'd done for them. . . .

Sam noted the expressions of the others in the attorney's office. Hopeful, fearful, expectant and resigned. Victor and Rich, their wives, Rosa, George, Reggie, and a few more she didn't know—all beneficiaries, apparently, of Paul Merritta's will.

Victor looked years older as he slumped in his chair. He was still under suspicion as an accessory in the murder of the agent three decades ago and also in the substitution of bodies in the auto accident in which Merritta's wife and daughter were supposed to have died. He'd refused to take a lie detector test but as yet there was no evidence he'd planned, executed or even knew of either. The Boston PD and FBI were not giving up though. He'd been put on notice.

Her glance moved to George. He looked apprehensive, too.

She admitted to her own apprehension. Her name—Samantha Carroll—had been on the list of beneficiaries. She knew she didn't want any part of Merritta's fortune, and she certainly didn't want the baggage it carried.

All she wanted was an explanation of why Paul Merritta had called her here, and the will was her last hope for communication between her and her biological father. Whoever inherited would have access to all of Paul Merritta's papers, safe deposit boxes, bank records.

They would have the kind of power that would either be the ultimate protection or the ultimate death sentence.

The attorney, an older man who put on thick reading glasses, plodded through the preliminaries. Then he got down to the crux of the will. A locked box sat on the side of his desk.

Pushing his glasses up on his forehead, he fixed each person with a smile. "This is the last will and testament of Paul Merritta. He made it at ten o'clock the night before he died, somewhat secretly, I must admit. I attended him and can attest to his mental faculties. His butler, Reggie, and the cook witnessed the document.

"He leaves the bulk of his estate to a charitable trust, which is to be administered by his son Nicholas Merritta and his daughter, Nicole Merritta, also known as Samantha Carroll. This includes all his businesses, his home and his bank accounts with the exception of $100,000 a year to each of his brothers, his son George, and his niece Anna for a period of ten years. After that, he feels they should be able to support themselves." The attorney paused, then added, "Mr. Merritta didn't think either Miss Carroll or his son Nicholas either needed or would accept any part of the estate. He did hope they would work together on the trust."

Gasps came from the family members.

"He can't do that," George blustered.

"He can," the attorney corrected, "and he did. He wanted to end the Merritta family's 'notorious' legacy. He paid for both George's and Anna's educations and believed they have excellent prospects in business."

No one mentioned that Anna's prospects had just been reduced to a federal prison.

The attorney obviously felt the sudden chill in the room, paused, then continued. "Paul Merritta said that legacy destroyed his life and almost destroyed his son's life. He wanted it stopped now. If you try to fight it, you will lose what is provided for you in the will."

Abruptly the attorney opened the box and took letters from inside to Samantha. He stood and walked over to Sam. "He wanted you and your mother to have these."

He handed them to her and returned to his desk.

Sam was stunned. Nicholas, she noted, showed no surprise at all.

So he had known something about the will.

Sam looked at the others in the room, all of whom seemed to be holding their breath.

"I would like to read it in private," she said.

After a long silence, they reluctantly filed out. Their faces were angry, bewildered, defiant, defeated. Obviously the new will was the last thing they had expected.

Nate and Nicholas remained with Samantha as she opened her letter, setting aside the one for her mother.

When she opened the envelope, a map fluttered to the floor. Nate leaned down and picked it up.

Samantha read the letter slowly.

Nicole———

I hoped to tell you this in person, but if not . . .

I loved your mother. I loved you. Always remember that.

I was weak and could not fight my father. I tried. But he always won. He made sure he'd win with the murder of a federal agent. My fingerprints were on that gun as well as those of an officer named Terrence McGuire.

I stood by when the murder took place. My father had ordered me to kill him, had told McGuire to give me a gun, but I couldn't pull the trigger. McGuire took it from me and shot him. My father kept the gun as insurance to keep a hold over McGuire and me. He didn't need that hold. I died that day. Then I discovered your mother had heard everything. My father wanted to kill her. I told him I would make sure she never talked, and he would still have Nicholas. It was the only way I could save your mother.

She took the gun, but I knew it was worthless without a body. I knew, though, where my father had the body buried, and made sure McGuire knew I knew. That kept him away from you all these years when he suspected your mother and you didn't die in the car crash. But now he's more powerful and he wants all the evidence that ties him to that day. I was afraid I couldn't protect you any longer, that he would find you and come after you.

I had to know whether you were strong enough to take it to the authorities. When I met you today, I knew you were. You and Nicholas.

Hopefully you will work together with the trust and get to know each other as you should have done throughout your lives.

I don't regret what I did all those years ago. I had no choice. I do regret that I missed those years watching you become the woman you are today. I am proud of both of you.

Your father,
Paul Merritta

Sam caught her breath at the last, touched by that final sentence more than any other. She felt a hand on her shoulder and glanced up, seeing Nick beside her, his mouth tight. Wordlessly she handed the letter to him.

A muscle moved in his cheek as he finished the final two paragraphs as if he too was moved by his father's simple statement. He handed the letter back to her.

Suddenly feeling the oppression of the room and of the proceedings that had just taken place, Sam picked up the map that had fluttered to the floor and passed both documents to Nathan. The expression on his face didn't change as he read the letter, then studied the map. His face told her he recognized the area. With any luck, the bullets would match the gun registered to a young patrolman named Terrence McGuire.

He held out his hand. "Let's go," he said as she rose, and he wrapped an arm around her.

"It's over," Samantha said.

"Not quite," Nate said. "There will be an arrest and trial."

She glanced at a stoic Nick. "The publicity isn't going to end, is it?"

Nick shook his head. "It's not going to be pleasant, but I'm used to it. You're not."

"Neither is our mother."

Nick didn't say anything and instead turned to Nate. "If you want to get back to your office, I'll take her to the hotel with the shadow."

Sam watched Nate's expression. After a fraction of a second, he nodded, and she breathed again. It meant he finally trusted her brother.

Nate and Gray, accompanied by four other agents, appeared in the chambers of Judge McGuire. They brushed by the secretary and a protesting clerk, briefly showing their credentials.

They had worked all night. They had found the skeletal remains of the officer and the bullet that killed him. Nate had contacted Patsy, who appeared several hours later and turned over the gun she'd kept locked in a Chicago bank safe deposit box all these years. The bullets matched.

She also identified a photo of McGuire as a young man.

Federal officers probing McGuire's finances were finding some interesting deposits.

It was more than enough, Woodward said, for an indictment.

Gray and Nathan led the small detachment of agents into McGuire's chambers.

Barker was not among them. Checks of phone records showed that Barker and McGuire had exchanged numerous phone calls in the past five days. Barker had admitted that he had given information to McGuire without informing his superiors, information that had almost caused the death of a fellow agent and a civilian. There was no evidence that he had done it for any reason other than that of an FBI agent trying to make points with a federal judge.

He was on his way to a very unpleasant posting until an investigation was completed.

McGuire entered his chambers from the courtroom. He barely looked at Nathan and the other agents. "Can I help you?"

"Indeed you can," Nathan said. "You can turn around and put your hands behind you."

Bushy dark eyebrows shot up. "What is this? A joke? I can assure you it's not funny."

"I have an arrest warrant for Terrence McGuire for the murder of a federal agent thirty-four years ago. You have the right to remain silent . . ." He recited the revised Miranda warning.

"I *know* my rights, Agent McLean. I also know you'll lose your job over this. Everyone knows you're a loose cannon."

"Do they?" Nate said. "Then you have nothing to worry about, do you? Now please turn around and put your hands behind you."

"Handcuffs aren't necessary," McGuire said. "I'll call my attorney and turn myself in."

"Sorry, sir. Procedure."

Gray went over to McGuire, pulled his hands back and locked the handcuffs.

"You'll be very sorry for this," McGuire said. "I've helped the Bureau . . ."

"I'm sure Agent Barker will testify to that," Nate said.

McGuire's face flushed. "I'll be out before you get home tonight," he said.

"Maybe," Nathan said equably. "Let's go."

Sam waited impatiently for Nate's return. Afternoon had turned into night, then into dawn.

She couldn't go to sleep.

She knew he had risked his job and even more for her. And she had to know what was happening with McGuire.

She made a cup of coffee. An agent was in the room next door to her, another in the hall outside. Her mother was in a room down the hall, Simon still fulfilling his role as protector with the backup of a federal agent.

Nicholas had gone to his office to conduct what he called damage control.

Finally, a knock. She ran to the door, opened it with the chain on until she saw who it was, then unlatched it.

Nate's eyes were bloodshot, the lines around them emphasizing his exhaustion. He gave her a crooked grin. "He's behind bars. Something tells me his appointment will be withdrawn by morning."

"Can they keep him there?"

"I think so, not only for the sake of justice but to protect him as well. A whole lot of law enforcement officers are going to be pissed off when they discover their hero was smearing egg on their faces while shaking their hands. They don't like cops who kill fellow cops." He touched her cheek. "I think it's over, love."

Love?

She cleared her throat around the lump that suddenly formed at that one word. "And you? Your job?"

"Never more secure," he said. "Gray and I bagged a federal judge and a Merritta." He grinned at her. "Not the one I expected, true enough, but my boss is happy."

"I'm glad," she said. She meant it, and yet she didn't.

His job would preclude a relationship with her. He was in Boston. She was in Colorado. He was law enforcement. She would be tainted forever.

He raised his hand and caught a curl, gently tugging on it until she looked directly at him. "They are happy enough," he said, "to give me a choice of assignments after we complete this investigation. I'm picking Denver."

Her heart bounced against her rib cage. Time ceased moving. So did breathing. "Are you saying . . . "

"I want to head in your direction if that's okay with you."

"My . . . the Merritta family." She held her breath, afraid to hope.

"To hell with that. An accident of birth. The Bureau isn't going to hold that against you."

She breathed again. Her blood started racing.

"There's something you should know first," he said.

She waited.

"I told you my wife died. I didn't tell you why."

A muscle twitched in his cheek as she waited for him to continue.

He led her to the bed, sat down beside her on the edge.

"When I married her, she was a social drinker," he said slowly. "During our marriage she started drinking more and more. Because of my job, she said. Because I was never home. Because I was obsessed with the Merrittas.

"We grew apart and I hated to go home. I never knew what I would find. I tried to get help for her, but she wouldn't take it. I worked even longer hours, and she drank more. One day, she drove the car into a tree."

Sam's heart seemed to stop. There was so much pain in his voice, in his face.

"I should have done more to help her," he said. "Instead I blamed the Merrittas for my own failure and went after them even more relentlessly. At one point, I would have sold my soul to take them down."

"You can't help someone who won't be helped," she said softly.

"If I had been home more, it might have been different. I failed her, just like I failed my mother."

Sam stilled. For the first time, she really understood his obsession. He hadn't just blamed the Merrittas. He had blamed himself for not protecting his mother. A boy who had lived with that guilt all his life. Then his wife's death had compounded it. Sam swallowed hard. "You couldn't have protected your mother, any more than you could've protected your wife against herself," she said. "For God's sake, you were a boy."

"I wasn't a boy when my wife died."

"No, but you had no more control then than you did as a boy. You can't help someone who doesn't want to be helped." She paused, then asked, "She knew what you did before she married you?"

"Yes, but she never realized the demands." His gaze bored into her as if searching for an answer to his unspoken question.

She knew what he was telling her. "Well, you don't have to worry about that with me," she said tartly. "I received the comprehensive indoctrination of an agent's life in the past few weeks."

"I can quit."

"No," she said. "It's who you are. And I love who you are."

"Can you open a branch of Wonders in Denver?"

"We've been considering that," she said. At least it had been mentioned once. And she could conduct the Internet business anywhere that had an electrical outlet and a phone line.

He leaned down and kissed her, his lips roaming over hers, then traveling across her face with a feather-light tenderness.

"I love you," he said. "But I want you to be sure. It might be the adrenaline and . . . even gratitude."

"I don't think so," she said. "I'm grateful to a man in Steamboat who once helped me change a flat, but I didn't once think about marrying him."

"Is that so? I thought *you* knew everything about flats."

She flushed, then grinned. "I just know how to cause them."

"Ah, shoot. I thought I had a real winner."

"Well, I'm decisive. That's something you should know about me. And I'm bossy. I told the guy how to change that tire. He couldn't wait to get away from me."

"I like bossy."

"Then I think you should take me to bed."

"You're shameless, too," he observed with obvious delight.

"I'm afraid so."

"And something *you* should know about *me*. I'm very good at taking orders."

"No, you're not," she disagreed.

"Well, maybe just *your* orders." He kept his fingers busy taking off her blouse, then her bra. He leaned down and kissed her left breast, then her right. "See?" he said.

She did.

She ran her fingers through his hair, then touched the hard planes of his face. Emotion flooded her in waves. She couldn't believe he loved her, that he was offering a heart that she now realized had been repeatedly battered. She silently promised that she would take good care of it.

She held her arms up to him. It was her way of telling him she was giving him *her* heart.

A slow, lazy smile spread over his face. Still, he hesitated.

"Bed," she reminded him.

"Only if you'll marry me," he bargained.

She leaned back and looked at the tired face she loved,

at the man who was so much better than he believed he was.

"That is an excellent—"

The rest of the sentence died in a kiss.

And the promise of forever.

epilogue

Nick, a small smile curving his mouth, looked out at the mountains from the patio of Sam's Steamboat Springs house.

He had arrived at Samantha's house with Nathan, who'd finished winding up the Merritta investigation and had just been transferred as second in command to the Denver field office. They had flown from Boston together.

Sam, delighted at their truce, had invited Simon and Patsy to join them for supper.

The case was all but over. Judge McGuire had somehow acquired a gun in jail and had killed himself. Anna had made a plea bargain in exchange for a lighter sentence. She would serve three years in a federal prison.

"So now it's really over," Nick said. "The Merrittas have been neutralized and the family dispersed. The other families can have our territory. And Pop can rest easily."

"Why did Paul Merritta talk about my mother as he did when I saw him?" Sam asked. "He sounded as if he detested her."

"A mask he could never afford to put down," Nick said. "I didn't know myself until I talked to him during your isit to the house that Saturday. I saw him before dinner and he told me everything."

"Why didn't you say anything?"

"The same reason he didn't. Neither of us knew you, knew what your reaction would be. My father wanted to ake your measure and I agreed with him. He had to know whether you should be hidden again, possibly under a different identity, or whether you were strong enough to take he information he had and use it in the right way."

Her brother hesitated. "I think he realized it was a mistake after he contacted you. He'd thought his reputation would protect you. He wanted you to know he'd tried to ake the family into legitimate businesses as much as he could without showing weaknesses to other families. But pain and drugs dulled my father's caution those last few months. He wasn't aware that McGuire had access to FBI apes. He believed his protection was enough. What he didn't realize was that McGuire had just heard he would be nominated for the federal appeals bench and was desperate o find Patsy and eliminate one of the three people who new what happened that night."

Sam mulled that over. It was horrifying to think a man ike that would be elevated to a federal bench. She wished he thought away. "And my mother? How did my . . . faher feel about her?"

"I think he always regretted losing . . . my mother." Nicholas looked at Patsy, who gazed at him with wistful eyes. "You know he never married again. He told me her oss was like a raw wound, even after all those years. But Victor had a relationship with McGuire, and he'd told him Patsy had the gun. As McGuire became more and more powerful, Pop knew he could never approach either one of you without putting you in danger."

Nick paced the patio, then turned back to them. "When he heard he had only a few months to live, Pop felt he had o find you. He knew the key was Patsy's sister, and he had

her monitored. It took a month, but then Patsy's sister me
your mother and he was able to locate both of you."

Sam listened intently. "And so did McGuire."

"Yes."

Nate broke in. "McGuire also had an arrangement with
my boss. He approved warrants and wire taps, and milked
Barker for information. He knew one day he might need
Barker's help.

"When McGuire learned—through Barker—tha
Patsy's daughter had suddenly appeared in Boston, he
feared she also knew about the killing thirty-four year
earlier. Just the hint of corruption would destroy him. I
was his chance to take her out, and at the same time lure
the mother out of hiding."

"So the attempts were meant to kill me, not just scare
the wits out of me?"

"Several came from Victor trying to scare you. He
wanted you out of Boston. But that gave Anna deadlier
ideas and she went after you in earnest," Nick said.
"Strangely enough, Anna claims she wasn't aware o
McGuire's interest. She had hoped to inherit most of the
estate because she knew I didn't want it. McGuire, on the
other hand, wanted to find both of you and obtain the gun
in case Gaberra's body ever surfaced. They were at cross
purposes until McGuire figured out what was happening
and let the Carrolls' whereabouts slip to Victor. He made
the trip to Chicago to keep you there. Then he would let the
Merrittas do the dirty work and consume themselves."

"And now you're free, too," Patsy said.

"Pop was the reason I stayed in Boston. He was the only
family I had. Not much of one, but sometimes he tried."

"And now?" she said.

"I'm ready to leave. The Merritta name isn't worth
much in Boston now. My partner and I can locate anywhere, and we both like this part of the country. It will also
make it easier to administer the trust with my sister."

My sister. Samantha liked the sound of that. She'd liked him showing up on her doorstep to tell her in person what was happening.

"You had something to do with that trust, didn't you? Before you knew about me?"

He nodded. "Pop and I had come to an understanding. He knew George and Victor would take the family back into narcotics. He didn't want that. Both he and I understood I could never cleanse the family. Not completely. And not without a war."

He hesitated, then continued. "But I didn't know about you, or that he intended to involve you. Unfortunately, he died and never really had a chance to get to know you. I talked to him the afternoon of the dinner, then the morning he died, though, and he was excited. You were everything he'd hoped for. You weren't easily intimidated, he said, and you're smart as hell."

"Do you think he was murdered?" She hated to voice her suspicion, yet somehow it had become important to know. To have everything in the open.

A prelude to a fresh start for all of them.

"Yes," Nick said softly. "I think Anna was afraid he would change his will. But I don't think it can ever be proven. He was taking so many medications."

Patsy took several steps in his direction. "Are you really going to move to Colorado?"

"We're thinking about Colorado Springs," he said. "Because we have such a large international business, we need proximity to an airport. I'll be up to Steamboat, though, to see my mother." His eyes twinkled in a way Sam had never seen before. "There's a certain young lady there, too. I think it's time to do some courting."

Patsy's eyes glistened with tears. She touched her bracelet, the one with the little flower that she always wore. Sam never thought it very pretty, but she knew it was her mother's most cherished piece of jewelry. Now Patsy took it off and fingered it for a moment, then opened it.

Sam had never known it opened.

Patsy held it out to Nick. "When you marry . . ."

Nick looked at it, and a muscle flexed in his cheek. Sam moved over and looked at it.

There was a tiny photo of two babies, not more than several days old.

"Paul gave that to me," Patsy said. She looked at Nick. "You were always close to me. Always. It broke my heart when . . ."

Sam leaned against Nate's shoulder as a tear wandered down her mother's eyes.

Nick's fist closed around the bracelet. "Thank you," he said in a husky voice.

Her mother's lips parted in a brilliant smile. Sam knew it would take a long time for the two of them to be easy with each other. But they had made a beginning.

So had Nicholas and Nate. They had flown to Denver together, then rented separate cars. But they even *smiled* at each other now. Her brother and her husband-to-be.

"Will you be here in time to give me away?" she asked.

Nick grinned. "Try to keep me away."

"And I'll be moving to Denver to be with Nate. Mother and I plan to open a second Wonders. We can see each other often."

Nick and Nate exchanged glances.

Maybe she was rushing things a bit, but now everything seemed possible. Still, it was a truce.

A truce. Not only a truce, Sam thought, but a covenant. Both men had conquered their demons, and perhaps she had, too. She would never again expect perfection from human beings. Not from her mother. Not from her brother. Not from her husband.

Not from herself.

She'd been so busy trying to create the perfect life,

he'd never really lived, or felt, or cared enough to look eyond the surface. She'd judged her father and Nathan nd Nick. They'd all made mistakes, but they'd all been ying to protect her.

What greater love . . .

She stood on her tiptoes to kiss Nathan. "Thank you," he said, then turned to Nick. "You, too."

Then it was Simon's—they would all always think of im as Simon—turn. "You're invited, too, of course," she old him.

"I'll be there. Wherever you have it. David always said is daughter was something special." He looked at her nother. "And his Patsy."

Sam looked at her mother. The lines around her eyes ad smoothed out. When she looked at Simon, she wore a mile Sam hadn't seen in two years.

"For the first time in thirty years, I feel free," Patsy said.

"I bet Dad is smiling up there," Sam said.

And suddenly she realized there were probably two ads smiling. At least she hoped so.

One she knew. One she'd never had the chance to know.

But now she knew that both had loved her.

She swallowed hard, and Nathan took her hand.

His lips skimmed over hers as if he read her mind.

"I imagine they are," he said.

And she knew that the very last shadow had left them.

In 1988, **Patricia Potter** won the Maggie Award and a Reviewer's Choice Award from *Romantic Times* for her first novel. She has been named Storyteller of the Year by *Romantic Times* and has received the magazine's Career Achievement Award for Western Historical Romance along with numerous Reviewer's Choice nominations and awards.

She has won three Maggie awards, is a three-time RITA finalist, and has been on the *USA Today* and Walden's bestseller lists. Her books have been alternate choices for the Doubleday Book Club.

Prior to writing fiction, she was a newspaper reporter with the *Atlanta Journal-Constitution* and president of a public relations firm in Atlanta. She has served as president of Georgia Romance Writers and as a board member of River City Romance Writers, and is a former member of the national board of Romance Writers of America.